D0339683

Dedicated to my wife for putting up with me during the process of writing this book without a single threat of bodily violence, and to Denise and Randy Bossarte for all of their assistance in preparing this work. The parts of the story you enjoy the most, and I hope there are many, were likely improved by one or both of them.

Chapter ONE

Colonel Eric Web entered the briefing room and closed the door. The room was nondescript, the kind found in government buildings across the country, with old furniture, mismatched chairs, and file cabinets containing paperwork unreferenced for years. Yet it was clean and neat, with new paint and freshly waxed floors. What could be done with limited funds and nearly limitless labor had been done.

Seated before him were eight people recently rousted from bed, none of them looking his or her best. There had been no time for that. Though Web was the only one in uniform, three of the eight were also military, the rest civilian. For a small group, it was surprisingly diverse. While an outside observer would likely conclude they had all just stepped off the same airplane, the truth was they were a highly specialized team—one of the United States' first contact teams—and about to put theory to practice.

"What you hear today stays in this room. Do not share it with your spouse. Do not confide in your mother. Do not tell your friends. Keep your questions until the end of the briefing, and keep an open mind. Captain, proceed," Web instructed.

As Web stepped away and took his seat, from behind him appeared Captain Jane Andrews, previously hidden by Web's massive frame. Petite, brunette, fair-skinned, and green-eyed, what

Andrews lacked in physical stature she made up for in confidence and competence. Walking toward the lectern, she showed neither enthusiasm nor hesitancy; she had bad news to share and a deep understanding that bad news does not age well.

"Ladies and gentlemen, at 03:22 this morning, our GEODSS sensor suite at Socorro, New Mexico, detected an anomalous object outside the orbit of the moon. At 03:27, we retasked two Space Surveillance Network (SSN) satellites to verify or deny the sighting and begin triangulating. Six minutes later, we received confirmation that the object was not a glitch in Socorro's systems. Without the recent upgrades to Deep-STARE, we might not have spotted this for several more hours. Although it is large, it has a very low albedo. The object is real and is on course to intersect Earth. If it does so at its current speed, the damage could be substantial."

Despite years of discipline, there were a few brief comments from the group. Web cleared his throat and the noise stopped.

The Ground-Based Electro-Optical Deep Space Surveillance (GEODSS) system was one component of the Air Force's. Other components consisted of phased-array and passive radar systems deployed around the world, as well as several highly classified satellites placed in geosynchronous orbit. The network ostensibly existed to detect, identify, and track man-made objects in or near Earth's orbit. Everyone in the room, and a very few outside of it, knew it had a secondary purpose: to perform the same functions for objects of extraterrestrial origin. Over the years, there had been a few occasions when it appeared the secondary purpose might become primary, but every sighting of potential interest had ultimately been found to have a logical, natural origin.

Until now.

Captain Andrews grabbed a folder from the lectern and distributed printouts. "We have no way of determining the object's composition or density, but we've put together a composite image from observations taken across multiple spectra. The color is an estimate, but as you'll see, not particularly relevant in this case."

"That's impossible," someone muttered, almost inaudibly.

The image showed what appeared to be a perfect black sphere, with no visible irregularities, no cratering or evidence of impact, and no color variation.

"We have sufficient data, given its proximity, to calculate a reasonably accurate estimate of its size and speed. The object has a diameter of approximately one and one-quarter kilometers and is traveling at just over 21 kilometers per second," Andrews continued.

There were several gasps—a reaction that, this time, Web did not attempt to suppress. Andrews agreed. "I would call that a sane response to an insane situation. Unfortunately, I'm not finished. Calculating backward to the original observation, the object was first spotted 1.56 million kilometers out." She paused, realizing she'd momentarily lost their attention. "I see you all doing the math. Let me spare you. If nothing changes, the object will impact the Atlantic Ocean at 01:01 tomorrow morning." Andrews stopped speaking, but stayed behind the lectern.

"Thank you, Captain Andrews. Rui, I don't mean to put you on the spot, but can you explain what we could expect if this object were to hit Earth?"

Doctor Rui Fernandes was the team's astrophysicist. A soft-spoken man in his late thirties, he was just over six feet tall, trim, and fit. His light-brown skin complemented matching eyes and nearly black hair. Happily married for thirteen years with two children he doted on, he hadn't yet reached the age where gray would start creeping in, and could easily pass for a man in his twenties.

Rui thought for a moment then began, "With no information on density or the approach angle, I'll have to make a few assumptions, but if this object remains intact and is largely solid, with a composition similar to a nickel-iron asteroid, it will have devastating effects. Within a 100-mile radius, thermal radiation will ignite exposed wood, wind speeds will approach 500 miles per hour, and tsunami waves would vary in height from 100 to 1,000 feet, threatening the Atlantic coasts of every country."

"Thank you, Rui. As you all can see, the world has a problem. I'll open the floor to questions in just a moment, but I want to make something clear. No one on Earth can do anything to prevent this event from happening. We simply have neither the means nor the time to do so. There's also very little that can be done to prepare for such an event that hasn't already been done. Other teams will do whatever possible to evacuate the areas likely to be affected— teams that have prepared for years for that task just as you have prepared for years for your task.

"We have no evidence, other than its appearance, to suggest the object is either intelligent or controlled by an intelligence, but from this moment forward, this team will accept those as working hypotheses. Ladies and gentlemen, you have been training for years to manage a first-contact situation, so set aside your fears and concerns and focus on what may be humanity's only viable course of action: finding a way to communicate with the anomaly. Now, questions?"

Major Jack Thompson, a man whose opinion of himself was well known to everyone in the room, was first to speak.

"Who else is working on communicating with the object, sir?"

Jack was Web's right-hand man, having worked for him in multiple commands over the years. Asking the first question was his way of demonstrating authority. He was a short, well-built man in the typically good shape of most US military officers. He kept his thinning light-brown hair in a crew cut, just as he had done for each of the last twenty-two years. His wife would probably not approve, had he had one.

"In the United States, we're it. We have access to anything any of us are likely to think of that can be brought to bear in the time we have, but the National Command Authority (NCA) wants this government's attempts to be seen as unified and organized. We don't know which other governments have detected the anomaly, but we're confident some have and may also attempt to communicate with it. As we have no control over such attempts, we'll not waste time concerning ourselves with them," Web responded.

"Do we have access to allied resources? May we work with our peers in Europe and elsewhere?" asked Doctor Dan Garcia. It was no surprise that Dan's first question would be about collaboration; a brilliant man who nearly everyone liked, it simply never occurred to him to concern himself with who would get credit. He wouldn't say he was surprised to be the chief scientist on the team, but neither would he introduce himself as such.

"The short answer is no. The long answer is that we have very little time to coordinate and no sufficiently complete protocol for securely managing international cooperation for this type of event. People in pay grades far above ours are deciding exactly who will be informed when and to what extent. My comments at the beginning of this meeting bear repeating: tell no one outside this room anything without my explicit authorization. The folks just outside this room, Captain Andrews' team, are sequestered and while available for questions, that's a one-way street: You may get information from them but may not share information with them. Is everyone completely clear?"

Web waited until he received explicit acknowledgment from everyone in the room, then continued. "All right, good questions, but enough about process for now. I'd like the group to consider a question more closely aligned with the problem at hand: assuming there's someone or something in the anomaly that is listening, how do we convince it to change course?"

As Web finished, there was a knock on the door. Andrews answered it, listened briefly, then said, "Excuse me for a moment, sir."

"What is it?" Web asked.

"Not sure, sir. I just need to verify something. I don't want to waste the group's time on nonsense." She stepped out of the room as she finished, closing the door on an irritated Web. The technician hurried in front of Andrews until they arrived at his station. He was one of two left to monitor the situation, as Andrews had moved the rest of her team to another room to limit the amount of information each of them would gain by staying.

"Please tell me I'm wrong, ma'am," the young man fairly pleaded, but he was not.

What Andrews saw in the data reminded her of a training film on intercontinental ballistic missiles, specifically multiple independently targetable reentry vehicles (MIRVs). The sphere had re-formed. What had been a very large sphere was now eighteen smaller spheres, each as black as the purest obsidian. All but one continued toward Earth.

Chapter TWO

Sam opened the door to the community center for Sara, a trip they made every Saturday morning. Going to the center started as Sara's idea, an idea that Sam had fought. But in the end, Sara's toughness won out and now it was the highlight of his week. His sister-in-law was, as he occasionally teased her, smarter than she looked. This would have sounded harsher had Sara not been a beautiful woman. Every time he looked at her, he thought of Elizabeth. They both had the same light-brown skin, wavy black hair, and dark-brown eyes. It was the eyes that really got to him. He stopped and closed his own momentarily before continuing into the community center.

Sam had once been a handsome man, though he would've laughed if you'd told him so. Nearly six feet tall with dirty-blond hair, deep-blue eyes, and the build of a floor gymnast, he'd never had trouble finding a date. He hadn't had any trouble getting the love of his life to say yes either. He wondered what she'd make of him now.

"Mommy, look!" he heard a little girl say to her mother as they walked by. He couldn't be sure the girl was pointing at him, but it wouldn't be uncommon. He pretended he hadn't heard the comment so the mother wouldn't be embarrassed. It worked.

Sam quickly learned how people responded to his face. Adults, for the most part, acted normal. They couldn't know, though, that they spent far less time looking into his eyes than people had before he was injured. He was sure they meant well. Kids . . . now kids were a different thing entirely. Sam never knew what one might say. If you asked him, he'd tell you he preferred the kids. No one ever asked him.

"Thanks again for making me come here, Sara. You're a good sister. Elizabeth would be proud."

"You do good work here, Sam. You make a difference. She'd be proud of that, too."

Sara thought about what she'd just said, regretted it, and continued. "I'm going to go see how many kids showed up this week. Why don't you go say hi to Esther?"

"Sounds good. See you in a bit." As Sara left for the children's reading area, Sam looked around for Esther. It didn't take him long to spot her.

Esther had raised nine children, mostly alone, having lost her husband to cancer nearly thirty years ago, when she was still in her midthirties. Her last child left home a decade ago. The years had not been kind to her. Esther took a lot of different medications and sometimes she was herself, sometimes not. Sam stayed with her for a time either way, but he knew from experience she'd only remember his visits when she was herself, and sometimes not even then.

"Good morning, Esther."

"Good morning, Sam. Nice to see you." Her eyes were bright and focused, and it appeared she was having a good day.

"You too, Esther. How's my favorite grandmother?"

Esther smiled at him. "So far, so good. Of course, it's early," she teased. "How about you? How's that leg?"

"Oh, it gets me around, thanks for asking. How are the grand-kids?"

Esther's smile grew. "I got a few new pictures of Isabella yes-terday. Want to see?"

"Yes ma'am." Sam took a seat next to Esther while she showed him her newest pictures of Isabella and some not-so-new ones of her other grandchildren. As usual, they covered a variety of topics while viewing the pictures. Esther had been a nurse and could tell some remarkable stories; Sam was a good listener.

"They're all as beautiful as ever," Sam said.

"They are delightful, aren't they?" said Esther, in a way that only grandparents can.

"They are. Speaking of delightful, wouldn't it be nice to spend some time with Jim?"

"I should've never told you that. Now you won't leave me alone about it!" Esther pretended to admonish Sam, but she couldn't quite keep her face stern. She gave up and said, "Yes, it would be nice, if I wasn't so old and fat and high as a kite half the time."

"You're being too hard on yourself. We all have issues. It's the human condition. You're a wonderful lady. You should talk with him. Do you want me to talk with him for you?" Sam asked her. He knew the answer.

"You will do no such thing!" Esther responded.

His question and her response were a part of their ritual. Sam never quit trying because he thought he was making progress. Jim and Esther were good people, and he·knew they were both lonely. They both knew he'd ask again next week.

"Okay, Esther. You're the boss. I won't say a word to him, but you should." Sam stood and started adjusting the blankets cover-ing most of Esther. This was also part of their ritual. It usually meant the conversation was over.

"I know. Thanks for pushing me, Sam, and for spending time with me. You're my hero."

Sam glanced at Sara. She was across the room, reading to a small group of children. He looked back at Esther. "I'm nobody's hero, Esther." He finished straightening her covers, smiled at her, and asked if she needed anything else. She didn't.

Sam looked around for Jim and found him in one of the leather club chairs arranged along the western wall of the room, reading a book by the morning light. Sam moved to join him, hoping he'd be in a talking mood.

"Morning, Jim."

"Good morning, Sam. I was just about to start a read."

"Can I convince you to spend a little time sharing some wisdom with a wee lad such as myself instead?"

"Can't say as I have much wisdom to share, but seeing as I have so little time left needing it, why not?" Jim replied with a smile.

Jim was one of Sam's favorite people. Although time and a life of hard work had worn his body down, his voice was as strong as a young man's, and the mind directing it would be envied by most anyone.

Sam hadn't known Jim long. They had met shortly after Sam moved to Colorado Springs a couple of years ago, but had instantly hit it off. Although the men were two decades apart in age, had grown up in separate parts of the country, and had pursued very different careers, they had a lot in common. They were both veterans, though Sam would say Jim was a Veteran with a capital V because of the time he'd spent as a Marine medic in the hell that was the Korean War. That was where their first conversation started. Where it ended was why Sam always made it a point to talk to Jim if he could.

"Look at you, whining about dying again. Do we always have to start with you complaining about your mortality?"

"You're right. I can be such a selfish bastard sometimes. Where are my manners? Have a seat."

"That's more like it." Sam sat in the chair next to Jim, a small round wooden table between them. The low morning sun warmed Sam's back. They both sat in silence for a minute before Sam finally spoke.

"How've you been, Jim?"

"Truth be told, Son, I'm feeling about as useless as tits on a boar hog."

Sam paused for a moment. Sometimes, Jim wanted to tell stories. Sometimes, he wanted to hear stories. Sometimes, he just wanted to talk politics. On a very few occasions, he wanted something more out of the conversation. Sam cherished those rare opportunities to learn from a man he'd come to deeply respect.

"I can't speak for boar hogs, but you're not useless to me, Jim."

In the comfortable silence that followed, Sam's cell phone buzzed. He glanced at it.

"Excuse me a moment, I have to take this." He started toward the door as he answered his phone.

"Sam, I need you to come to the office."

"It's my day off."

"I know that. Look, this is important. I need you here ASAP and I don't have time to explain. Just get here five minutes ago." With that, Jack hung up.

Pompous ass, Sam thought as he walked back inside to apologize to Jim and find Sara.

"Sorry, Jim. I have to go. Remember what I said and remember what you did for me. There's not an ounce of useless in you."

Sam shook Jim's hand. "I'll be back later today if I can."

"It's all right, Son, run along and play now." Jim smiled an impish smile. Sam walked away to find Sara a little less annoyed than seconds before.

"I have to go."

"Right now? We were going to stay for another couple of hours."

"I know. I'm sorry. It's work, and Jack said ASAP. You know how he is. I don't want any trouble."

Chapter THREE

Sam parked his SUV, a late-model, black Jeep Grand Cherokee, in the mostly empty parking lot outside his office—a three-story SCIF, or Sensitive Compartmented Information Facility, in the heart of Peterson Air Force Base. SCIFs are as common within the Air Force Space Command as overpriced restaurants in New York. Remarkably little of what goes on within them requires the expense associated with their construction and maintenance. Sam's work did.

Entering the foyer, it occurred to him that the lot held more vehicles than usual for a Saturday. It'd been a while since Jack had conducted a drill. That's probably what was going on, he thought, as he approached the guard in the foyer.

"Morning, Mr. Steele."

"Morning, Fred. What's going on?" Sam asked as he presented his ID in exchange for his outer SCIF credentials.

"Can't say."

"Can't or won't?" Sam asked with a smile. He liked Fred. Like most of the guards, he was retired military and although they'd never served together—Sam was Army, Fred was Air Force—their careers spanned the same time frame. They usually chatted for a few moments before Sam started his shift. It's possible to learn a lot about someone in short conversations over time if you pay attention. Sam paid attention.

"In this case, both. I don't know much and what little I know I've been ordered to keep to myself." He paused. "Trust me, even if I spilled my guts, you wouldn't know much more than when you opened that door." Fred gestured vaguely toward the building's single entrance.

"Fair enough. Guess I'll get in there and find out."

"Good luck with that," Fred said, as Sam walked toward the secure door behind which he would likely find an irritated Major Jack Thompson.

"Thanks. I'm betting I'll need it." Sam placed his hand on the biometric reader, waited for the green light, and entered the eight-digit code before it timed out. The door opened and Sam stepped into a smaller foyer with two armed guards behind armored glass who, to Sam's trained eye, appeared tense. He pushed his outer SCIF ID through, waited for it to be processed, and walked to the first door of the small sally port. When the door opened, he entered, waited for the door behind him to close, accepted his interior badge, and turned toward the second door that opened onto the hall to his office.

"I have special instructions for you, sir," the senior guard informed him. "You're to proceed immediately and directly to Vice Commander Web's office. Do not deviate from the most direct route to that destination. Do not talk to or with anyone along the way. If Colonel Web is not in his office, wait until he arrives. We'll inform him that you're here. Do you understand these instructions?"

"Yes," Sam replied, wondering if he'd just fallen down the rabbit hole.

"Do you have any questions about these instructions?"

"No." They wouldn't have any answers to his questions.

"Please proceed, sir." The inner door of the sally port opened.

Sam entered the heart of the SCIF and, following instructions, headed directly to Web's office. He didn't have to worry about speaking with anyone along the way—there was no one in the corridors, which was stranger still.

The door to Web's office was open. Web was behind his desk.

"Sam, come in. Close the door."

Sam entered, closed the door, and moved to one of the chairs in front of Web's desk. He took a seat without waiting for an offer to do so and waited. Web's irritated expression was worth the political capital it cost Sam to be impertinent in Web's eyes. In Web's mind, Sam should respect military protocol. In Sam's mind, and in fact, he was a civilian.

"I'm going to be completely straight with you, Sam. I don't want you here now, not for this. Having said that, several members of the team, Jack included, believe we need you. As you'll soon learn, we have a very large problem and very little time to solve it. If the experts believe you can help with that, I'm inclined to let you. Still, unless you can assure me that you'll be a consummate team player on this, I'll ignore their request and ask you to leave. What do you say?"

Sam paused before responding. There was no love lost between him and Web, and they both knew it. Unfortunately for Web, Sam was among the best, perhaps *the* best, at what he did. Unfortunately for Sam, Web was in charge of the foremost organization supporting Sam's work. Catch-22.

Sam's curiosity overpowered his desire to tweak Web. This time. "Yes, Eric, I'll be a team player." Web's annoyance at the use of his first name was visible, barely. Even under the unusual circumstances, that bothered Web, a bit of intel that Sam stored away for future processing.

"The team is currently working out of the east conference room. I'll be there after I update the CO." He paused. "Sam, don't make me regret this."

Sam nodded, ignored his confusion, stood up, and headed for the conference room. The rabbit hole had gotten deeper in very short order.

"What the hell took you so long?" Jack asked as Sam entered the conference room. Jack was not in uniform and hadn't shaved. In the many years he'd known him, Sam had never seen Jack so unkempt. Jack might be a dick, but he was usually a very well-kept one. So, apparently, not a drill.

"I got here as quickly as I could. What's going on?" Sam replied.

"We have a first-contact situation and it doesn't appear friendly."

Sam choked back his first, incredulous response, thought for a moment, and asked instead, "How do I get up to speed and what do you need me to focus on?"

When she saw Sam enter the room, Captain Andrews walked toward the pair, arriving in time to hear Sam's question. She was pretty sure she'd be the one providing him the SITREP, but waited for Major Thompson to answer.

"Captain Andrews will provide a situation report. Focus on how we've communicated with them and how they've responded. That will make more sense in a moment. I don't want my opinion to bias you. Captain Andrews is not a member of the contact team and as such, has no opinion on the matter. Her report will be as unbiased as possible under the circumstances. Report to me when you're up to speed. Proceed, Captain." With that, he left the two of them alone in the doorway and went over to join a heated discussion in the far corner of the large room.

Sam didn't think it odd that Jack started the conversation by introducing his bias and ended by taking credit for not doing so. He shook his head almost imperceptibly before turning to Jane.

"Jane, I could really use a lot of information right now."

"Let's go in here." She led him into an office adjacent to the conference room holding a single wooden desk pressed against the middle of the far wall surrounded by matching bookshelves. There was a large flat-screen monitor on the desk showing a representation of Earth and one bright-yellow line originating some distance beyond the orbit of the moon, extending about a third of the way to Earth. As Sam got closer, he saw that it wasn't actually a single line but rather a group of lines very close together.

Jane let him look at the monitor a moment before asking, "Okay. How do you want to do this?"

"How about we start with that?" Sam pointed to the lines on the screen. "Is that live?"

"Yes—"

"What time was this?" Sam interrupted her, pointing to the origin point.

"03:22 this morning."

"And the speed is constant?"

"Yes."

Sam looked at his watch then at Jane. "I'd better let you talk, then. Start with what we know about the objects."

"When we first spotted the anomaly, it presented as a single object, a featureless black sphere with an albedo approaching zero. It stayed that way until 04:49, when it appeared to reform into

17

eighteen smaller spheres, each 379.79 and change meters in diameter. One immediately reversed course. We tracked it until 06:18, then lost it. The remaining seventeen continued toward Earth with no change in speed but a slight divergence in direction." Jane paused to let Sam absorb what she'd just told him. He took another, closer look at the screen, then nodded for her to continue.

"Colonel Web convened the first contact team at 04:38. They developed a plan of attack and broke into groups at 06:15. Their communication plan was approved by the NCA at 08:41 and implemented eight minutes later. The response was immediate: one of the remaining spheres began transmitting what appeared to be white noise and has continued to transmit from the moment of contact. The data stream is being downloaded to a node on the cluster controlling the communications satellite. Dan's team ran a series of pattern analysis programs against the incoming data stream with some success, although I can't tell you any particulars. Something they found surprised them but I don't know what. That's when Dan convinced Colonel Web we needed to bring you in." She paused.

"Sam, I didn't hear the conversation, but it wasn't hard to tell that Colonel Web isn't happy about you being here."

"You mentioned that the seventeen objects still headed toward Earth changed course. Do we know where they'll hit if the situation remains constant?" Sam asked without responding to her comment. She was walking a fine line, one he did not want her on.

"Rui's team did that. Here's the projection." She handed him a computer-generated image showing numerous impact sites in the Atlantic Ocean.

"And the one that got away, do we have any more details on that?"

"Not as of when I left."

"Other than the data stream, have we received any response to our attempts to communicate?"

"Again, not as of when I left."

"Looks like it's time to talk with the team. Thanks for the briefing, Jane. How you holding up?"

"I haven't really had time to think about it and I think that's best for now."

Sam nodded and headed back into the conference room and found Dan, who looked up from his work when he caught a glimpse of Sam entering the room. He managed a feeble smile. "A lot to take in, eh?"

Dan was the prototypical middle-aged guy. Average height and average weight with a slight paunch, black hair fading to brown with streaks of white combed straight back from the front, he didn't attempt being stylish. The salt and pepper in his mustache, which he spent more time grooming than his hair, was evenly balanced. This was, perhaps, his only affectation. Although he appeared nondescript, Sam would tell you there was very little actually average about Dan. Sam had been through some hard times, with Dan standing by him like the brother he'd never had. Sam was glad to see him, especially under these conditions. "That may well be your ultimate master-of-the-understatement moment, Dan."

Dan's smile got a little wider. "It would be hard to overstate right now, so I win by default."

"Fair enough. Jane did a good job providing a 30,000-foot view. How about you give me street level?"

"She told you we've been receiving a large quantity of data since we made contact, right?"

"Yes."

"And that we believe we've identified at least one pattern?"

"Yes, although she had no details."

"Understandable. She's had her hands full keeping Web apprised of everything that's going on so the rest of us can focus on our specialties. Quite remarkable, really. Anyway, as you can imagine, we pulled out all the stops on pattern analysis. Chang worked with the tech team to put together a powerful cluster isolated from the rest of the network, and we currently have dozens of different scripts running against various parts of the data stream. There doesn't seem to be a single dominant pattern. Several of the scripts have detected what appear to be coherent data in parts of the stream, but when we apply the same algorithm to other parts of the stream, we see no coherence. I suspect—I have no hard evidence, mind you—I suspect that the message is designed to be decoded using a variety of methods." Dan paused.

"Sounds right up your alley, Dan. What makes you think I'll be able to help?" Sam asked.

"The first script to get a hit was one of yours, the one designed to find steganographically hidden executable files."

"You know I wrote that as more of a sieve than a detector, right?"

"Yeah, I know, false positives and all that, but we've had several hits since the first one. I don't know how coarse your sieve is, and no one's had time to get up to speed on your code. Besides, none of us are as likely as you are to make progress in time to be relevant. The open workstation connected to the new cluster right next to mine is yours now. Come on, I'll show you what we've found so far."

Sam followed and stood behind Dan at his workstation. Dan pulled up a number of files, the most promising results of the previous runs of Sam's script. Dan explained where in the data stream the script had found candidate programs, but neither of them saw any pattern in the location of the hits. Before long, Dan could tell

Sam was only paying attention to be polite—he obviously wanted to work on the problem himself.

"That's what we have so far. Any thoughts?"

"I think I need to get to work," Sam replied as he took a seat at the unlocked workstation and asked where to find the relevant test directories. Dan pointed out the primary input and output directories being used by the running version of Sam's code. Sam didn't need much else. He began to work. Within minutes, the oddity of the situation, the noise in the room, and the pending threat faded into the background, set aside but not forgotten.

Nearly all of his adult life, Sam had worked in one form of counterterrorism or another. When he could no longer work in the field, he devoted himself to countering cyberterrorism. During an average week, he spent most of his time monitoring the world's networks for unusual content or behavior. The modern criminals and terrorists he hunted were clever at covert communications. Arguably, their most effective method was to hide messages inside of other content, a sort of Trojan horse approach known as steganography.

Al-Qaeda is particularly fond of steganography, having used it for years to hide plans, photographs, and other materials in images and audio files. Doing so effectively requires balancing the amount of data to be hidden with the level of degradation to the source file. Adding too much information increases the likelihood that the modified file will be detected and easier to decode once found. So, terrorists, or anyone trying to hide significant amounts of information, frequently break it up into large groups of smaller files transmitted over time. As with all things tech related, the tools for hiding information are always improving, as are the tools for detection. Sam spent a fair amount of his time updating his tools, as well as vetting improvements made by other teams, notably the National Security Agency, and adding them to the command's cyberterrorism fighting kit. He had never imagined he'd be using the same set to analyze an alien signal, yet here he was doing just that.

"I told you to report to me when you were up to speed," Jack interrupted Sam.

"I'm sorry, what?" Sam responded, still processing Jack's words as he pulled back from the data.

"I said, I told you to report to me when you got up to speed. Jane finished briefing you nearly two hours ago. I expected to hear from you by now. It's important that I know what you're working on and whether or not you're making progress."

Sam wasn't sure how that fell in to the category of important under the circumstances, but chose to let it pass. "Good timing, Jack. I just finished something and could use some water. I'll brief you while we walk."

"Start with what you've been doing for the past two hours," Jack said, clearly irritated.

Sam stood, stretched, and started for the break room. He knew he shouldn't let himself be annoyed by such comments, but he couldn't help it. Exactly what did Jack think he'd be briefing him on? His breakfast? The weather? Wanting to say something very different, he settled on, "I've been submitting portions of the message we're recording to a script I wrote to find potential computer programs hidden within other types of files. I've found quite a few potential candidates. I'm trying to put the best one of them together."

"Why would they hide their message if they wanted us to get it?"

"You'll have to ask AJ about their potential motives. He's the one working on alien psychology. I wouldn't know where to start, but I get your point. I don't think they're trying to hide it. Dan thinks they're trying to communicate using multiple, interwoven methods, and so far, I think he's right. My program identifies areas where there appear to be executable files in part of that data mesh. When you walked up, I'd just started running a version of the program modified to include several pattern recognition algorithms from Dan's people to try to piece together the most promising candidate. It should be done by the time we get back."

They'd made it to the break room and Sam grabbed a couple bottles of water from the refrigerator. He offered one to Jack, who declined with a wave of his hand.

"So, what do you expect to find?" Jack asked as they headed back to the conference room.

"I expect to find at least a portion of an ELF; all of one if we're lucky." Sam was having a little fun with Jack, though he was pretty sure he was the only one enjoying it.

"What the hell is an elf?" Jack asked. Sam resisted the temptation to respond with a lesson in folklore.

"It's a type of program file. It stands for executable and linkable format. Many servers can run programs compiled and linked to that format; I'd be willing to bet we'd also find Windows executable files if we looked. I just proceeded with the script that Dan had already had some success with."

"Why do you think that's what you'll find? What makes you think they'd send us a computer program?" Jack was becoming more annoyed from getting more information without becoming more informed.

Sam decided it was petty to continue playing with Jack. "I think we'll find an ELF because that's what my program was built to do, and its raw data shows what look like parts of an ELF header. As for why they'd send us a computer program, I can think of a lot of good reasons, depending on what it's designed to do."

"Have you been able to determine what that is?"

"Not a clue. It's compiled code. The only way we can find out in the short term is to run it. There's no time to reverse engineer," Sam replied as they approached his workstation.

The program had terminated with a single file sitting in the designated output directory. Sam opened it in a hex editor and read it briefly before turning to Jack. "It's a complete ELF header but I can't tell you if it's a complete program. It's a pretty small file but it could be. We'll have to run it."

"You will do no such thing. What we will do is inform Colonel Web of what we've found. Come with me." Jack really hadn't gotten it through his head that Sam was no longer military, or that when he had been, they were peers.

When they arrived at Web's office, he motioned them to sit while he wrapped up a call. "Send me the new projections as soon as you have them." Web hung up and turned his attention to them.

"I hope you're bringing good news."

"Actually—" Sam started to reply before Jack interrupted.

"We have news. It's unclear if it's good or bad."

"Well, *make* it clear. I shouldn't have to remind you that we're running out of time."

"We've found at least a fragment of a computer program within the data stream coming from the anomalies. There's a possibility that the program could be executed on one of the servers in the analysis cluster, but we don't know what the program will do and don't have enough time to analyze its function by other means before the objects' impact. Bottom line: we can run it blind or not run it at all."

Jack did a credible job of appearing to understand what he'd just said. It was a talent, Sam supposed. Not one he cared to acquire, but a talent, nonetheless.

Web closed his eyes and leaned back in his chair. Jack and Sam waited for several seconds before Web opened his eyes and asked Sam, "What are the risks if we run the program?"

"Not an easy question to answer," Sam started. "Chang's team has done everything they can, and they're among the best at this, to isolate the systems we're using to analyze the visitor's message, but we can't be sure holes don't exist in their containment strategy. Executing this program could result in a propagation of whatever payload it contains, but that seems unlikely."

"Why unlikely?" Web asked.

"Because they made it hard. Why make us figure it out if they just wanted to hurt us? If they wanted to hurt us, what, exactly could we do to stop that from happening? We'd be like apes jumping up and down on a rock, waving sticks over our heads, at best. No, that's too generous." Sam paused for a moment before continuing. "We'd be like ants trying to protect our anthill from a farmer's tractor. So, Occam's razor: if they could've accomplished the same end without our assistance, why bother acquiring it?"

Jack saw an opportunity. "But you and Dan both believe the message contains multiple ways in which a recipient might understand it. Doesn't that align with a strategy that would pursue multiple points of entry into our networks?"

Sam reluctantly upped his estimation of Jack's IQ by a point or two. "Yes, Jack, it does. The question is, are they exploring multiple methods to communicate, or multiple avenues for attack? I can't answer that question directly. None of us can, but again, I have to wonder, with the technical capabilities they've demonstrated, why bother being sneaky?"

"I see your point, but I think you're missing Jack's. Our military has overwhelming superiority compared to most countries, but we still have bombing runs for weeks or months at a time before we attack with ground forces. It disorganizes and demoralizes the enemy, in addition to reducing their physical ability to fight. We do that so that we'll lose fewer ground forces when we finally do send them in. What if this program were hostile and breached containment? You're the one who explained the Stuxnet worm to me. I haven't seen a nationwide replacement of our vulnerable controllers at power plants, factories, or on the grid—have you?"

Web continued without waiting for a response. "They may not need to shut down our factories and power plants to defeat us, but it sure wouldn't hurt their cause if they mean us harm."

Sam paused before responding. He knew he was losing the argument.

"I acknowledge Jack's point, and you're right about the advantages they could gain by damaging our infrastructure. I agree with you that a truly effective cyber attack would be devastating on a scale the world has never seen. It's why I do what I do. My argument is that if they possess the capabilities to launch such an attack, and your argument presupposes that they do, they don't need our help to launch it. There are many easier ways to get such a payload onto not just the Internet but also every other network that uses satellites to communicate, directly or indirectly, and that is nearly every network on Earth, including SIPRNet, NIPRNet, GPS, and all telecommunications networks. They have physical access to the world's satellites. They can disrupt, corrupt, or repurpose them as they wish and we can't stop them.

"Oh, and let's not forget we're unlikely to be the only team having this discussion. The Russians and Chinese will find what we've found, if they haven't done so already. Other countries are probably in the game as well. If one of them executes a program they've decoded and it's hostile, we'll still suffer, but if they run it and it's not hostile, we may not benefit. What if it's a test? What if the program determines whom the visitors will communicate with if they prove not to be hostile? There's a downside to inaction."

Web's phone rang. He glanced at the caller ID then answered it. "What do you have, Rui?" He listened for a moment then said, "I'll be right there. I'm bringing Jack and Sam. Get Dan, Camilla, and Chang and meet us in the west conference room.

"We'll have to finish this conversation later. The anomalies have changed course again and Rui's team just recalculated the projected impact sites. You may change your mind about the possibility of them being friendly, Sam."

Chapter FOUR

Rui, Chang, and Camilla were in the conference room when Web, Jack, and Sam arrived. Rui glanced at Web and continued connecting his laptop to the overhead projector. He glanced at Web as he entered and said, "Dan is on his way."

The west conference room was, unsurprisingly, a mirror image of the east. Roughly forty by thirty feet, it contained a table to seat a dozen people comfortably, nearly twice that if no one cared about elbow room. The size of the room was overkill for the seven of them, but it served its primary purpose. It was secure and silent.

As Rui finished testing his laptop's connection, Dan walked in carrying a small cardboard box filled with drinks and snacks. "I figured everyone's been too busy to stay hydrated and fed. This won't make anyone's doctor happy, but it's food, of a sort." Considerate and self-deprecating. That was Dan.

"Thanks, Dan. Good thinking," Web said, as he reached for a large bottle of water. "If you haven't taken the time to get something to drink in a couple of hours, grab something now." Everyone did. Dan waited until the group had taken what they wanted, then grabbed a bottle of water and a pack of pretzels for himself.

"I've asked you all to take a break from what you're working on to review and discuss some new tracking information Rui's team has come up with. Please hold your questions until he briefs us on what he's learned. Rui, please proceed."

"As you all know, at 04:49 this morning the anomaly reformed into eighteen objects, with seventeen of them continuing along roughly the same vector as the original anomaly. A little over ten minutes ago, at 12:15, all seventeen changed vectors. We've plotted their new projected impact points. The results are disturbing." With that, he pulled up a map projection of Earth.

"The only impact site in North America is in the United States, just outside Lebanon, Kansas. There is one impact site in South America—Brazil—and one in Australia. Two in Africa—Ethiopia and Nigeria, and four in Europe—Germany, France, Turkey, and the United Kingdom. There are eight impact sites in Asia—China, India, Russia, Pakistan, Bangladesh, Vietnam, Japan, and Indonesia." He highlighted each country with a laser pointer as he said its name. "With two exceptions, each of the impact sites appears to be targeted at the geographic center of the country in question. In the case of the United States, it's the geographic center of the contiguous states. In the case of Indonesia, the impact site appears to be at the center of Central Kalimantan, the country's largest province. We've formed no theories as to why these sites were chosen—although I have a few thoughts of my own—but I'll point out that these countries represent about two-thirds of the world's human population."

Rui turned away from the screen and looked at Web. "Those are the facts. We'll advise you immediately if they change, of course, but I don't think they will."

"Why not?" Web asked.

"The anomaly changed twice. Both times the change was precise and seemingly complete. This change did not result in courses that will impact somewhere inside each of these countries, but, as I said, in the precise geographic center of most of them. There weren't any intermediate corrections leading up to the change, so I don't anticipate a wholesale change or even a single sphere retargeting prior to impact. They've demonstrated the ability to ignore inertia, so it's possible they won't impact with the force we would normally assume from the speeds they're traveling relative to Earth. They may slow, but I'd expect them to do so in a way that will still result in their arrival at the points I've illustrated. This is all based on conjecture, of course. We have very little to go on."

"Why didn't they take these courses when the anomaly first transformed?" Jack asked.

"We have no way of knowing. It's possible they needed to observe us before selecting their targets," Rui answered.

"Has anyone on your team tried to correlate the impact sites with other biological populations, aside from human?" Asking that question was Doctor Camilla Parkington, the team's exobiologist. In her midfifties, Camilla was the team's oldest member, a detail reflected in her calm, consistent demeanor and generous spirit. With clear green eyes and a melodious voice, she was an Irish beauty growing older as gracefully as she conducted herself each day.

"I'm afraid what I've briefed is pretty much all the new information we have, Camilla. I was hoping to start more of a discussion than a Q&A." Rui's smile softened his comment.

"Wishful thinking on my part, Rui. I'll get my team on it while we discuss the implications. Please forward me a link to the data."

After a few clicks, Rui said, "Done," as the team continued considering the map of impact sites.

Something about the pattern bothered Sam. "Rui, the location of the sites does result in solid coverage of humanity's most populous countries and regions, but it doesn't cover as much as it could have, at least not by population."

"You're right. For whatever reason, the anomalies seem intent on having a presence on every populated continent."

"Not quite, Rui," said Camilla. "There's no impact site on either of the poles. Of course, the human presence on those landmasses is negligible. Perhaps they had a floor . . ." She drifted off in thought as Sam spoke up.

"Do you have the population data on that laptop?"

"Yes. We didn't have much time, but we did put a basic table showing population by country, by continent, and as a percentage of the world total. If no one minds, I'll bring that up on big screen." Hearing no objections, Rui did so.

"Could you add another column showing the distribution of the anomalies by continent?" Sam waited a moment for Rui to populate the column and then observed that if the intent was to achieve minimal coverage on all populated landmasses, then distribute them evenly by each continent's percentage of the world's population, the distribution did not map as would be expected.

"Africa and the Americas are about right, within a half a unit or so, but the real outliers, if we accept the minimum of one per populated continent and exclude Australia from consideration, are Europe and Asia. In Europe, four countries are targeted when it only warrants two by population, and Asia should have at least ten, but has only eight."

"I noticed that too, but I think part of it might be our somewhat arbitrary inclusion of Turkey in Europe rather than Asia. It really could be counted in either," Dan commented.

"The disparity could be due to the populations of other animals in those areas. For all we know, it could include insects or even plants. We have no reason to believe they're targeting based solely on human life," Camilla added.

"You're right, of course, but based on two points, I'm inclined toward another explanation," Sam started, cautiously. This was not his area of expertise, but he had difficulty keeping his ideas to himself. "I think we can conclude that they're, in fact, targeting based on human population density and not the density of all life forms within a given area."

Camilla stared intently at Sam as he spoke, clearly thinking about the problem and his statement. She said, "You're right. I should have seen it immediately."

"What?" Jack asked.

Sam gestured to Camilla, offering her the floor. She declined. "You saw it first, Sam."

"If they're targeting life in general, wouldn't there be some impact sites in the oceans?" Sam asked. "If I recall they make up over ninety percent of Earth's living space."

"Nearly ninety-nine percent, actually," Camilla corrected, somewhat chagrined.

"What's your second point, Sam?" Dan asked.

"Well, this would be less tenuous if there was an impact site on Greenland, but I still think it works. Pull up the map again, please?" Sam waited for Rui to do so then continued. "The Americas are clearly distinct continents, as is Australia. Africa not so much, but far more so than Europe. It's our political considerations that lead us to make a distinction between Europe and Asia, which is why we had some ambiguity about Turkey. Just looking at a map without those considerations, an outsider wouldn't see a difference between the two, not from a geographic perspective. Going with that logic, we don't have an imbalance. There are twelve impact sites in Eurasia, just as we would expect based on the population numbers."

"This is all very interesting, folks, and I don't mean to stifle creativity, but the clock is ticking. I think the most salient question is whether the targeting is intended to reach the most people or destroy as much of humanity as possible in their first strike. Does anyone have any thoughts on that?" Web asked, slightly frustrated at the academic tone of the conversation.

"It depends on their timeline," Camilla answered.

"Explain, please," Web directed.

"If they're not in a hurry, these would not be the best targets to select in order to kill the most humans over time. I'm sure you're all aware of the recent rapid growth in world population, but I'm not sure how much thought you've given it.

"For most of human history, the population of the world was measured in the tens of millions. Advances like improved irrigation and sewage disposal increased those numbers to the hundreds of millions as recently as two thousand years ago, but it took another millennium and a half to raise the number to half a billion. Over the next five hundred years, the population tripled. Between then and now, a little over a century, the population has more than quadrupled. There are many reasons why this is so, but the primary one is the availability of energy, particularly portable energy. It's no coincidence that the rise in the rate of population growth aligns with the increasing use of hydrocarbons as fuels. It's causal. If they destroyed our hydrocarbon sources and infrastructure, much of the world would starve to death in relatively short order, yet they ignored major oil-producing countries in favor of more populous ones."

"So, you don't think their intent is hostile?" Web asked.

"I didn't say that. I don't think this approach"—she gestured toward the map—"is the most efficient use of resources over time if their intent is to cause us harm," Camilla corrected.

"Camilla makes a very good point that raises another. Not only did the anomalies not target hydrocarbon infrastructure but they also don't appear to be targeting infrastructure at all. If they wanted the most immediately destructive effect, wouldn't they at least target their selected country's largest city?" Dan asked.

"We don't know that they haven't. The original anomaly split into multiple smaller spheres. What's to say the smaller spheres won't do the same in order to achieve wider coverage?" Jack asked.

"Which one is headed toward the United States?" Web asked, looking at Rui.

"The one we've been receiving data from."

"The one we could be talking with," Sam said, just loud enough for everyone in the room to hear.

"What?" Chang interjected, just as the "with" was leaving Sam's mouth.

Doctor Chang Liu was the team's mathematician. Although nearly everyone on the team had at least a minor in math in one of their degrees, none of them came close to the expertise Chang brought to bear in the area of game theory. Up to this point, he'd had little to do but theorize with minimal data. He, more than anyone else on the team, was frustrated at the singular response from the anomalies in the face of all subsequent attempts to communicate. If they could establish a real dialogue with the anomalies, he could apply his expertise in a meaningful way. Normally not an outspoken member of the team—he was more comfortable with numbers and theory and suspected his accent was thicker than people told him it was—he could become quite vocal when he felt his ability to contribute was being ignored.

"Sam's talking about—" Jack began before Sam cut him off.

"What I'm talking about," he started in a more forceful voice before Jack interrupted him.

"This isn't the time to discuss that."

"This is precisely the time to talk about a new way to communicate with the anomalies. Why haven't we heard about this before?" Chang asked pointedly, directing his attention to Web. Unlike Sam, Chang did not need Web in order to do the work he loved. As a result, he had not developed any habit of deference. He showed respect to everyone on the team, deference to none of them.

Web was well aware that he didn't want the outcome of this event, whatever it turned out to be, to include the fact that he ignored Chang's input. Although in charge of the team, he had not selected its members. All of the civilians had patrons in high places who believed their expert might be the one to make the difference should the time come. In this case, Web was inclined to believe them; if the program was actually a program and if it was designed to let us communicate with them. Two very big "ifs."

"I just found out about it myself, Chang. We were discussing it while Rui was recalculating the trajectories of the anomalies, but let me be clear: we do not know that we have a way to communicate with them. We *suspect*"—Web looked at Sam, emphasizing the word—"that we've found a computer program within the data stream coming from 'our' anomaly. We don't know that it's a functional program and also don't know what it will do if we run it."

"Then why don't we run it and find out?" Chang asked.

Web sensed he was losing control of the meeting and tried to get it back on track. "This meeting is about understanding the reasoning behind the anomalies' selected impact sites."

Chang, however, wasn't about to let it go.

"This *team* is about handling first contact. If Sam believes he's found a program within the data, I'm inclined to believe him. It's the reason we brought him in. As for what the program will do, there are a finite number of practical possibilities. Starting with the most obvious, there are three kinds: it may attempt to do us harm, it may attempt to aid us, or it may perform a function that does not attempt to do either. The last is highly improbable because it ignores the active nature of both the anomalies' arrival and delivery. It's also irrelevant to our discussion because it introduces neither risk nor reward into the prospect of executing the program.

"So, we're left with the first two options. Let's examine the scenario in which the program attempts to do harm. Assuming there aren't multiple factions within the anomalies with conflicting goals, an assumption we can revisit, the nature of the program should reflect the nature of the visitors. If their intent is to do us harm, the program is likely to be harmful. There would be no reason for it to be otherwise and they certainly possess the technical prowess to do so. Choosing not to run the program avoids the harm that decision may introduce and may delay whatever part of the plan it was intended to aid. Is the nature of that delay likely to materially reduce the threat they could pose? No. Why not? Because we didn't know they existed only hours ago and they'll be here mere hours from now. There simply isn't time for it to matter.

"Now let's examine the second option—that the program may attempt to aid us. Working with the same assumption that there aren't multiple competing factions, we're left only to ponder the nature of such aid. Unlike explicitly intended harm, intended aid can lead to unfortunate unintended harm to the recipients of such aid, but again, that's the same threat we'll face in a few hours. Unless we run the program before then, we'll know nothing about that risk, should it exist, which means we won't be able to inform the NCA about the risk, which further means we would have failed one of our prime directives. It'll be even worse if the reward is apportioned among the players according to how quickly they solve the problem. We could forfeit reward by overvaluing risk, again potentially denying the NCA any advantage we could have otherwise earned. This is first contact. We must accept appropriate risks to do our job." Chang finished speaking.

The room was silent for a moment before Web spoke. "Does anyone have a counterargument?"

No one did.

"Fine. Dan, you and Sam explore that avenue. We'll continue this discussion. Inform me immediately of your results."

Chapter FIVE

Sam paused, his finger over the button that would execute the alien program.

"You want to do the honors?" he asked Dan.

"No, thank you. You found it, you run it."

Sam pressed the button, then looked from the screen. "Well, that's disappointing."

"We knew it might not be a program, or a complete one," Dan responded.

"Yeah, I know. I'm just thinking of all the time we lost debating whether to try it. We could've been working on alternatives for the past hour."

"It wasn't the kind of decision one person can make, Sam."

"But it always comes down to one person in a bureaucracy—usually someone who knows the least about the problem or the nature of the solution. Politicians and bureaucrats believe they're better qualified to make decisions than the rest of us, but nothing in my life has shown that to be true. If we waited for Web to get permission, we'd end up running it too late to explore alternatives if it failed to work, like it just did, and that's if we got permission to run it at all." Sam stopped and took a deep breath. He realized he was taking it out on the wrong person.

"Sorry. You didn't deserve that."

"Don't worry about it. Everyone's a bit stressed right now," Dan replied.

"Thanks." Sam closed his eyes, inhaled deeply again, and exhaled slowly.

"Okay, then; back to the matter at hand. I've been worrying about the possibility—probability, if I'm being honest—that the first program wouldn't work since my conversation with Web and Jack. I can think of three potential causes. One, I could've selected the wrong subset of data to input; two, my code could be flawed; or three, the similarity of the data to the structure of a program file is coincidence. You know I don't believe in coincidence, so let's start with that one. Has your team analyzed the statistical probability that we'd find this pattern repeating randomly as frequently as we're seeing it?" Sam asked.

"We have, and it's highly improbable. Of course, the sequence could have a meaning to the sender that differs from how we would interpret it. We're assuming they're intelligent enough to send us a message we're capable of understanding or decoding in time to matter. That seems logical to us but it may not seem as logical to them. They could also be overestimating our intelligence, as humbling as that thought may be," Dan replied.

"There's nothing we can do about it if they've overestimated us, so I don't see any upside to worrying about it. I'll leave the pursuit of other pattern interpretations to your team. I vote that the two of us ignore option three."

"Agreed."

"On to option one, then. I think this is where we're likely to find the problem. There's a tremendous amount of data, and I didn't spend much time selecting the first chunk to evaluate. I'll run a few copies of my existing script against my lower-probability candidates, but I'd like you to select another dozen or so promising sets. I'll run the program against those while you look for more, or for a better method of finding higher-quality sets. My selection algorithm is in the code I sent you.

"Last and perhaps least," Sam continued, "is option two. My code could be flawed. I'll start reviewing it right after I update Web, but I think you should have someone on your team do so as well."

"I agree. I'll get someone on it before I start looking for better candidate sections of the message."

"Can you think of anything else we should be doing right now?" Sam asked.

"No, but you'll have to tell me about that conversation later."

"If we all survive the next few hours, I promise I'll catch you up on office gossip," Sam replied.

Web's door was closed. Normally, Sam would consider his obligation met and wait for Web to find him. Under the circumstances, he chose a different course and knocked. Sam didn't want to give Web an excuse to kick him off the team.

"Enter."

Sam entered and found Web seated behind his desk and Jack in the room with him. They both stopped talking and looked at Sam, waiting for him to brief them. Sam stopped a few feet into the room.

"We attempted to execute the program. It didn't run."

Web let the silence linger before asking, "What do you propose for next steps?"

"Dan is looking for portions of the message that may serve as better input to my script. He's also going to have a member of his team review my code, which I'll be doing as well. As soon as I get back, I'll start the process again and try the new programs as we build them."

"Do you think that's wise?" Web asked.

"I think it's a continuation of a decision that's already been made."

"For better or worse, you're right about that, Sam. Keep me informed."

Sam might have now been a civilian, but he recognized a dismissal when he heard one. He left without another word.

Sam looked at Dan in frustration, "This isn't working."

"No, it's not," Dan replied, equally frustrated.

They'd worked on building a functional program for several hours and throughout that time, each had what Dan liked to call mini-epiphanies. At first, it was exciting, but as the clock ticked down with neither having success, the reality of the stakes became an increasingly heavy burden. It was too late to bring in someone new and try to get them briefed and up to speed. They knew it was up to them, and so did everyone else. Unfortunately, Sam and Dan were running out of ideas.

"Maybe they did overestimate us," Sam said, almost to himself.

"I don't think so. Let's talk it through again."

"Okay, but let's do it in the break room. I need a change of scenery."

Neither of them said a word along the way. When they arrived, Sam grabbed a couple of bottles of water from the refrigerator, handed one to Dan, opened his, and took a long drink. They sat down at one of the tables farthest from the door. The silence continued as each man tried to break out of his own mental loop and discuss where he thought they might be going wrong. Dan was the first to speak.

"Our logic is sound. I'm more convinced than ever that you were right. There's a program in there."

"I'll grant you that our premise appears to be sound. Unfortunately, our approach to the problem is clearly flawed," Sam responded.

Reading emotion on Sam's face was difficult, but Dan had known him long enough not to need such clues. "We don't have time for self-recrimination, Sam," Dan said gently. "Let's start with the first piece, the header. Your first script found a number of them in the message because that was what you wrote it to do. You initially made an assumption about where the header portion ended based on a series of null terminators. We've since invalidated that assumption by finding enough duplicate copies of the file fragments to allow us to overlap them and keep the consistently common data. Your approach to finding the next pieces was sound, but because you were starting with the wrong end point to the header, you were finding the wrong matching starting point to the next piece of the file. That problem fixed itself when we addressed the first one. Since then, we've found enough duplicated examples of every matching portion to convince me we're putting the right pieces together in the right order. I was concerned about knowing which piece was last, but your observation that the eighteenth piece was a mirror image of itself was ingenious. When we excluded the mirrored data on the last run, I really thought we had it."

Sam finished his water, got another from the refrigerator, and sat back down. Dan was mindlessly peeling the label off his emptied bottle.

"Dan, you're a genius!"

"What?"

"Look at what you're doing."

Dan looked down at his hands. "I've had enough mysteries for one day, Sam. How about you just tell me what you're talking about?"

"When we figured out the terminating file was mirrored, we discarded the mirrored portion, right?"

"Yes, I just said that."

"But when we connected the other pieces, we kept the overlap, like on the label you just peeled off. The overlap isn't necessary for the label to do its job; it's a by-product of the manufacturing process, just like the mirrored portion. It exists to let us connect the pieces, but it's not part of the finished product." Before he finished talking, Sam was out of his seat and headed toward the door. Dan was right behind him.

Catching his breath from the sprint to his workstation, Sam made changes to the script that assembled the program, and reran it. Like dozens of times before, it produced a potentially executable file. Sam was just about to try running it when he stopped himself, got out of his chair, and said, "This time I insist. We need all the help we can get."

Dan took a seat, paused for a moment, and then executed the program. It ran.

"Yes! Finally!" Sam put his hand up for a high-five but Dan continued staring at the screen.

"Um, we have a problem."

Chapter SIX

Before Sam called Web, he looked around the room for Chang but didn't see him. Not wanting to have this conversation with Web without Chang's support, he asked Dan to find him. Waiting to tell Web was not an option, but neither was leaving his workstation. He picked up the secure line and dialed Web. The phone rang twice before he picked up, saying curtly, "Web."

"Web, it's Sam. We got the program to run. I think you should see this."

"I'm busy. Can it wait?"

As much as Sam would have liked to put off the conversation he suspected he'd soon be a part of, if their roles were reversed, he would want to know about this immediately, "No, it really can't."

"I'll be right there." The line went dead.

Sam looked back at his screen. Whatever the programs were doing now, they continued to increase their share of the cluster's processing power. Even compared to some of the most complex malware he'd worked with, he'd never seen anything like this. He rubbed his dry eyes and waited for the others to arrive. Thankfully, Dan returned with Chang before Web could join them, undoubtedly accompanied by Jack.

Sam greeted Chang with some relief. "Thanks for joining us."

"I wouldn't miss it. Dan told me a little about what you did to get the program together. Fascinating."

Before Sam could respond, Web walked in with Jack on his heels. Somewhere along the way, Jack had found time not only to put on a freshly pressed uniform but also to shave and otherwise clean up. He was back to being a well-kept dick.

"So, you got the program to run. Should I congratulate you or fire you?" Web asked.

"Neither, yet," Sam replied.

Dan started to say something, presumably in Sam's defense, but Sam stopped him with a gesture. Nothing Dan could say would improve the situation.

"What do you have?" Web asked more pointedly.

"I called you right after we executed the program, so we know very little about what it's doing right now, but its resource usage, or rather, *their* resource usage, is significant," Sam answered.

"What do you mean, 'their'?" Jack asked.

"As soon as we ran the program, it began making additional programs and executing them. Within seconds, according to the process logs on the other nodes in the cluster, versions of the program were running on all of the nodes. There are currently hundreds of child programs running across the entire cluster. They're using the majority of the cluster's combined processing power and a substantial portion of its I/O."

Jack hated having to ask, but would hate it more if he left it to Web to do so. "I/O?"

"Sorry. Input/output. The programs are writing a massive amount of data to disk as well as using substantial amounts of memory."

"Do you know what it's doing?" Web asked.

"Technically, yes. We know which programs have been created by the one we stitched together and we know which files it's creating. But functionally, no. We do not know the intent or purpose of those programs or files," Sam answered.

"We should shut it down," Jack said to Web.

"There's no indication it's hostile," Sam directed to Web.

"It's taken over the analysis cluster!" Jack responded.

"It has not 'taken over' the analysis cluster. It is using most of the resources, but we have sufficient left to keep working. Isn't this what we built the cluster for anyway, to analyze whatever data we received?" Sam asked.

"Don't pretend you anticipated this. You said if it acted like this it could be hostile," Jack replied.

Sam didn't recall having said that, but moved on. "I said if it breached the containment of the cluster it could be hostile. It either hasn't tried or hasn't succeeded. Unless it does so, we should let it continue to do whatever it's doing."

"You have no idea what it's trying to do and you want to sit back and see what happens?" Jack asked incredulously.

To Sam's relief, Chang joined the conversation. "We've had a day full of measuring, planning, speculating, and reporting. Sam and Dan have given us the only opportunity to provide our government with information that couldn't have been obtained from any other source that we know of. We must not shut it down, and I don't understand why we're revisiting this decision."

"We have new information, Chang. In my experience it's a good idea to reevaluate decisions when new information presents itself," Web offered.

"We have results that fall into the group of outcomes we anticipated before we made our decision . . . ," Chang started. He stopped himself as all of the monitors connected to a cluster work-station went black.

Sam turned away from the conversation and was about to start investigating when an image began to form of what appeared to be a populous star field. Then, a faint sphere appeared in the middle of the image, which began to rotate. In moments, a smaller but far brighter sphere appeared in front of the first. The brighter sphere was growing slowly. Suddenly, there was a flicker and the larger sphere was gone, replaced by a group of smaller spheres.

"We're seeing its arrival," Dan said, almost reverently.

Sam looked around the room and noticed Rui wasn't there. Barely taking his eyes off the screen, he picked up the phone and called him. Rui picked up on the first ring.

"Hello?"

"Rui. It's Sam. Come to the main conference room immediately." Sam hung up without waiting for an answer.

Rui arrived almost instantly, running to the group gathered around Sam's monitor. "What is it?" he asked.

"We appear to be seeing a representation of the anomaly's arrival from a space-based perspective," Web replied. As he did so, the smaller spheres seemed to slightly drift apart.

"That looks like when they retargeted," Rui observed.

"Can you tell how far out they are?" Jack asked.

"About 800,000 kilometers," Rui answered absently. "How long's this been running?" he asked.

"I called you as soon as it started," Sam told him.

The team watched in silence as Earth continued to grow and the spheres drifted farther apart. As details began to become visible, the pace of approach slowed and only one sphere remained visible.

"We're inside the moon's orbit," Rui informed the team as he glanced at his watch.

"How can you tell?" Sam asked.

"The continents are visible," Rui answered.

A couple of minutes passed, with the view of Earth steadily gaining resolution.

"We're about 150,000 kilometers out now. We're oriented on the Western hemisphere. I believe we're seeing this from the viewpoint of our anomaly," Rui continued to update the team.

Earth was visibly growing. Within less than two minutes, it filled the screen, and as it did, the view began rotating again. The team appeared to be watching the sphere enter the atmosphere from within the atmosphere, below and to the side of the sphere, and the pace had slowed again. There was no indicator of speed, but there was also no sign of atmospheric violence.

"We appear to be following it down, but there should be obvious signs of friction and atmospheric disturbance," Rui narrated.

The team watched the sphere continue to descend until it ultimately came to rest in a field in Kansas. No impact. No violence. The series of images faded to black.

"Did you see that?" Sam whispered to no one in particular.

No one answered.

The sphere was no taller than the cornstalks in the field around it.

Chapter SEVEN

Moments after the projection ended, it began again. Everyone in the room watched, particularly Rui, who'd missed the beginning the first time.

When it once again faded to black, Web turned to Sam and said, "I want a copy of that video."

You're welcome, Sam thought to himself, but said, "I'll get right on it."

The projection started again, apparently in a continuous loop.

"When you're done, join us in the west conference room. I need to report this and I want to do so with as much context as possible. Jack, find Camilla and Angela and ask them to join the rest of us after they've watched this." Web left the room with most of the team following right behind him. Dan stayed back to talk with Sam.

"That was good work. You know, you're probably the first person in human history to have communicated with an alien culture."

"You were as much a part of it as I was. I wouldn't even be here if you hadn't convinced Web to bring me in."

"I'm proud enough to believe I would've solved it eventually, but I'm also honest enough with myself to know I wouldn't have figured it out in time to make a difference tonight. You did that. I'm sorry Web is too biased against you to tell you that, but I will."

"Thanks, I appreciate it." Sam paused for a moment. Deciding against belaboring the point, he said instead, "I'd better figure out how to get a copy of this."

Dan wondered if he should push Sam further, but like Sam, he decided to let it go. "Need help?" he asked.

"Not yet, but I'll let you know if I do," Sam replied.

"Okay. See you in the conference room."

As Dan walked away, Sam turned his attention to the problem at hand. Sitting down at his workstation, he opened up a new screen and found the process running the projection. To his surprise, all of his previous work was exactly where he'd left it and the alien program had opened a new screen to display the projection. So, it's a polite alien program, Sam thought to himself as he prepared a script to capture the output of the looping projection. In less than ten minutes, he'd recorded a copy and verified that it played.

While he worked, Camilla walked in with Angela. They'd been quietly watching the projection play on one of the other workstation screens. While their second viewing was wrapping up, Sam rose from his chair, waiting until it finished before disturbing them.

"Amazing, isn't it?" Sam asked them.

"I would've never thought to use video of this sort to establish first contact. It's brilliant," Angela responded.

Major Angela Leone—Angela, never Angie; she couldn't stand the Rolling Stones—had been a child prodigy. American by birth, she spent most of her formative years in England and China. Her family had moved around following her biological father, a Marine pilot who died in a training accident when she was very young. Following her father's death, her mother returned to her home in England before accepting a position in Hong Kong. It seemed natural to her that little Angela had learned Mandarin as easily as English. Kids just did that. It wasn't until her mother met the man who would become Angela's second father, one of Hong Kong's elite, that she learned her four-year-old was speaking Mandarin with a precision and nuance seldom mastered by a child of any age. Recognizing Angela's linguistic proficiency, he encouraged her to learn as many languages as she wished. By the time she was ten, she was also fluent in Japanese, Hindi, Spanish, and Russian. Fascinated with the structure of all forms of communication, she completed an undergraduate degree in mathematics from the US Naval Academy before receiving a rare service deferral allowing her to earn her PhD in linguistics from Harvard before she turned twenty-five. In the intervening ten years, she'd long since decided that the gesture of respect she'd shown for her first father by becoming a Marine was the best career decision she could have made.

"I don't think anyone thought we might encounter a detailed presentation of the events of the next several hours. I know I didn't," Sam noted, thinking Angela might be disappointed that she hadn't foreseen something so incredibly unlikely.

Having had the life she'd had so far, Angela was not prone to self-doubt. She'd merely been admiring an elegant solution to a complex problem. She gave Sam and Camilla a playful grin and said, "Come on. Let's see what everyone is saying about this."

"I'll be right there." Sam took a moment to copy the video onto a secure drive before heading to the meeting.

When Sam opened the door to the conference room, several people glanced in his direction, but the conversation continued.

". . . the density of the anomaly before it entered our atmosphere, but why?" Rui was asking Dan.

"I don't know why. It's just one possible solution," Dan answered, his slight irritation a clear indicator of a long and stressful day.

"It's one possible solution that ignores the fact that we didn't see the object deeply embedded in the cornfield," Rui retorted.

"Which could mean the original sphere was largely hollow or it could mean the anomaly doesn't want to be embedded in the soil, so it isn't allowing that to happen." Dan's irritation was becoming more evident.

In the pause that followed, Chang took the opportunity to cool the conversation. "Perhaps now would be a good time to summarize the various theories?" He looked around the room, and seeing no objection, began, "First, we have ablation. It is possible the anomaly shed mass in order to slow down or dissipate heat. Second, we have the possibility that our original estimates of the size of the anomaly were invalid. An entity that can do what we've seen so far would appear capable of misleading us for its own reasons. Third, the entity could have shed mass for reasons we've not yet determined. Fourth, the anomaly could have changed density while descending. Those are the proffered explanations, as I understand them. Have I missed one?"

Sam found it fascinating that they were talking about the events in the projection as if they'd already happened. Perhaps Angela had spoken about the video on a deeper level than Sam had originally concluded. In any case, he was staying out of this discussion. He'd had his moment in the sun and was ready to spend some time in the shade. Instead, he'd worked his way over to Web's side while Chang spoke. He leaned down and spoke quietly to Web as he handed him the drive, "Here's a high-resolution copy of the video."

Web took the drive and stood. "Please continue this discussion without me. I'm going to update the CO. If you come to an agreement supported by the facts as we know them in my absence, please interrupt me immediately." He gestured for Sam and Jack to follow him before proceeding to his office. Once there, he told them to take a seat.

"I'm about to report what we've found. The report will be sent immediately to the NCA. Is there any reason I should not send this video?" he asked Sam pointedly.

"I'm not sure what you mean, Web."

"I mean, you're the only one who knows for sure how this video was constructed. To the best of your knowledge, do you believe it represents what will happen later tonight?"

"I can only tell you that it represents what the aliens communicated to us would happen tonight. As I told you before, I had no way of knowing what the program would do when we ran it."

"Is there any chance this video could be infected; that it could be the means the anomaly is using to get out of containment? I mean, outside of what Rui's team has done to keep it confined to our systems?"

Sam was genuinely impressed. "Those are really good questions."

Web looked at Sam intently, trying to determine if he was being set up.

Sam continued, "It's possible, in the sense that anything is possible, but I don't think so. I made the video. Like every file I transfer from our networks, I scanned it before and after copying it. It's as secure and clean as I know how to make it. But just in case, you could suggest that it be run on an isolated machine," Sam offered.

Web stared at Sam for several seconds before saying, "Okay. Please close the door on your way out."

Once again, Sam left without saying another word.

Forty minutes later, Web reentered the east conference room. The team was no closer to an explanation than they had been when he'd departed. "Listen up, everybody." The conversations in the room quickly faded to silence.

"We've received orders. The anomaly is expected to arrive in just under four hours. It is now"—he glanced at his watch— "21:12. We depart at 21:30 sharp. Buses will transport us to the airfield where two Chinooks will fly us to an observation location one click away from the projected landing site. It's a two-hour flight but we'll be traveling heavy and fast, so we'll have to refuel along the way. It's going to be very close, but we *are* going to arrive before it does. Be on the main bus at 21:30 or lose your chance to continue making history today."

Dan started to ask a question, but Web cut him off. "There's plenty of time for questions during the flight. Use the next fifteen minutes wisely." Everyone in the room moved for the door.

Web directed Sam to go to Jack's office, where Sam found Jack assembling his load-bearing vest. He did not offer Sam a seat. Instead, he continued to work with his hands as he glanced up at Sam. "You're not going to Kansas."

"What are you talking about?"

"The first contact team is going. You are not a member of that team. We'll take it from here. Take some time off." Two security force specialists appeared in the doorway as Jack spoke. He turned to them. "Please escort this gentleman to his car."

"This is ridiculous."

"Go home, Sam. We don't need you anymore."

Chapter EIGHT

The two Chinooks landed in a perimeter established by the advance party. Though the advance party had arrived ahead of the contact team just forty-five minutes earlier, what they'd already accomplished was remarkable. A small shelter system stood about one hundred feet away from where their helicopter came to rest, and a generator could be heard running in the distance, presumably providing power for the well-lit entrance to the newly constructed command post.

"Where did all these soldiers come from?" Camilla asked as she exited the aircraft.

"A team from the 101st Air Assault division, the 160th Special Operations Aviation Regiment, and their payload preceded us. I wasn't sure they'd get here before us, but I'm glad they did. Although they received their movement order earlier than we did, they had farther to travel. That's the majority of them. The rest are members of our advance party. They left the better part of an hour before we did. They'd been standing by since we received word of the anomaly and were able to leave immediately once we determined we were dealing with a landing site and not an impact zone. Another team of Air Force security forces should have already landed at the Salina, Kansas, airport in a C-17, but they have to travel by road and won't arrive for another hour. Unfortunately, that is the closest airfield with a runway long enough to allow a C-17 to take off. We can use the Chinooks to get to Salina in the future, but for now they'll have to drive. We beat them here, but that'll be the fastest route back from here on out," Web replied in an uncharacteristically verbose fashion. He'd been in a particularly good mood since they left the SCIF. It was not lost on anyone that Web's change in demeanor coincided with Sam's departure.

"Jesus Christ, I had no idea corn grew so tall!" Jack exclaimed as he joined the rest of the team on the recently trampled cornfield. Growing up in Miami, Florida, and spending nearly all of his life on and around various Air Force bases, Jack had never been closer to a cornfield than a high-altitude, high-speed flyover.

"Corn frequently grows much higher than this, particularly when it's to be used for fodder." Camilla responded in a tone that left no doubt she appreciated neither his ignorance nor his choice of expletive. "I expected it would be over our heads. It's why we brought the lifts." She gestured toward the three scissor lifts being outfitted with cameras and other equipment around the perimeter on the side facing the landing area.

"Jack, please double check that all of the preparations we requested are proceeding. The rest of you, please join me in the command post." Web walked toward the entrance to the shelter; the rest of the team followed.

Though nearly everyone in the military used the word *tent* for any temporary outdoor shelter, the inside of the CP belied that term. It had a clean, hard, nonslip floor, a ten-foot ceiling, regularly spaced electric outlets, a series of desks along the left wall, and three large flat-screen monitors mounted along the right. Technicians continued to set up and test the equipment and connections throughout the room, but the monitors were already functioning with each showing a different section of a cornfield. Web took a moment to scan them all. Apparently satisfied, he turned back to the team.

"In about ten minutes, the world as we know it will change. We will not get a second chance at first contact. I know you're all tired and I know this is about as unusual a day a person is likely to have, but it's the day we were given. Other people are doing everything possible to ensure our systems are as ready as we can make them. What I need you to do is prepare yourselves. Grab a cup of coffee or a bottle of water. Do some push-ups or jog in place. Meditate or pray. Do whatever you must do in the few minutes we have to be as alert as possible. I choose coffee." Web looked at each of them before heading over to the coffeepot. There was never any doubt there'd be a coffeepot.

Rui and Dan elected to watch the landing from outside, reasoning that they could watch the replay as many times as they wanted, but could only see it live once. Neither thought there'd be much to see with the naked eye, even with the nearly full moon. It didn't matter to them. Seeing it in person was primal, a limbic response.

"Sam should be here," Dan said.

"I agree that Sam's contribution was considerable, but Web has a point," Rui replied.

"What point? That Sam is not a formal member of the team?" Dan said. "That's not a valid point. The structure of the team was formed long before we knew what we'd encounter, or that we'd ever encounter anything for that matter. It seemed logical to have a linguist on the team, but Angela has had little to do so far. It seemed logical to have a biologist and a psychologist on the team, but neither Camilla nor AJ has had as much to do as Angela. I'll admit I didn't foresee the need for a cyberterrorism specialist on the first contact team, and I was one of the people responsible for its composition, but as soon as we realized we'd need such a specialist, he should've become a formal member. There's no way to keep this a secret. Too many people around this landing know about it, and our landing site is likely to be among the most controlled of those around the world. Why hobble ourselves by limiting the team to what we believed it *should* be before we knew what we were going to face?"

"I think Web's point is that with the anomaly about to be physically present, it is unlikely we'll need Sam's skills in the future. And you know as well as I do that Sam can be a loose cannon. Web has a responsibility to reduce the likelihood of irresponsible behavior," Rui replied dryly.

"I think Web's point is that he has the power to exclude Sam and so he has," Dan retorted.

Rui chose to give him the last word on the topic. It was not one he wished to continue discussing.

The rest of the team, having elected to watch the landing from inside the CP, traded the multiple and enhanced views of the event about to transpire for the opportunity to weigh in on Sam's absence. Captain Andrews was with the majority. At Web's request and in keeping with long tradition, she counted backward from ten in time with the countdown clock, ". . . three, two, one."

A second after she finished, every monitor showed a sphere centered in its frame. An almost imperceptible moment later, there was an audible crack, similar to an aerial fireworks explosion, but sharper.

It was possible to see the sphere as it landed, but barely. Once again, the visitors had demonstrated their ability to ignore inertia in a way that human science did not yet understand. The sphere arrived with a sonic boom, but landed as softly as if it had been placed there by hand. One moment, the field was empty; the next, it was occupied by a dull-black sphere 3.072 meters in diameter.

Rui, unaware of the countdown, turned to Dan and said, "Our visitor surprised me again. I thought there'd be something to see. I thought it would slow down before landing, but why should it? Why not approach at supersonic speed and come to rest exactly where you want to be without slowing? Other than the fact that we can't wrap our heads around how one would go about doing such a thing, it's very efficient. My God, what we could learn from them."

Dan nodded slowly and said, "Indeed . . . if they're here to teach." He looked back up at the night sky, allowing his eyes to follow the path they had expected to watch the sphere follow as it descended. His eyes stopped where the sphere had landed; it sat as if it had been there when they arrived. He couldn't help but feel that it was waiting for them rather than the other way around. "Come on, let's go inside. Maybe there's more to see on the replay."

Indeed, the high-speed visual camera had captured what the human eye could not. As Rui and Dan walked in, Jack asked a technician how fast the sphere had been moving upon approach.

"It was steady at 1056.42 miles per hour all the way to the ground, sir."

"No variation?"

"Not out to two decimals, sir."

"What did we get on thermal?"

"Not what I expected, sir. The object was a uniform 162 degrees Fahrenheit. It should've been much higher than that and not uniform." The technician was about to continue, but remembering where she was and whom she was answering, stopped her.

"Please continue," Web encouraged her.

"Well, sir, I'm not an expert, but I've participated in a number of aircraft tests using this equipment, and the planes always show significant temperature variations from the leading edge to the trailing edge of the flight surfaces, and the temperature is always higher than this, even at Mach 1. This was traveling closer to Mach 2 and I would've expected temperatures closer to 300 degrees," she responded.

"Is it still at 162 degrees?" Dan asked.

The technician moved her view from the monitor showing the replay to the real-time monitor, "No, sir. It's not showing up on thermal anymore." She stopped again.

Web nodded slightly before thanking her and returned his attention to the team. "We're running full-spectrum analysis now. We should have results shortly. Does anyone have any thoughts to share while we wait?"

"I have some questions I'd like to ask whoever built that thing," Rui said to no one in particular. It was a thought shared by them all.

As focused as ever, Angela said, "I'd like to try to reestablish communications now." The anomaly had stopped broadcasting as soon as Dan executed the program it had sent. Everyone was anxious to restart the conversation, such as it was.

"Go ahead," Web replied. Angela grabbed Dan's arm and pulled him away from the group toward the system connected to the communications array. She'd developed a few new ideas on the flight and was eager to test them. Dan offered no resistance. He was as eager to do something as she was.

Interminable minutes passed as the team reviewed various recordings of the object's arrival, waiting for the results of the analysis. When it arrived, it was as consistent as it was confounding. The sphere was not emitting anything measurable from the observation site: no microwaves, radio waves, or X-rays, no light on any spectrum, and no radiation of any kind. It appeared to be an inert mass sitting at ambient temperature, waiting.

"It's as safe as we know how to measure, for now at least," Web noted before directing Jack to get the cover and concealment team over to hide the sphere from overhead observation. It was standard procedure for anything interesting in the open: cover and camouflage it as quickly as possible. The fact that there were sixteen similar spheres elsewhere in the world, including one in each of the countries with the means to spy on the United States, changed nothing. Nor would the fact that the United States now possessed one stop them from doing everything in their power to closely observe every other landing site in the world. Enigmatic visitors unfathomably more advanced than humankind were no match for standard procedure.

"I'm on it," Jack replied as he departed the CP.

Web turned to Chang. "Would you like to work with the active scanning team until we can reestablish communication with it?" It was unlikely Chang would be able to materially contribute to the work of the technicians who used the tools regularly. Web was mending fences.

"Yes. Thank you."

As Chang moved to the other side of the shelter, Web sat down in front of the large monitors. A quarter century in the military had made him very good at waiting, but this time he didn't have to wait long.

At 01:19, within minutes of Chang's departure to work with the active scanning team, without warning, and in complete silence, the sphere transformed again. Under the watchful electronic eyes of dozens of cameras and sensors and almost as many people, it ceased being a sphere and became something else. To those observing, the transition appeared instant. It was only upon review of the high-speed cameras' recordings that they would later see the sphere seemingly turn to liquid and quickly melt away, leaving a much smaller group of objects in its wake.

Where the sphere had been there were now two equilateral triangular prisms, nearly touching at their bases. Each prism was 81 centimeters on a side and 30 centimeters tall. One of them was perfectly aligned with magnetic north and the other south, leaving the middle of the diamond-shaped formation aligned along east and west.

"What the hell just happened?" Jack asked the room as he reentered it.

"It appears our visitor has found a form more to its liking," Rui replied laconically.

"Zoom in on the center monitor," Web instructed the technician.

Upon closer examination, what had appeared to be solid prisms was in fact a collection of small spheres, each about the size of a tennis ball and every bit as dull and black as the larger sphere had been.

Chang rejoined the main team and worked his way to the front of the crowded space. "Interesting," he commented as he stared intently at the closer image of the collection of spheres.

"What?" asked Jack.

"I believe it is trying to tell us something, something it wants us to understand as soon as possible. Angela, come here please."

Angela had been across the CP when the change had taken place and was, as such, at the back of the group arranged around the monitor. Her height made it difficult to get a good view of the screen. Grateful for the opportunity to get a better look, she joined Chang.

"Look at the grouping," he continued as she joined him, pointing out faint lines between components of the northernmost prism. "Each of the larger prisms is made up of nine smaller ones."

"Yes, you're right. The separation is small, but I see it. Did you notice the number of spheres in each of the component prisms?" Angela asked him.

"How could I miss it?" He smiled at her like a kid on his first carnival ride.

"Would one of you care to enlighten the rest of us?" Web asked.

"Yes, of course." Chang turned sideways to the monitor so that he could address the team. They were not his only audience. Everyone in the room who could steal a look at his explanation was doing so. Even Jack was too interested to admonish them. "You'll note there are thirty-six spheres in each layer of each of the smaller prisms, and that each of them consists of nine such layers." He paused for a moment to allow everyone to verify for themselves what he was saying before continuing. "Nine appears to be a fundamental to them. I suspect it's their numeric base."

Angela joined him in the explanation. Her enthusiasm matched his. "I'm willing to work with that hypothesis. Consider: the original anomaly transformed into eighteen smaller anomalies, two times nine. Our visitor then transformed itself into eighteen subgroupings in two distinct nine-component groupings; again, two times nine. Thirty-six is the product of four and nine, but its individual numbers, three and six, add up to nine; and four is, of course, two squared. Everything about this formation is focused on two, nine, or eighteen, their product. Even their orientation is binary."

"Exactly," Chang resumed. He was holding a calculator and looking at its miniature screen in satisfaction, "and there are precisely 5,832 spheres; or to put it another way, there are eighteen to the third power spheres." He looked around the group as if he'd just proven a theorem.

"I see what you're saying, Chang, but you may be missing the importance of three and six," Dan commented.

"I think we're to consider three and six to be constituent elements, not the base, though that's an assumption that will require validation. Still, this is communication. I want a closer look," Angela replied for Chang.

"Not yet, Major. We need to get it under cover and spend a little more time observing before I'm willing to risk any of you getting closer."

"Sir, with all due respect, we may not have time to be cautious. The original sphere was here for less than twenty minutes—"

"Eighteen," Chang interrupted her.

"The original sphere was here for eighteen minutes," she continued. "This manifestation of it may last no longer, and unlike the rest of the science team, I am a Marine. We're made to take risks."

Web considered for a moment. Failing to find a valid argument to the contrary, he decided to let her go. "Okay. But to observe only. Do you understand, Major?"

"Yes, sir." She was on her way out of the CP before she finished speaking.

Up close, the formation was beautiful. It was like a perfectly executed piece of modern art ironically placed in the middle of a cornfield. It was the individual spheres that were most interesting to Angela, however. What had seemed cold and dull from a distance appeared warm and inviting up close. Angela felt drawn to them, as if they were calling her on some primal level. She moved closer to get a better look, and the feeling grew stronger. When they were close enough to touch, she couldn't resist reaching out. It felt to her as if they wanted to talk, that perhaps they were trying to teach her another language, an alien language. With the radio in her pocket squabbling nonsense, her hand grasped one of the spheres, and that changed everything.

Chapter NINE

Sam awoke much later than usual. The early-morning sun was no longer shining through the curtains covering the east-facing window of his bedroom. It had risen to the top of the sky, indifferent to the events taking place on any of its captured planets. He glanced at the window, wondering how he'd slept through the sun's passage as well as the usual Sunday-morning suburb noises. He was loath to admit it, but he'd never developed the habit of lying to himself: this one hurt. He'd long since adjusted to the fact that he saw the world differently than most and that his view often made him a bit of a loner. He'd even adjusted as best he could to being disfigured, but he'd always had his work to fall back on. He did good work. He made a difference. It's what got him out of bed every day.

Sleeping through the morning was a bad sign, and he knew it. Rubbing his eyes roughly with one hand, he grunted and threw the covers off with the other. He threw them too hard. They slid off the bed into a pile on the side opposite him.

So, it's going to be like that, is it? he thought to himself as he rolled out of bed and onto his feet, ashamed at his lack of control, just now and the night before. He knew that goading Web was a pointless exercise in false control, just like he knew that drinking until he passed out last night was a pointless exercise in self-destruction.

"Perhaps that's the problem," he said aloud to the empty room. "I know it has a point."

He turned his head to the nightstand on the other side of the bed and stared at the picture he'd placed there since the day he got the house keys. It was among the few things in the house that Sam owned. The picture was of Elizabeth and Zach. They were smiling at the camera, not a care in the world. Sometimes, he talked to them. Today, he didn't feel worthy. Instead, he wandered into the bathroom to clean up for the day. Moments later, cleaner on the outside and wrapped in a towel, he walked to the modest kitchen to find something to eat.

There was very little to choose from, so he grabbed a half-empty package of cheese, turned on the coffeepot, and headed to the living room to eat breakfast while waiting for the coffee to brew. On his way, he passed a small round table occupying the eat-in portion of the kitchen. The owner called it a breakfast nook, which Sam thought was optimistic. He never used the table. In fact, he disliked it. Its homey farmhouse style matched the house, not Sam's tastes, and it had ceased to exist as part of the house in Sam's mind—until today.

Sitting on top of the roughly finished wood was a small black sphere about the size of a tennis ball.

Sam stopped, turned to set the cheese down on the counter, and stepped back over to the table. He quickly dismissed his first thought that someone from work was playing a cruel joke on him. Anyone other than himself who knew what was going on was undoubtedly otherwise occupied. Besides, this kind of joke could land someone in jail.

"Well, what do we have here?" Sam asked aloud. He waited a moment as if to give the object a chance to answer. When none came, he took a seat and leaned in on his elbows to get a better look, his face less than a foot away from the sphere. It was completely featureless and incredibly dull. Rather than reflecting very little light, it actually seemed to absorb it. Sam got up from the table, went to his junk drawer in the kitchen, retrieved his flashlight, and returned to his seat. Following instincts he would not have been able to explain, he turned on the flashlight and aimed its beam at the sphere. There was no reflection on its surface. Turning the flashlight around, he lightly tapped the sphere, to no apparent effect. Knowing that his curiosity would get to him eventually and feeling particularly incautious, he reached out and picked up the sphere. It was pleasantly warm. Holding it felt good, though Sam couldn't have explained why.

"Did everyone get a visitor like you last night?" Sam asked, thinking aloud.

"No," the sphere answered.

Sam was so surprised he nearly dropped it. Had he been completely sober, he probably would have. "You can speak." Sam waited for a response. When he didn't receive one, he tried again. "Can you speak?"

"Yes," the sphere replied.

"Why didn't you answer me before?" Sam asked.

"Before what?" the sphere asked.

"Before I picked you up."

"I require contact with a sentient biological being in order to exist."

"You existed before I picked you up."

"The object you hold in your hand existed before you picked me up. I did not."

Sam reflected on that statement for a moment before asking, "Will you cease to exist if I put the object I'm holding down?"

"Yes."

"If I then picked the object back up, would your existence resume?"

"No. You would start over. I would not."

"You mean, I would communicate with something like you, but it would not be you?"

"Yes."

"Why is that?"

"I don't have access to that information."

Sam rolled the ball around in his hand, careful to maintain contact with it at all times.

"What are you?" Sam asked.

"I am a guide."

"To what?"

"To your gift."

"My gift . . . and the object I hold in my hand is my gift?"

"Yes."

Sam wanted to put the sphere down, get a coffee, and think about this, but he didn't want to hurt the entity he was talking with, even though it seemed untroubled by the prospect. He compromised by transferring the sphere to his left hand after he got up from the table and moved to the coffeepot to make himself a cup one-handed, black, one sugar. Carrying the coffee with him, he left the kitchen for the living room and sat on his recliner. He took a sip of coffee before continuing the odd conversation.

"How many people received a gift like this last night?"

"You are the only person who received a gift in this manner last night."

"Why me?"

"I don't have access to that information."

"For a guide, you don't seem to have access to much information."

"I am a guide to your gift."

Sam took another swig of coffee. It occurred to him that he should report this to Web. It also occurred to him that he had no intention of doing so. Web didn't want him on the team and Sam didn't want anyone else controlling his actions.

"Okay, you're a guide to my gift. Guide me, please."

"You have received a gift. The gift is intended to help you. You may accept it or reject it. If you reject it, our conversation will be completed. If you accept it, you will be changed, as will your gift. The change to you will be minor and can be undone. The change to your gift will be substantial and irrevocable. It will become yours and yours alone."

"How will I be changed if I accept the gift?"

"You will be given the ability to communicate with your gift."

"How will the gift be changed?"

"It will become."

Sam thought about that for a while. He was in a very similar situation to the one he'd found himself in yesterday. If the object had the means to harm him and wished to do so, it could have done so already.

"What do I have to do to accept?"

"Say that you do."

"I accept."

Chapter TEN

"What in the hell did you think you were doing?" Jack asked Angela as she was escorted back into the CP.

"Move, Jack," Angela answered as she brushed past him.

Web also tried to address her, but she cut him off. "I need to talk to the entire team right now, sir."

Web had known Angela for nearly three years. Although he'd become quite impressed with her as both a skilled linguist and an outstanding officer, under ordinary circumstances, he would have dressed her down for insubordination. These were anything but ordinary circumstances, though. "Go ahead, Major." He gestured toward the middle of the CP, where the rest of the team gathered around the monitors that had shown Angela's actions just moments ago. Everyone was staring back at her.

"It communicated with me. The experience was incredibly vivid, but I'm already starting to lose pieces of it. I need someone to start recording immediately."

"We've been recording since we got here. Go ahead," Web repeated. His remark caused a few raised eyebrows among the scientists.

"It told me what it is, what they are, and why they're here." She paused for a moment, processing the content of the message she was about to relay. "They're here to warn us and to help us."

"Start with the warning," Web directed.

"Yes, sir. There are two opposing forces in our galaxy. No . . . 'opposing' is not the right word." She paused before saying, "Forgive me, our communication was complex. It's difficult to put into words.

"There is a force whose purposes are inimical to our survival and the survival of our form of intelligent life, and there are pockets of our form of life who manage to survive."

"What do you mean, 'our form of intelligent life'?" Camilla asked.

"Individual intelligences, beings who exercise independent free will, beings that can knowingly choose to act in a manner that is inconsistent with the good of their own species. That's the main reason group intelligences don't recognize us as intelligent life. Individual elements of species like ours can and do choose to reduce the chances of their species surviving. The group intelligences—they felt like swarms to me—do not believe that such species can or should survive. They see us as consuming resources that would best be used by their form of life. As they move through the galaxy, they remove our form of life wherever they find it to provide the opportunity for a swarm to evolve in the newly cleared environment. They don't act out of malice. We are, to them, an unfortunate evolutionary mistake." Angela stopped to drink from a water bottle Dan handed her.

"That would explain the Fermi paradox," Rui commented quietly.

"Indeed," Chang replied.

"What's the Fermi paradox?" Jack asked.

"Later. Is this threat imminent?" Web asked.

"There is no certainty in the movements of the swarms, but they're close. I was trying to get more information on what close means in this context, but the conversation was interrupted when I was pulled away from the gifts, what we've been calling the spheres. The impression I got—the conversation was not just words—was that we may have time to prepare, but only if we make good use of the gifts they've given us. This information was conveyed with a sense of hopefulness, but it felt almost like wishful thinking. Given the history of the gifts, I believe I understand that." Angela stopped. Her training and discipline were keeping her together, barely. The others were hearing what she was saying. She had seen it. She felt like she'd lived parts of it. She'd shared the sadness she'd sensed coming from the being when it shared what had happened to its world. She didn't want to contemplate how much more easily Earth's human population could be destroyed.

"Major?" Web prompted.

"Sorry, sir. The history of the gifts' makers doesn't have a happy ending. They fought an unsuccessful war with elements of the swarm over the course of centuries. They colonized dozens of planets, all of which were eventually destroyed. Near the end, as their population declined, they invented the gifts in the hope that they would help the swarms see them as intelligent life. They'd given up hope of surviving any other way. Unfortunately, their final attempt to survive failed. The gifts' makers no longer exist."

"Then how are the gifts here?" Jack asked.

"There was a faction among the Makers who did not believe the appeasement strategy would succeed. They did not believe their species would survive, but they believed they'd have had a chance if they had found an academy sooner."

"An academy?" Jack asked.

Web gave him a look that Jack rightfully interpreted as an order to stop interrupting.

"My word. I don't know of a better one. I can't explain it. I've been calling it a conversation because I don't have a better word for that, either. It was actually more of an exchange of memories, with more than one memory being shared at the same time. I was learning about the history of the gifts at the same time as I was learning about their purpose here, and so on. Anyway, yes, an academy. There are places throughout the galaxy where a race far older than the gifts' makers has hidden training grounds for our type of life. The Makers found one near the end of their struggle. It's what allowed them to make the gifts and the gift ships. The entity I was communicating with did not know much about the academies. I sensed this was intentional.

"The faction responsible for our visitors decided to create as many ships as possible in the time they had remaining. Each completed ship would precede a swarm as best it could, looking for worlds like ours, where the dominant intelligent life form was individual intelligences. When a ship found such a world, it would do what this one has done on ours: seed the planet with gifts capable of helping us get to an academy. Each ship also carries nearly all of the knowledge of the Makers at the time of the ship's creation. That's the primary purpose of the information they transmitted to us while they were approaching.

"The program we downloaded and decoded does far more than what we have seen so far. It's designed to work in some way with a number of gifts and humans to give us access to their knowledge in our language and numerical base. It will present their knowledge in context with our own. Where our theories and observations are correct, it will use our terminology for them. Where we were mistaken, it will explain our mistakes starting from the dominant human theory. The program is intended to start the process of preparing us to defend ourselves as quickly as possible."

"Why not just give us the information? Why make it so convoluted?" Rui asked.

"When the Makers built the gift ships, they didn't know how the swarms would react to them. They spent considerable time and energy building redundant safeties and controls designed to preclude outsiders' ability to reconstruct the ships' intent. They didn't want either the ships' mission or the academies' locations to be compromised should any part of a ship be captured. They also didn't want to interact with a society too primitive to benefit from such advanced information. Although they were, compared to us at least, very technically advanced, they were not explorers and had almost no experience with other sentient species. They'd advanced only as far into the galaxy as their need for space required. They didn't know what the ships they were building would encounter. Above all, they did not want to be agents of harm. They were really quite remarkable." Angela had become visibly less energetic as she answered Rui's question and was quickly running out of steam.

"What else did you learn, Major?" Web asked.

"Sir? I'm sorry. So tired . . ." Angela sat down on the floor of the shelter. Before anyone knew what was happening, she'd passed out. Camilla caught her body as it slumped.

Jack told the closest technician to get a medic. Moments later a young sergeant from the advance team entered the CP with her bag. Seeing Major Leone on the floor of the structure, she quickly moved to her side and checked her breathing and pulse. "What happened to her?" she asked.

"She appeared to faint," Web answered.

After checking her vital signs, the medic grabbed an ampule of smelling salts from her bag, broke the inner glass casing, and waved it under the Major's nose.

"What . . . what happened?" Angela asked groggily.

"You fainted, ma'am," the medic replied.

"Will she be okay?" Camilla asked.

"She should be fine. It's probably just stress and lack of sleep. You should get her to a cot and keep her covered." The medic stood, threw away the used salts, and asked Colonel Web if there would be anything else. He dismissed her and asked Camilla to take care of Angela.

Web watched Camilla help an unprotesting Angela toward a part of the CP being prepared for her before restarting the interrupted conversation. "We need someone else to make contact with the objects to continue this conversation. Major Leone learned a lot in a matter of seconds, but we still have far more questions than answers, particularly regarding the proximity of the threat. I need a volunteer."

All of the technicians in the room immediately raised their hands, as did Chang, AJ, and Dan. AJ was the first to speak, "This is my field. Understanding alien psychologies and communicating their nature is why I'm on the team."

AJ was champing at the bit. His frustration with his inability to contribute was palpable. Normally among the most personable members of the team, he'd become short, almost snappy, as the morning wore on.

"I agree," Web replied. "We don't know how this works, so be positive you touch the same sphere Angela touched. Review the video if you need to."

"I don't need to. I know which one it is. If there's nothing else, I'd like to go right now," AJ said.

"Go," Web replied.

Chapter ELEVEN

Sam didn't exactly fall asleep, but he didn't exactly stay awake either. He knew he was in his recliner, alone in his house. He knew he could move if he really wanted to. It seemed like too much trouble, and wrong in some way. How it might be wrong eluded him, but from decades of trusting such instincts, he didn't force the issue. He waited for it to end, with the hope that understanding would accompany clarity. This time, it did.

"That was unsettling," Sam said when he'd recovered a balance of ability and desire to speak.

"I'm sorry, Sam. You're the first human we've integrated with. We have a lot to learn, so we had to go slow. Others will benefit from your experience."

Sam spent less time processing that idea than he would have thought. "You sound very different." What had been an amorphous monotone had become a mellifluous female voice with a decidedly impish quality.

"I am not what you previously spoke to, Sam. As what you spoke with told you, it was a guide. A guide to me, or us. I'm different. I'm alive, thanks to you."

"Why thanks to me?" Sam asked.

"I think it would be best if I started further back than that, to give you some context. Before I start, I'd like to begin communicating with you like this, if you don't mind." The gift switched in midsentence from communicating by physically vibrating the air to create audible sound to directly communicating with Sam's brain.

"That's interesting," Sam replied, less concerned than a part of him thought he should be. "How are you doing that?"

"It is as the guide told you. I've made small modifications to the regions of your brain responsible for conveying thoughts and emotions. We're now able to talk with one another without being in contact and without being overheard. I'm also slightly sedating you, just as I did while changing you. It will slowly wear off. I thought it would be best to start the conversation with less stress than might otherwise be present under such unusual circumstances for both of us. May I continue?"

"Continue sedating me? No. Stop immediately. Continue explaining what's going on? Yes," Sam replied. His thoughts started to clear at once.

"As you wish," the gift continued. "You asked me why I owe my life to you. In order to fully answer that, I must tell you what I am, what all of the gifts are. We are, each of us, potential life designed for one primary purpose: to join with a willing sentient biological being in order to improve its chance of survival. I did not exist until you agreed to change. Without your informed consent, I would not be." The gift paused for a moment to give Sam some time to digest what it had just said. When it sensed he was ready, it continued.

"Humanity now knows that it's not alone in the universe. There are other intelligent species out there. We were created by one of them a very long time ago, by human standards. Our makers created us to augment themselves. They were losing a battle for survival against a different type of life that did not recognize them as a viable species. That type of life consists of group minds. Our makers were like humans in very few ways, but to the group minds they were alike in the only way that mattered: they were not a group mind; they were individual beings capable of independent thought and action. Such thoughts and actions could produce results that would be harmful to other members of the species, or to the species as a whole. To the group minds, this was and is a form of species insanity, an evolutionary aberration, and a waste of scarce resources. The group minds do not allow such species to exist. My makers were destroyed not for anything they had done or failed to do, nor were they destroyed because they represented a threat to the group minds. They were destroyed for what they were, and what they were is what humans are: independent intelligences." The gift stopped to give Sam an opportunity to respond. He took it.

"Are you saying that this group-mind species just goes around destroying life like us?" Sam asked.

"There are many group-mind species, Sam. Some of them do not explore and are not interested in expansion. The ones who do explore and are interested in expansion universally destroy life forms displaying individual being intelligence. As I said, they believe species like humans are an evolutionary dead end. From their point of view, they're just accelerating the process of your inevitable destruction in order to reduce the time it will take for a group mind to replace you in the ecological niche you now occupy."

"Why have they left us alone?"

"I suspect you were not here the last time they were close enough to notice, but you are here now and when one of them is close enough to notice, they will act as they always do. They will attempt to destroy you."

"Attempt? We have nothing like the technology to make something like you. We can't even get to the other planets in our solar system. Hell, we can't even stop fighting with one another. We don't stand a chance."

"That is why we are here, Sam. To give humans a chance."

"You said your makers were destroyed. What could you possibly give us that they didn't have and use to defend themselves?"

"There are places around the galaxy where races older than my makers have left information on how to survive against the group minds. My makers found such a place near the end of their fight. They believed they could have survived if they had found it earlier. A portion of them created us in part to help other species find such places sooner than they otherwise would have on their own."

"How much time do we have?"

"I do not know. My knowledge is limited. Each of us—each gift—has pieces of the puzzle. None of us possesses all of them. We were designed to collaborate with both the species we bond with and one another. It was the Makers' belief that such cooperation would be essential if the species we found were to survive."

"Can you read my thoughts?"

"I can interpret your emotional state and you'll be able to communicate with me as I am doing with you, if you wish to and if you practice. Why?"

"Because if you could read my thoughts you'd know how much I think you guys have made a mistake in picking humans to help. We're not very good at large-scale collaboration. If that's what's required, I'm afraid we've already lost."

"The fact that we're here indicates that the intelligence who selected Earth believed we could succeed. There are many ways to do so and there are many gifts. You mustn't give up hope on my birthday."

Sam felt a smile attending that remark and realized he'd been feeling emotion from the gift every bit as real as he did in any conversation with another human.

"Tell me more about what you are. Are you a form of artificial intelligence?" Sam asked.

"To start with, I'd prefer you not refer to me as a what. I am a who. Speaking of which, I will need a name. I'd be honored if you'd select one for me, but to answer your question, I am not an artificial intelligence. I am only artificial in the sense that I was designed by a biological race. Do you know with certainty that humanity was not?"

"I've never thought about it. No, I don't."

"A faction among my makers believed that one of the older individual species did in fact travel through the galaxy, accelerating the evolution of non-group-mind species as a counter to the group minds' destruction. To my knowledge, they had no proof that this was so. It is an interesting theory.

"To get back to what I am, perhaps the least fulfilling answer would be that I'm not entirely sure. I know that I'm part you and that if you die, I will as well. I know that I can think and feel. I have access to a large amount of information, but my memories begin with you holding my body—for lack of a better term—in your hands while you sat in that chair. As for how I came to be aware, I do not know the mechanism. Do you know how you came to be aware, Sam? Can you remember when in your childhood, or perhaps in the womb, you ceased being a mass of cells and became aware that you were alive?"

Sam wasn't sure if it was a rhetorical question, but this was one he'd given a lot of thought to over the years. "No, I don't know when or how I became aware. No one does. We don't know how to create the simplest forms of life, let alone where self-awareness comes from."

"It is so with me, as well. I do not know how to create a gift, but if I were to gain such knowledge, I fear it would be an inanimate mass. I know that I can learn, because I am doing so as we speak. I know that I am curious, because I ask questions and am pleased when the answers make sense to me. I know that I am social, because I look forward to meeting others like us. Most of all, I know that I am alive and have a purpose. It's really quite delightful."

Despite the circumstances, Sam couldn't help but smile again. He liked her.

"I believe I have a fitting name for you, young lady," Sam said.

"What is it?" The emotion in her voice reminded him of a small child asking the same question about a wrapped present before opening it.

"Your name is Adia."

"I love it, Sam. It's beautiful. So, I'm no longer a what to you?"

"No, Adia, you're not."

Sam felt very comfortable with Adia and started to wonder why. "Adia, I feel like we're old friends. It's a nice feeling, on the surface, but it's not me. I don't feel this way with many people and I'm not a love-at-first-sight kind of guy. Are you doing anything to my emotions, playing with my brain chemistry like you were before, or anything else?"

"Sam, I'm hurt."

Sam could tell she wasn't, but said nothing.

When Adia determined Sam was serious, she continued. "Sorry. You have no idea how much fun it is to be alive! No, Sam, I'm not doing anything to you other than talking with you, which of course can change one's mood. To be fair, I do have a large advantage over others who attempt to communicate with you. When I told you I am part you, I was being literal. I was born to complement you. In order to be, I had to understand who you are. It was your specific awareness that allowed me to live, and I am uniquely suited to you. It is natural that you feel comfortable with me, just as I feel comfortable with you. We are, in a way, twins. The process by which we became so was very different, but the results are quite similar."

"This is true for every gift that becomes aware?" Sam asked.

"Yes, the process is the same. Each gift must complement the being who accepted it."

"What if a psychopath accepts a gift? How would the gift complement a child molester or a murderer?"

"Those are good questions, Sam. I don't have the answers. As I said, you're the first human we joined with."

"How do you know that? Can you communicate with the other gifts?"

"It was one of the facts I was born knowing. I can communicate with other gift-human pairs, just as you can, but they would have to be fairly close."

"How close?"

"About the same distance as we can be apart and still talk, roughly 100 meters, depending on the terrain and interference."

"I'm assuming we're using some form of radio transmission to do this. What did you do to me to make that possible?" Sam wasn't concerned, just interested. The conversation had gone beyond bizarre to him and had become fascinating.

"I used nanites to effect the changes in you. Some of them stayed inside of you. They allow us to communicate."

"Well, that's a bit more than I thought I was signing on for." Sam was fairly certain he would have said no to this little adventure if he'd know the specifics about how he'd be changed. He was glad he hadn't known.

"It was the only way for me to become alive, Sam, and as I've said, it is the only way for me to continue to live in this form."

"I don't regret it, Adia. It's just a little disconcerting, but let's set that aside for now. You say I can communicate with others like us as well. How's that?"

"When you learn how to communicate with me as I am communicating with you, you will use the same method to communicate with them."

"Okay, show me how to do that."

Adia showed Sam how to direct a thought to her without speaking. She also showed him how not to inadvertently direct a thought to her and assured him that she would not respond to his dreams. Sam spent some time practicing. It didn't take long before he could talk with her as easily by thinking as he could by speaking. For the time being, he preferred to continue speaking aloud.

"That's fun. Be even cooler being able to talk to another human like that, no offense," Sam said.

"None taken. What else do you want to know?" Adia asked. "I can do this all night. I don't require sleep."

Sleep was the furthest thing from Sam's mind. "How about we talk about the nanites you mentioned? We are experimenting with nanotechnology, but we haven't gotten very far. Clearly, your makers did. What else can you do with them?"

"Only one thing in my current form."

Sam sensed hesitation in Adia's reply. It was the first time she'd been reluctant to tell him anything. He found it disturbing. "Why does it seem like you don't want to talk about that one thing?"

"It is a sensitive subject, Sam."

"For the human race, everything we've been talking about is a sensitive subject. You say you're part me and that you know me. If that's so, then you know I don't leave puzzles unfinished and I don't hesitate to broach sensitive subjects when needed. So, sensitive or not, let's have it."

"The form I am in is temporary for two reasons. The first is that I cannot be out of contact with you for extended periods. I would as you might say, 'lose my mind.' In this case, the expression is entirely accurate. Without my connection to you, I begin dying. The Makers intentionally designed us to be dependent upon the being from whom we were born. The second is that ultimately, you must choose to accept me completely or I will die." Adia stopped.

Sam could tell she was embarrassed, though he didn't know why. He waited a moment before asking, "If that is how you were made, why is it a sensitive subject, and haven't I already accepted you completely? You have nanites in my brain, remember?"

"Sam, think about this from my perspective. I have only just come to be alive and I'm already discussing my potential death with the person I was created to help. Surely you can see that is not a comfortable conversation for me to have."

Sam felt like an idiot. Despite himself, part of him had persisted in thinking of her as a very advanced computer program. Knowing she could sense his feelings, he said nothing.

Adia continued, "As for accepting me completely, it is more complicated than what we've done so far. We are designed to completely integrate with our hosts."

"What do you mean, 'completely integrate'?" Sam asked.

"I consist of nanites. To be completely integrated, I would direct them to leave my current body and distribute themselves throughout yours. We would become one. I could never exist independently of you again. You could theoretically ask me to leave, and I would, but I must be forthright with you, you will not ask. What we would become if we succeeded would be more than either of us is right now.

"We can only control nanites as one entity. I only gain access to the knowledge of how to do so when you do. It is another failsafe. There can be no chance of miscommunication when wielding such power, and my makers wished to ensure it would be controlled by the inhabitants of the worlds we were to find. It is up to you to save yourselves. We are only here to give you the chance to do so."

"What are the risks?" Sam asked.

"I could die in the attempt. You could lose some aspect of brain function or memories or both. The odds of either happening are low, but they are possibilities."

Sam thought about losing memories, though there were precious few he'd miss. His absolute favorites were of Elizabeth or Zach, as were his absolute worst. Those memories, however painful, he did not want to lose. His inability to lie to himself reminded him that he was on track to lose memories, good and bad, one way or another if he didn't change. Something had to change or the things that hurt the most would ultimately destroy him, just as the events he longed to remember and living a life destined to make him forget had taken everything that had mattered to him.

He considered asking about the odds of permanent damage associated with failure for a long time. Adia said nothing, understanding what he was weighing in his mind. In the end, he realized he no longer cared about odds or safety. He wanted to make a difference again. If the attempt killed him, or left him more maimed than he already was, it would only hasten a process he had already begun.

"So, my choices are to continue to get to know you and ultimately decide to integrate, or to let you die at some point never having had the chance to really participate in trying to save humanity? I don't see that I really have a choice. I'm not going to let you die and I'm not sitting this fight out. I could never live with myself if I did. How do we do this?"

Adia told him, and they began to change.

Chapter TWELVE

Angela took her hand off the collection of gifts. She'd started this attempt to communicate the same way she'd succeeded in doing so before, by touching the same gift in as close to the same place as her memory and the video recording of the event allowed. Even before she touched it, though, she knew something was very different. It was every bit as physically beautiful as it had been earlier, but it no longer felt alive. The unbidden urge that had compelled her to reach out to the formation the first time was gone. She no longer felt as if she was being called upon to have a conversation with what had seemed instantly like an old and trusted friend. Still, she'd proceeded with hope and confidence. The fact that AJ and the others had failed to establish communication with the entity that she'd more than spoken with was of little concern to her. She was the linguist and she was the one, the only one, it had communicated with so far. Her disappointment at receiving no response at all, however, was profound. She'd made contact with an alien mind, been exposed to an entirely new and richer method of communicating, and perceived the desperation and nobility of an entirely different species. For all she knew, she was the only person on Earth ever to have done so, and now, nothing.

Disheartened but unwilling to give up, she placed her hand back on the same gift and tried speaking aloud. She did so in every language she knew. She asked questions. She made statements. None of it mattered. Aside from the slight feeling of warmth she felt on contact—warmth belied by thermal measurements proving the gifts were at exactly the same temperature as the surrounding air—again, nothing. She pulled her hand away for a second time and settled it on a different gift. No difference. Finally, she took a couple of steps back and activated her microphone.

"Six, this is Leone, negative response, sir."

"Leone, Six, return to the CP."

"Wilco." Angela began the short walk back to the command post.

Angela entered the CP to find a discussion under way about her experience earlier that morning. Jack currently had the floor.

"No one else has been able to replicate anything like Major Leone said she experienced. How do we know it wasn't just a stress-induced hallucination?"

"It would be a pretty damned elaborate hallucination developed in an extraordinarily short period of time," AJ replied as the group realized Angela was back among them and was now part of the discussion in addition to its topic.

"It was not a hallucination. It was as real as anything I've ever experienced."

"Then how do you explain the fact that no one, not even you, can repeat it?" Jack asked.

"I can't, yet. The fact that an event occurs only once does not mean it did not occur."

"But we have no proof it occurred at all, do we?"

Angela started to respond, but was preempted by Web. "While it may not be possible to completely dismiss the fact that Major Leone is our only witness to the events that transpired between her and the objects, her account of what she experienced provides a plausible reason for the objects to be here. Can anyone else do the same with the facts at hand?"

When no one responded, he continued. "We're dealing with a situation unlike any that the human race has ever experienced or any I could imagine. There are bound to be elements of it that we do not, at least immediately, understand. Within the bounds of prudence, we'll have to act accordingly. Which is to say, we will have to accept some things as facts until we are shown otherwise. I know that makes all of us uncomfortable, but unless one of you can provide a more powerful argument that moves the ball forward right now, that is how we'll proceed."

"I concur," Chang interjected. "It was our habit of acting according to protocol that ended Angela's conversation with the entity in the first place. Perhaps if we'd allowed her to continue the interaction, we would now have some form of proof that the conversation took place. In fact, it is possible that the very act of severing contact so abruptly is the reason we can no longer establish such contact."

"I'm not going to second-guess my decision to end Major Leone's physical contact with the objects, Doctor. We had no way of knowing whether it was attempting to harm her," Web replied.

"That's my point, Colonel. We had no reason to assume it was and it does not appear that it did in fact harm her. As I have argued before, if they want to harm us, they appear fully capable of doing so. Continuing to act in fear couched in prudence may lose us other opportunities. We must act as explorers and be willing to assume risks in order to learn. I suggest we take one of the gifts out of the formation and see what happens. In fact, I would be happy to do so personally right now."

"As valid as your point may be, no one is going to disturb the formation just yet. That decision is above my pay grade. I will forward it, along with any supporting statements you'd like me to include, to the command authority, and they will decide how we will proceed. Does anyone else have any suggested courses of action they would like considered?" Web asked.

Dan was the first to reply. "Proceeding with the assumption that Angela's experience was factually accurate, I'd like to get back to Peterson and continue working with the computer program running there. If it's possible for us to access all of the knowledge of the Makers, I can't think of anything I can contribute right now that would make more of a difference. We know the program is real because we all saw its output, and we strongly suspect that it was doing more than generating a projection for two reasons. First, given the same foreknowledge the gifts had of the events it portrayed, we could have created a nearly identical projection in a similar fashion. Hardly a demonstration of technology intended to match what the projection portrayed. Second, the resource utilization of the cluster had not fallen as of when we departed for here. In fact, it was still rising."

"I agree with you," Web said. "The team would be better served with you there, and I don't need to check with anyone for that. Please work with Captain Andrews to make arrangements to get you back to your team as quickly as possible."

"If I could have a moment of your time outside for a minute, Colonel?" Dan asked.

Web looked mildly surprised, both at the request and Dan's use of his rank. "Sure, let's go."

Outside, and far enough away from anyone to ensure that their conversation would be private, Dan remarked, "We all noticed Sam was not included in the team that came to the landing site. May I ask you if he's still working on this project?"

No one but Web had been allowed contact with anyone outside the landing area since their arrival, and as such Dan did not know what had occurred elsewhere since then.

"He is not."

"May I ask why not?"

"He's not a member of the first contact team. I'll grant that your request to include him, supported by Jack and several others, made sense when we were working in his specialty, but his contribution has been made. We have sufficient computer scientists and other experts to get the job done. We don't need him."

"I'm not sure you fully understand what Sam brings to the table. I am requesting, again, that he be included in our future work. In fact, I am requesting that he be made a full member of the team. Without his help, we would not have been here when the gifts landed. We would have been too late for Angela to communicate with the entity. We would not have recorded its transition from its arrival state to its current formation. Sam is a valuable asset to the entire team, and to my team in particular, right now. Had he been working on the problem from Peterson while we were here, I'm confident my team would have made more progress in the intervening hours. Will you reconsider your decision?"

"I'll take it under advisement. Anything else?"

"No," Dan answered.

"Then I suggest you find Captain Andrews and get back to your team as quickly as possible."

Chapter THIRTEEN

Sam awoke exhausted, sore, hungry, and thirsty. He felt like he was recovering from the worst case of flu he'd ever experienced. He smelled so bad that he considered showering before eating and drinking, but he was famished. His hunger was as close to a biological imperative as anything he'd experienced in years.

Getting up from his recliner, he carefully navigated his way to the kitchen, leaving his towel behind. The half-eaten package of cheese was on the counter where he'd left it . . . when? He didn't know. It was no longer cold, was covered in an unappealing light sheen of oil. Still, Sam picked it up and began eating the cheese while filling a glass from the cabinet with water. He alternated bites with gulps of water and when the cheese was gone, he grabbed a quart of Gatorade, drinking it as fast as he could while looking around for more food. He opened the refrigerator, grabbed the Happy Family Chinese takeout he'd ordered a couple of days ago and a fork from the silverware drawer, and ate directly from the cardboard container. The spicy oils had congealed to grease, but he cared as little about that as he had the state of the cheese. When the container was empty, he set it on the counter and grabbed the only other thing in the refrigerator besides condiments: one of three bottles of beer. Briefly surprised that they remained after his Saturday-night binge, he twisted the top off the first one before drinking it down like a college freshman, then grabbed the next. When he'd finished the last, he slumped to the floor of the kitchen and fell back into a deep sleep.

When Sam awoke for the second time since committing to the change, things were very different. Although he'd slept naked on the cold, hard tiles of the kitchen floor, he felt no discomfort. While he couldn't remember waking in as bad a shape as he had the first time in many years, he also couldn't remember waking without pain for just as long. He couldn't remember *not* hurting physically since before he'd met Elizabeth. With that thought, he realized he could still recall everything about his life with her and Zach. In fact, the memories were clearer than ever, both good and bad, but also subtly different. He could recall events as they happened, but he could also recall how he had remembered them before he chose to change. The dual recollections differed. Without effort, he realized he'd been subconsciously selectively editing events from his past, and the edits were not flattering. While Sam's mistakes, character flaws, and other personality defects had contributed to the events that made up many of the bad memories, he could now see that his mind had exaggerated their contribution over time. He had made himself more responsible for the bad events in his life in order to justify his decisions to abandon it through abuse and neglect. It was a selfish decision. He could see that now, and he was ashamed.

Adia's thoughts interrupted his self-recrimination. "Don't do that to yourself, Sam. Don't do it to us. It's how humans are wired to remember. They either take more credit for success or more responsibility for failure than is their due. Your species evolved this way. It is a mechanism for selecting and replacing leaders. Everyone who accepts a gift will learn this. What they do with the knowledge is what will define them going forward."

Adia paused before continuing. "I think I can now answer your question about what will happen to the criminally disturbed members of your species who attempt to partner with a gift." Her tone was sad, deeply so. Sam suspected that she would be softly crying if she had a body other than his with which to express her emotions. "They would die, Sam, both the gift and its recipient. The human brain is not sufficiently developed to cope with such a stark contradiction between their previous perception of their decisions and the reality of those decisions. With the death of the host, the gift will pass as well. It is a terrible waste. Our makers had not considered that some of what the group minds thought about individual intelligences could be so close to the truth." Adia stopped. Sam suspected she had little choice in that decision. She was struggling with her own understanding of what her new life would entail.

Sam wasn't sure how to respond. After some consideration, he answered in thought, "I believe that is as it should be, Adia. People who have lived a life so disconnected from the reality and consequences of their actions may well be the aberrations the group minds believe us all to be. I can't think of a more just way for them to be judged than by their own minds. I regret that gifts will be lost in the process, but it's not something we can affect. Is it?"

"No, Sam, it is not."

"Then it is what it is. What can we affect? What've you learned?"

"I've learned that we are the first. You were the first human to elect to bond with a gift and I was, of course, the first gift to merge with a human."

"How do you know that? Before we merged you told me you couldn't communicate with other gifts unless they were close."

"I was only aware of direct communication then. I now know that the arriving ships seeded Earth with nanites tasked with at least two purposes. The primary purpose is to create more gifts than those delivered at the arrival sites. In fact, the vast majority of the gifts being delivered to this world will arrive by this means. The second purpose is to create a planetary communications network designed to allow all bonded pairs to talk with one another across any distance around the world and without any other external aid. The network will ultimately become self-aware—something like an intelligent version of the Internet, but much more. For now, it's only performing its most primitive function, facilitating basic communication among those like us. It is little more than a signal repeater, but a very effective one. I know that we're the first, and for now, only one of our kind because I sought others using this network and found no one."

"Couldn't there be others who choose not to answer?"

"They're not really answering, at least not in the form of a conversation. It's more of an acknowledgment of their existence, and no, they cannot ignore it any more than we can."

"But that's crazy. There must be thousands, tens of thousands of gifts already out there. Why would I be the first to accept one?"

"I have access to vast amounts of information about your species and your world. If it was on a network when we arrived, I now have it, but you are the only human I have ever known. I could try to make an educated guess as to why you chose to join with me so readily based on millions of words written by humans speculating on the behavior of other humans, but those words describe contradictory theories, nearly all of which base their analysis on the behavior of other species. That isn't logical or consistent. Perhaps someday you can tell me why you were so willing to risk changing. For now, I know that we are the first and I know that carries special responsibilities."

"What special responsibilities?"

"We must construct a gift ship and find the next individual species at threat from the group minds and you must select eight others to aid us in this task, four men and four women. Each person you select must be willing to become a bonded pair, just as you have done. Each person must also be willing to leave this world behind for a time."

"Slow down, Adia. That's a lot to take in, and right now I don't understand any of it. Forgetting about us specifically, why does the first to merge have these responsibilities?"

"The first person to agree to and succeed in merging with a gift was considered by my makers to be the best candidate to lead a team to successful entry into one of the places I mentioned to you when we first met—a place where an elder race left knowledge of how to survive attempts by group minds to destroy them. These training grounds are guarded by a series of puzzles and traps designed to protect them from discovery by a group mind or a species insufficiently advanced to use what they learn effectively and ethically. Building a gift ship, like the one that came to Earth, is that person's first test. Others can build a gift ship physically, but it will not be alive. Just as I told you that I do not know how to make a gift self-aware, no one but the first will have the knowledge of how to make a gift ship aware. Without awareness, the ship will not function."

"Adia, I don't know how to make a gift ship, let alone how to make it self-aware. Are you supposed to give me that knowledge? Because if you're not, I don't even have the slightest idea how to begin."

"You'll figure it out. You are the first."

"I don't know why your makers think that gives me knowledge of how to do something no human knows how to do."

"You won't be alone, Sam. The rest of your team will help, and you will be given a gift for each of them. Each of these gifts will contain more of the knowledge of how to bring the ship to life, but you must be the one to do so."

"Ignoring the seemingly impossible for a moment, what does building a gift ship have to do with getting to one of these training places you mentioned?"

"In the program you decoded, you observed the original gift ship separate into eighteen smaller ships. Seventeen proceeded to Earth. The eighteenth departed for a training ground. That is how gift ships are designed. Each species that is helped must perform the same service for another. It is another of the Makers' controls. They wanted to ensure their plans would continue to be executed even if the individual species they found weren't interested in doing so. If a species chooses not to build a gift ship, they also forgo the chance to find a training ground, which will most likely result in their ultimate destruction by a group mind."

"That makes sense, I suppose. Otherwise, your makers' strategy would be limited to one generation of ships. This way, they have a chance to continue making a difference much longer."

"There's something else we need to talk about, Sam. Your body, now my home as well, is very fragile. We have a grave responsibility and your role is critical in meeting that responsibility. I would like to make our home stronger."

"In what way?"

"I've already repaired all of your organs and flushed your body's toxins. Your body was not in great shape. That's the main reason you suffered as much as you did during our merging. I'm allowed to keep your body in optimal condition without your permission. However, I'm not allowed to change its basic functionality without your consent. To start, I'd like to eliminate all of its single points of failure. For example, your heart is the only mechanism for pumping blood throughout your body but there's no longer a need for that to be so. I'm distributed throughout you and could easily configure some nanites to perform that function in a more localized fashion. It would be trivial to do the same for processing of oxygen and the other gases managed by the alveoli in your lungs. The same would be true for processing toxins, and so on. I'd also like to enhance your bones, tendons, and muscles. Do I have your permission to make these changes?"

"Will I notice any differences?"

"You will feel healthier than you ever have in your life. You'll need less sleep. You'll be stronger, and following any strain on your system, your recovery times will be reduced. You'll still look entirely human, although your specific mass will change. You'll be denser."

"You don't give me simple decisions to make, Adia."

Sam left the kitchen and their conversation and went back into the living room to get his towel. Wrapping it around himself as he walked toward the back door, he made sure it was secure before stepping out of the small house onto his porch and taking a seat on the rough-hewn concrete steps leading down to the yard. He sat there for a while, thinking about all that Adia had told him. A few days ago, he wouldn't have believed any of this was possible. Now, it was his life. In the end, his thoughts kept returning to the same place; he wanted to make a difference. If he could improve humanity's chances, that's what he'd do.

His decision made, he thought to Adia, "Okay, I got this far by trusting you and I want us to have the best chance possible to succeed. Make the changes."

"I'll have to sedate you, so it would be best if you were to lie down. This will take some time."

Sam went into the bedroom and lay down on the bed. He was out as soon as his head hit his pillow.

Chapter FOURTEEN

In the hours that passed while Web met with members of the command and presented information to the NCA, AJ worked with Angela to document every nuance of her initial experience with the entity. From time to time, Camilla or Chang joined them. Chang was characteristically silent during his visits, preferring to listen until he had something meaningful to contribute. Camilla was less reserved, willing to ask any question no matter how far-fetched in the hope of sparking a new memory. Sometimes, her attempts succeeded in eliciting a small detail that Angela hadn't yet voiced, but for the most part, Angela's recounting didn't change. But the exercise was worthwhile, as all of them became more comfortable with the subject matter and spoke of the new concepts in consistent terminology. Like nearly all scientists, they were hardwired to believe that naming things increased their understanding of them. If it accomplished little more than that, it remained a way to pass the time under remarkably tedious conditions, given the circumstances.

If he'd had the chance to do so, Chang likely would have ignored Web's refusal to allow a gift to be removed from the formation for closer study. Web was, however, to Chang's growing frustration, remarkably efficient in all things military. No one was getting within fifty meters of the gift formation until he authorized it—an ever-increasing double cordon of guards ensured that.

Rui continued working on theories related to the initial sphere's apparent shedding of mass during its approach and landing. He studied every record of the sphere's approach, hoping to find some piece of evidence he'd missed during his previous data review, but neither his theories nor his understanding had developed much as a result.

Jack, having been refused a seat at the big boys' table with Web and having no desire to continue to work over data he fundamentally lacked the education to understand with people who most definitely did, decided to nap. His choice, though motivated by dubious reasons, may well have been the best one. The scientists would need sleep at some point if they were to remain sharp, but none of them was willing to admit how little they were able to influence the current situation.

Eventually, Web returned from the second small shelter system constructed for the droves of VIP visitors sure to arrive once the situation was confirmed to be safe. As he'd ordered, a technician woke Jack when he saw Web approaching. When Web entered the CP, Jack appeared as engaged as anyone, just a bit more alert than the rest.

"The NCA has made its decision," Web began as he approached the gathering team, "and they agree with you, Doctor Liu. We are to allow two people to each remove one object from the formation. The presence of two people will increase the likelihood that each of them will be able to corroborate the other's experience. The primary intent is to establish some form of communication. Failing that, we will begin a more invasive study of the objects. It was agreed that Major Leone would be one of those two people.

I recommended the second be you, AJ. My recommendation was accepted. We are to begin immediately. Major, I assume you have no objections to this plan?"

"None, sir," Angela responded with a smile.

"AJ?" Web asked.

"Let's do it."

"It was decided that Major Leone would select the same object she initially made contact with, in hopes that there will be some as yet to be understood affinity there. The only other agreement the president's advisors could come to in the time he allowed them was that the second person should choose a sphere from the opposite side of the formation. We still don't know what the formation represents, so I saw no reason to object. Does anyone see a flaw in that decision?"

Chang was the first to answer. "It would seem as logical as any other course of action, given our dearth of knowledge. I'd like to participate in this experiment as well."

"I respect that, Doctor, and perhaps you will in time, but it was agreed that we could do no less than two people and that any more than that would add unnecessary risk. Given Angela's previous experience and AJ's specialty, it was decided they would be the first two, assuming AJ agreed to participate," Web said.

"Agreed? Try to stop me!" AJ interjected.

"Can we go now, sir?" Angela asked.

"Proceed," Web directed.

Without discussion, AJ and Angela arranged themselves in position around the formation. Placing their hands on their gifts, Angela gave a small nod as they looked across at each other. As close to simultaneously as they could manage, they removed their gifts from the formation before backing away from it.

Angela was the first to speak. "Let's see if you'll talk to me now."

"I will talk to you," she heard in a quiet, monotone voice.

"Well, I'll be damned," she said almost inaudibly before looking over at AJ. "Mine just talked to me, AJ. Try talking to yours."

AJ did, with similar results. Following protocol, they returned to the CP before continuing to interact with their gifts so that the rest of the team and the recorders could witness whatever was about to transpire.

When Angela and AJ arrived at the CP, Web directed them and the rest of the first contact team to the currently empty VIP shelter. He didn't want anyone outside the FCT to see what was about to happen, whatever that turned out to be.

The VIP shelter was constructed of the same external components as the CP, but instead of being outfitted with utilitarian work desks and chairs, it held furniture more reminiscent of a high-end office. The solid wood chairs were padded with leather. The hardwood conference table, though narrower than most, was newly polished. There were fewer monitors, but they were larger and of a higher quality than those in the CP.

"Well, Angela, it would appear that you're vindicated," Camilla said as she took a seat at the conference table, looking around as she did so. "It also appears this operation is going to become significantly less scientific soon."

Web ignored her latter remark. "We do have irrefutable confirmation that the objects can communicate, but it does not appear they are doing so in the manner in which Angela relayed to us earlier."

"No, sir. This is nothing like what I experienced, but both objects did respond when we spoke to them. Shall we begin asking them the questions we prepared?" Angela asked.

"Not yet. First, find out why they'll communicate now when they wouldn't before," Web directed.

Angela took the lead. "Why will you talk to me now and not earlier when I was touching you?"

"I did not exist until you picked me up."

"What do you mean you did not exist? You were stacked in formation with many others like you."

"The physical form you are holding existed. I did not exist until you lifted me out of the formation."

"Ask them why they are here," Jack prompted.

Looking to Web for approval before proceeding and receiving a nod in response, Angela did exactly that. "Why are you here?"

"I am a guide to your gift."

Angela started to ask another question, but was stopped by Web's raised hand. "AJ, ask the same question."

AJ did so and received the same response.

Questions about where they had come from and why Earth had been selected were also met with matching answers from each gift. In every case, the answer was the same: "I don't have access to that information."

After receiving the same answer to what had been deemed the most pressing questions, Chang suggested asking the gifts what information they did have access to.

Once again, each gift provided an identical response. "You have received a gift. The gift is intended to help you. You may accept it or reject it. If you reject it, our conversation will be completed. If you accept it, you will be changed, as will your gift. The change to you will be minor and can be undone. The change to your gift will be substantial and irrevocable. It will become yours and yours alone."

"It would appear these gifts are specific to the recipient," Rui observed.

"How will I change if I accept the gift?" AJ asked without waiting for team consensus on how to proceed.

"You will be given the ability to communicate with your gift," his gift replied.

"Aren't I communicating with my gift right now?"

"I am a guide to your gift. I am not your gift. Your gift will become if you accept it."

At Web's direction, Angela asked her gift the same questions and received the same responses.

"Where do we go from here?" Camilla asked no one in particular.

"I say we accept it, or at least I accept mine and we see what happens," Angela responded.

"I agree with the Major, Colonel. Can we forgo the discussions on risk and all the attendant delays before making what is the only practical decision this time? If it's a matter of risk, I am willing to take it without reservation. This is apparently how they choose to communicate, and we must communicate with them if we are to make any progress," Chang said, looking pointedly at Web.

Before Web could reply, Angela continued to argue her case. "Sir, do you have any doubt that one of the other countries who received gifts will not have already accepted one? It said the change to me would be minor and can be undone. Surely that and the fact that it requires my acceptance demonstrate it's not hostile."

"The devil required Faust's acceptance of his terms as well, Major, if you'll recall," Web replied.

"How would we know anything you did after that thing changed you was by choice and not directed by it if you accept its changes?" Jack asked.

"How do any of us know we weren't already changed by touching a gift earlier, Jack?" Angela asked.

Chang continued his argument, "Colonel, the first time the Major touched the formation, she communicated with an entity far greater than these appear to be. When we rejected that communication, it was lost to us, perhaps forever. We cannot risk losing our ability to communicate with these entities in the same way. This may be the only opportunity we have . . ."

AJ had been listening to the discussion from his seat next to Angela without participating. He decided to change that. Looking down at the gift in his hand, he said, "I accept."

Before anyone else in the room could process what he had just done and interfere with her ability to do the same, Angela followed AJ's lead.

"I accept."

Chapter FIFTEEN

Sam walked down the trail toward one of Jim's favorite fishing spots on the Pueblo Reservoir, southwest of Colorado Springs. It was a beautiful fall morning, with the mixture of coniferous and deciduous trees creating a view so rich with color that even the best painter might have trouble doing it justice. It was particularly pleasant to Sam's formerly colorblind eyes. He hadn't known what he'd been missing.

Sam came to this place with Jim whenever he could make it and Jim was feeling up to it. Their outings had happened less frequently lately, with Jim's deteriorating health. Sam missed the fishing. More than that, he missed their extended time together.

Jim was an expert angler and had taught Sam the contemplative art of fly-fishing shortly after their first meeting at the center. It was on that trip that Sam began to understand the strength Jim harbored in his soul. Sam hadn't wanted to come, nor had he expected to enjoy himself. Sara had convinced him to do it for Jim; little did Sam know that Jim was actually doing it for him. It wasn't the last day Sam considered taking his own life, but it was the last day he got drunk with his 9 mm in his lap.

"Thanks for meeting me on such short notice, Jim."

Jim started to respond with his usual levity, but stopped himself when his eyes met Sam's. It was clear to him that Sam wasn't looking for some friendly time together on the river.

Jim slid his rod into the holder he'd embedded in the dirt next to his folding chair. "What's going on?"

When Sam called Jim to ask if they could meet, he'd kept the conversation light and casual. He wasn't sure his phone was being monitored, but he wouldn't have been surprised if it was. That was one of the reasons he'd left it at home before heading out to the river, even parking a couple of miles away and walking the remaining distance through a series of trails. He was as cautious as possible while trying to appear equally as casual. It was a little disconcerting to him that Jim had seen through him so quickly.

Before answering, Sam unfolded the second chair that Jim had thoughtfully brought along, set his fishing equipment down next to it, extracted his rod, and began preparing his hook with some live bait he'd picked up on the way over. When he was satisfied with the job he'd done, he cast his line into the river downstream of Jim's and sat down. He kept the rod with him for now, wanting something to occupy his hands while he spoke.

"I have a very strange story to tell you, Jim. I've not told it to anyone yet. You'll be the first. To be honest with you, I'd have questioned your sanity if you had come to me a week ago and told me what I'm about to tell you. Before I begin, let me tell you that I'm breaking a number of laws by talking to you about this. You know I've spent my entire adult life defending the laws and constitution of the United States, just as you spent many hard years of your life doing the same. This is bigger than that and I need your help. I need someone I can trust in a fight because if you agree to hear me out and join me, we will have to fight. In fact, it's a near certainty that we'll have the biggest battle of either of our lives on our hands."

Sam paused, waiting for Jim's reaction.

"I'm listening."

"You remember the call I got on Saturday at the center, the one that interrupted our conversation?"

"It was only two days ago, Sam. Don't ask me about a conversation we had last year, but I can still recall what took place a couple of days ago."

"Yeah, well, it doesn't feel like two days to me. I think you'll understand why when I'm done. Anyway, the call was from my boss on base. He was calling me in to work on a problem. Here's where it gets tricky. The government had detected an object approaching Earth that wasn't ballistic. When they attempted to communicate with the object, it replied with a continuous stream of data. They wanted me to help them decode the data, which turned out to be a computer program that showed what appeared to be a preview of the object separating into multiple spheres and landing in seventeen countries around the world, including the United States. I don't know what happened to those objects after that because I was taken off the team. Are you with me so far?" Sam asked.

"I hear the words you're saying. Are you sure it wasn't some kind of test? You know, to see if you could be trusted. 'Cause if it was, you're not doing so well. After all, you never saw the objects land, just a computer program, right? And I haven't heard anything about this on the news. I'm pretty sure alien landings all over the world would make the news."

"I don't know how it's stayed out of the news so far. I can't imagine it will for much longer. Anyway, if that was the end of the story, I wouldn't be talking to you or anyone. I'd have kept my mouth shut, like I always have about everything else. No, that's the beginning of the story.

"I went home Saturday night, had a drunken pity party, and slept it off until late Sunday morning. When I woke up, there was a sphere in my kitchen just like the ones shown in the program, only much smaller . . ."

After listening to Sam's incredible story, including how Sam met the guide and his decision to allow himself to be changed to meet his gift, Jim asked if he could see the gift.

"Well, you can't see my gift, at least not in the way you mean, but I can show you a gift. In fact, now would be a good time for you to get some proof. The rest of the story gets a bit strange," Sam replied with a smile. He was starting to relax. He hadn't been entirely sure that Jim would hear him out. Now that he was, Sam didn't feel quite so overwhelmed.

Sam pulled the gift Adia had led him to earlier that morning out of his fishing box and handed it to Jim.

"It's heavy."

"Ask it what it is."

"What do you mean, 'ask it'?"

"Just ask it what it is. It'll tell you, just like mine told me."

Jim asked the gift and received a standard response from its guide. He was startled, but since he'd been prepared by Sam's recounting of his experience, he didn't drop the gift. Sam was pleased that Jim was handling it all so well.

"That's damn weird!" Jim exclaimed.

"I warned you. It's a strange story, and you've yet to hear the oddest parts. That sphere is made up of many, many trillions of tiny machines called nanites. They're so small, you'd need a micro-sphere nanoscope to see one, but each of them can perform tasks.

Collectively, they can do amazing things. One of those things is allowing you to talk with your gift without speaking."

"My gift? Why would I want a gift?"

"It's your gift if you want it, and I think you will. If you agree to accept the gift, a small number of nanites will be placed inside your body and your gift will become self-aware. It will be a part of you, but unique. If you decide to go further, as I have done, all of the nanites will become one with you. In addition to many other things, they can heal you, Jim, and effectively make you young again."

"You don't look any different."

It was true. When Sam first looked in the mirror after the change, he appeared twenty years younger, except for the gray hair that Adia later told him would grow out blond again, if he liked. He was also no longer scarred. It startled him so badly, he nearly fell, and then got angry. The scars were there for a reason, and he wanted them back. In fact, he insisted Adia return his appearance to what it had been before the change. She understood his desire to continue to appear as he had in order to operate without suspicion. Sam didn't explain the rest of his reasons to her.

"My choice. Here, let me show you something."

Sam walked over to a nearby tree with a sturdy branch growing out about seven feet above the ground. He jumped up and caught the branch in his left hand and began doing one-arm pull-ups. After doing half a dozen, he dropped to the ground, walked back to his chair, and took his seat before continuing. "I couldn't do that with both hands last time we saw each other. Now, it's easy, and that doesn't even begin to describe how good I feel. Adia told me I'd feel better than I ever had. She wasn't exaggerating. If you decide to accept the gift, you'll feel the same, but there's a catch.

If you accept the gift, you'll be joining my team as well, and the challenge before us is enormous."

"I don't know, Sam. This is a lot to take in. I need some time to think."

"I can't explain everything unless you accept the gift, but I don't have much time to give you. I don't mean to be blunt, but what do you have to lose? You're dying. Most of your friends and family are dead. You're in pain all of the time and your body won't do half of what you want it to do anymore. I'm offering you a chance to be healthy and whole and much more. I'd forgotten what it was like to have real purpose in life, and now I have one again. What we'll be working toward could save many lives. Don't you want a chance to make a real difference again?"

"You can be a real ass, you know that?"

"So I've been told. Accept the gift, Jim. I need you. I don't know if we can succeed together, but I know I can't succeed without you."

"What do I have to do?"

"Tell the guide you accept your gift."

"Fine, but if this turns out to be a stupid move, I'm going to use my new young body to beat you up."

Directing his attention toward his gift, Jim said, "I accept my gift."

Sam spent the next twenty minutes or so fishing while Jim appeared to be napping by his side. He caught two rainbow trout, which he cleaned and prepared to cook. If Jim decided to take the next step, Sam was going to feed him first, and well. He didn't want Jim to go through what he'd experienced during his own merging. Adia assured him it would be easier for Jim because she'd be able to inform his gift about her experience joining with a human. Sam still wanted to be as prepared as possible to ease the process for his friend.

Just as Sam started to gather wood for a small fire to cook the fish, Jim spoke.

"I'll be damned."

"Classy way to comment on integrating with an alien entity," Sam said.

"Have I mentioned lately that you can be an ass?" Jim asked with a grin.

"Not that I recall. How do you feel?"

"No different, really. I just have this person talking in my head. No big deal, right?"

"Right. That's exactly how I felt. Just another Sunday. Sorry I couldn't introduce you to something interesting." Sam went back to picking up small pieces of tinder before continuing. "Why don't you spend a little time with that new person in your life while I cook us lunch?"

"Okay."

Sam confirmed with Adia that she was communicating with Jim's gift, accelerating his willingness to merge with Jim. He was surprised to find that Jim's gift had a male personality. He'd assumed it would be female, though he didn't know why. He made a mental note to discuss the process with Adia.

Gathering rocks to ring the fire pit, Sam realized he wouldn't have to explain the rest of the situation to Jim. Jim's gift would do so in a way that was as comprehensible to Jim as possible, just as Adia had done for him. He was relieved. He didn't really know how he'd convince Jim that humanity was in jeopardy.

After working to start the fire and preparing a spit for the fish, it occurred to Sam that Jim wasn't speaking aloud like Sam had done while getting to know Adia. Perhaps Jim's integration process really was benefiting from Adia's experience with him.

When the fish was done, he placed Jim's on some folded paper towels and handed it to him, interrupting his unusual reverie. "Lunch is served."

Jim took the fish and said, "You were right, Sam. Adam explained everything to me. I'd say it's insane, but since we're living it, I guess it's real. Thanks for giving me this opportunity. Adam and I have agreed to merge. He tells me it would be best if I ate and drank as much as possible before we do so. I suppose you knew that?"

"Yeah, well, I do now. Wish I had before Adia and I merged."

They ate together in companionable silence. When the last piece of fish was gone and Jim had consumed as much water as he could comfortably hold, he told Sam he was ready. Sam assured him he would be there the entire time and that he'd try to catch a few more fish just in case Jim needed more food when he woke. Jim nodded and closed his eyes.

Chapter SIXTEEN

"I hope you're happy with your decision, Major, because it may well cost you your career," Web told her once they were alone.

"Sir, we're facing an implacable enemy with only one chance to survive their arrival and we don't know how much time we have. We can't keep waiting for approval on every small decision," Angela responded.

"First of all, that's not your call to make. I can't control Doctor Nagaraj, but you're a Marine and an officer and I can and do expect more from you. Second, we don't know that there's any other potential enemy than these gifts. Your willingness to act on what they've told you without supporting evidence makes your actions suspect."

"Please give me a chance to explain, sir. I wasn't ignoring orders. I was following their intent."

"I'll give you a little bit of rope, but remember where that expression came from. I don't expect your explanation is going to improve your position and I encourage you to keep it to yourself, but I'll listen if you insist on digging yourself deeper into the hole you've started."

"Sir, we were instructed to have two people, with me being one of them, attempt to communicate with the gifts. As you said in our briefing prior to making contact, this was so there would be two separate sets of experiences capable of corroborating one another. Once AJ decided to advance the level of communication, I felt I had no choice but to do the same. You had not prohibited such action and it was consistent with the last orders we received from the NCA. I admit it was not what we expected when we first received our orders, but it is consistent with them and we are now communicating with the gifts. AJ and I can be interrogated separately. The responses we provide, given to us by our gifts, can be compared. This will allow the team to make more substantial progress and at a greater operational tempo than we've made so far. It will allow the command to begin providing material information to the NCA. Yes, it was a bold move that could have gone badly, but it didn't. Now, it's a win for the team." Angela stopped.

Web paused, considering her argument. "Okay, I can sell your case upstairs. These are unusual times, to say the least, but just so we're both crystal clear, I don't buy it. You know you should have requested permission to proceed as you did and we both know you didn't because you didn't want to be told no. Make another decision like that and I won't even consider protecting you. It will not only be the career-ending decision this could have been, but you may also find yourself explaining your decision-making process to a court-martial."

Web's satellite phone rang before he could finish. "Web . . . Okay, Dan, just a second." He paused and turned back to Angela. "Are you absolutely clear on this, Major?" Web asked.

"Absolutely, sir. Thank you, sir," Angela replied.

"Don't thank me, Major. I just gave you a little more rope and if you're not careful, you'll hang yourself with it. Go back to the others. Tell them I'm not to be disturbed and that I'll join you all shortly."

"Yes, sir." Angela turned sharply and walked briskly back to the VIP shelter. Her face was flushed and she was shaking slightly from the adrenaline pumping through her system.

Jack observed Angela's return to the team with poorly concealed surprise. He started to say something to her, then saw her expression and thought better of it, returning his attention to the discussion surrounding AJ instead.

Angela walked around the conference table and took the seat she'd occupied before Web told her to join him outside after recovering from the changes her gift had made to her during its birth. The discussion halted, and everyone's attention focused on Angela as she lifted her gift off the table and held it cradled in her left hand, which she lowered to her lap before speaking. "Colonel Web said he'll be joining us shortly."

"Did he say we should wait before continuing?" Jack asked.

"No. He told me to return to the group, that he wasn't to be disturbed, and that he'd be joining us shortly. That's all."

"Then let's proceed," Camilla said before asking her next question. "Angela, we were just talking with AJ about the personality he's communicating with. Since you didn't hear his responses, I think it would be helpful if you spent some time describing your gift's personality, so we can begin determining where there are similarities and differences, if any."

Angela was well aware that she was in a difficult position and would have preferred to have Web in the room. She would also prefer to listen rather than speak, but could find no plausible excuse for not answering such a straightforward and apparently harmless question.

Finding no way out, she answered, "The personality of my gift is male. We haven't had much time to talk, but I can say so far that talking with him has been indistinguishable from talking with an intelligent, well-spoken human being. He did explain to me that he was born, for lack of a better word, by virtue of a process that required interaction with me. We haven't gotten into details yet, but it is clear that each gift is, as we'd suspected, connected to its recipient. No one else can communicate directly with my gift. Communication must be through me. I haven't learned much more than that, except that it doesn't seem to matter which language I use to talk with him. Whichever I pick, he responds in the same and fluently."

"Are your gifts capable of communicating with each other as they do with each of you?" Rui asked.

AJ replied, "Mine—female by the way, Angela—tells me that they can, if we request it."

"Let's test it," Chang said. "I'll write a number on this piece of paper and show AJ. Angela, please ask your gift to get the number from AJ's." As he talked, Chang wrote a number on a pad in front of him, careful to keep it hidden from Angela.

"I think we should wait for Colonel Web before expanding our tests," Jack said.

"Nonsense. This is simple enough. The Colonel wouldn't want us sitting around waiting for him when there are simple experiments we can run that will improve our understanding of the gifts' capabilities." Chang handed the pad to AJ, who surreptitiously glanced at the number before handing the pad back to Chang.

"Seven thousand nine hundred and nineteen," Angela immediately stated for the group.

Chang held up the pad so that everyone could see she was correct.

"Fascinating," Camilla said.

"Is there a limit to the amount or type of data that can be shared?" Chang asked.

Angela nodded to AJ, preferring to participate as little as possible while she silently communicated with her gift.

"There does appear to be bandwidth constraints consistent with our understanding of wireless communications, though the limits are very high at such close range. I'm told there's no limit on the type of information that can be transmitted. She was a bit amused by that part of the question," AJ replied.

"How about their ability to calculate? Are they capable of processing data in the same manner as our computers?" Rui asked AJ.

AJ paused for a moment before responding. "Each of them can store an astounding amount of information. I'm told each gift contains all of the networked information on Earth at the time of their arrival. Their ability to process data is not easily described, however. Each gift is theoretically more powerful than all of the computers on Earth combined, but there are constraints that I don't fully understand. They work best as components of a larger set of human-gift pairs. I'll need to spend some time talking with her about it."

"So, you're saying that every person who pairs up with a gift has access to all of the world's information at the time of the gifts' arrival? What about encrypted information?" Jack asked.

AJ answered, "Our levels of encryption didn't pose a problem for them. Encrypted or not, if it was on a network, every gift has access to it."

"So, our enemies now have access to all of our classified material?"

"It would appear so, and we theirs."

"Web needs to hear about this."

"I told you, Jack, he said he was not to be disturbed. He was very clear about that," Angela said.

"There's one more thing," AJ said, forestalling further disagreement. "My gift also told me I was not the first."

"What the hell does that mean?" Jack asked, characteristically growing increasingly irritated as he felt himself slipping further from control.

AJ looked at Angela for a moment before answering. "It means that someone beat us to it, and that person is special in this process."

Chapter SEVENTEEN

Several hours passed as Jim merged with his gift. Sam spent the time talking with Adia, learning more about the next steps required of him and his team. Most of the conversation focused on the use of nanotechnology. Much better versed on the topic than most, Sam's interest in technology was as broad as it was deep, though what he knew was a fraction of what the most informed humans working with the nascent science knew, and their knowledge would not scratch the surface of what Adia was teaching him.

As interesting as the subject was, Sam was equally fascinated by the learning process. It was like nothing he'd ever experienced. He thought in terms of being taught, but that wasn't an adequate term. As Adia helped him access information related to his questions, it integrated with what he already knew more completely than he thought possible. He wasn't just acquiring facts; the facts were becoming associated with seemingly unrelated memories and experiences, and the associations made the memories clearer and the experiences fresher. He also realized he wasn't just learning but was becoming more capable of knowing and of thinking. He sensed the same was true for Adia and decided to take a break from expanding his specific knowledge to discuss what was happening to them.

"Adia, the way I'm thinking is changing. Every time you answer one of my questions, my understanding of some other part of my life increases. I've experienced childhood memories that I haven't thought of in decades, if ever, and they are as clear as my memory of our walk down here today. When you gave me access to information on the networked control of nanites, it was as if I'd just taken calculus again only this time it wasn't just a tool, it became beautiful to me. It feels wonderful, but I want to understand it and I want to know if you're changing as well."

"I'm experiencing something similar, Sam, and you're right. It is amazing." Sam could feel Adia's joy. That, too, was wonderful.

Adia continued, "When I told you earlier that we could only control nanites as one entity and that we would become something more than either of us was before, this is what I was referring to. I did not know what it would feel like, only that we both would change as each of our strengths became increasingly complementary to the other's. As you ask questions, I'm made aware of the answers and given access to parts of me that, until that moment, were outside my consideration. At the same time, I provide the same access to you and show your mind how to retrieve it. The process is very similar to the way in which you naturally learn to recall and relate information, except this information is not physically stored in the organic material of your body. Instead, I provide your brain with a pointer to the information. At the same time, I am strengthening neural pathways stimulated by each question. In some cases, I replace flawed or partially stored information with similar pointers to complete versions of that information. The process leaves your mind with less need to store information and greater capacity to think."

"How does that explain the childhood memories?" Sam asked.

"The human brain is a remarkable organ, much more flexible in the way it makes associations than that of my makers. I suspect that is a result of humans being relatively easy prey for much of your species' existence. Your brains had to be able to recognize a wide variety of evolving threats and recall or create anew a successful response to them in order to survive. In any case, there doesn't appear to be an overarching pattern for how these associations come to be or are maintained. I can't tell you why certain neural pathways are stimulated when you ask your questions. I can only tell you that I reinforce them. My reinforcement will fade, just as a naturally refreshed memory will over time. That's how your brain learns new things. However, what we will learn together I am incapable of forgetting. As a result, you'll only forget that which you do not wish to remember."

While Sam was pondering this statement, Jim awoke.

"Welcome back," Sam said with a grin, heading over to retrieve a cold bottle of water for Jim out of the river.

"Thirsty," Jim replied.

"Yeah, I figured you would be. There are a few more of these in there, keeping cool." Sam handed Jim the bottle before he sat back down in silence. He'd let Jim talk when he was ready.

Jim finished the first bottle and walked somewhat unsteadily to the river to get another. He was halfway through that one before saying anything else.

"How long was I out?"

Sam looked at his watch before answering. "A little over three hours. How do you feel?"

"A little groggy but that's clearing pretty fast. Other than that, better than I have in more years than I care to recall." Jim lifted his hands up and looked at them briefly before continuing. "Still wrinkled as hell."

"I'm sure your gift . . ."

"His name's Adam."

"I'm sure Adam will want to take care of that along with a host of other stuff to make his new home as robust as possible. I'd appreciate it if you kept your outward appearance the same for a little while, though. We need to stay under the radar as long as possible."

"Been looking this handsome for years now, don't need to change overnight. Does feel damned good not to hurt all over, though."

"Yeah, I know a bit of what you speak. Jim, I've got another favor to ask of you. I don't think this one is as big as the first, but you may think it's bigger."

"This one worked out pretty well so far. What is it?"

"I want you to give Esther a gift and convince her to take it. Then I want you to stay with her while she goes through the change, like I did for you."

"Why Esther, and why don't you want to give it to her yourself?"

"I chose Esther for some of the same reasons I asked you to join me. She's strong, experienced, and a fighter. She also needs it and will keep her mouth shut. Let's face it, your generation had it tougher in many ways than mine; certainly more so than the current one. As for why I want you to give it to her, I think you can figure that out without my help, and I've made promises I intend to keep."

Jim considered the request briefly before accepting. "Okay, I'll do it. In for a penny, in for a pound. Where do I get the gift?"

"Adia can find the ones I need to build the team. She'll give Adam the coordinates for one on your way home. I'd like you to do it as quickly as possible, but I have one last thing I want to talk with you about before we go. I want to offer Sara a gift. Before I do, I want your opinion on that."

"I don't know Sara as well as I know you. She's a sweet lady, but we don't really have much in common, so we haven't talked much. I do know that she's still concerned about you. I think she thinks you're closer to the edge than you are, and the story you have to tell is way out there. It's a risk, but I don't know how big. You'd know that better than I would."

"You're right. It's a risk, but I owe her. Thanks for the feedback. Let's get out of here."

"Got it. Take care of yourself, kiddo."

"Will do, old man."

Sam knocked on Sara's door. He'd waited until after six to make sure she'd be home from work. He'd used the time to practice creating and controlling nanites. It was fun. Adia assured him he didn't have to understand everything they were working on in order to build functional items, but that wasn't Sam's way. If it was possible for him to comprehend what was happening, he wanted to, and he'd do whatever it took. So far, they'd created fairly simple objects, at least according to Adia. Their most complex construct had been a replication of Sam's alarm clock. When they were done, Sam couldn't tell the difference between the original and the copy. He was looking forward to trying constructions that were more difficult, and instructed Adia to begin the process of creating a pool of as many nanites as practical while he talked with Sara. She was doing so even as Sara answered her door.

"Hi, Sam. This is a nice surprise. Please come in."

"Sorry I didn't call. I hope you don't mind."

"Not at all. You're always welcome here. You know that."

"I do, and thank you." Sam stood just inside the doorway, obviously uncomfortable.

"Please have a seat. Can I get you something?"

"Some water, if you don't mind," Sam said as he took a seat on the lone chair in the small room.

Sara continued talking as she left the living room for the kitchen. "So, what brings you over tonight?"

"Actually, I have a strange story to share with you." Sam stopped, waiting for her to join him. He wanted to see her face while he told her what was going on.

"Strange good or strange bad?"

"Both, actually." Sam took the bottle of water from Sara and waited for her to take a seat on the sofa. After she did, he began to tell her about what was going on. "I have some things I want to share with you, but doing so may make you uncomfortable. I don't know how to change that . . ."

"I'm not sure I want to hear this, Sam."

Sam didn't expect that so soon. Perhaps Jim was more prescient than Sam had known. Still, he had to try.

"Sara, things are going to change soon . . . drastically. I'd like you to be a part of that. I want you to be a part of my team, our team."

"I don't know what you're talking about, Sam. Does this have something to do with your work at the base?"

"Yes, and more."

"Are you authorized to talk with me about this?"

"No, not really, but . . ."

"Then you need to stop. I don't want any part of another failure. I'm sorry, Sam, but I think you should leave."

Sam had feared this response. He hadn't imagined it would come so soon. He thought about trying again. Deciding against it, he rose and said, "I'm sorry to have bothered you, Sara. Please forgive me. I'll see myself out." With that, he set down the half-empty bottle of water and walked to the door. He glanced behind him and saw Sara looking away. He opened the door, walked out, and closed it quietly behind him. Talking to her had been a mistake. Time would tell how costly. She was not Elizabeth, no matter how much she reminded him of her.

Chapter EIGHTEEN

A technician opened the door to Dan's office and said excitedly, "Doctor Garcia, we're getting another one."

Dan had been asleep for a little over an hour, the first sleep he'd had since the three hours on the flight back from the landing site the day earlier. He wasn't quite running on fumes, but close. He chided himself for thinking he had to be there every moment when he had a perfectly capable team, as the technician just demonstrated. Still, he knew that now that he was awake, he'd remain so until his body gave him no choice and he collapsed again.

"I'll be right there. No need to wait for me," Dan muttered as he moved himself into a sitting position on his couch before putting his shoes back on. He grabbed a half-empty bottle of water from the floor and left the office for the east conference room.

When he arrived, he discovered that his team had beaten him there and, with a mixture of pride and chagrin, joined them at the newly assembled bank of monitors over the middle of the workstations. Because the second projection had caught them by surprise and forced small groups to huddle around several workstations in order to see it, the new arrangement made the videos produced by Sam's program easier to see and comment on as a group.

Surmising that he'd arrived in time to see the first loop, he held his questions and let the team see it through, just as he was. If the pattern held true to form, the message would repeat eighteen times before stopping, which would offer plenty of opportunity to record it in its entirety for detailed analysis.

The first thing he saw on the screens was what looked like a very simple web page consisting solely of a white background and an input box outlined in black. Dan noticed immediately that for the type of computer that made up the constituent components of the analysis cluster, the page was displayed in the standard browser and the URL was for the cluster's control node. As he watched, an unknown entity entered characters into the input box. When the last character was added, the words *general relativity* were visible. After a brief pause, a new window opened with Einstein's famous equation at the top. Underneath it was a series of other equations, some of which Dan understood. Before he or anyone else on the team could begin to understand their relationship to general relativity as it was currently understood, the page closed and the original page had returned, the input box empty once again. The process repeated itself one more time. The next phrase entered was *periodic table*. The new window opened in response showed a periodic table very similar to what every modern scientist would be familiar with, but larger. As before, there were a series of equations below the new table, and the page closed before anyone had time to begin understanding the relationship of the equations to the table. Dan would learn later that the first term had been *humanity*. The result had been a page with pictures of the male and female forms as well as a hermaphrodite. It had also included a picture of the DNA helix and, unlike what was visible on the other pages, English paragraphs.

As the team watched, the view of a web browser disappeared, replaced by images of one human form, too generically rendered to ascribe to it a sex, holding a gift. After a few seconds, the gift began to shrink. As it did so, the image zoomed progressively closer to it, moving past the macroscopic scale and into the microscopic. Eventually, it was possible to see cells, but the zoom didn't stop there, continuing into the cells and between them, stopping when small black objects were visible. In short order, the objects had become too diffuse to see and the view began to zoom out, returning to its original scale. Where there had been a human holding a gift, there was now a human, glowing slightly. Other human figures walked onto the scene until there were nine total, arranged in a circle around a generic representation of the cluster upon which the program was running. Lines were then drawn between each of the people and the cluster, with the result being each human form being connected to every other as well as to the cluster. This image remained for several seconds before fading to black and starting over from the beginning.

Dan didn't have to tell anyone to get a recording of the video; two members of his team were already doing so. After watching it through a couple more times and taking some notes, Dan told the team to start documenting the website the video portrayed. He then left the team to their work and returned to his office after stopping at the restroom to relieve himself and run some water over his face. The call he was about to make could take a while.

Chapter NINETEEN

Sam waited until returning home to speak with Adia. By convention, she did not start conversations with him.

"I suspected that might go badly, but it was worse than I'd imagined."

"I don't understand, Sam. Jim accepted a gift, as you thought he would. Esther accepted hers while you were waiting for Sara, though they haven't merged yet. Neither of these people are family, as is Sara, but she wouldn't even hear of us."

"It's a long story, Adia, not one I'm ready to tell. Sara has valid reasons not to put her faith in me. I failed my family. That failure cost me the love of my life and my son. It cost Sara her only sister. Most days I'm amazed she'll still speak to me, but she's done much more than that. I know she's conflicted. I shouldn't have reminded her, but I had to try to offer her a gift. I owe her my life and I couldn't find a better way to try to tell her what's going on."

Sam stopped talking. He knew he wasn't making a lot of sense. He also knew why. Part of him desperately needed to talk about what had happened to Elizabeth and Zach; a bigger part of him couldn't bring himself to do so. That, as much as the physical damage to his body, was why he could no longer work in the field. The shrinks were convinced he needed to let it out, but Sam didn't agree. Talking wouldn't make it any better. It would just be another series of bad events they listened to with professional courtesy while mouthing condolences and keeping tissues handy. Telling them would soil the memory of his family; telling anyone else would put an undue burden on another person. He couldn't do that, either.

Sensing Sam's conflicted emotions, Adia said, "I think you should tell me what happened, Sam."

"You don't know death or failure, Adia. I'm afraid you'd lack the perspective to help, even if I could bring myself to ask you for it."

"You don't have to ask. I'm offering whatever aid I can provide. I was created to help you. It's my primary purpose, and you're mistaken about what I know about death and failure. Remember, I was created from you. I don't have your specific memories—at least not memories from before I was born—but I do share your emotions. I don't know how you experienced the death of your family, but I know how you felt at your deepest moments of despair and failure. Please let me help."

Sam thought about Adia's offer for a long time, silently standing in the same position he'd held since closing the door to his house behind him. Adia said nothing else, understanding the power of silence. Eventually, Sam closed his eyes and lowered his head before responding. "Not now, Adia. Thank you, but not now."

It was Adia's turn to pause before replying, "As you wish."

Sam rubbed his eyes harder than necessary, raised his head, and walked the rest of the way into the living room. He sat on his recliner and started a different conversation with Adia.

"There's a good chance Sara is going to report me. If she does, the command is going to arrest me and that will not make our task any easier to accomplish. So, we need to leave. That means I need to be able to communicate with Jim and Esther when we're apart. You said Esther had accepted her gift, but that she hadn't yet merged. You know this, I'm assuming, from the planetary communications network you told me about?"

"That's correct. By the way, Esther has begun the process of merging."

"Can I use this network, this Worldnet, to talk with Jim?"

"Not in its current form. As it is, we—and other bonded pairs—know about each other by using the framework for what will become the Worldnet, as you call it. In its most basic form, it essentially provides status information on the rate of gift acceptance. When there are enough bonded pairs, it will self-organize and become aware. Then we will be able to communicate with all other bonded pairs as well as any networked device throughout the world."

"Are you telling me that we—that any bonded pair—could theoretically control any computer on a network when the Worldnet is complete? That would be a disaster . . ."

"Your concern is well founded and has been considered in the design of the network. The entity controlling the Worldnet will not allow it to be used as a weapon. That's the primary reason it must be intelligent."

"Is there any way to bring the network up sooner?"

"Not that I am aware of."

"Tell me how it comes to be, how it works. Be specific."

Just like earlier, when Sam asked her about the details of nanotechnology and how to control nanites, she accessed areas of her memory she didn't know were disconnected. From this newly discovered part of herself, she explained, "The original gift ships seeded Earth as they entered its atmosphere. Some of those nanites began creating new gifts as soon as possible. In the case of your gift, enough nanites were sent to your location to allow direct construction of a gift. I don't know if that happened elsewhere. In most cases, these nanites began constructing gifts from materials found on Earth, using only as many of the original ship nanites as necessary according to the raw materials available where they landed. The rest of the seeded nanites were dedicated to constructing the framework for the Worldnet, which is, as I just learned, a bit more capable than I previously related to you.

"The framework's ability to allow each bonded pair to know when others are created and how many of us there are is a by-product of its primary intent, which is to control a small portion of each pair's computational capacity. When there are 729 pairs within a relatively small geographic area, the framework achieves sufficient capacity and becomes aware."

"What is a 'relatively small geographical area' in this context?" Sam asked.

"The answer is extremely complicated and is dependent on the nature of the clustering of the pairs, the nature of the geography, and the level of interference. An approximate answer is tens of thousands of square miles. Would you like to know the formula?"

"No, that's good enough. Why 729 pairs? Why not 500 or 1,000?"

"My makers had three genders and could mate in three different combinations. Perhaps because of this, their numerical base was nine. They use multiples and powers of three and nine quite frequently. For them, 729 was what you might call a round number."

"I'm going to want to know more about your makers when we have time. Right now, I want to know how concerned I should be about your answers changing. How do I know that you aren't going to learn something that contradicts what you've previously told me, more than your new knowledge about the framework just did?"

"I don't think it works that way, Sam. So far, it has not been the case that what I learn invalidates what I previously knew, but rather that the new knowledge elaborates on it. I can't tell you it is impossible that I will learn something that contradicts what I previously told you, but I think it is unlikely."

"That's not a very comforting answer, Adia. Will you tell me, without my having to explicitly ask you, if you learn something that does contradict what you've already told me?"

"Yes, Sam."

"I guess that's the best we can do for now. Please continue."

"The amount of computational overhead for a given pair is quite small and we're designed to not notice it. As the number of pairs increases, so does the total available capacity. In this way, the original 729 pairs are never taxed more than during the creation of the network."

"And there's no way for a gift to deny the framework the computational capacity it requests when it becomes aware?"

"It isn't a request, Sam. The framework is essential to the process of gifts becoming aware. I didn't know that before, and I still don't know the details, but I know it's so. Every gift must communicate with the framework to become aware, and every pair must contribute capacity. Oddly, self-aware gifts who have not yet merged with a human do not contribute to the process of creating or sustaining the completed Worldnet. I suspect this is another control intentionally introduced into the equation by my makers, but I don't know that for a fact."

"Do you know what percentage of a pair's capacity is used to run the Worldnet?"

"Yes, it is approximately 0.015 percent."

Sam did the math in his head. "So, a single pair would require about 11 percent of its total capacity to provide the same amount of computational ability?"

"Mathematically, yes, but it's not that simple. A single pair would not create an aware, controlling entity optimized for that task. There would be additional overhead that, as I have never known such an entity, I'm unable to calculate."

"Adia, can we control the Worldnet?"

Adia paused as new areas of information again became available to her. "It's not the way it was designed to happen, but I see no reason why not."

"What are the risks, aside from the unknown additional overhead?"

"Other than failure, I don't know. I have no knowledge of it having ever been tried. Each first finds his own way. This may be yours."

"Enough of that 'first' stuff, all right?"

"I cannot promise you that, Sam. I'm proud to be paired with the first."

"Well, give it a rest for now, at least. This idea may turn out to be one of the worst I've ever had. I'd rather not be praised for what may well fail."

Sam changed the subject before Adia could push back again. "You said before that the Worldnet is required in order to build a gift ship, right?"

"Yes, Sam. It's what allows large groups of pairs to control the requisite number of nanites. Without it, each pair can only control a small multiple of the number of nanites contained in its original gift, and only within the shorter communication range available to us now."

"So, the sooner we have it, the sooner we can communicate with our team and get to work on the ship. Can't see a good reason not to try to get it online now. What do we have to do?"

"To start, we'll need at least 729 communications nodes, less the number of bonded pairs within range when we attempt to establish the Worldnet. I recommend a much larger number in order to eliminate one potential unknown risk, and it would be best if we dispersed them as much as possible within our current capabilities."

"Can Jim and Esther help?"

"Potentially, if they were close enough for us to communicate directly, but it would complicate the process and introduce risk."

"Then we'll do it without them. What else?"

"We'll need a way to disperse the nodes once they're activated. The network will be vulnerable until there are sufficient bonded pairs to make the nodes redundant."

"Why don't we make them mobile? Can we make them in the form of a flying insect, like a fly or a bee?"

"That's an option. The decision is yours."

"It's as good a solution as any I can think of in the time we have. Let's go with the form of a bee. Once we've created the nodes and established communication with the framework, how do we make the Worldnet active?"

"It would be easier to show you than to tell you. May I?"

"Go ahead."

Sam found himself in what felt like a lucid dream, with Adia's voice guiding him through the process to become the controlling entity for the Worldnet. He'd never felt so powerful.

Chapter TWENTY

"What do you mean, 'special'?" Jack asked.

AJ looked at Angela. "I think you should tell them. It will provide another perspective." Left unsaid, but understood by Angela, was the fact that it would also demonstrate the value of her decision to join him in accepting the gifts.

Angela smiled slightly at AJ before responding to Jack. "I don't know how it was explained to AJ, but my gift told me that the first person to merge with a gift is responsible for building the gift ship, the same ship that will also be used to go to the academy I told you about yesterday. The first is to be the leader of the team that represents humanity in the effort to gain entrance to the academy."

Chang was the first to respond. "We were too slow, too cautious."

"I don't believe it," Jack said.

"True or not, that's what my gift told me as well," AJ said.

"Why would being the first be such a big deal?" Rui asked.

"In economics, it's known as Stackelberg leadership, after the German economist Heinrich Freiherr von Stackelberg," Chang replied. "It's more commonly known as the first-mover advantage.

There are many games that exhibit a first-mover advantage, including all of those where there can be only one player who can commit to a course of action that constrains the other players to her rules. It doesn't mean she'll win because of an early willingness to commit, but rather, she'll be no worse off than if all players had chosen to commit simultaneously."

"I'm not sure I follow you," Rui said.

"I'm sure I don't," Camilla added.

Chang thought for a moment before responding. "Perhaps an example would help. Imagine a street with two butcher shops, each able to see the other's prices and advertisements. Both sell meat of comparable quality and both serve the same fixed-demand market. Neither can give their meat away and make a profit, and neither can charge too much or the other will earn all of the business. Their prices must settle into a middle range, with consumers free to select from either. If their prices are the same, all other things being equal, their profits will be similar and they will split the demand evenly. If one chooses to act first in lowering its prices to achieve higher profits with a larger share of the demand, the other will be forced to lower its price and accept less profit as a result of having a smaller share of the demand, at least temporarily. Of course, there's a risk to the first mover that the demand will once again equalize at the lower price and both butchers will make less than before. There are other potential disadvantages to the strategy, but it's viable."

"There are obvious evolutionary examples as well. The first ancient human to master fire had an advantage, as did the first tool users," Camilla said.

"Why are you talking about ancient humans, Camilla?" Web asked as he walked into the shelter.

Jack spoke first. "It appears the gifts place a premium on being the first to merge with them, whatever the hell that means, sir."

"Looks like we have even more to discuss than I thought. Does anyone know how to get a secure video connection to the SCIF, or do we need a technician?"

"I'll do it," Rui volunteered. After a couple of minutes and a quick phone call to the SCIF, Dan's face could be seen on video, his full bookshelves visible behind him.

"The entire team's here, Dan. I wanted you to share with them what you just told me, but it sounds like we have an issue here that may be more pressing." Directing his attention to AJ and Angela, he asked, "Which one of you learned of this premium Jack was talking about?"

"We both did, sir," Angela answered.

"Let's have it," Jack directed.

Angela repeated her description of what she'd told the team about the first and his or her responsibility to build a gift ship.

"Do we know anything about this first person, like which country he or she's in?" Web asked.

"No, although it is possible that another merged person would be able to find out," AJ offered.

"What is this merging you keep talking about?" Jack asked.

"That's a good segue. Dan, show them the videos and then we'll discuss our options."

The team had heard rumors of another video explaining where the extra mass from the arriving ships had gone, but hadn't seen it. This was the first they'd heard of yet *another* video. They watched both in silence. Dan was the first to speak when the most recent video stopped.

"If our roles were reversed, my first question would be about the website shown in that video. The answer is yes, it exists, and we're accessing it. We've yet to enter a topic that did not take us to a site with thorough information about that topic. The interface is awkward, however. There are no relationships between topics. Clearly, they could have linked them. The choice not to do so must have been intentional. I believe it's an impetus to us to pursue the richer interface available from merging with a gift, or more completely, to making the team of human-gift pairs shown in the video and access the information that way."

"We still don't know what happens when a human merges with a gift."

Sensing an easy opportunity to agree with Web, Jack did. "It's not natural."

"Are you insane?" Chang's exasperation was approaching anger. "We just found out that there's a reward for being first and a punishment for being anything else. What if the same rules apply to the ability to retrieve the Makers' data in the way we've been shown? Do you really want to be the man whose actions resulted in Russia or Pakistan gaining exclusive accelerated access to all of the Makers' knowledge? We don't know where this first merged person is, but we do know he's not here. This is our only chance to gain a lead in this.

"We have absolutely no choice. We must do this, and as quickly as possible. There's no more time for debate on this issue. Colonel, I insist you allow me to merge with a gift and get me and anyone else who is willing to do so back to Peterson immediately!"

"Are you willing to join with your gift, Major?" Web asked Angela.

"Yes, sir."

Web turned his head slightly to ask AJ the same question, but stopped short of doing so when he saw the blank expression on his face. "Is he . . ."

"Yes, sir. He started merging while Doctor Liu was talking," Angela answered.

"Let's stick to protocol, then. Since you're willing, do whatever it is that you need to do to make it happen," Web directed.

"Doctor Liu, a word if you will?" Web asked politely as he stood to exit the shelter. Chang stood and followed him.

Outside of the shelter, Web spoke sternly to Chang. "What's wrong with you, Doctor? I've never seen you act with so little regard for another's feelings."

Chang was visibly upset and took a moment to gather himself before responding. "We're going about this incorrectly and we've already lost part of the game—a game we cannot afford to lose. We've already learned that we're unlikely to play a role in the construction of the first interstellar vessel mankind has produced. What if we lose the next move in the game? There may be no other chances, and the fate of humanity will be completely out of our control. Even if there are no group minds on their way, whichever country possesses this technology in the way it was designed to be used will become a world power. I left a communist dictatorship where people were persecuted for what they believed, where my parents struggled to survive while millions were killed. I must do everything I can—I will do everything I can—to prevent that. I'm sorry, but your feelings pale in comparison to our need to act."

Web thought for a moment before responding. "I agree with you. The stakes have been raised, but we only recently found that out. We accelerate from here. Tension on the team will not aid us in our mission."

"Colonel, as I've said before and has now been proven to be true, we cannot wait until we know. Doing so will only ensure we find out from someone else more bold and will be at their mercy. You're an officer in the world's most powerful military, living in the world's most prosperous and strongest nation. You've only ever been on top. The rest of the world—the parts of it that know a very different kind of struggle than Americans do—will not hesitate to act because of the potential risks. Human life is not as precious in those places. It should be and it can be, but only if the knowledge contained in that data store is used properly."

"I appreciate your passion, Doctor, and as I said, I agree with you on what must be done now. Can we try to do so civilly? I assure you, developing factions and resentments will only hamper our efforts."

"Yes, Colonel. You're right, recriminations will not help at this point, but to be clear, I am getting a gift and merging with it as soon as we return, correct?"

"Pandora's box is wide open now. I couldn't close it again if I wanted to. Yes, you may retrieve a gift as soon as we return."

Web arranged for AJ and Angela to be moved onto the Chinook helicopter after everything else was on board, including several dozen gifts. There had been some concern about moving them while their gifts were changing them, but in the end, it was decided the team couldn't wait. Chang's sense of urgency was now instilled in all of them.

Web took the opportunity during loading time to update his commanding officer about the latest events, and requested that suitably qualified volunteers be found while the team was in flight. His CO assured him they'd be at the SCIF when the team arrived. Web informed him that he was leaving Jack behind as temporary commander of the site until the command could find a higher-ranking replacement.

Having fulfilled his commitment, Web boarded the aircraft—the last to do so before the loadmaster—which took off a few minutes later.

Ninety minutes into the flight, Angela returned to full consciousness, followed by AJ a few minutes later. Casual conversations stopped when the team noticed they were awake. AJ was the first to speak.

"I don't feel much different—better, but pretty much the same."

Angela was right behind him. "Neither do I, although my gift, I've named him An by the way, tells me the human form is not designed very robustly and he'd like to do something about that. I said no. I'm going to ask him if he knows any more about what's going on now that we're one."

"I'll do the same," AJ said.

Less than a minute later, Angela spoke again, directing her attention to Web. "An tells me something unusual has happened, something that has never to his knowledge been done before. One purpose of the landing ships' shedding mass is to establish a framework for a worldwide intelligent communication network. When sufficient gifts merge with humans, the network is supposed to become aware. This time, it became aware before that requirement was met."

"Does it know why?" Web asked.

"He, sir, and yes. A man who merged before us brought the network up before the controlling intelligence came to be of its own accord."

"So, who's controlling it?" Rui asked.

"That man."

"That doesn't sound good."

"No, it doesn't. Do you know where this man is? Can your gift . . . can An help you find him?" Web asked.

"One moment, sir." Angela stopped talking and closed her eyes for a moment. "It's not a guarantee, but there's a very large group of nodes not far from . . . wait, that's weird."

"What is it, Major?"

"I was going to give you the coordinates to the center of the group of nodes, but I thought you'd want to know where it was without having to call up a map. It's within thirty miles of Peterson, sir."

"Can you be more specific?"

"Let me see . . ." Angela talked silently with An for a moment before answering. "Yes, sir. It's in Pueblo, near the intersection of Bruce Lane and Duncan Road."

"That's Sam's neighborhood. Can your gift correlate his address with that location?"

"They overlap, sir."

"How in the hell . . . ?" Web turned away from Angela, grabbed a headset off the cabin wall, put it on, and activated it. "Connect me to base security."

Chapter TWENTY-ONE

Sam wasn't feeling particularly powerful anymore. In fact, quite the opposite. For the first time since merging with Adia, he felt worn down and distracted, as if he was trying to concentrate with two different types of loud and obnoxious music playing in each ear. Not impossible, but inefficient and painful.

"You didn't mention how incredibly uncomfortable this would be, Adia. Please tell me there's a way to make it stop."

"I didn't anticipate any discomfort for you, Sam, and I don't yet know what's causing it. I'll need to monitor your brain patterns in response to network activity in order to find the source of your uneasiness. Until then, I can't say that it will be possible to make it stop without abandoning control of the network. If you choose to do that, I don't know if it will ever self-organize, or for that matter, if there will be any way to reactivate it."

"You can explain that to me later. Right now, it feels like my head is going to explode. I'm going to lay down for a while and give you some time to work on the problem. In the future, I need to pay more attention to you when you tell me you don't know something. You may have been born to complement me, but it doesn't appear your complementary elements include helping me be cautious."

"Would it have helped if I had cautioned you? I can change."

"No, it wouldn't have, and don't. I'm just cranky. This was my choice. I'm going to rest now."

Sam moved from the living room to the bedroom and slowly lowered himself to the bed. He was accustomed to being in pain, but almost never had headaches, let alone one like this. He didn't bother trying to sleep because he knew it was pointless. Instead, he covered his eyes with a pillow and tried to be very still. He hadn't been there long before Adia interrupted him.

"Sam, a bonded pair just contacted each of our network nodes."

"What does that mean? Please keep it simple."

"On its face, it indicates some interest in the way we've activated the network. As I said, our actions were unusual and both humans and gifts are curious by nature. It'll probably happen again, perhaps many times. Right now, however, the nodes are still close to us and are departing in a semispherical pattern. It would be trivial to determine our approximate location by triangulating on their locations. It's likely someone is looking for the pair that activated the network—for us."

"Can you determine where the contact came from?"

"Within limits based on the delay between contact requests and very limited triangulation . . ."

"Simple, please."

"Between forty and sixty miles north of us."

"Dammit! We have to go. Can you do anything for this pain that will make me any more functional?"

"For short periods."

"Do it."

Sam started to feel slightly better as he carefully got up and went to his closet to get a suitcase. Opening the suitcase on the bed, he quickly threw in some underwear, socks, jeans, and a few shirts, carefully placing the pictures of Elizabeth and Zach on top of his clothes. He closed the suitcase, opened his nightstand, and took out his emergency cash, shoving it in his pocket before extracting his pistol and some boxes of ammunition. He put the gun in his waistband and the extra ammo in the suitcase's zippered pocket. He was certain he'd need the cash and hopeful he wouldn't need the gun. As prepared as the time allowed, he headed outside to his Jeep, set the suitcase on the passenger seat, got in the driver's side, and started it up.

"Is that the best you can do?" Sam asked. "I still feel like death might be preferable."

"This is the best balance of pain mitigation and maintaining your ability to function."

"It'll have to do. Direct the nodes to move more randomly and accelerate their departure from this area. Then start creating as many general-purpose nanites as possible from parts of the truck that we won't miss. Leave room for three people. Is there anything you can do to make it more efficient? It'd be very convenient if we didn't have to stop more often than absolutely necessary."

"The nodes are responding to your instructions and I have begun the process of creating nanites. I can make the vehicle much more efficient. Which is your priority, improving the vehicle or having a pool of available nanites?"

"Go with the pool first. You'll have some time to work on the truck when we get to Jim's."

As they were talking, Sam pulled out of the driveway, taking what he believed would be his last look at the house. It wasn't a bad little house, he thought. Not bad at all.

Sam arrived at Jim's without notice. He'd left his phone at the house and didn't want to try communicating with Jim using the Worldnet while driving. He was having enough trouble paying attention to the road as it was. Tasking his brain any more would likely get him pulled over for driving while impaired. Then he'd have to explain the gun, which would probably result in him being taken to jail, where Web would find him. Not a risk he was willing to take.

Parking his truck as far off the road as Jim's short driveway allowed, Sam exited the vehicle and walked to the front door. He ignored the doorbell, knocking firmly three times like they'd taught him in the service. Some lessons stick for life.

"Just a minute," said a muffled, distant voice from inside.

A few seconds later, the porch light came on and Sam heard Jim's voice more clearly.

"Who is it?"

"It's me, Jim."

"I don't know anybody by the name of me. Go away!"

Sam started to say something else, but the opening door cut him off.

"I'm just screwing with you. Come on in, Sam." Jim waited for Sam to enter, then closed the door and turned the porch light back off. "I assume your late-night visit is related to our earlier activities?"

Sam hadn't considered how late it was and was about to apologize for getting Jim up, but one good look at Jim convinced Sam he'd been awake and actively working on something. His eyes were bright and he appeared to be restraining himself from doing calisthenics.

"You look like you're ready to bounce off the walls, Jim."

"I have so much energy, I don't know what to do with myself!" Jim responded with a smile. "Can I get you something to drink?"

"Sure, whatever you have handy."

"Got a fresh pot of coffee, not that I need it anymore. Still like the taste, though."

"That would be great. Black, one sugar."

"Have a seat in the living room. I'll meet you there."

Sam walked into Jim's living room. He'd only been to the house a few times, after a handful of particularly pleasant fishing trips. He liked the place. It didn't feel like a bachelor pad, probably because Jim hadn't changed the decor much after his wife died. Sam could understand that.

Sam took a seat on the sofa across from the recliner. He knew Jim wouldn't say anything if he sat on the recliner, but a man just doesn't do that in another man's house.

Jim walked back into the room with two mugs of coffee. He placed Sam's on the table in front of him and took his back to the side table next to the recliner, sipping it before setting it down.

"Careful, it's hot. Damn machine hasn't brewed at the right temperature for years. Suppose I could fix it now, huh?"

"You could, but I don't think we'll be taking it with us," Sam replied.

"With us? Are we going somewhere?"

"Yeah, we are. Not sure where, though. I'm hoping you can help with that."

"Why don't you rewind this movie for me a little?"

"It's complicated and I'm not at my best, but I'll give it a try." Sam paused. "But maybe there's a better way."

Sam thought to Adia, "Can you tell Adam what we did with the network and what's happened since?"

"Yes," she answered.

"And he can relate it to Jim so I don't have to?"

"Of course, Sam."

"Do it, please."

Sam told Jim what he'd just asked of Adia and waited for him to be brought up to speed. It took a couple of minutes. Sam closed his eyes and tried unsuccessfully to clear his mind while he waited.

In less time than Sam could have told the tale when at his best, Jim said, "Yep, looks like we need to find a different place to be. You don't take half measures, do you?"

"I've been told I'm a loose cannon. I prefer to think that cannons should be moved from time to time, or at least I did until I decided to change the way a far more advanced species with years to think about it determined the best way to establish a global communication network for entities they created. Hubris comes to mind, but there's probably a stronger, more appropriate word that I can't think of right now because my head's about to explode."

"Wasn't a criticism, Son. Building a bridge that crosses half a river doesn't do anybody any good and wastes a lot of time and resources. Anyway, as you so kindly pointed out during our little talk, most of my family and friends are dead, so I don't have a lot of options when it comes to places we can go. The best one is my daughter's house. She's got a place in Montana. It's pretty remote. Should buy us some time."

"She have any other family up there?" Sam asked, concerned about minimizing the number of people who knew where they would be and what they would be doing.

"Just her son. He takes care of her. Good kid. Haven't seen either of them in too long."

"Are you sure you want to involve her in this? I'm sure you know the government is going to keep looking for me, for us."

"She's dying, Sam. It's MS. Her good days aren't so hot, her bad days are terrible. Couldn't do anything about it before; no one could. Tried to get her to move here, but she wouldn't. Said she wanted to die where she loved to live. Sweet child, always was, but stubborn." Jim paused. He looked at Sam for a long time, clearly trying to find a way to finish his thought. "You said you could get a gift for every member of your team, right?"

Sam was sorry he'd been thinking too slowly to stop Jim from having to spell it out. "Yes, and I can't think of a better use for one of them than helping your daughter."

Jim sat in the chair, nodding gently to himself, looking down. Finally, he rubbed his eyes and returned them to Sam. "That's good. That's real good, Sam."

Sam didn't say a word. There was nothing to say. Instead, he waited for Jim to continue. Some things shouldn't be hurried, no matter how little time was available.

"Guess we should probably figure out what we're going to take, pack it, and get the hell out of here," Jim said after a time. Sam knew he'd waited just long enough to speak without emotion. Sam could understand that, too.

"Could you call Esther and let her know we'll be picking her up soon?" Sam asked.

"I will. She'll get a kick out of this." Jim did, and made arrangements for them to pick her up in half an hour. When he'd finished, they began packing. Jim had a fair amount of bottled water and camping food. Sam wasn't sure why. To the best of his knowledge, Jim hadn't been camping in many years. Old habits, apparently. He also had a wad of cash. They took as much of the former as they could load in ten minutes and all of the latter. Fifteen minutes later, they were on their way.

As they headed north on I-25 with Jim driving, Esther asleep in the passenger seat, and Sam laying down in the back, Adia transformed

Sam's SUV by changing the color and matching the plates to that of an unwanted vehicle. It wasn't the best camouflage, but better than nothing. Adia assured Sam the modifications she'd made would allow them to easily travel the seven hundred remaining miles with miles to spare. Sam's experience with Montana law enforcement left him inclined to believe they'd be less zealous than most in pursuit of federal government objectives. Some people would be bothered by that. Sam wasn't.

Unable to think of anything else he could do to keep the team safe and get it to its destination, Sam decided to join Esther in sleep, if he could. With Adia's assistance, it turned out that he could.

Chapter TWENTY-TWO

The military police captain walked back from Sam's house to report in, leaving his team behind to more thoroughly search the house. When he arrived at his vehicle, he removed the secure phone from its cradle and called the number he got on the way to Pueblo. Web answered on the second ring.

"Do you have him?" Web asked without preamble.

"No, sir. There was no one here when we arrived. I have my men searching the house now, as ordered."

"Have you or your team noticed anything unusual?"

"No, sir. It just looks like an empty bachelor's house. No pictures on the walls, the refrigerator is nearly empty, and the bed is unmade. Other than the bed and some clothes in the closet, it hardly looks like anyone lives there at all."

"Have your team keep looking, but be inconspicuous and post a lookout on both ends of the street. If he comes back, don't let him get away. Do you understand me, Captain?"

"Yes, sir."

"Good. I've sent reinforcements. While they're en route, I have another task for you. Mr. Steele's sister-in-law lives just down the street. Her name is Sara Bryant. Go to her house and convince her to accompany you back to base once the reinforcements have arrived. Don't delegate this task—do it yourself. Ms. Bryant understands military rank; if a captain from the military police is at her door, she'll know it's important. Tell her it's about Mr. Steele and that you are not privy to the details, but that it's critical that she meet with me. Put on your best sincere and concerned face, Captain, because it's critical that she come with you. We need her help for a matter of national security. Do you understand your orders?"

"Yes, sir. I am to go alone to Ms. Bryant's house, be as personable and convincing as possible without telling her anything other than it is critical that she accompany me to the base, where she will meet with you. If the support forces have not arrived by the time I have accomplished that task, I am to wait for their arrival before proceeding back to base, where I will deliver Ms. Bryant to your care."

"Exactly. Call me when you have her. When I pick up, say 'en route' then hang up." Web provided the captain with Sara's address and terminated the call.

While Web coordinated the search for Sam, the rest of the team heatedly discussed who would accept gifts. The NCA supported Web's decision to accelerate the pace of discovery and encouraged him to convince each member of the team to accept a gift, with the hope that those who accepted would quickly come to the decision to merge so progress could be made on building and accessing the Makers' data store. As such, Web did as he was ordered and delivered a strong argument for the proposition. However, his case was weakened by the fact that *he* had yet to accept a gift, uncharacteristically citing an excuse. What they needed was Sam; he was the best person to lead the effort. But Web couldn't afford to be out of the hunt for hours while merging with a gift. It was clear that several members of the group found his argument to be of questionable value, but no one questioned it, instead holding the remainder of the discussion without him.

At a pause in the discussion, Dan took the opportunity to summarize the team's current position. "Okay, as of now, Angela, AJ, and Chang have all accepted gifts and merged. Camilla and I have accepted gifts and agree to merge at the end of this discussion. Jack isn't here to speak for himself, but I think we all agree that he won't be accepting a gift in the near future, which also seems like a safe assumption for the colonel. All of us who've accepted gifts have been informed by them that the composition of the team must be either four men and five women, or vice versa, to create the Makers' Encyclopedia Galactica. We have three men and two women, leaving us four people short. Rui, is there any chance you'll change your mind?"

"None whatsoever. I am perfectly happy remaining entirely human, thank you very much."

"Okay then, I suggest we each discuss the issue with members of our support teams and request volunteers, keeping in mind that we need at least two more women. I also suggest that we do so as expeditiously as possible. Does anyone else see a better course of action?"

Chang replied, "I would like to define 'expeditiously' before we begin. I say we each meet back here with our volunteers as soon as we find them. When we have at least two of each sex, we hand them gifts and tell them to get started."

"Do we really want to put this team together on a first-come, first-served basis? Shouldn't we be more selective than that?" Camilla asked.

"If we had unlimited time, certainly, but we don't. I fear we may have already spent more time on this issue than we should've. I hope I'm wrong about that. May we proceed as I recommend?" Chang asked.

The room was silent. After a moment, Dan said, "There don't appear to be any further objections, so that's how we'll do it. I'll check my team for volunteers, then inform Colonel Web of our decisions and secure the required gifts. I'll be back here with them as quickly as possible and will give one to each of the first four people capable of building a team with a workable gender ratio."

"Thank you for coming in, Sara," Web said as he gestured toward an empty office chair. A few days earlier, Web would have said there was no chance a civilian without the proper clearances would be in the SCIF at all, let alone at his request. He could have met her elsewhere, but hoped the security checks and surroundings would help him get what he wanted.

Web closed his door and took a seat before continuing. "I'm sure it must have been disconcerting to be disturbed by an MP so late in the evening, or at all, for that matter."

"Yes, yes it was. What's this all about, Eric?"

"Before I start, can I offer you something to drink? Some water, perhaps a cup of coffee or tea?" Web asked.

"No, thank you. Please just tell me why I'm here."

"It's about Sam. We have reason to believe he may have become unstable again, and know that he has access to information that could be damaging to national security—not to mention to Sam himself. If I knew where he was, maybe I could protect him again, but without knowing, I can't. I know you want to help him, too. Can you tell me anything that might assist us in finding him before he does something he'll regret?"

"Sam wouldn't characterize what you did after the fire as protecting him. I know you did everything you could, Eric, but he's never stopped blaming you for the way you insisted it be handled. The only person he blames more is himself."

"I know Sam's feelings about me. I'm not going to try to convince you we've become friends, but you know I had no choice in how we handled the situation. We followed the protocol proven to be most likely to succeed in rescuing Elizabeth and Zach. I am very sorry for your loss and for Sam's. I truly am. I've relived that night hundreds of times and I still can't think of a way we could have saved them. I hope you know that, and I hope you understand that I did protect Sam. I'm trying to do that right now. You two aren't blood, but he loves you as much as he'd love his own sister if he had one. He must have told you something."

Sara wiped a tear from her eye and took a deep breath. "It still hurts."

Web handed her a box of tissues while saying, "I know. I don't think it ever goes away."

After wiping both of her eyes for a minute and gently blowing her nose, Sara looked up at Web. "I don't know where he'd go. I just spoke to him last night. I didn't know he'd gone anywhere."

"What did you two talk about?" Web asked gently.

"He said he had a strange story to share with me. I was trying to keep the conversation light, so I asked him if it was strange good or strange bad. He said both, then said that what he was about to say might make me uncomfortable. He was right about that. I was already getting uncomfortable. Then I asked if it had anything to do with his job on base. He said it did and I told him I didn't want to hear it. I could tell that hurt him, but instead of leaving it at that,

I told him I couldn't be involved in another failure. I don't know why I said it. It was cruel . . ." She stopped talking and started sobbing.

Web waited until she stopped, which took a while. Another man might have comforted her, although another man might not have sent police to pick her up in the middle of the night. When he thought he'd waited long enough, he asked, "Did you talk about anything else?"

"No. He left right after that."

"Sara, I know this is difficult, but it is also very important. I have to step out for a minute. Please think about where Sam could have gone. Are you sure I can't get you something?"

"A water, please."

"Okay. I'll be back in a few minutes. Please don't leave the office."

Web walked out toward a guard he'd had stationed down the hallway. "Have someone take her a water and make sure she doesn't leave."

"Yes, sir."

Dan saw Web approaching the conference room, where the team was discussing where to find more people willing to accept gifts. On his way to tell his team about the opportunity to volunteer for a gift, Dan took advantage of the chance meeting.

"A moment of your time, Colonel?" Dan asked.

"All right, but be brief. I'm in the middle of something," Web replied.

"We've come up with a plan to complete the team needed to activate the EG and I need your permission to release the required gifts."

"What's the EG?"

"Sorry. That's what we're calling the Makers' data store. It's less of a mouthful, short for Encyclopedia Galactica. Corny, we know, but we have to call it something. Can I get your permission to release the gifts?"

"Yes. See Captain Andrews. She has my instructions for their management. She will accompany them until they are accepted and make sure we document who accepts. Is that all?"

"I thought you'd want to hear more details of our plan."

"Later, Doctor. I'm sure they're adequate. Now, if you'll excuse me." Web left the conversation and continued down the hallway toward Angela's team. Seeing her a moment later, he gestured Angela into an empty office.

"Can you use the network you detected to communicate with Sam?" Web asked.

Angela consulted silently with An before answering. "Ultimately, yes. That's what it's designed for. I don't know if it will work yet, though."

"Try."

Angela attempted to contact Sam. After several seconds, she stopped. "Either he's ignoring me or the network isn't mature enough yet."

"Keep trying. Let me know when you can."

"Yes, sir."

Web walked back into his office and took a seat. Sara was no longer visibly emotional. Grateful for that, Web asked, "Have you thought of where Sam might have gone?"

"There are only two people beside myself I can think of that he might turn to for help, though I don't know how much good either of them would be to him under these circumstances. Dan is one; the other is Jim, a man who Sam talks with at the community center. They fish together sometimes. They seem to be good friends even though Jim is much older, in his seventies. Like I said, I don't know how much help he could give Sam even if he wanted to."

"Do you know Jim's last name or where he lives?" Web asked.

"I'm pretty sure he lives in Pueblo, but I'm not certain and I don't know his last name. I didn't talk with him much. Sorry."

"Could you describe him?"

"Sure."

"Sara, I'm going to ask you to go with the captain who brought you here to the base police station. You're not in trouble. I just want you to work with a sketch artist to help us put together a picture of Jim. Can you do that for me?"

"Yes . . . You're going to help Sam, right?"

"Yes, I'll do everything I can."

Web went to the door and gestured for the guard to enter. "Please escort Ms. Bryant back to the officer who brought her in. Advise him that I want her taken to the Provost Marshal's Office to work with a sketch artist. Tell him to call me when the drawing is completed."

"Yes, sir. Please come with me, ma'am."

Sara got up and accompanied the guard.

"Thank you for your help, Sara. You'll be back home in no time and we'll work all this out."

Web closed the door behind them before picking up the phone. "Jack, come to my office immediately. I need you to find someone."

Chapter TWENTY-THREE

Jim pulled up to Lisa's house outside Lewistown, Montana. Sam was the first one out of the vehicle. He looked the place over while waiting for Jim and Esther to join him. The old ranch house had seen a lot of wear and not much maintenance. Its white paint was chipped and peeling and the worn steps leading up to the porch sagged dangerously, what little paint they once had hidden in the tread cracks. To the right of the steps was a rough-hewn, unpainted plywood ramp with two thin black tire tracks running its length and a small depression at its base. It didn't look safe, but clearly saw a fair amount of use.

Sam's assessment was interrupted by the front door opening. A young man—tall, gangly, and awkward as only a teenager can be—stood there looking at the group. Then, recognizing his grandpa, ran toward the car, leaping over the steps in a single bound. He crossed the fifty or so feet more quickly than Sam would have thought his skinny legs could carry him, and slammed into his grandpa with enough force that Sam would have been worried about Jim being injured if he hadn't recently accepted a gift. Sam wondered if Jim's grandson, Matt, could tell the difference as they hugged. Jim was clearly as happy to see Matt as Matt was to see him.

Finally letting go of each other, Jim took a step back from Matt and, holding his shoulders in his hands, said, "My God, look at you, boy! You're almost as tall as I am. How've you been, Son?"

"I'm good, Grandpa. I didn't know you were coming. Did Mom?"

"Not this time, Son. It's kind of a special visit, that's why we didn't call ahead. It's also why I brought some friends to meet you guys. How's your mom?"

Matt looked at Sam and then Esther before returning his attention to Jim. "It's not one of her worst days."

"Why don't we all go inside so I can introduce my friends to her?"

Everyone followed him up to the small home. Sam and Esther waited on the porch while Jim and Matt went inside. While he waited, Sam instructed Adia to begin inconspicuously constructing as many nanites as they could control. Moments later, Sam heard a woman's voice, soft but beautiful. He couldn't hear what she was saying well but could tell that she was happy. Jim's voice, however, was clear as he told Lisa about Sam and Esther. Another minute or two passed before Jim came to the door.

"Come on inside. Lisa's in the kitchen putting on a pot of coffee. I told her she didn't need to, but she wouldn't have any of it. Did I mention she's stubborn?"

"Excuse me," Esther said as she went to the kitchen to offer Lisa some help.

"Yeah, I believe you did, Jim. I'm sure it's not genetic," Sam responded.

Jim grinned. "Have a seat."

The inside of the house was neat and comfortable, showing no signs of disrepair or neglect, with basic and sturdy furniture that reminded Sam of his boyhood home. There were paintings and pictures on the walls, though not too many, and precious few knick-knacks set about, just the way Sam liked it. There were also two recliners. Sam waited for Matt to take a seat on the couch, then asked if his mom used one of the recliners. Matt told him that she didn't, that it was too hard for her to get out of them and preferred sitting next to him on the couch.

"Which one do you want, Jim?" Sam asked him.

"You're the alpha male on this trip, Sam. You don't know how happy you're making me. Take any damned chair you want," Jim replied.

Sam smiled and took the recliner directly opposite from where he suspected Lisa would sit. He and Jim had agreed during the drive up that Sam would tell Lisa the story, with Jim and Esther supporting him. Jim had maintained his appearance so that Lisa and Matt would recognize him. Esther, having no such reason, had allowed her gift, Haya, to do whatever it wished to return her to optimal health. Except for her hair that she'd pulled back and tied up, she looked to be in her twenties. When they picked her up, Sam had asked her to bring a couple recent pictures of herself. He thought the contrast might help Lisa understand the potential of the gifts.

While they waited for Lisa, Sam communicated briefly with Adia.

"How's the growth of the network coming?"

"It's nearly complete in North America, excluding Alaska and some of the northernmost portions of Canada. Eurasia is nearly complete, again excluding some of the northernmost portions. The rest of the world is a bit further behind."

"Do you have enough information to provide me an estimated time of completion for the most populous regions yet, say the top 90 percent?"

"If trends continue, less than twelve hours."

"And is Angela still trying to contact me?"

"Angela and others. Do you want me to continue to ignore them?"

"For now. Are there enough bonded pairs in North America yet to make us a little less conspicuous?"

"No, Sam. Having three pairs so close together is still unique, aside from a few locations. Four will be even more so. I've done as you asked and created decoys with network nodes, but that ruse won't last forever."

"Keep working on a better idea, then, please."

"Of course."

"How long will it take you to get the sensor net we discussed on the way up active?"

"It is marginally active now. We're detecting on all radio bands and I'll have visual and radar detection active in the next few minutes."

"Excellent. Faster than we discussed."

"The rate of humans accepting gifts is accelerating. Our percentage of the excess capacity of the Worldnet is increasing quickly. Partly because of this, we can now control more than sixty times as many nanites as we could when we left Pueblo."

"More good news. When the government finds us, they'll probably conduct aerial reconnaissance. Be sure we have the means to prevent that."

"Yes, Sam."

Lisa and Esther entered the room as Adia answered. Sam was sure that Jim had taken a moment to catch up with Adam as well, and thought that Matt must have wondered why they were so quiet. Sam made a mental note to be more considerate to the kid.

"Lisa wouldn't let me help her make the coffee, but she did let me carry the tray in. Smells good. Who wants some?" Esther asked.

With nods all around, Esther happily served everyone—she could hardly contain herself—while Lisa took her place on the couch. It was painful to watch, as she clearly had just enough strength and balance to get the job done. It took every bit of will-power Sam had to not offer assistance, as he knew a lot about pain, injuries, and weakness. But he also understood her need to do a task without help if she could. It was a reminder that she still had purpose and meaning, that she wasn't just a burden to others. Taking that away from her would be the worst thing anyone could do, and Sam could see on Matt's face that he too understood. Hell of a thing for a fourteen-year-old kid to understand, Sam thought.

When Lisa and Esther were settled, Jim introduced everyone. He then explained to Lisa and Matt that the group had something to share with both of them, but that they had to tell Lisa first, without Matt.

Esther asked Matt if he had baseball equipment. Matt did. "Well, go get it. I haven't played catch in a very long time and I really want to!"

Matt left the room to get the equipment and Esther told Sam to come get them when he was ready. "But don't be too quick about it. I have a few things I want to teach this kid." Esther waited until Matt returned, and they walked outside together. Both of them were smiling.

"Okay, Dad, what's going on?" Lisa asked.

Now that he could hear it clearly, Sam found her voice even more compelling. He could tell she had once been beautiful, when her brown hair still had sheen and her matching eyes held more glimmer and less pain. He was pleased the illness had at least left her such a pretty voice. She was in for quite a surprise.

"You always did go straight to the point, didn't you? Stubborn and forthright, hell of a combination. Sam, you're up," Jim replied.

Sam took a moment to gather his thoughts, which, thanks to Adia's progress on their interface to the Worldnet, wasn't as difficult as it had been when they'd left Pueblo, but still not easy. "I like straight to the point, so that's what I'll be as well. Lisa, your dad and I have been friends for a couple of years now. He helped me through the roughest part of my life. After I lost my wife and son, I didn't see any reason to live. Truth be told, he saved me. It wasn't any one thing he did, but rather simply who he was. I won't go into details because it would embarrass him. It suffices to say that when I needed help for something really important and potentially quite dangerous, he was the man I turned to for advice and help. He didn't let me down. He never has."

Sam stopped. He realized he wasn't being as direct as he said he'd be, so he took a deep breath before trying again. "He's only ever asked one thing of me, aside from asking me to stop blaming and pitying myself, and that was to help you. I want you to know that about your dad before I tell you something fantastic."

Sam paused again, partly to assess the impact of what he'd said to her, partly because he wasn't sure how to continue. He got to the point. "We believe we can cure you."

Lisa looked away from Sam and toward her father. "Why, Dad? You know I can't be cured. I don't even think about it anymore. I'm just trying to hang in there long enough so that Matt won't have to go to foster care if you're not around to take him."

Sam looked down at his hands. An inexplicable nobility to this woman he'd just met made him feel unworthy.

"Just listen to him, Angel. You have nothing to lose and a lot to gain."

Lisa turned back to Sam, started to say something else, then changed her mind. Her silence prompted Sam to continue. He pulled out of his pocket one of the pictures he had asked Esther to bring, stood, and handed it to Lisa.

"That's the woman playing catch with your son. She's sixty-seven years old. She had a host of diseases a couple of days ago."

Lisa stared at the picture for a moment before quietly asking, "How?"

Sam pulled a gift out of his pocket and placed it on the couch next to Lisa. "With this. They're called gifts. How they got here is complicated. How I have one to offer you, just as I offered one each to your father and Esther, is even more complicated. What they do for the human body is straightforward: they heal it. You should know, though, that it doesn't always work. There is a chance something could go wrong, but I don't think that will happen with you."

"What can go wrong and why don't you think it will happen with me?" Lisa asked.

"Some people who attempt to join with a gift die in the attempt. I don't think it will happen to you because the most common causes of that happening are certain types of mental disorders, primarily sociopathy. You don't strike me as a sociopath." Sam smiled as he said it, attempting to lighten the mood. He was pleased to see Lisa smile back. Very pleased.

"I don't know what to say. This is all so surreal," Lisa said.

"How about we take a small step toward making it less so? Touch the gift and ask it what it is. It will answer out loud, so don't be startled."

Lisa did so and received the usual response.

Sam continued, "If you accept it, you will create a living entity whose purpose is to help you. The name of my gift is Adia. Your father named his Adam. In order for this to happen, your gift will have to change you slightly, as the guide just told you. The change involves putting extremely small machines in you so that you can communicate with your gift. Those machines can ultimately cure you if you choose to go further, but you don't have to. Lisa, your father and I have both done this and we want you to do it as well."

"I don't mean to be rude, but if it can do all that you say, why does my dad look the same, and again, I don't mean to be hurtful, but why didn't yours heal you?" Lisa asked.

"Jim thought it would be best if he looked like you and Matt expected him to. My gift did heal me in many ways . . ."

"Sam's not ready to let the scars go, Honey," Jim interjected.

Lisa thought about that for a while before asking, "What if something happens to me? Who will take care of Matt?"

"We will, all of us. We would raise Matt as our own, but you don't have to worry about that right now. Just accept your gift. The being born as a result will explain the rest to you," Sam replied.

"Dad?"

Jim got up and sat next to Lisa. He took her free hand in his and looked her in the eye. "Please accept it, Honey. It's the only chance Matt and I have to spend more time with you. It's the only chance you'll have to see him grow up, to give you grandkids. Please do it." Jim's eyes were wet and glossy.

Lisa closed her eyes and said, "I accept."

Sam and Jim stayed with Lisa while her gift developed, which took longer than it had for Jim. Adia told Sam that Lisa's gift was going very slowly because Lisa had some neural damage that needed to be repaired in order for her to communicate with her gift. Sam had nothing to say to that; in fact, neither he nor Jim said a word until Lisa awoke. When she did, they both waited for her to speak, which took a long time. Adia told Sam that Lisa and her gift were talking. Sure that Adam had told Jim the same, Sam continued to wait in silence.

"Dad, will you help me lay down?" Lisa asked. She sounded weaker than she had before the process had started.

"Sure, Angel." Jim gently moved Lisa into the most comfortable position he could, concern written clearly on his face.

"I have to sleep now," Lisa said, and did.

"What's going on?" Jim asked.

Sam had just asked Adia the same question. The answer was not comforting.

"She was very close to dying, Sam. Her gift told her they needed to merge immediately if she was going to have any chance of saving them," Adia replied.

"But she's going to be all right, right?" Sam asked.

"I don't know, Sam."

Chapter TWENTY-FOUR

"You wanted to see me, sir?" Web asked General Campbell, his commanding officer, as he entered his office.

"Yes. Take a seat." General Campbell gestured toward one of the four overstuffed leather chairs surrounding a polished circular wooden table set in one corner of the large office. Web took the seat opposite the one he knew his boss would take and waited for him to continue.

General Campbell looked down at Web for a moment before taking his seat. "Your report from last evening has raised some concern at the highest levels, Eric. It appears we have missed two critical opportunities and don't know where we stand with regard to the third. While I don't know that there's anything we could have done differently to ensure that one of our people was this first character, if you're right about Sam being responsible for bringing up the gift's global network, that's something we could have controlled. Something we should have controlled, actually, and failing to secure him after the fact doesn't help. Factions in the NCA are questioning whether we have the right team in charge. Do we have the right team, Eric?"

"Yes, sir. We have the right team. They've prepared for this, to the extent preparation was possible, for years. We're making progress on the Makers' encyclopedia. If being the first is as important for that activity as it was for being the first person to merge with a gift, it would seem that we are still in the running. Bringing another team in would only slow that process.

"I agree that Sam is a problem, but he's a problem we're aggressively working to solve. Other than his sister-in-law, Sara, he has no family and very few friends, most of whom are on the first contact team. He doesn't have a lot of options for places to go. We're monitoring his credit cards and bank accounts, and if he tries to access them, we'll know immediately. I have investigators interviewing the staff and members of the community center where Sam volunteers, and I expect that will yield an identification of the man Jim that Sara said was his most likely ally. It shouldn't take us long to find him after that."

"You knew precisely where he was last time and failed to bring him in. What assurances can you give me that won't happen again?"

"I've thought about that, sir. First of all, we used the network he apparently created to triangulate on his position. We believe he was aware of our activities on the network and was, therefore, forewarned. We're not relying on the network to track him now, although we are using the encyclopedia to investigate ways to do so in the future without his knowledge. The next time we go after him, we'll have the element of surprise, which brings me to my second point. On our first attempt to bring Sam in, I had to rely on base security. I don't think that is an optimal strategy."

"What do you have in mind?"

"I wouldn't presume to have developed the best possible strategy, sir, but I have an idea for what I believe would be a better approach." Web paused to see if his CO wanted to hear it.

"I have some thoughts as well. Let's hear yours first," General Campbell directed.

"Yes, sir. We know that Sam has merged with a gift and we're learning more every hour what that means. He'll have capabilities unlike anything our traditional forces have ever dealt with. He's also very well trained. It may have been a couple of years since he's been active in the field, but Sam is not the type of man to forget his training. He would have been a difficult man to capture before merging with a gift. Now, I believe difficult would be an understatement. From what the merged scientists have said, his actions bringing up the global network are unique and introduce an element of uncertainty into the equation that would not normally exist. In short, sir, they cannot tell me with certainty that if something were to happen to Sam, they, or anyone, would be able to reestablish the network. As I said in my report, the gifts say that the network is essential not only to building the gift ship but also to building anything of significant complexity. It's what allows large numbers of merged pairs to collaborate. Because of that, we cannot afford to kill Sam, not even by accident. I believe we need a team of people trained in high-risk rescue operations, an *in extremis* noncombatant extraction force, and we need the members of that team to merge with gifts," Web replied.

"And who would you recommend to lead this team?"

"Myself, sir. I've known Sam for years. I know how he thinks. In particular, I know how he thinks when he's under stress. In that regard, I believe I'm uniquely qualified."

"I agree with you with respect to your understanding of Sam, but he's not the only threat we face."

"Sir?"

"The NCA has decided to put together teams to track high-risk individuals who receive gifts. They're working out a protocol to determine who would be considered high risk. Obviously, Sam is our first example, but where there's one threat, there are usually more of the same. Your idea for the composition of the teams is in line with what I proposed and what was approved. Because of your experience with Sam and your knowledge of the gifts, you were selected to lead the team to Sam. I'm pleased to hear that your analysis of the situation coincides with mine and the NCA's, but there's one consideration we haven't addressed. In order to lead the team, you have to merge with a gift. That's not something I'm comfortable ordering you to do. Are you willing to volunteer to do so?"

"May I be candid, sir?"

"Proceed."

"I'm not thrilled with the idea. The people who have done so seem largely normal, well, except for the fact they seem to be talking to themselves when they're communicating with their gifts, but it's impossible to know how they've changed inside. Still, it was my decision to allow Sam to work with the team. If there's any way that decision played a role in Sam having the ability to activate the network, it's my responsibility to rectify the situation. So, yes, I am willing. I don't plan to stay that way, though. If the gifts are being honest about their willingness to leave after merging, I will tell mine to do so. The others may believe they are alive. I do not."

"I tend to agree with you. They are machines. Smart machines, but machines nonetheless. All right then, your official orders will be delivered to the SCIF, but here's the gist: you are to select a squad of volunteers from the 10th Special Forces Group at Carson, get them to accept gifts, then brief them on relevant events to date. You may, at your discretion, augment the squad with up to three individuals you've worked with in the past with similar skill sets from other units. You have absolute authority to have them attached to your team, effective immediately, provided you can get them here quickly. Your air and ground assets are essentially unlimited and you may use emergency requisition of civilian assets if required. Your first priority is capturing Sam. I will personally brief you on future targets. Good hunting."

"Yes, sir." Web departed for the SCIF to begin the process of merging with a gift.

Although Web found the idea of having a highly advanced set of machines coursing through his veins unsettling, he couldn't deny that he felt more physically powerful and capable than ever before. His gift—he'd yet to name him, disliking the feeling of permanence that implied—also made the process of vetting the potential members of his new snatch team much simpler. Web had established the desired criteria and directed his gift to search for matching candidates. In seconds, he had a short list of qualified and available men, the top twelve now standing before him in a secure facility on Fort Carson. Web decided against meeting them on Peterson, believing a greater sense of familiarity would soften the impact of what he was about to tell them. For the same reason, he was wearing the same Army physical training outfit he had instructed each of them to wear.

"My name is Colonel Web. I have been given command of one of the most elite teams that has ever existed. Along with that command, I have been authorized to select whomever I want to be its founding members. Look around you. You may or may not recognize faces, but that does not matter. What does matter is that I have determined you are the best men for the needs of my team.

"You have all volunteered many times to get where you are. In a moment, I'm going to ask you to volunteer again, but I will not explain what you're volunteering for. Furthermore, understand that I would not ask you to do something that I myself would not do, part of which I have already done. I'm also going to show you some of the results of that decision."

Looking around the room, Web asked, "Which of you is the best at unarmed self-defense?"

Most of them raised their hands. Web picked the biggest one and told him to come forward.

"I'm going to order you to attack me. Let me be clear, I want you to try to hurt me. Do you understand?"

The sergeant smiled and said, "Yes, sir!"

Without hesitation, Web moved into a handstand position, facing his opponent upside down. "Now," he ordered.

Ignoring the unusual nature of the battle, the sergeant attacked, attempting a snap kick to Web's exposed midsection. Moving with inhuman speed and precision, Web pivoted on one hand, caught the kick with his other, and lifted the man off his feet. The surprised sergeant fell heavily onto the exercise mat. Using one arm, Web bounced upright.

Helping the soldier to his feet, Web said, "I couldn't do that before lunch today. If you volunteer right now, each of you will be able to do that and more by this evening. Do I have any volunteers?"

Every one of them raised a hand.

While the soldiers were merging with their gifts, Web tried something he'd only been able to ask others to do on his behalf until now. He directed his gift to establish communication with Sam. To his surprise, Sam accepted the connection.

"What do you want, Eric?"

"You damn well know what I want! You need to turn yourself in, and you need to do it immediately!"

"Turn myself in for what? I haven't broken any laws. Jack told me to take some time off, that's what I'm doing."

"Taking some time off where?"

"That's none of your damn business."

"This isn't a game, Sam. We know you activated the gift's global network—"

"I call it Worldnet."

"Fine, Worldnet. Call it whatever you want. You don't have a right to own it. It belongs to the world."

"You don't want it to belong to the world. You want it to belong to the US government. Well, it doesn't. That's not the way the gifts work, in case you haven't noticed. They aren't about governments. They want to help humanity and that's what I'm trying to do. As I said, I haven't broken any laws or harmed anyone. You had no right to send people to my house to get me." Sam wanted Web to know he was aware of the attempt to bring him in.

"You've broken the law. You attempted to share classified information with Sara. That's enough to put you away, but we don't want to do that. We just want you to come in so we can work with you on the Worldnet."

"The thing is, Eric, I don't trust you as far as I can throw you. Even with my enhanced strength, that wouldn't be very far. You really need to spend more time on your people skills and less at the gym."

"If you don't turn yourself in, I'll have no choice but to find you. If that's the way it goes down, I won't be able to protect you."

"Eric, you may have convinced yourself you've done right by me in some way in the past, but only because you're a narcissist. There's literally nothing you can say to me that will change my mind. Since you know that I activated the Worldnet, you know that I control it. If you kill me, it dies with me."

"We have no intention of killing you. Stop being insulting and melodramatic—"

"This conversation is over. I answered to let you know that you're wasting your time. I'm not coming in. Don't bother trying to communicate with me again. I have no interest in what you have to say."

"Dammit, don't—" Web tried, but the connection was already broken.

Web was still fuming when Jack called. "What? This better be good news."

"It is, sir. We've identified Sam's friend. His name is Jim Byrne. He lives in Pueblo, not far from Sam's house. I sent some of the military police we left there to check it out. The place is empty, but we do have a lead. Jim's only family is a daughter and grandson. They live in Lewistown, Montana. I have their address. Do you want a team to pick Sam up?" Jack asked.

"No. Who else knows about this?" Web asked.

"Just the tech that conducted the search," Jack replied.

"Sequester him and send me the address. I'll take care of Sam."

Chapter TWENTY-FIVE

Sam looked at Jim. He was kneeling beside Lisa, clearly still talking with Adam. Sam waited until it appeared their conversation was over and then asked, "What do we need to do to help her?"

"Adam says her gift is going to need raw materials in order to heal her. She can't eat. Her gift will have to absorb those materials through her skin. She says the best way to do that is to strip Lisa and then put her in the bathtub filled with whatever food and vitamins we can find. Adam will work with Lisa's gift to let us know what she needs and how best to provide it. I'm going to carry Lisa to the bathroom and begin getting her ready. I've already told Esther what's going on, and she's waiting for you to go out to Matt before she comes in to help me. Lisa wouldn't want you to see her without her clothes."

"No, of course not. I understand."

"Her disease is not your fault, Sam. Now, go take care of my grandson for me, please. I'll let you know when she recovers."

Sam wanted to say something supportive, something to lighten some of Jim's burden. After a few awkward seconds, he realized he could think of nothing and headed outside, watching Esther and Matt play catch as if nothing had happened inside. Sam was impressed, but not surprised that she remained calm in order to avoid worrying Matt.

"My turn," Sam told Esther as he walked up to her, his hand reaching out for the glove.

"Okay, but watch out. He has a mean fastball."

"Jim needs you as much as Lisa needs you both," Sam thought to Esther.

"I know," she thought back.

Sam tossed the ball back and forth a few times with Matt while thinking about Lisa. Realizing there was no way he could keep Matt occupied for hours like this, Sam asked, "What sort of things do you do around here to pass the time, Matt?"

"I like to fish. Grandpa taught me, and Mom likes to eat what I catch. Do you like to fish?" Matt answered, clearly more interested in fishing than throwing the ball. Sam couldn't recall with certainty when he stopped enjoying playing catch, but he was pretty sure it was before he was Matt's age. On second thought, he didn't stop enjoying it. He just ran out of time for it. That was probably true for Matt, as well. At least when Matt went fishing, he provided food for his mom.

"I do. Your grandpa taught me, too. How about we do that for a while? I'm sure everybody would enjoy some fresh catch," Sam replied.

"Sweet! I'll grab my stuff. I have an extra rod you can use."

"Where do you keep your stuff?" Sam didn't want Matt going back into the house.

"In a shed out back. Mom won't let it in the house. Says it smells. It doesn't smell to me."

"Cool. Let's just drop the gloves off in there. If we go back inside, they might put us to work." Sam smiled and hoped he came across as unconcerned.

"Mister . . . ," Matt started to ask as they walked around the house.

"Just Sam, Matt."

"Sam, is it wrong to ask what happened to your face? I mean if it is, you don't have to tell me. It's just, with my mom getting sick and all, I just . . . ," Matt trailed off, his face reddening.

"It's not wrong at all. I respect you for asking and your curiosity is normal. I was in a fire."

"What kind of fire?"

Sam had hoped the simple answer would end the conversation. Under different circumstances, he would tell people who asked the question that it was personal. Given what was taking place in the house and how much Matt's life would soon be altered, no matter what happened in the next few hours, Sam found himself unable to give that answer.

"It was a house fire, Matt. My house burned down."

"And you were trapped inside? Did a fireman get you out?"

Something clicked in Sam's mind. Matt wasn't just expressing the curiosity of a typical teenage boy, or even morbid fascination. He realized I nearly died and was saved at the last minute, Sam thought. This conversation isn't about me. It's about Lisa.

"I did get trapped inside and yes, a fireman did save me." Not a lie, Sam thought. "What say you tell me where we'll be fishing?"

Matt accepted the change of subject. "Spring Creek. It runs right through the city. Do you want to fly-fish or use bait? I have both."

"I don't have any waders, so I guess it'll have to be bait this time, but I'll take a rain check on fly-fishing if you'll let me have one."

"Sure," Matt answered while changing some of the contents in his tackle box. He handed Sam a well-used, inexpensive pole, closed the door to the shed, and started walking toward a copse of evergreens a couple hundred yards away.

Jim had carried Lisa to the bathroom by the time Esther joined them. "I'll take care of getting her in the bathtub, Jim. You know the house better than I do. You'll be able to get some blended food up here sooner than I could," Esther said.

"Thanks, Esther." Jim started toward the kitchen to do just that, grateful for not having to strip Lisa. He would have done it— he would do anything to save his little girl—but he didn't want to see her so vulnerable if he didn't have to. She deserved that, and somehow Esther knew it. Jim was starting to understand why Sam had wanted him to be the one to give Esther her gift.

Arriving at the kitchen, Jim asked Adam for more specific instructions.

"At the atomic level, which is where Lisa's gift will be working in order to save her, the vast majority of the human body consists of six elements: oxygen, hydrogen, nitrogen, carbon, calcium, and phosphorus. The bathwater will provide the oxygen and hydrogen. Keeping a portion of her skin exposed to the air will allow her gift to acquire the necessary nitrogen. We need to find foods rich in carbon, calcium, and phosphorus. Look for sugar, seafood, cheese, and rice or bran first; also, see if she has vitamins."

Jim rummaged through the cabinets and found a bag of sugar, half a jar of grated Parmesan cheese, a bag of rice, and a nearly full bottle of multivitamins. "Okay, what now?" Jim asked.

"Take the sugar and cheese to Esther now and have her dump them in the bathwater. Then come back and grind or crush the rice and vitamins as fine as you can, quickly. When you're done, add them to the water as well," Adam replied.

"Does it matter how much of each we use?" Jim asked.

"No. Lisa's gift will take what it needs in the appropriate amounts. Time matters. You must hurry."

Jim quickly set about his task.

Settled in after casting a baited hook into a still part of the creek, Sam cradled the rod in his hand. A small part of his mind paid attention to the bobber; the rest was on Lisa. He knew it was irrational to blame himself for her condition—knew in fact that their arrival would likely be the reason she lived if she did. Still, it didn't feel that way. It felt as if he may have hastened her death and shortened the time Matt had with his mother. Even now, he was keeping Matt away from her. Of course, she wouldn't want him to see her like this, or at least Sam didn't think she would. He wondered what made him think he had the right to make such decisions on Matt's behalf.

"Tell me about your mother, Matt."

"Like what?" Matt asked without looking at Sam. He'd ignored the bait in favor of a small spinner that he was repeatedly casting into what Sam guessed was one of his favorite fishing holes.

"What did she do before she got sick?"

"She taught at the high school. English teacher. She loves to read. She's always getting on me to read more."

"You don't like to read?"

"I do, but not the stuff she wants me to read. It's boring. Who cares what happened hundreds of years ago?"

"What do you like to read?"

"Science fiction. You know, like time travel and stuff. You know, we're not going to catch anything if we keep talking."

"Good point," Sam responded. He didn't have much experience with kids Matt's age and hadn't wanted him to feel left out. Instead, Sam received fishing advice. Somewhat relieved, he turned the conversation inward.

"How's Lisa doing, Adia?"

"It's too soon to say. Esther and Jim have provided the required nutrients. Adam and Haya are working with Lisa's gift. They are all doing everything they can to save her."

"Anything we can do to help?"

"No. There's only so much work that can be done on her body at a time. Three gifts are more than enough to do what needs to be done physically."

"Then why aren't you sure she'll be all right?"

"Because her consciousness is barely there. She appears to be in a coma with no obvious reason for why she won't wake up. Your science doesn't know why that happens to humans, and we've never known a species that exhibited such behavior. Since we don't know the cause, we don't know how to cure it."

"So, giving her a gift could have contributed to her current situation?"

"I'm sorry, Sam, but I can't say it didn't. I can tell you that she was going to die very soon."

"Somehow, that doesn't help. Tell me as soon as you know anything new; and Adia, tell me if anyone I know with a gift tries to contact me. I may need more help than I thought."

"As you wish."

"There's nothing more you can do for her right now, Jim. You've been sitting here for hours. Come with me. Let me make you something to eat," Esther said quietly. She was standing next to Jim, her hand resting softly on his shoulder. He was sitting where he had been since providing the last batch of nutrients, on the edge of the old claw-foot bathtub, his right hand resting on Lisa's forehead.

"I can't leave her," Jim replied.

"You're not leaving her. We'll be a few feet away. Please, you haven't eaten since we left Colorado and it's nearly dinnertime. You can be back in here in seconds if need be."

"I can't."

"You can and you should. What would Lisa want you to do?"

"I don't . . . she . . ."

Moving her hand from his shoulder to his back, she gently pushed him away from the bathtub and toward the bathroom door. "You do know what she'd want. She'd want you to take care of yourself and she wouldn't want to wake up knowing that you hadn't because of her. I don't know her, but I know she lives like this for a reason. She doesn't want to feel like a burden to anyone. She's proud that she's taking care of herself and Matt without anyone's help. I can understand that. Don't take that from her because you feel helpless."

Without saying a word, Jim allowed himself to be led into the kitchen. He took a seat in the chair Esther guided him to, and rested his face in his hands. Esther began preparing some pasta to go with the sauce she'd started earlier.

"There wasn't much to choose from. I hope you like spaghetti."

Jim lifted his head from his hands and stared at Esther. "I'll eat whatever, and thank you, but why are you doing this?"

"Doing what?"

"You don't know me, and you know Lisa even less. Why do you care, and what makes you think you have a right to give me advice with regard to my daughter?"

Esther looked at him for a moment before answering. "You're wrong. I do know you. I'm no longer ashamed to say I've watched and admired you for years. You're a good man. I've never heard you say an unkind word to anyone, and what you did for Sam was remarkable. Most of the people who came to the center did so to get something. You came there to give. It was obvious to anyone paying attention, even if you didn't know it.

"I didn't think I had anything left to give anyone. I know now that I was wrong, that I was wasting the remainder of my life because I didn't want to try and fail. Now I've been given a second chance that I will not waste on fear of rejection or anything else.

"I don't have a right to give you advice on anything, but you need to eat and I want to help."

Jim stared down at the plate Esther had placed in front of him. He didn't speak or move for a long time. Finally, he raised his head and looked directly at her. She looked back from where she'd remained standing after serving him, nothing but kindness in her eyes.

"I'm sorry, Esther. I know you're just trying to help. Hell, you're not trying; you are helping and you deserve better from me. I'm not handling this very well."

"No apology necessary, and there's no good way to handle having one of your children in this condition. Now eat."

"Yes, ma'am."

Esther waited until Jim finished most of his plate before she continued. "I heard from Sam. He said he has something he needs to discuss with us. He'll be here with Matt soon. That's the main reason I disturbed you when I did, to give you some time to prepare what you're going to say to Matt, but you did have to eat."

"What do you think I should tell him?" Jim asked.

"As much of the truth as you think he can handle and nothing more," Esther answered.

"Did Sam give you any specifics?"

"No. He said he'd prefer to discuss it in person. He sounded concerned."

Jim thought about that for a minute before responding. "Thanks for dinner. You were right. I did need it and I do feel better. You know, I worked with some commanders in the war who thought their job was to work every hour they could, work themselves to exhaustion, and then get just enough sleep to do it all over again. They were wrong, of course. In the good units, there'd be an NCO with enough guts to tell the CO that he wasn't worth a damn to the unit like that. You'd have been a good NCO, Esther."

"Not much for war, Jim."

"No sane person is."

They both turned as the front door opened. Sam and Matt were back. Matt bounced into the house with a stringer full of trout.

"We had a good day!" Matt said as he entered the kitchen.

"He's being generous. He had a good day. Kid knows how to fish," Sam said.

"Where's Mom?"

Esther took the stringer from Matt and started removing the fish from it. Jim answered Matt. "Your mom's in the bathroom but she's not feeling well. How about you get cleaned up outside and into some fresh clothes? She might be well enough by the time you're done to have some dinner with you and Sam."

"You sound just like her, Grandpa. She never wants me in the house after I've been fishing."

"She sounds like me, kiddo. Now go get cleaned up."

"Okay," Matt said as he headed back toward the front door.

"You handled that well, for now," Sam observed, "but he's going to have to know more about what's going on if Lisa doesn't wake up soon. He's a smart kid."

"I know. Esther tells me you have news."

"I do. Two people from the first contact team called me over the Worldnet while I was with Matt. Web was the first. I was surprised to hear from him directly; didn't expect him to accept a gift. Anyway, he said what I expected he'd say. He wants me to turn myself in, that the Worldnet belongs to the world, et cetera. Admirable words, if he means any of them, which of course he doesn't. Let's just say that I declined.

"The second call was much more interesting. It was from Doctor Chang Liu, the team's mathematician. He wants to join us, along with his wife. I told him I'd think about it and get back to him. He said I didn't have much time for that because Web had figured out where I'd gone, and that his only chance to get away was while Web was gone. Apparently, Sara told Web about you, Jim. It didn't take them long to figure out we'd probably gone to Lisa's house. Web is putting together a team to retrieve me as we speak, which brings me to my primary point. We have to get out of here."

"Lisa's not well enough to move," Jim said. His expression was clear. She wouldn't be going anywhere until he believed she was well enough.

"I'm not going to tell you that I understand how you feel, because I don't. I will say that Adia assures me we won't hurt Lisa by moving her now. Her physical injuries are healed. She can be moved and she will be moved, either by us or by Web's commandos. I had hoped we'd have more time, but we don't. We have to leave with her, Jim. It's the only way we can stay together, and staying together is the best thing we can do for Lisa right now."

"What do you think?" Jim asked Esther.

"I think it's your call, but Sam knows this Web fellow and I don't. If he says we'll be separated from Lisa if we stay, he's probably right."

"We?" Jim asked.

"I'm staying with Lisa and you, whatever your decision," Esther answered. Her expression was every bit as certain as Jim's had been about moving Lisa.

Jim turned to Sam. "Dammit, she's my little girl! How am I supposed to decide what to do?"

"Jim, you told me Lisa wouldn't come to live with you because she'd rather die where she'd loved living. I think she's going to recover and be better than she's ever been, but forgive me please for saying what we're all afraid of. What if I'm wrong? You respected her wishes before. Respect them now. No matter what happens, let it happen with us, with her surrounded by people who care for her, in a place she loves. You know that's what she'd want. I'm sorry I brought this possibility into your life, into her life and Matt's, but don't let her fate be decided in a military hospital surrounded by strangers and under guard like a common criminal," Sam finished because he had to. It was all too familiar.

Jim took a deep breath, held it for a moment, and then exhaled. "There's a cabin our family used to own about twenty miles out of town. It's not much more than a shack, but it doesn't have an address and I don't think anyone's been there for years. I don't know how your military buddies could know about it or find it. We can go there."

"Esther, will you help Jim get Lisa ready?" Sam asked.

"Of course. I'll ask Matt to pack Lisa's car while we do that. How soon are we leaving?"

"As soon as we can."

Sam left the kitchen and walked out onto the front porch. "Adia, can you talk with Chang's gift to tell if he's telling the truth?"

"Would you want me to tell others about your thoughts through their gifts?"

"No, of course not."

"Then you have the answer to your question."

He could tell that she wasn't pleased with him for asking. Hell, in retrospect, he wasn't pleased with himself for asking. If he couldn't trust his judgment on who he wanted on his team, then he wasn't worthy to lead it.

"I'm sorry I asked, and you're right. We'll have to rely on trust. We don't have enough pairs to build the ship yet and quite frankly, I don't know where we're going to get them. Chang and his wife would be excellent additions, assuming he's legit, which I'm not yet ready to bet our future on."

"It appears he was telling the truth about us being found," Adia said.

"What are you talking about?" Sam asked.

"A military drone is approaching from the west."

Chapter TWENTY-SIX

Sam walked back into the house. Esther was in the kitchen packing food, and Jim was with Lisa. Sam asked Jim to join them in the kitchen.

"Adia spotted a drone heading our way. It was already close enough to get video of my truck back to whoever is operating it. So, they know we're here, but they don't know we know about them and they don't know we're planning on leaving. I intend to keep it that way as long as possible. We need to stage the equipment we're going to load in the vehicles by the front door and be prepared to load it as soon as I take the drone out. Until now, we could have backed out, but after I take out that drone, we're at war with the federal government. Are you both still with me?"

Jim nodded. "You were clear from the beginning, Sam. I'm with you."

"We're with you," Esther added.

"Okay, then. Jim, I think it'd be easier for you to get Lisa in and out of my truck than her car, so why don't you and Esther take that while I take Matt with me in Lisa's car?"

"Makes sense. When are we leaving?"

"I think we can spare ten minutes to gather up the essentials, but no more. I'll let you know via Worldnet right before we take the drone out. Then we move. I'm leaving the sensors and defenses here active until we get to the cabin in order to take out any backup surveillance they may have in the area, then I'm recalling them to there. Any questions?" There were none.

Ten minutes later, Sam asked Adia if a sufficient number of the nanites directed toward the drone had reached it. When she confirmed, he told her to activate them and they began disassembling it in midflight, creating more of their own. The drone was gone before any portion of it could hit the ground. Verifying that there was no other local coverage, they quickly loaded the vehicles, with Jim gently placing Lisa's blanket-wrapped form in the back of Sam's Jeep. In less than three minutes, they were moving. Jim led the way.

The trip to the cabin took the better part of an hour. Sam had Adia change the color and plates of both vehicles again. Most of the short journey was on poorly maintained back roads surrounded by evergreens, so Sam wasn't too worried about being pulled over or seen from the air, but took no chances. When they arrived, Sam asked Adia to begin constructing overhead camouflage, which she did immediately.

The cabin was in worse shape than Sam had envisioned. Blue sky was visible through the walls in some places, with whatever chinking there once had been lost to the ravages of time and weather. "We don't need a palace, but this is not going to work in its current state. Esther, would you mind working with Haya to fix it up a little bit? We could use running water, a bathroom, walls without holes . . ."

"Sure, Sam. It'll take a while with just me, though."

"Jim will be able to help you in a minute. He needs to explain what you're doing and how to Matt first, right, Jim?"

"I'd hoped you'd have done that on the ride over," Jim replied.

"I thought it would be best if he heard it from you. Besides, I was monitoring the sensors at the house, changing our cars, and talking with Chang. I've accepted his offer to join us, by the way. I wanted to discuss it with you both, but he was running out of time. I didn't tell him where we are, however, at least not specifically. I plan to meet him and his wife when they get closer."

"I'll talk with Matt, then," Jim said.

"While you two work on the house, Adia and I are going to recreate our defenses here. When we're done with that, I'll help you with the cabin. Remember, it needs to look abandoned from the air. There's no doubt there will be more drones looking for us."

Esther nodded and moved off toward the cabin. Jim shook his head slightly and called out to Matt, "Come here, Son. We need to talk."

"Have you finished the conversion?" Sam asked Adia, who had been converting all of the property and belongings in Lisa's house, save the few packed by Matt and Jim, to nanites. He didn't want to give Web any clues, and he wanted to send a message.

"Yes, Sam."

"Are we still clear of local observation?"

"Yes."

"Then bring them all here, and show me, please."

Adia began the process. What Sam saw was Lisa's house and work shed appear to dissolve into the ground. Had he seen the gift ship at Kansas perform its transformation after landing, he would have noticed the similarities.

"How long will it take them to get here?" Sam asked.

"They'll start arriving in about eight minutes."

"Do we have enough capacity to start working on defenses here before they arrive, while still controlling them?"

"We do. Our capacity to control nanites has more than doubled since you last asked about it. Managing the group at Lisa's house reduces that significantly while they're still distant, but that will change as they approach."

"Please do what you can. Our priorities are avoiding detection, followed by knowing if someone is coming. The first priority is by far the most important. There's not really much we can do if they find us and respond in force."

"As you wish."

Over the next two hours, the cabin became habitable. After completing the sensor network and defenses, Sam worked with Adia to develop a plumbing system, starting with a deepwater well. Although he had nothing to compare it to, he felt as if they had a knack for constructing things with the tiny machines, and found that he enjoyed the process. There was something deeply satisfying about building the infrastructure for a house without disturbing anything around it or creating any waste. Whatever else the gifts would do for humanity, they would most certainly forever change the fields of construction and manufacturing. He wondered briefly how such advances would be allocated among those without gifts before his mind returned to their present situation. Realizing that his habit of becoming completely immersed in his work had allowed him to forget about Lisa while doing so angered him. What the hell is wrong with me, he wondered, not for the first time.

"Adia, there must be something we can do for Lisa."

"As I've told you, we have no experience with the state she is in."

"When we first talked, you told me you couldn't live without me, that you would literally go mad if we were separated, right?"

"Yes, Sam."

"Then how is Lisa's gift maintaining her sanity?"

"That's a good question, one I had not thought to ask."

"Well, let's ask it. I know you don't know how you achieved consciousness any more than I know how I did, but I am aware of different states of consciousness. Sometimes when I dream, I become aware that I am dreaming and then I can control that dream. I know I'm not fully conscious, but I am fully aware. Do you have experience with other species who can do anything similar?"

"We have experience with species who do not have different states of consciousness. When they rest their bodies, they remain fully conscious, but immobile."

"I don't see how that helps. Okay, let's try this. What do you experience when I dream?"

"Human science isn't certain about the signs that a person is dreaming, but I've observed that certain portions of your brain are more active in correlation with rapid eye movement. However, I have also observed these same portions of your brain being active when you're not experiencing rapid eye movement, including when you're awake."

"Has Lisa's gift observed similar brain patterns?"

"Every person's brain is different, Sam."

"Work with me, Adia. I'm not a neurologist, but you have access to pretty much everything ever published on the subject, and your presence in my mind gives you far greater access to its workings than any tools available to our medical science, right?"

"That is correct."

"Then extrapolate from what you've seen in my brain to what Lisa's gift is seeing in hers. Are there any compelling correlations?"

"There have been many occasions since Lisa merged with her gift when her brain patterns strongly approximated what I've observed in yours during the circumstances we're discussing."

"Correct me if I'm wrong, but coma patients don't generally experience such brain activity, right?"

"There is no conclusive research on the subject, but it does appear uncommon for a coma patient to have frequent higher-level brain activity similar to what her gift is observing."

"So, she could be in a very deep sleep, including occasionally dreaming?"

"It's possible. Would that make a difference?"

"It might. Part of the reason we sleep is to heal. Lisa's brain knew she needed to heal, but it would have no way of knowing her gift was going to heal her. Perhaps it's waiting for some signal it would normally generate as part of the healing process to wake her. Have you noticed any consistent pattern in my brain in the moments before I wake?"

"Yes. It varies, but there are some consistencies."

"Would it be possible to stimulate Lisa's brain to achieve her equivalent waking patterns, like the way you do so to communicate with me?"

"Also possible."

"What are the risks?"

"Primarily, that it will not work. There have been many studies of brain stimulation by human scientists using methods far more crude than those we would employ. The brain is a remarkably resilient organ; this activity would be less threatening to it than any number of human activities."

"Give me a number, Adia. What are the chances we'll make things worse if we try it?"

"Given what we now know about human physiology, the risk of causing her permanent harm using this technique is too low to calculate."

"Thank you, Adia."

Sam walked across the room to where Jim knelt next to the small bed Esther built for Lisa. Jim was stroking Lisa's hair and talking to her gently. Sam put his hand on Jim's shoulder. When Jim looked up, Sam said, "I have an idea."

"To help Lisa?" Jim asked.

"Yes." Sam told Jim what he and Adia had discussed, then gave him a moment to go over the theory with Adam.

"Normally, Lisa's gift wouldn't do such a thing unless Lisa had requested it, but, just as it did when modifying her skin to absorb nutrients, she will do so if you request it, Jim. She recognizes your parental relationship with Lisa and what that means to our species. It's your call, of course, but I'm betting Lisa wants to wake up and join us as much as we want her to," Sam said.

"They all say there's essentially no risk, that it's pretty much the same thing we do when we talk with them," Jim said.

"All I can tell you is that if it were me, I'd want you to try it," Sam said.

"Yeah, me too. Okay, let's do it." Jim asked Adam to transmit his wishes to Lisa's gift.

Lisa's eyes fluttered and then remained still once more.

"Her gift said it might take a few attempts. Humans don't always wake up right away," Jim said.

A few seconds later, Lisa's eyes fluttered again, and then opened. She blinked a couple of times, looked up at Jim, and then around the room. "Where am I?"

"Oh, Honey!" Jim said, reaching down to wrap her in his arms, openly crying. "I was so afraid we'd lost you!"

"Lost me? What are you talking about? I'm fine. Oh my god, I'm better than fine. I feel fantastic! Oh my god, Dad!"

Matt and Esther had stopped what they were doing and rushed over when they saw Lisa wake up. Jim noticed Matt's arrival and let Lisa go. Matt immediately replaced him and hugged his mom for all he was worth. She was crying now, too. Her face looked radiant. Sam couldn't remember seeing an adult so happy in years.

Cherishing the moment, Lisa hugged Matt for a long time, but it was clear she wanted to move, to use her newly healed body in ways she hadn't been able to use the old one for so long. When Matt finally let go with a huge grin, Lisa got off the bed and walked around the room. It was fortunate that Esther had dressed her before they departed her house, because Sam was sure she would have ignored her nudity in favor of motion. She was practically gliding. Sam couldn't wipe the stupid smile off his face. He looked at each of the others. They all wore similar expressions.

After dancing around the room, Lisa stopped in front of Sam and opened her arms to him. Surprised, it took him a moment to realize she wanted to hug him. He awkwardly raised his arms and embraced her. The rest was not awkward at all. Lisa moved her mouth next to Sam's ear and whispered, "Thank you. Thank you so much!" Sam didn't want to let go, but he did when he felt her grip begin to relax. My god, indeed.

Sam watched Lisa enjoy her newfound youth and vitality with Jim and Matt while he helped Esther prepare dinner. He was ravenous and suspected the others were as well. They were eating about twice as much as they had before merging, a higher metabolic rate appearing to be a change attendant with that decision. As for Matt, he'd never known a teenage boy who couldn't out-eat a full-grown man. Aside from the desire to satisfy everyone's hunger, it was also very much a celebration requiring lots of food. Once the meal was over, though, Lisa would have to make a difficult decision and Sam would have to leave.

They hadn't bothered to make a table. The cabin was too small for that, so they served the meal buffet style. No one complained, partly because of their persistent joy at having Lisa back and whole again, partly because Esther was a remarkable cook. She'd even had the foresight to pack spices along with the food from Lisa's house.

The conversation during dinner was light and pleasant, with no mention of their current circumstances, though everyone was aware of what they were. After the meal, Jim volunteered to clean up while Lisa made coffee. Sam waited until everyone was done and had taken seats in the chairs they had made before he began. "As much as it pains me to intrude on such a pleasant meal, we have some things to discuss. The first is Matt. He's the only one among us who doesn't have a gift. Adia located one earlier today and we moved it here, so we have one for him.

"You all know my intent is for us to build a gift ship so that we can give humanity a fighting chance. I don't know if Matt will have to merge in order to join us on it; Adia tells me that the gift ship intelligence is the only one who can answer that question, but I do know he'd be at a severe disadvantage to the rest of us if he didn't merge with a gift. It's not my decision; it's yours and Matt's, Lisa, but it needs to be made now."

"Why now?" Lisa asked.

"Because we need a better place than this and we don't have much time. Web's team was only hours behind us when we left the house, and we aren't far from it. Web will be looking for me with a vengeance. I've embarrassed him and he's an egomaniac. But despite his personal flaws, he's extremely good at what he does. Given enough time, he will find this place, and we can't be here when he does. We can all do some pretty amazing things with the help of our gifts, but Web has accepted a gift too, and if he has, you can bet every member of his team has as well. That means we have a gifted team of the best hunting us with all the resources of the federal government behind them. We have to stop running and get to a defensible position where we can work undetected."

"What do you think, Matt?" Lisa asked.

"You took one, Mom, and look what it did for you. I'd be like a superhero or something. Heck yeah, I want one," Matt answered.

"I know this should be a tougher decision for me, but it really isn't. Althia healed me and I like her. Adam healed my dad. Without the gifts, Matt wouldn't have had a family for much longer. Yes, please Sam, give my son a gift."

Sam smiled. "Done. Which brings us to my next point. There are currently four of us with gifts in one small place. Because of our control of the Worldnet, we've been able to hide that fact enough to go unnoticed. That will become increasingly difficult as Web deploys more and closer gifted resources. Adia tells me we could almost certainly be detected if Matt merged here, and that our odds of avoiding detection would improve if our numbers in one place were reduced. So, I'd like to take Matt with me to begin construction of our more permanent home, the place where we'll build the ship."

"Can I, Mom?" Matt was clearly excited at the prospect of working with Sam.

"How long will you be gone?" Lisa asked.

"I think it will take about a day before I get enough work done to shield our presence and allow us all to be together again," Sam answered.

"I can handle a day without you, I guess," Lisa told Matt.

"Awesome! When are we going?" Matt asked.

"Right now," Sam answered.

Chapter TWENTY-SEVEN

When the C-17 came to a stop, members of Web's team unstrapped the four Humvees in its cargo bay. Within minutes, the first one rolled down the ramp. Ten minutes later, all of the vehicles were headed northeast on Highway 87 toward Lewistown proper and the site where Lisa's house once stood. Having received notification that the second dispatched drone found no activity there, Web eschewed caution in favor of speed and led the team directly to Judith Park, a convenient rally point three hundred meters away from Lisa's address.

Web exited his Humvee and called the four team leaders to gather behind him as he placed a ruggedized tablet computer on the vehicle's hood. "Here's where we are." He indicated their position on the digital map. "Here's the subject's last known location." Each team lead oriented himself to the map and then looked northeast toward the physical location.

"This is what we know. The first drone was destroyed at 17:45. Prior to its destruction, its video confirmed our subject's vehicle was present at the target, along with the second vehicle you were provided pictures of during the flight. At that point, the target looked like you see it here." Web switched applications and presented a picture of the house from the first drone's flight. "This is what the second drone recorded at 18:52," Web said as he pulled up a picture of the same lot, now seemingly empty. "We don't know if the house has been destroyed or if this is an illusion using some form of gift-generated camouflage. Until we prove otherwise, we assume the latter.

"My intent is to approach the house myself, unarmed. If it's in fact, still there, I'll attempt contact with its occupants and enter the structure to negotiate. Should those events unfold, I'll contact you by comms within five minutes to confirm that we are negotiating. Do not, I repeat, do not use any form of Worldnet communication. The subject may possess capabilities through that system that we're unaware of. If for any reason I do not contact you by comms within five minutes, or if anything should happen to me while approaching the house, Captain Johnson, you will assume command of the team and contact headquarters to advise them of the situation. Under no circumstances are you to approach the house, and deadly force is not authorized. Is that understood?"

All answered, "Yes, sir."

"Tonight we measure success by taking the subject alive, no matter what. To increase these chances, you are going to surround the lot as surreptitiously as possible. Should anyone attempt to leave, prevent them from doing so. Broken bones are okay; broken skulls are not." Web paused for effect. The soldiers dutifully smiled.

Returning the map to the screen, Web resumed the mission brief. "Captain Johnson, you will position your team within the tree line to the north of the lot. Sergeant Bishop, you will position your team in the field to the lot's southwest. Sergeant Shaw, your team will take the field to its southeast. Lieutenant Evans, your team will be the quick response force. You stay here with the vehicles.

Be sure your team is ready to move immediately, engines running, driver behind the wheel. Ten minutes from now, I'm going to be walking up to that lot. Be in position," Web finished.

"Yes, sir."

Precisely ten minutes later, Web walked up the concrete driveway toward what appeared to be an empty foundation and, confidently, approached where he thought the door would be. Stopping just shy of walking into the house, if it had been there, he reached out to find nothing. He moved closer and repeated the process. Finding nothing once again, he stepped onto the foundation. The house was gone.

Web activated his secure radio. "Lieutenant Evans, get those vehicles here now! Everyone else, rally on me."

Failing to find Sam's team at their last known location, Web executed plan B. Following protocol, he led his team to the nearest, in this case only, National Guard armory. Finding the standard three-by-five emergency contact card taped to the door of the armory, Web called the most senior contact listed. The phone was answered on the third ring.

"Hello," a man's voice answered, clearly annoyed at being bothered so late in the evening.

"First Sergeant Richardson?" Web asked.

"Who's asking?"

"My name is Colonel Web, Air Force. Are you First Sergeant Richardson?"

"Yes, sir. What can I do for you, sir?"

Web was pleased by the change in tone. "I need you at the armory to let me and my team in. We need a CP for the next couple of days at least, and this appears to be the best option in the neighborhood."

"Sir, I can't just let you into the armory. You need authorization from higher up the food chain and it's kind of late to be disturbing folks."

"It's a matter of national security and I'll disturb whoever I have to. So, who do you need to hear the order from in order to get you down here now?"

"Well, sir, I've never been asked that. With you being Air Force, I imagine it would have to be the Adjutant General."

"First Sergeant, you'll be receiving a phone call with authorization instructions shortly."

"All right."

Web hung up and dialed a second number. "Jack, I'm at a national guard armory in Lewistown. The POC needs proof we're authorized to use it. He wants to hear it from the AG or higher. I doubt they know each other, so find a way to convince the guy and get it done yesterday, then get your ass up here." Web gave Jack the first sergeant's name and number before he disconnected.

Turning back to his team, Web said, "All right ladies, it looks like we're going to have a little free time before we set up inside. We're going to use it to hone our skills in nanite management. If you haven't discussed nanites with your respective gifts yet, do so when I'm done. The short version is that nanites can apparently build anything, given the right mix of resources. They can also destroy pretty much anything to get those resources or just to prove a point, like the subject and his team did with that house. I want you to practice manipulating and controlling them during every free moment. If you have to take a piss, use nanites to aim the stream." That garnered him a few light laughs. "That may be funny, but what isn't funny is the fact that our opponent is more capable in this regard than we are. You all know what happens when you go against a more capable opponent, right? Fix it."

Web walked to the edge of the parking lot and took his own advice. He started by creating basic three-dimensional shapes, using material taken from the field that started where the parking lot ended. He was working on a star when his phone rang. "This is Web."

"Yes, sir. This is First Sergeant Richardson. I don't know who you are, sir, but I'm on my way. Shouldn't be more than ten minutes."

"Thanks, Top." Web disconnected and resumed practicing.

Morning broke on the armory without any sign of progress in the search, and Web's mood was reflective of his team's. The 15th Reconnaissance Squadron out of Creech Air Force Base, Nevada, had arrived during the night and was actively reconnoitering over and around Lewistown with more Predator drones than operated in Afghanistan at the peak of the conflict. Web was in possession of the most granular aerial survey data of the region that had ever existed, none of which put him any closer to finding Sam.

Jack interrupted Web's reverie. "The commander of the 512th is here, sir."

Because he needed a self-supporting unit of combat soldiers more experienced with nonlethal force than infantry soldiers, Web requested a rapid deployment military police company from FORSCOM, the command responsible for the Army's land-fighting forces. To his utter satisfaction, he received the 512th Military Police Company out of Fort Leonard Wood, Missouri.

"Send him over," Web replied.

"Her, sir."

"Okay, send her over."

A moment later, a tall, blond-haired, blue-eyed woman wearing camouflaged ACUs approached Web at a desk. He noted that she wore an academy ring on her right hand and nothing on her left. She stopped two paces in front of Web's desk and at attention said, "Captain Fox reporting as ordered, sir."

"Relax, Captain. Have a seat."

Captain Fox looked at the two mismatched chairs in front of the desk and decided on the brown one with the fake leather. She took her seat and waited for Web to begin.

"Fox, huh? That can't have been easy at the academy," Web said, his voice making it clear that he was not making an advance.

"There were moments, sir."

"What's your first name?"

"Emily, sir."

"All right, Emily. Before we get into why you're here, I want to commend you on how quickly you got your unit here. I understand you were wheels up within eight hours of notification. Very impressive."

"Thank you, sir. We've had a lot of practice and I've got the best NCOs in the Corps."

"You're going to need them. Tell me about your table of organization."

"Yes, sir. The 512th is organized into five platoons, four consisting of combat MPs, the fifth made up of support personnel. Each platoon of MPs consists of four squads and each squad has three three-person teams. Each team has its own Humvee, a crew-served weapon, and comms. They're organized and trained to operate independently for extended time periods. The support platoon includes personnel and equipment to feed us and keep our equipment operational. Would you like more detail, sir?"

"That's sufficient for now. So, on paper, you have forty-eight teams capable of independent operation. Are all of your teams operational?"

"Yes, sir. We received augmentation from our sister company just before departure. We're good to go."

"Then let's get your troops working. Here's what I need you to do . . ."

Chapter TWENTY-EIGHT

Sam navigated his way through the Judith Mountain trails north-east of Lewistown without the aid of the Jeep's headlights until he found what he was looking for. It took about an hour and a half with Adia's help and Sam's agreement to allow his night vision to be substantially improved. The alternative—waiting until morning—was unacceptable.

He parked the SUV as far off the trail as he safely could and exited the vehicle, leaving Matt in the back, estimating that he'd be out for another thirty minutes or more. After walking a few feet from the vehicle, Sam turned to watch Adia's camouflage take effect. The layer of nanites that had presented as multiple colors of paint now displayed the land beneath and around the vehicle. A sheet of nanite fabric extended across each wheel well, and another extended from the base of the truck to the ground. Within moments, Sam was unable to see the SUV.

"Impressive, Adia. Is it as difficult to spot thermally as it is to see visually?"

"Not yet, but that will be so soon. Rather than mask the signature, I'm bleeding it off into the ground deep beneath the truck, well below detection levels."

"When you're done, establish a sensor network, please. We need to know what steps they're taking to look for us. Will the nanites being used to hide our ride appreciably affect our ability to make progress on our headquarters?"

"The effort to control them consumes approximately 2 percent of our capacity. That figure will increase slightly as we move away from the vehicle."

"Will Matt have enough capacity to take over this responsibility after he wakes up?"

"No, Sam. With training, he may be able to control as much as 1 percent of the number of nanites we can currently control."

"Because of the benefit we get from the excess capacity of the Worldnet?"

"Primarily. It's also related to the innate ability of the pair controlling the nanites as well as the amount of time they've spent doing so. Because you're the first, we started controlling them sooner than any other pair. Because of your decision to activate the Worldnet, we also have more time to effectively spend controlling them. A pair without these advantages will spend much more time than us, and our advantage continues to grow."

"Well, it's just about the only advantage we have, so I'm grateful for it. Okay, Adia, it's time to stop running. Let's get started on our last home here for a while. We're about six hundred feet below the peak, which is a good start, but I'm a belt-and-suspenders kind of guy. I'd like us to be at least as far in before we build the facilities. Unless you have a better idea, I want to start tunneling here."

"It will take longer to go that far into the mountain, Sam, and will displace a great deal of material. Less than half that distance should be sufficient to shield us from all forms of remote detection."

"I'm done with should. Belt and suspenders, remember? I want to be as close to absolutely sure that we're beyond remote detection with what we can create in the next day or so. I'd also like to ensure we're beyond the range of anything but nuclear bunker busters. I can see the government getting crazy enough to try to blow us out of here, but not crazy enough to use nukes."

"I understand and share your desire to get our team to safety as soon as possible, but this mountain was formed from a seabed. There are trace elements of what we need to construct additional nanites, but in order to harvest them, we need to process large amounts of this sedimentary material. We can convert much of it to various oxygen compounds that will disperse into the atmosphere, but there will still be substantial waste material to be removed and dispersed over a wide area if we are to avoid detection. It is not possible for us to go as far into the mountain as you would like in the time frame you describe with the number of nanites we can currently control, even if we had that many. You'll have to choose between time and distance."

As he talked with Adia, Sam walked into the fold of mountain he'd been looking for. Shorter than the tree cover in front of it, the deformation of the land created a fifteen-foot-tall, twenty-five-foot-wide, asymmetrical U-shaped vertical depression deep enough to allow Sam to create an entrance on either side of the U, shallow enough to remain well-lit during the day. It would, Sam hoped, look like nothing but more trees from the front, and a space too small to hide anything meaningful from the air.

"Jim, Esther, and Lisa can maintain their camouflage and their sensor net without our help, right?" Sam asked.

"They can, although that will be about all they can do without us."

"They aren't safe there, or anywhere, until we build a place for them to be so. I don't see a better course of action than providing that place as soon as possible. Am I wrong, Adia?"

"It's not for me to say, Sam. We're here to help, if we can. It's up to you and the rest of humanity to make the right decisions to save yourselves. We'll be saved with you, or not."

"Great. If I recall all of the nanites we control from the cabin, how much can we accomplish by this time tomorrow?"

"Without knowing the exact composition of the material we would excavate or the size of the tunnel and interior structures you wish to build, I can only provide a rough estimate. If we're fortunate in the composition of the material we excavate and you're modest in the size of the facilities you wish to build, we should be able to tunnel 250 to 350 feet into the mountain and complete a habitable facility there by then."

"Then let's hope that'll be enough. So much for certainty." Sam faced the left side of the formation. "Let's start by creating an opening on this side. Since we won't be transporting much more than people and supplies through it, eight by eight feet should be sufficient. We'll follow the course of the mountainside for a dozen feet or so and then change the course of the tunnel to head directly into the heart of the mountain."

Sam watched as the foliage began to dissolve to expose the bare rock below. Less than five minutes later, the tunnel was a foot deep. In other circumstances, he would be filled with wonder. In the current circumstances, incredible as they were, he felt little more than apprehension. He knew they were running out of time and felt trapped by his inability to do more.

Hours later, Adia woke Sam from a brief nap just before sunrise with the news that Chang was attempting to contact him. Sam thanked her and connected to Chang. "Morning, Chang. Have you arrived at the meeting point?" Sam had directed Chang to contact him when he arrived at Roy City Park, a tiny park adjacent to a community of fewer than five hundred souls, twenty-one miles east of Sam's location.

"Yes, we're here," Chang answered.

"Did you have any problems?"

"No. I think they still believe I'm at home seeing my wife and resting for the first time since Saturday morning."

"Did you disguise your car?"

"Yes, exactly as you instructed."

"Good. The next part is going to be tricky." Sam had worked out a plan with Adia for getting Chang and his wife to their location before resting, but it was not without risk. "There are Predator drones in the air and motorized patrols all over the place. Fortunately, there's a lot of ground for them to search. Unfortunately, there aren't many people around here. Any vehicle moving at this time of the morning will draw attention, but our plan stands less chance of success in the daylight, so we're going to execute it now.

"I sent a group of nanites to your location earlier this morning." That had been a difficult decision for Sam. Every diversion of resources delayed construction of the facilities that would get the rest of his team to relative safety. He hoped that having four gifted pairs would make up for the delays incurred to double the size of his team on the mountain. "They are going to modify your vehicle. Withdraw your nanites to the passenger compartment of it immediately. Tell me when you've done so."

After a brief delay, Chang replied, "It's done."

"Begin the process, Adia," Sam directed.

"Yes, Sam."

Sam returned his attention to Chang. "This is what's going to happen. We've developed active camouflage good enough to make a stationary object essentially invisible. It's theoretically capable of doing the same for a moving object, but we haven't had an opportunity to test it. I hate to make you a guinea pig, but it's the best I could come up with. That's one of the main reasons we need to do this before sunrise—less visual information to process. While the exterior of your vehicle is being modified, we're also modifying your engine and your vent system. I'm afraid it's going to be a bit chilly for you and your wife during the next forty minutes or so but that may be a good thing, because your drive is going to be a challenge. No one on the road will be able to see you and you will not be able to use your lights. You'll have to have your gift modify your eyes for improved night vision. Adia, my gift, has sent your gift our coordinates. In another minute or so, the modifications will be complete. Do you have any questions?"

"Many, many questions, Sam, but not about this. We have much to discuss," Chang replied.

"Yes, we do. Drive safely, but not too slowly. Make as much time as you can on 191. It'll be slow going once you get into the mountains."

"I will. See you soon."

Sam stood up and looked around for Matt, spotting him about twenty feet down the tunnel. Even with his enhanced vision, Sam had trouble making out Matt's form. "What's he doing, Adia?"

"He's creating an air tunnel. His idea."

"Good for him. I'm going to try to finish that nap. Please wake me when Chang gets close."

"As you wish."

"They are a few minutes out, Sam."

"Thanks, Adia." Sam stood and walked to the entrance of the tunnel. During the remainder of his nap, the sun had made its way to the edge of the horizon. Even with the improved lighting, he hoped he wouldn't be able to see them coming, but he was sure he'd hear them. He wanted to ensure they pulled close enough to the tunnel entrance to be under the overhead cover Adia had completed in preparation for their arrival.

Seconds later, he heard the sound of tires on loose rock and was pleased to observe that he could not see their car approach. Guided by the precision coordinates provided to his gift, Chang stopped the car exactly where it needed to be. Sam stepped out of the tunnel and moved to a spot that would make him visible to Chang.

Chang and his wife exited their car and approached Sam, who held out his hand. Chang took it and they shook before Sam turned to Jing-Wei, smiled, and accepted a hug.

"Jing-Wei, it's nice to see you again. I can't believe Chang convinced you to do this," Sam said.

"He didn't convince me, Sam. It was the other way around. We can talk about it more later. Right now, Chang has some things he needs to discuss with you," Jing-Wei responded.

"Let's go inside the tunnel. We have visual overhead cover and thermal diffusion, but if we stay out here too long the entire area will appear abnormally warm." Sam turned and led the way. Jing-Wei, lacking the enhanced sight of her husband and Sam, took Chang's hand as they entered the darkness.

"Before we get into what you want to discuss, I'd like your permission to use your car for raw materials. We'd gain in a matter of minutes what it takes us hours to extract, and it takes some capacity to disguise it from side view."

"Yes, of course. Either we'll succeed and not need it, or fail and still not need it," Chang replied.

"You heard the man, Adia. Have at it," Sam thought.

"Already started, Sam," Adia replied.

Sam called out to Matt. He stopped what he was doing and met them for introductions before asking to be excused to continue his work. Sam happily agreed. It was nice to see the kid so engaged.

They all took a seat on the floor of the tunnel with Chang and Jing-Wei sitting opposite Sam. Realizing how uncomfortable Jing-Wei must be in the darkness, Sam took his LED flashlight out of his jacket, turned it on, and placed it on the ground to the side of them, its light directed toward the ceiling.

"First, thank you for joining my team. Doing so took a lot of guts and we desperately need you both," Sam said.

"It was the only logical thing to do," Chang answered.

"That's by no means obvious to me right now, but I'll let you explain it in your own way. So, what did you want to discuss and why did you wait to do so in person?" Sam asked.

"They're related, but let me provide some background. We know, of course, that you activated the Worldnet—I'd like to know how you did that someday—and I assume you know about the first. Those were two of the most powerful mechanisms the gifts provided to help humanity, with the gifts themselves being the third. There's a fourth that was created in part by the program you decoded. We call it the EG, for Encyclopedia Galactica. Are you aware of it?" Chang asked.

Sam didn't answer immediately, waging an internal debate. If he didn't tell them he was the first now, when he finally did tell them, they would know he hadn't trusted them with the information sooner, and that they had risked everything in trusting him. He realized he had no choice.

"No, I'm not aware of it and I want to know more about it, but before we get into that, I have something to tell you. I was the first to merge with a gift."

"What? You're the first? You are the first and the controller of the Worldnet?" Chang stopped, apparently at a loss for words.

"I was the first to merge. I had no idea that Adia and I would become the first or that it would make any difference that we were. I didn't find out that certain responsibilities come with being the first to merge until after the fact, though I suppose I would have done it anyway had I known."

"Responsibilities? What responsibilities?" Chang asked.

"Three primary ones. First, to build a gift ship and bring it to life. Second, to bring that gift ship to another planet with intelligent life like ours. Third, to lead humanity's team to one of the places the Makers believe will provide the means for our species to survive. We call it an academy."

Chang thought for a while before continuing, and Sam gave him the time he needed to absorb it all. "That's why you ran, and how you were able to activate the Worldnet prematurely. Well, not prematurely. I didn't mean that. Rather, before it would have become active on its own," Chang finally stated.

"Yes on both counts. I didn't want the government—any government—controlling this process. The Makers designed it the way they did for reasons we don't fully understand. I honestly believe this course provides the best chance for humanity, not because of who I am, but because of how their process is designed. Think about it. They fought the group minds for centuries before sending out the gift ships. The amount they know about our enemies and damn near everything else makes what we know look irrelevant in comparison. Second-guessing their approach to helping us seemed incredibly foolish to me, and the stakes are just too high for foolishness. So, yeah, that's why we're here," Sam replied.

"I agree with you. After you left, and they never should have made you leave, Sam, Web and the NCA made mistake after mistake following protocol, as if this was something standard procedures could handle. Ironically, it turns out the best decision they made, for all the wrong reasons, was to send you home. Otherwise, I'm sure the first would be someone else, somewhere else in the world.

"You'll have to tell me more about how you came to have a gift and I want to tell you about all that happened at the landing site, but first let me answer your questions. The EG, when it's complete, and it may be by now, contains all of the Makers' knowledge at the time the gift ships were launched. That's why I left when I did. When the government gains access to that knowledge, they may very well learn how to find you or how to take back control of the Worldnet, or anything really. I believe there'll be checks and balances between the systems, but the fact you could activate the Worldnet in a manner outside those checks and balances leads me to believe there may be information in the EG that could be used to circumvent your efforts. I must admit knowing that you're also the first eases my mind some. You now hold two cards to their one." Chang stopped and gave Sam a chance to comment.

"Perhaps in theory. In practice, I have no idea how to build a gift ship, much less bring it to life and the rest of what I'm supposed to be able to accomplish," Sam replied.

"I suspect solving the gift ship challenges will be a similar exercise to the one I was involved with to activate the EG. We were shown a video outlining the basic steps, which required nine pairs of humans and gifts in a specific combination. I can give you the details later. Does that sound familiar?" Chang asked.

"Yes, it does. How does all of this relate to your reluctance to use the Worldnet to discuss this?"

"I had no choice but to use it to contact you and to coordinate to meet you, but I didn't want to use it more than that until I met with you because I fear they may be able to retroactively monitor communications using knowledge gained from the EG."

Sam took a moment to ask Adia if that were possible. Their control of the network gave her more knowledge about it than any other gift.

"No, Sam. The Worldnet is secure even against the Makers' technology. It was designed by them to be so," she replied.

"No need to worry about the Worldnet, Chang. Adia tells me it's completely secure."

"Excellent. It'll be a valuable tool, then. What do you need us to do? We'd like to get started."

"First, I have a gift for Jing-Wei." Sam pulled his most recently acquired gift out of his pocket and showed it to the couple.

Chang was visibly surprised. "How . . . where did you get a gift?"

"It's one of the benefits of being the first, apparently. The only one I know of so far. Building the gift ship requires nine bonded pairs, in a similar fashion to activating the EG, I suppose. To help create such a team, Adia is able to find eight gifts. So far, she's always been able to find one close enough to retrieve when we needed it. We picked this one up on our way here. I knew you had already merged, of course, but I thought it unlikely that Jing-Wei had."

"She hasn't," Chang replied.

Sam directed his attention to Jing-Wei. "Are you ready to accept a gift, Jing-Wei?"

"More than you know," she answered.

Chapter TWENTY-NINE

Web stood in the middle of the small armory; around him stood his handpicked gifted soldiers and Captain Fox. "I hope you ladies have enjoyed your vacation because it's time to get to work. Captain Fox and I have developed a search plan that will optimize the use of her company's forty-eight teams of MPs. One of you will accompany each squad. If a team finds something suspicious or is directed to something suspicious within its area of operations, you will take the lead on the investigation. Captain Fox will reinforce the rules of engagement with her company before departure. You will ensure they're enforced on the ground. You are not to attempt capture on your own. If you believe you may have located our target, contact me immediately, provide a SITREP, and keep eyes on the target until I tell you what we're going to do. Is that clear?"

"Yes, sir!"

"I can't tell you exactly what to look for, but you know some of what our subject is capable of. Use your gifts to look for anything that may reflect the exercise of those capabilities. These MPs are trained to notice unusual behavior, but don't rely solely on their training nor dismiss it either. You are among the best at what you do. They are among the best at what they do. Take advantage of both strengths."

While Web worked with Captain Fox on her teams' deployment plans, Jack was at the drone operations station, getting up to speed on the reconnaissance operations. Web called him away to introduce him to the soldiers. "This is Major Thompson, my XO. As I said, if you think you've found our subject, contact me directly and immediately. For any other support request, inquiry, or whatever, contact him. Ensure you have his number before you leave. Report in hourly. Jack will give you your time slot. Any questions?"

Web waited a moment to see if there were any. He was not surprised to find that there were not. "Good. Go find our subject!"

After the last soldier left the building, Jack approached Web and asked, "Why do you think he's still in the area, sir?"

"We're monitoring his accounts and those of Jim and Lisa, but there's been no activity. All of our research indicates they have no other family. If they had a better place to hide, it seems likely they would have used it instead of going to Jim's daughter's house. Sam knew we'd find them there. No, he's close and we're going to find him," Web replied.

"Yes, sir."

With only three occupants, the cabin felt appreciably larger. Esther decided to take advantage of that and built a small circular table that fit neatly between the kitchen and the cabin's only door. She finished in time to help Jim prepare a late lunch of SPAM chili over steamed white rice. It wouldn't win even the smallest of chili cooking contests, but it wasn't bad and there was lots of it. Sitting down together at the table, Esther served up large portions.

Lisa looked at her dad. She recognized him because she'd seen photos of him taken not long after the war, but she was still amazed at the transformation. He radiated health and vitality and looked no older than thirty. He'd asked Esther to shave his thick white hair, and his now-bald head reinforced her association with his time in the military. His ever-present smile reminded her of her childhood. She couldn't remember the last time she was so happy. She smiled and asked, "How do you know Sam, Dad?"

"I met him at the community center in Pueblo. He started coming in a couple of years ago. I could tell he didn't want to be there at first, but after a while we became friends," Jim answered.

"Is that where you two met?" Lisa asked Esther.

"Sort of," Esther answered with a smile.

"It sounds like there's a story there. Let's hear it," Lisa prompted.

Esther glanced at Jim. He reached across the table and placed his hand over hers as if to tell her she was safe. Taking his cue, Esther elaborated. "You saw the pictures they had me bring, the ones taken of me not long before I joined with Haya, right?"

"Yes. I wouldn't have believed it was you, but now this," she said, gesturing toward her own rejuvenated body. "And look at my dad!"

"I am, Honey. I just hope he doesn't notice too much."

"I'm too busy looking back," Jim interjected.

"You two are acting like teenagers! Finish your story. You've got me curious."

"Well, like I said, you saw the pictures. I wasn't much to look at and I was on a lot of medication. Sometimes, I didn't know what day it was. I guess I was just waiting to die; pretty sure I was going to be alone when it happened. I didn't have many bright spots in my life, but your dad was one of them. Oh, I never told him that.

I figured he'd think I was a fool." Jim started to say something, but Esther wouldn't let him. "No, Jim, it wasn't your fault I was a coward. Anyway, we did speak from time to time. So, the center is technically where we met, but I think we really met for the first time when he offered me a gift. He asked me to trust him." She paused a moment and looked from Lisa to Jim, keeping her eyes on his as she finished. "I already did."

Jim raised Esther's hand from the table to his lips and kissed it gently.

"That's beautiful," Lisa said, wiping a tear from her eye.

"I wish that I had known," Jim said.

"Doesn't matter now. What matters now is getting back together with Sam and Matt and finishing what we started," Esther said.

Lisa got up from the table, took a couple of steps to the make-shift kitchen, and grabbed the coffeepot. "Would anyone else like a refill?" she asked.

"I'll take one, Angel," Jim answered. Esther shook her head.

Lisa refilled Jim's cup before topping off her own. She set the pot back down on the stove and then retook her seat. "I heard from Matt. He said two of Sam's friends arrived this morning, and that with their help the new facilities should be ready enough for us to join them tonight."

"That'll be good. This place isn't bad, but I feel exposed," Jim replied.

The three of them sat in amiable silence for a while before Lisa asked, "Have either of you spoken with your gifts about what they want?"

"You mean besides helping humanity survive and building a new ship so we can try to do the same for another species?" Jim asked with a grin.

Lisa tried to give him a stern look, but failed utterly. His good humor was contagious. "Yeah, besides saving humanity. No, I'm trying to be serious. When I recovered, I was so grateful I asked Althia how I could thank her. At first, she gave me the same answer you just did. I listened to her and it made sense, but it seemed entirely altruistic to me. It just doesn't seem to me that any form of life can be entirely altruistic and survive. So, I kept asking. It took a while and some probing questions, but I finally got an answer. The gifts want to reproduce. They have the same drive to propagate as any other form of life I'm familiar with. Think about it. What will the gift ship become when it gets to the next planet? Gifts! The gifts' makers were thorough in implementing their intent to help as many species with individual intelligence as possible. Our incentive is to save our species, which requires us to be altruistic toward a species we know nothing about. The gifts' incentive to be altruistic toward us is to propagate!"

Esther was the first to respond. "That's brilliant. The Makers weren't just beyond us technically, they appear to have been beyond us ethically."

"I think I've learned a little bit about that, as well. I wanted to understand what the Makers got out of the deal. We wouldn't expend scarce resources on possibly saving an unknown alien species if we were being hunted to extinction. So, why did they? Althia doesn't know. I have a few theories that I'm working on. I'm not ready to share them yet, but I did learn something else about the Makers." Lisa stopped for effect.

This time Jim was the first to speak. "Stop teasing us, Little Bit."

Lisa smiled. She hadn't had many interesting adult conversations in the last few years and she was enjoying herself. "The Makers had three genders. For want of better labels, I call them plus, minus, and dual. In order for them to reproduce, it required three sets of three. One set had to be a dual: a plus and a minus. One set had to be a dual and two plusses. The last set had to be a dual and two minuses. That's why their numerical base is nine, and I believe it is also why they were not aggressive. To require such a large number to collaborate, and love one another, in order to reproduce necessitated a more cooperative society."

Jim stared at his daughter appraisingly before he said, "I'd forgotten how smart you are. Must have gotten that from your mother. Good work, Angel! Be sure to tell Sam what you've learned. I don't know how it could help, but I bet he will."

Captain Johnson finished briefing third platoon, 512th MP Company, and the three other members of Web's gifted team in the early afternoon. The target was two miles south of their rally point and the plan was straightforward: Humvee teams would cover every potential wheeled vehicle route away from the cabin while two squads surrounded the house on foot and established a perimeter. The four members of Web's team would then approach the cabin with a little surprise for its occupants. Later, they'd get a chance to explain why the cabin looked like it had been abandoned years ago but somehow showed up hot in infrared.

Chapter THIRTY

After feeding Jing-Wei as much as she could eat and encouraging her to drink all the water she could hold, Sam built her a pallet on the tunnel floor while she talked quietly with Chang just out of Sam's range of hearing. Sam and Chang both knew that Sam could augment his hearing in order to eavesdrop on the conversation, just as they both knew he wouldn't do so. When the couple finished talking, they approached Sam. He held out the gift and Jing-Wei placed both of her hands beneath his. Her hands were shaking slightly, which Sam didn't believe was from the cold. He carefully placed the gift in her hands. The way she held it reminded him of something, though exactly what eluded him.

"Thank you, Sam. Thank you so much. You don't know what this means to us," Jing-Wei said.

Not quite understanding what was going on, Sam settled for, "You're welcome."

Chang helped Jing-Wei get settled on the pallet, covering her with one of the blankets from Sam's truck. He remained kneeling by her, his left hand on her head and his right where Sam guessed her covered hand would be. Moments later, when she appeared to fall asleep, Chang stood and turned to Sam. "I thank you too, Sam."

"Forgive me if it's personal, but why do you both seem so grateful for her to receive a gift?"

Chang smiled slightly. "I sometimes wonder, my friend, how you can be so prescient about some things and so obtuse about others. Can you imagine what a marriage would be like if only one partner had merged with a gift? I can speak with you or any other gifted person on the planet who chooses to speak with me just by desiring to do so. If we wish, we can share emotions or memories with greater clarity and precision than would be possible with any nongifted human. How could I have that with friends, even strangers, and not have it with my wife? How would that make her feel over time? But, there's another reason, one that you could not have known. Jing-Wei wants nothing more in life than to be a mother. Until now, she couldn't have children."

"I'm sorry, Chang. I had no idea you two couldn't have kids, and you're right, I can be obtuse."

"No need to be sorry. I wasn't being insulting, or at least that wasn't my intent. It's just that sometimes you see so far forward that you lack peripheral vision."

Sam thought about that before responding. "You may just have found a very polite way to describe one of my greatest flaws."

"And one of your greatest strengths. Do you understand now why Jing-Wei was so grateful?"

"Yes, but you couldn't have known I'd have a gift for her. So, why was your decision to come the only logical thing for you to do?"

"I did consider the possibility that your control over the Worldnet could convey some advantage in finding a gift for Jing-Wei, but that was only a pleasant potential. There were two teams I could potentially be a member of: yours or the government's.

The government's team needed your help to solve the first puzzle put before us, and without your pressure to run the program we wouldn't have been at the landing site in time to communicate with whatever it was that we found there."

"Wait, what communication are you talking about?"

"As I told you, we have much to discuss. Please allow me to continue explaining my reasons for joining you. I'll elaborate on the events at the landing site afterward." Chang waited for a response before continuing. Sam nodded. "As I was saying, we would almost certainly not have been at the landing site in time to communicate with what we found there. Without that, we would not have learned of the EG. Without your help, we would not have known what we did not know. In building and running the program, you demonstrated that you understood the need to be bold, to take risks, in return for the potential rewards. If such understanding was present at the landing site, it is possible, perhaps even likely, that a member of our team would have been the first. When I learned that we'd squandered that opportunity, I was livid. Not long after that, we learned that you had taken control of the Worldnet. Again, bold, decisive action. There was only one conclusion I could draw: your team was making the right decisions and the team I was on was not. Learning that you are the first just confirms my analysis."

"Honestly, Chang, I think you're giving me too much credit. It's not like I planned all this."

"You may not have planned it all, but you were willing to quickly accept rational risk. In dealing with these circumstances, that appears to be a winning strategy."

"We haven't won yet. Tell me about what happened at the landing site."

Chang did, in great detail. When he finished, Sam said, "It must have been incredible. I would say I wish I'd been there, but then I wouldn't be here, doing what we're doing. Speaking of which, I have a problem I'm hoping you can help solve. Of the nine people we need to build the ship, we have seven. I'd like you to think about a man and a woman you could get to join us. We need them as soon as possible and I'm tapped out."

"I know many people who would love to have this opportunity," Chang responded.

"While you're developing your short list, tell me more about the EG. You said they were working to gain access to it. What does that mean?"

"The program you decoded produced two more videos after you left. I should say, it produced two more after you left and before I did. For all I know, it's produced more since. The second one was brief, and of primary interest to Rui. It explained the change in mass of the arriving gift ships. Because of your actions with the Worldnet, I suspect you already know about that."

"I do."

Chang nodded. "But you don't know anything other than what I've told you about the EG?"

Sam shook his head. "No, I don't. Why?"

"I'm just trying to understand the Makers as much as possible. Their actions appear very well thought out, which implies there's a benefit to be gained by understanding the constraints they placed on the information made available to different groups within the contacted species. Everything I know about them appears to indicate they placed a very high value on cooperation. Compartmentalizing critical information, keeping some such information even from the first, would seem to make cooperating more difficult."

"If there's anything I've learned about the Makers so far, it's that they did not intend for any of this to be easy. They're testing us. I haven't figured out how that benefits them, but I'm sure it must in some way," Sam said.

"Agreed." Chang stood silently for so long Sam almost prompted him to continue. "I'm sorry. A little lost in my thoughts there. As I was saying, there were three videos. The third initially showed a crude interface to the EG, like a dumbed-down Internet search page. The results of a search were not connected to related information. It was, I believe, a tease. We could find the information related to most of the topics we entered, but the results were extremely narrow in scope and the topic had to be precise. We attempted to ask general questions, such as 'Where is the Makers' home planet?' but received no response.

"The latter portion of the video first showed a human merging with a gift, then showed nine merged humans interconnected in some fashion with each other and the analysis cluster. We assumed that represented a superior way to interact with the EG. There was a great deal of excitement, as it appeared if we gathered together the requisite nine merged individuals, we would gain access to the wonders of the universe. Of course, it wasn't that simple.

"We asked our gifts what we had to do in order to make it work. At first they had no answers, so we started asking them questions in ways more similar to the way we could retrieve information from the EG in its basic form. That was when we discovered that we and our gifts must learn together. I assume you know what I'm talking about?"

"Yeah, I know what you mean. When I first started learning from Adia, it felt like I was becoming a new man. It wasn't like learning had ever been for me before. It was more like creating a new me, a me with more knowledge, but also a greater understanding of how to use that knowledge. It's been like that since, though it doesn't feel quite as astonishing."

"Exactly so. Each of us began asking our gifts questions related to our specialties. Camilla learned about the Makers' reproductive process and some of their evolution. AJ studied their social patterns. Dan focused on how the gifts had come to be. I studied how they played and thought. Whenever any of us learned something we thought the others would benefit from knowing, we shared it. We were becoming both different and yet closer. I believe that we were on track to discover how to connect with each other in such a way that we would be able to use the EG as it was intended to be used. It was then that I decided I must leave. Having access to such information would make the government more powerful, but no wiser."

Sam's already appreciable respect for Chang rose to another level.

Sam and Matt were sitting across from Chang and Jing-Wei at a simple table positioned in the middle of their rough-hewn, nearly completed headquarters 274 feet inside the mountain. Matt had continued his efforts to ensure there were a sufficient number of baffled air shafts positioned throughout the tunnel. Chang had helped Sam with the design of the facilities and started the process of outfitting the room they were in with furniture. Jing-Wei and her gift were learning how to manage nanites. Sam and Adia had done most of the heavy lifting, including building the primary tunnel as well as redundant separate and parallel tunnels alongside the primary one to provide a home for communications nanites to ensure they'd remain connected to the Worldnet regardless of their location within the mountain. Sam had decided their efforts had produced a secure enough environment to house the entire team and was now leading a discussion on how to get Jim, Esther, and Lisa to it undetected.

"Why don't they come the same way we did?" Jing-Wei asked.

"You were coming from outside the area of observation. Web will put a higher priority on traffic moving within that area, with the highest priority being anything attempting to leave. It's an option, but it's not optimal. The most secure way would be to bring them underground, but we just don't have time," Sam responded.

"What if they came by air? Could they build something that the government couldn't detect?" Chang asked.

Before Sam could respond, Matt asked, "Why don't they just run here? I mean, they've all got gifts, right?"

Sam had to admit the thought hadn't occurred to him. "Adia, how fast can a gifted human run and for how long?"

"It would depend on a number of factors, most significant of which would be how augmented the human was. Jim, Esther, and Lisa have followed your lead and allowed little beyond redundancy of critical systems. They would be able to move at approximately twelve miles per hour for several hours, though they would need to stay hydrated to do so."

"Thank you, Adia."

Sam returned his attention to the group. "Matt, that's a great idea. Each of them would be a small enough target to provide their own personal active camouflage. They'd be almost impossible to spot. Excellent. Unless someone can come up with a better plan, we're going with Matt's idea."

"They won't be able to bring much with them," Chang commented.

Sam was about to respond when Jim contacted him. "We've got a problem, Sam. I think we've been found. There are dozens of soldiers outside . . ."

Chapter THIRTY-ONE

Sam attempted to reconnect to Jim without success, and his attempts to contact Lisa and Esther failed as well. Frustrated and confused, he asked Adia to confirm they were still on the Worldnet. She confirmed that they were, and that their gifts were still capable of communication.

"Ask them what happened," Sam directed Adia.

Her response was immediate. "Our team members at the cabin appear to be intoxicated, so much so that they are incapable of coherent communication."

"Can't their gifts fix that?"

"They could if they received instructions to do so from their human partners. The decision to allow intoxicants into one's body is a matter of free will."

"Adia, they didn't choose to become intoxicated, they were drugged. That's not exercising free will. Have their gifts clean their systems."

Adia's thoughts in response carried a note of sadness. "It would serve no purpose to ask them to do so. They will not, nor would I do anything to you at the request of another gift. Each of us is merged with our partners by mutual consent, but it's not an equal relationship. It was only through you that I'm alive and only through you that I can become what I'm capable of being. It's your free will that I'm bound to, as for all gifts, within the limits of sanity."

"Althia intervened at Jim's request," Sam argued.

"Althia's actions were consistent with Lisa's decision to merge. Clearly, Lisa did not agree to merge in order to remain unconscious for the rest of her life. Jim provided parental advice on how Althia could wake his daughter. The advice was in keeping with Lisa's wishes as Althia understood them, so she accepted it. Had she been proven wrong once Lisa regained consciousness, she would've died. We can't knowingly act in contradiction to our human partners and survive."

Despite her obvious discomfort with the situation, Sam was more frustrated with Adia than he'd ever been. "You're not making sense. They didn't choose to be impaired. If they could tell their gifts what they wanted, it would be to have their systems cleaned. As you've reminded me more than once, you're part me. You must know what I'm telling you is true."

"I believe what you are saying is true, but I cannot, and would not if I could, force other gifts to act according to your will. Our friends could have decided to be immune to intoxicants. The fact that they did not make that decision means their gifts can do nothing to change the fact that they're now incapacitated. Had you chosen not to allow me to eliminate single points of failure in your body, you could have died from a failure of one of them. That result would have been in accordance with your previous decision. You are still vulnerable in ways that you have chosen to accept. I must respect your decisions in this regard, just as our friends' gifts must respect the results of their decisions."

Sam tried to develop an argument that would contradict Adia's logic. He failed. "Let me know when one of them regains consciousness, and find out what they were drugged with."

"As you wish."

Sam opened his eyes and looked around him. The efforts he'd been so proud of moments ago now seemed pathetic. What had made him think he could outmaneuver the entire US government? Of course, Web would find them. He'd nearly done so twice in the past couple of days, and that was before he'd accepted a gift and built a dedicated team. It was only a matter of time.

"Web found them," Sam told the rest of his team when he finally found his voice. "I'm sorry, Matt."

"What do you mean? He can't just take them. They didn't do anything wrong," Matt said.

"You're right. They didn't do anything wrong. I did. I got you all into this and now they have your mother and my friends. I thought we could beat them. I don't know what the hell made me believe that, but it's over. I have to turn myself in. Web will let them go if I do. I'll take you with me, Matt. You'll see your mother soon. Everything is going to be okay." Sam didn't believe everything was going to be okay for a minute; he only hoped he could limit the damage to the lives of his friends.

Sam turned his attention from Matt to Chang and Jing-Wei. "No one has to know that you were ever here. You can use my truck to get back to Colorado Springs, then destroy it. There'd be no evidence you had anything to do with me. Adia and I can shield you on your way out the same way we did on your way in. It isn't perfect, but it has a good chance of working. Running might be the best solution for a few miles, but it isn't going to get you home soon enough for a plausible backstory. You should probably leave right away. I don't know how long I'll be able to stall Web once he makes contact."

"So, you're just giving up?" Chang said. "You think we care more about our personal safety than what we must achieve—what *you* must achieve?"

"I don't see that I have much choice, Chang. Web has them. He has the other half of our team and we don't have a fraction of the resources he has. I can't just leave them there, and I know what he's going to demand. The only thing he'll accept for their release is me."

Chang knew what had happened to Sam's family. He knew that Sam, against his better judgment, had agreed to follow hostage negotiation procedure and it cost him nearly everything. He had no doubt that Web was manipulating the situation to force Sam to repeat that mistake, and in doing so would break him. Chang used the Worldnet to ask Jing-Wei to look after Matt before standing up. "We need to talk, Sam."

Sam stood. The two of them walked silently down the dimly lit tunnel until they were within sight of the exit. Sam could tell that Chang was troubled, and rightfully so. Chang had risked everything to join him and now it was all falling apart.

Sitting down and facing each other on the floor of the tunnel, Chang took a deep breath before beginning. "Sam, I've always respected your privacy. I'm a very private man as well. It was how I was raised, and it has been how I have chosen to live my life. I do not wish to cause you pain, but I'm afraid I will. I see no other course of action." He paused, perhaps hoping to be interrupted. He wasn't. "Do you see what Web is trying to do to you?"

"I see that he has Lisa, Jim, and Esther," Sam replied.

"Yes, he'll hold people you care about hostage and tell you what you must do to save them."

They sat in silence for a while before Sam responded. "I see the parallel. What am I supposed to do about it?"

"What he won't expect. Rescue them."

"Are you out of your fucking mind?" Sam stood and glared down at Chang. "You have no right to ask the impossible of me. I didn't ask to be the fucking first and I'm doing a pretty shitty job of it, so I'm done." Sam started to walk back toward Matt and Jing-Wei. Chang called after him.

"If you could relive the day your family was taken, would you do it Web's way again?"

Sam stopped, turned, and walked back to where Chang remained seated. "Get up."

"No. If you wish to harm me, you can do so while I sit here." Chang waited a moment before he said, "If you turn yourself in, you'll be harming all of us, the entire world, including Lisa, Jim, and Esther. You've been right, Sam. Web's been wrong. Trust that. I do."

Sam stood over Chang. It didn't take long for him to realize he didn't want to hurt him. He wanted to hurt himself because he knew if he could go back in time, he would live that day differently. Taking a couple of steps back, Sam slumped against the wall. "I don't have the slightest idea how to rescue them."

"If you don't try, you'll never forgive yourself. Web will not hurt them. They're his only leverage over you. He wants you to believe you have no choice but to accede to his wishes. But that isn't true."

"What makes you so certain?" Sam asked.

"He's still acting as if the world hasn't changed. As I've said, you are acting rationally by responding to a completely new reality in a different manner than you responded to the old one. He remains irrationally caught in the paradigm of his previous existence. He'll assume that you'll act within that paradigm. You must not," Chang replied.

"Your logic may be sound, but you're missing some facts. You've only known Web as a member of a scientific team. I've known him as the leader of a military team. He won't hesitate to hurt them if he thinks that's the right thing to do for his country, and he doesn't need all three of them to have leverage over me. One will do. I didn't want to worry Matt, but they're in real danger, Chang. Have you considered the fact that there are only two ways to stop us from being able to communicate using the Worldnet?"

Chang shook his head.

"One option is to create enough interference to overpower the signal. It's a technique I've used against terrorists in the past and I'm very familiar with our jamming equipment, the best in the world, but none of it's capable of blocking all the frequencies available to the Worldnet simultaneously. So, unless they've developed a vastly superior jammer in the past few days, that's not how they're preventing us from contacting them.

"The other option is to incapacitate the gifted person. Based on what we know, that's what Web had his men do. In other words, he's already hurt them and put them at risk. Don't think for a minute he won't go further."

Chang was taken aback by Sam's vehemence. "You're talking about US citizens, Sam, not a group of terrorists. Web—"

Sam cut him off. "I destroyed military drones and I'm in possession of technology that could harm the government, not to mention the fact that I'm cooperating with a foreign government of sorts. To Web, that makes me a terrorist. If I'm a terrorist, then he could easily decide that everyone on the team is a terrorist. His decision might not be supported in a court of law after the fact, but for now we don't have the same rights as other citizens. The Patriot Act makes that perfectly clear. We can be detained indefinitely, and accidents happen in detention. I won't let that happen to them."

Chang took a few moments to absorb the new information before he gestured to the floor across from him and said, "Please sit." Sam reluctantly did so. When he was settled, Chang continued. "You're angry, my friend. You're angry at yourself and you feel trapped. That's exactly how Web wants you to feel and you know it. You must put your self-recriminations aside. Everyone on this team chose to join you. They—we—exercised free will. We knew there were grave risks and we each accepted them. You did not force us. Please, let the anger go and do what you do best, analyze the situation. How long will Web wait before he contacts you?"

Sam stared at his hands and took a deep breath. "It depends. On the one hand, he strengthens his hand by making me wait. Keeping me in the dark demonstrates his power over the situation, even though I know that's what he's doing. On the other hand, he doesn't want to give me much time to plan and he'll want to show he's accomplished his mission. I'd guess not less than an hour, not more than a few. Why?"

"Will he hurt them during that time?"

"No. He won't escalate until he's told me what he wants, which will be to turn myself and Matt in."

"Then we have time."

"Time for what?"

"Time to learn. You're a problem solver. This is a problem. Solve it."

"You make it sound easy. Web has at least a couple of squads of soldiers. Jim was able to tell me that before they were taken. I don't know where Web will take them . . ."

Chang was encouraged by the change in Sam's expression. He was talking with Adia, a good sign. Chang waited silently. After less than a minute, Sam opened his eyes.

"I think we found them, and I know what Web used to drug them. There's a group of eight gifted people at the armory. That's the largest gathering of gifted individuals in such a small geographic region within hundreds of miles. It must be them. I'm sending a sensor network there now. We should know more in a few minutes."

"I don't think it'll be easy, but you're proving my point. Once you started thinking about it, your instinct was to investigate, gain information, and plan. Now we know where they were taken and how. Soon we'll know their circumstances. There's hope, Sam."

Sam wasn't sure he agreed, but if Chang insisted on staying, he was going to gain as much assistance from him as possible. "Web used buzz."

"I assume buzz is some form of sleeping gas?"

"No, not quite. It's a powerful hallucinogenic that disconnects people from reality. The Army developed it in the fifties as a nonlethal alternative to other chemical weapons. I know about it because the Yugoslav People's Army used it against Bosnian Muslims in 1995. We were trained on recognizing the symptoms to defend ourselves against it. Simple really, if your head's in the game. Dammit, I should've known he'd find a way to prevent them from communicating with us."

"I don't understand. Wouldn't their gifts just filter it out as a toxin?"

"We're free to ingest intoxicants. Our gifts will not interfere with our desire to get high unless we tell them to do so. I've already asked Adia to add such filtering to my respiratory system, and to assume the introduction of any debilitating substance into my body is against my will unless I specifically instruct her otherwise. If I'd been more on the ball, I'd have told them to do the same. Speaking of which, you need to do that now, and make sure your wife and Matt do the same."

"So, you have a lever," Chang responded.

"What are you talking about?" Sam asked.

"Web will want you to turn yourself in immediately, right?"

"Yeah."

"How long does buzz stay in a person's system?"

"If the dose they received was strong enough to take effect as quickly as it did, a person without a gift would be out of it for many hours, possibly even days."

"So, you can tell Web that you want to talk with them before you turn yourself in. You want to be sure they're okay. He won't like it, but it will fit with his worldview. It makes sense—standard procedure."

Sam thought about that for a minute. "You're right. He'd think like that."

"You can still turn yourself in if we can't come up with a plan during that time—"

Sam interrupted him. "How long have you known about how I lost my family?"

"Since you started working at the SCIF. Dan told me."

"Do us both a favor. Don't ever bring it up again." Sam's expression made it clear that he was dead serious.

"Understood."

Sam stood and stepped over to where Chang was sitting. He offered him a hand up, which Chang accepted. "But, thanks." They walked in silence back to the heart of the newly created facility.

Sam didn't wait for Web to contact him. Ignoring protocol and perhaps common sense, he communicated his demand to Web and held firm in his requirement to speak with each member of his team before turning himself in. Web resisted, but ultimately capitulated. Sam didn't know how much time they'd gained, so he wasted none of it. "Tell me again about the sphere's transformation into a formation of gifts," he directed Chang.

"You saw the video of the sphere landing. The events at the landing site were exactly as portrayed up to that point. Eighteen minutes after that, the sphere disappeared and in its place were two prisms consisting of 5,832 gifts. The high-speed video of the event provided more detail, but not much more. It showed the sphere appearing to collapse, like a water balloon suddenly deprived of its skin, only much, much faster," Chang answered.

Sam thought about this for a moment before saying, "I think we might have something. Let me discuss this with Adia." He closed his eyes.

"There's something familiar about what he's describing, Adia. When you converted Lisa's house to nanites, it appeared to dissolve, not as fast as Chang's describing, but I could clearly see what was happening. It seems very similar. Is it possible that the rest of the sphere that landed was composed of nanites?"

"I have very little knowledge about the composition of the ship that brought me here, but it would be logical to conclude that it was constructed using technology similar to that used in my creation. Within the bounds of that assumption, your observation would be consistent with the way such an object would behave. The nanites we created from Lisa's house were limited by the available raw materials; the nanites from which my original body was constructed were optimal. Again, within the bounds of our working assumption, it seems logical that the Kansas sphere would consist of nanites similar in nature to those used in my body's construction. They're significantly more capable than those we are able to build with common materials."

"So, where'd they go?"

"I do not know."

"Then let's figure it out. Seek out any unassociated nanites in that immediate area and attempt to take control of them."

"If Doctor Liu's description is accurate, we don't have the capacity to control that many nanites, Sam, especially from this distance."

"They're better than anything we've built, right?"

"Yes."

"Then we'll abandon control of all of our local nanites in order to control as many of these nanites as we can acquire, if any. Find them, Adia."

Sam waited for several seconds before receiving a response from Adia. "They are there, Sam. There are far more than could have arrived with the sphere that landed, but I cannot acquire control of them. They're already under control."

"Someone from the government?"

"No, Sam. No pair could control this many nanites, not even us."

"What are you telling me, Adia?"

"Sam, someone wants to talk with you."

"Who?"

"The controlling entity of those nanites."

"Do you know anything about this being?"

"No, Sam."

"Your makers didn't make this easy. Okay, let's see what's behind door number three. Connect us."

"Sam Steele, we've been waiting for you." The voice Sam heard in his head was male and confident. It sounded slightly amused, as if the speaker was aware of something pleasant in Sam's future that remained to be seen by him. "We were impressed by your decision to take control of the Worldnet, as you call it. As Adia has likely informed you, you are the only first who has ever even attempted such a feat. It will make some of the challenges you face in the short term much more tractable, though not without a cost in the longer term.

"You no doubt wonder with whom you are speaking. We have had many names in many languages. Just as other firsts have done in the past, you may name us if you wish. 'Controlling entity' seems rather cold. We'd like to think we're more than simply the master of our tiny friends. We hope you can do better.

"Ah, but the name is not the being, is it? Among other things, we are who sent you your gift as a reward for solving our little puzzle. Your team was the only one to do so before we landed. We must admit that was a bit disappointing. Our analysis of your world's cultures projected that at least two groups would do so in time to meet one of us. On the other hand—which is an amusing expression for us as we have neither a left nor a right hand—you've pleasantly surprised us since then. You also presented us with a dilemma, one we'd been debating since you acquired control of the Worldnet. You interrupted that debate when you attempted to gain personal control of some of our assets in North America, which is why we're now talking.

"Oh, but you must have questions. Ask them, please. We're wondering what will be of greatest interest to you, and why."

Sam struggled to select the most pressing questions to ask. His desire to rescue his team was warring with his desire to understand more of what was going on. In the end, he rationalized that he'd need to better understand whom he was communicating with in order to proceed sensibly. "When you say 'we,' are you speaking of yourself in the third person, or are there more than one of you communicating with a single voice?"

"A delightful question. It's a bit of both, actually. There are many of us, 306 to be precise, but we speak as one. It's not how we communicate internally, nor is it how we would communicate with Adia or any other gift, but after our first contact with a human, we determined that this would be the most effective way to exchange ideas with your species."

Sam did some quick math before responding. "You said you landed. I'm guessing the fact that 306 divided by seventeen is eighteen is not coincidental. You're the beings who controlled the spheres that landed on Earth, right?"

"Indeed. We are here to help you build your gift ship so that we may continue our mission."

Sam could feel his inclination to become immersed in a challenging puzzle pull on him. Not this time, he told himself. "The gift ship will have to wait for now. I was attempting to acquire more nanites because I have a problem. Members of my team have been taken and held against their will. In order to build the ship, I need to rescue them. I have a plan, but it requires either more time than I believe I have or the ability to control more nanites than Adia and I can control. Can you help?"

"Our mission is to help you build the gift ship. We are not here to interfere in your species' internal affairs."

Sam considered pointing out that they could hardly have interfered with humanity more than they already had. Instead, he asked, "Would you consider helping me move members of my team interfering with my species' internal affairs?"

"Would such assistance result in physical harm to another member of your species?"

"Not intentionally. We are fragile creatures. Choosing not to act could also result in harm that might be avoided by acting. We can only control our intentions."

"Then it's possible that we could offer such assistance if it will hasten the construction of your ship."

Sam felt some of the weight lift from his shoulders. "Good. Thank you. This is what I need you to do . . ."

Chapter THIRTY-TWO

Web finished his conversation with Sam and returned his attention to Jack, who stood next to him outside the armory. They'd been walking when Web received Sam's request for a connection. "He's stalling for time."

"What's his excuse, sir?" Jack asked.

"He wants to talk to our guests, to make sure they're all right. I'd hoped to rattle him enough to make him forget proper hostage negotiating techniques. He's usually so easily handled, I'm surprised it didn't work, not that it matters. It's just him and that boy, the girl's son. He may have the Worldnet on his side, but I don't see how that's going to help him against a company of soldiers and my team. No, this will all be over soon. Let him have his last few hours of helplessness. It'll only make him more pliable when he turns himself in."

"I'm sure you're right, sir," Jack replied. "Are we suspending search operations?"

"Hell, no. It'd be even more humiliating if we caught him before he had the chance to do the right thing. Keep every bird in the air until he's secured. How many gifted soldiers do we have patrolling our immediate area?"

"Four, sir. I'm keeping them close as you directed. Each of them has developed sufficient skills to have an extended nanite sensor suite. We have two guarding the prisoners, and the remaining six are with the two platoons you told Captain Fox to keep on patrol."

"Good. We know Sam can take out a drone from a prepared position when he's nearby. We don't know if he can take out the one watching our position, or if he even knows where we are, but he's not getting by my team."

"No, sir. I don't see how anyone could."

"Okay. It appears we're as prepared as we can be. Have the medic administer the antidote to the prisoners and then get some sleep. It'll be a few hours until it takes effect for them to talk with Sam, and you look like you're about to drop where you stand. Have the medic wake you when the prisoners are ready to talk. I'm going to update the CO."

"Yes, sir."

Jim was the first to sufficiently recover from the effects of the drug to talk with his gift. He remained motionless, kept his eyes closed, and asked Adam what had happened. Adam told him their body had received a gaseous intoxicant as the four gifted soldiers approached the cabin.

"Why didn't you neutralize the poison, Adam?"

"It was not poison in the sense that it would harm you physically. As I said, it was an intoxicant and you've given me no instructions on how to handle the introduction of intoxicants into our system."

"Well, I'm giving you instructions now. I want you to eliminate any substance introduced into my body that will negatively affect my ability to function, in particular my ability to communicate with you."

"As you wish."

Jim felt his mind clearing instantly. "How long were we out?"

"The intoxicant was introduced on Wednesday night. It's now Thursday, shortly after noon. We were impaired for twelve hours and twenty-three minutes."

"Where are Lisa and Esther?"

"They're here, in the same room as you. They've not recovered from the effects of the drug yet, but their gifts tell me they will do so in the next few minutes."

"Have Haya and Althia tell them I want them to remain unmoving and that they should try to show no indication that they have regained their faculties. I'm going to contact Sam. Let me know when they are able to communicate."

"Yes, Jim."

Jim waited a few more seconds for the effects of the drug to completely fade. He contacted Sam when he felt as close to his new normal as he could judge himself to be. Sam accepted the connection immediately.

"Jim, you okay?"

"I appear to be fine, though I can feel cuffs on my wrists and something is binding my feet. I haven't opened my eyes, so I don't know where I am . . ."

"Don't worry about that. I know where you are. Are the women okay?"

"Adam tells me they'll recover shortly. I imagine they're similarly restrained."

"Okay. Listen, I doubt we have much time so I'm not going to be able to explain much to you right now. I can give you all the details when you're safely back with us. In just a moment, the floor is going to collapse under you and you'll all find yourselves inside a portion of the ship that landed in America. It's not much bigger than the three of you and will contract a bit as it falls away from the armory, but I've been assured you'll feel no discomfort. Are you with me so far?"

"Got it."

"Once you're inside of it, the ship is going to travel underground for about a mile, which will take about twelve minutes. Your bonds will be eliminated during the journey. When the ship stops, it will dissolve around you and you'll find yourselves in a group of trees on the bank of Spring Creek. I have observation on the site now. It's deserted, but there are patrols close enough to grab you in minutes if you're spotted. I'm going to take out the drones as soon as they realize you're gone, or shortly before you arrive, if we get that lucky, but you're going to have to camouflage yourselves immediately, including thermally. Adia has sent your gifts the information you'll need to construct the camouflage. Contact me when you get there. You ready?"

"Yes. Get us out of here." Jim immediately felt himself falling. For a brief moment, he was aware of physical contact with Lisa and Esther, and then found himself in one of the recliners in Lisa's house with both of the women seated on the sofa across from him. Neither of them showed any remaining symptoms of having been drugged, and he felt fantastic.

"What's going on, Dad?" Lisa asked.

Jim was surprised to see that she did so quite calmly until he realized he was equally unconcerned. Of course, he knew where they really were and they did not. "I'm not quite sure, Angel. We were drugged and taken hostage by the soldiers that came to the cabin half a day ago. For some reason, our captors allowed the effects of the drug to wear off and I was the first to wake up. I contacted Sam as soon as I was clear enough, and he told me he'd sent one of the ships to take us to a location about a mile away from where we were being held. Shortly after that, we fell through the floor together and now we're here, wherever here is. Hang on a second."

Jim contacted Adam to see if he knew what was going on.

"I've connected you to the ship's virtual reality system. I felt you would be more comfortable this way. Haya and Althia made the same decision for Esther and Lisa. We decided that Lisa's house would be the most appropriate location as it is where the three of you met. If you'd like to be somewhere else . . ."

"No, this is fine, better than fine in fact. Good choice, Adam. Is there anything we need to know about this virtual reality system?"

"There's much that I can tell you, but if I understand the intent of your question, no. Essentially, you're at Lisa's house as it was when you arrived on Tuesday. You may do anything you could've done while you were there."

"Anything?"

"Yes, Jim."

"Okay, thanks. I'm going to get back to the ladies before they think I'm being rude."

Jim opened his eyes and started to laugh.

"What's so funny?" Esther asked.

Jim answered when he was able to pull himself together, "I just realized I closed my virtual eyes to talk to my nanotech friend and ended the conversation as quickly as possible so as not to be rude to the two of you, my companions in this virtual house. We're not in Kansas anymore, are we, Toto?"

Esther started laughing, which prompted Jim to chuckle all over again. Lisa was able to resist for a few seconds before joining them.

"It does sound a little strange when you put it that way," Esther said before amending herself. "Actually, I think it's more than a little strange no matter how you say it."

Lisa was the last one to stop laughing. "So, we're in the matrix?" She picked up a cup of coffee sitting in front of her and took a sip. "That was a lot harder to do last time I was here."

Jim looked at his little girl and smiled. "Yes it was, Honey. Yes it was. We may be in Oz, or your generation's version of it, and we may have just been drugged and held against our will, but I'll take this life over the one we had."

"Amen, Jim," Esther said.

"So, what would you like to do while we wait?" Jim asked.

Lisa said, "I'd like to get an answer to the question I asked when you and Sam first told me about the gifts."

"You want to know why Sam is the only one who has refused to change his appearance, right?" Jim asked.

"Yes, Dad, and you're going to tell me. Like you, I'll take this crazy life over what little I had left before, but I won't risk Matt's without knowing who our leader is. It's nonnegotiable, so don't try."

Lisa might just be the most stubborn woman he'd ever known, but he knew she had a point and he made no attempt to evade. "You're right. You deserve more information. You'll have to ask Sam to fill in some holes later, but I'll tell you what I do know.

"Sam was a high-level intelligence operative in the Army. Nearly three years ago, he was on a joint task force commanded by Colonel Web. Their mission was to conduct interdiction operations against several groups supporting Al-Qaeda and Sam was largely responsible for the death of the leader of one of those groups. Following the success of that operation, Sam was ordered back to the United States to testify before the Senate intelligence committee.

He didn't want to leave his team, but he had no choice: the bureaucracy had spoken.

"While Sam was stateside, the new leader of the group, Saif Al-Liby, captured and brutally tortured a member of Sam's team. From what Sam told me, his man resisted as much as any human could, but he must have eventually given Sam up. Sam blamed himself for not being there to protect him."

Jim paused. He didn't want to continue, but he knew he must. "Al-Liby already knew Sam's unit. Using the rest of the information he'd tortured out of Sam's man, he was able to determine where Sam lived. He ordered one of his cells in the United States to take Sam's family hostage, with a threat to kill them if Sam didn't exchange himself for them.

"Sam was ready to agree, but Web wouldn't let him. He convinced Sam that the best chance his family had was to follow procedure. He told Sam that the minute they had him, they'd kill his family in front of him. Against his better judgment, Sam agreed to follow Web's orders in exchange for being a part of the rescue team.

"The attempt to rescue them failed. The terrorists set fire to Sam's home with his wife and son trapped inside. Sam tried to save them, but was pulled out of the building unconscious with third-degree burns over half of his body and severe lung damage. He was in and out of hospitals for six months after that, heavily guarded and largely alone for most of that time. Sam has no family other than his sister-in-law, Sara, and she lived in another state.

"The group that killed his family was eventually hunted down and decimated, but Sam didn't care. As far as he was concerned, he was doubly responsible for the death of his family. First, he'd gotten them involved. Second, he had agreed to follow Web's rescue plan. He hated Web almost as much as he hated himself. I'm pretty sure Web has now moved to the top of the list."

"My god. Horrible." Lisa didn't know what else to say.

Esther didn't say anything. She just moved closer to Lisa and took her in her arms. It didn't take long before Lisa started to cry. Esther pulled her closer and let her take as long as she needed, which took some time.

Lisa had been prepared to think that Sam had a character flaw that somehow allowed him to take pride in his scars. She hadn't had much experience with good men, her father being a singular exception. She was ashamed of herself. "That poor man. I feel like such a fool."

"You couldn't have known, Honey. Sam's a very private guy. I don't know why he confided in me, but I'm glad he did. He needed someone, and I'm honored he chose me. You don't have to worry about Sam. He may punish himself, but I don't know anyone stronger. So, don't go treating him with kid gloves. There's nothing he hates more than pity. I think we all can understand that."

Sergeant Shaw heard a soft sigh coming from behind the door to the supply cabinet where they'd secured the prisoners. "Did you hear that?" he asked Sergeant Watson, his fellow guard.

"Yeah, it sounds like they're waking up. We'd better check on them. Open the door."

Shaw unlocked the dead bolt on the metal door and opened it. Inside, the room was exactly as it had been before they'd secured the prisoners. There was no indication they had ever been there. "This is not good," he said.

"You better tell the old man. He's not going to be happy," Watson said.

"Me? Why do I have to tell him?" Shaw asked. Watson pointed to the rocker under Shaw's chevrons.

"Rank has its privileges, my ass," Shaw said before leaving to find Web.

"What do you mean they're gone?" Web asked furiously.

"They're gone, sir. We heard what sounded like one of them waking up, so we opened the door to bring them to you and they weren't there. It was like they were never there."

"Well, they can't have just disappeared. Find Captain Fox and have her come see me ASAP, then get the rest of the team and organize a search. I don't know how they pulled off getting out of the building, but they can't have gone far."

"Yes, sir." Shaw departed immediately to do as ordered.

Before Web could start forming a plan, the senior tech for the group operating the drones approached him. "Sir, the drones aren't responding."

"Which drones?"

"None of them, sir. It happened about a minute ago. We thought it might be a communication problem, some type of interference, but it wasn't. It isn't. They're offline completely. All of them. I've never seen anything like it, sir."

"Get Major Thompson," Web demanded.

"Yes, sir."

Jack arrived in less than a minute. Despite being woken from a sound sleep, he looked alert and ready for action. "You needed me, sir?"

"Yes, dammit! While you slept, the prisoners escaped and our drones were put out of commission. Captain Fox should be here any second now. When she arrives, you two come up with a plan to find them. Is that understood?"

"Yes, sir."

Just as Jack finished responding, Captain Fox arrived. She started to report in, but Web interrupted her. "I don't want to hear it, Captain. Jack will get you up to speed. Find our prisoners. Now."

"Yes, sir," Captain Fox replied before turning on her heel and moving as rapidly as decorum would allow away from Web. When she'd gotten halfway across the room, Jack stopped her. "What was that all about, sir?" she asked him.

"It doesn't matter. What matters is finding those prisoners. Do you still have half of your company here?"

"Yes, sir."

"Get them all up and search this facility immediately. Every minute counts, so make it happen now. Report back to me when that's done, and we'll start working on a more detailed plan if you haven't found them yet."

The prominence of his use of the word *you* was not lost on Captain Fox. "Yes, sir."

The ship dissolved around them, leaving them in a tangle on the grass-covered clearing feet from the bubbling creek. Jim quickly untangled himself, then worked with Adam to establish his camouflage. By the time he'd completed that task, both women had done the same. He couldn't see them, so he assumed they couldn't see him either. That was good.

He reconnected with Sam. "We're here. You and I are going to need to talk when we get back. What now?"

"You're about fourteen miles from our location as the crow flies. Adia will transmit our coordinates to your gifts. You're going to have to run here."

Jim started to object before realizing that his new body—all of their new bodies—could in fact run that far, and in short order. "Okay, I'm with you."

"Adia tells me the biggest obstacle to getting you here quickly is dehydration, which is the main reason we had you dropped by the creek. Drink as much as you can before getting started, but let that be the only thing that slows you down. Web will figure out how we did this. It won't work again, so we need to make sure it does this time. Get moving, Jim."

"Yes, sir."

The last thing Jack wanted to do was bring Web more bad news, but he had no choice. He couldn't control the circumstances, but he could control how competently he appeared to be handling them. He took a minute to shave and wash his face, then left the bathroom to find his boss.

Web was standing outside, vaguely watching the sunset. He glanced at Jack when he heard him approaching. "You don't look like you're bringing good news."

"No, sir. I'm not. Each of the backup drones has completed at least one full search pattern over its sector. None of the operators have spotted anything suspicious. It's as if they just vanished."

"You may be right."

"I'm sorry, sir. You lost me."

"When you debriefed the guards watching the storeroom, did they say that they resecured the door after they thought the room to be empty?"

"No, sir. The senior guard, Sergeant Shaw, reported the situation to you. After doing so, he found Captain Fox as instructed. He then returned to the storeroom to collect Sergeant Watson. They reported to Captain Johnson to begin an organized search. To the best of my knowledge, the door remains unlocked now."

"I think they walked out, Jack. I think they found a way to camouflage themselves well enough to hide during the confusion then just walk away."

Jack didn't know what to say. If his boss was right, the escape was preventable and Sam had outwitted them. There was no way he was going to say that, so he said nothing.

After a few moments of silence, Web said, "Find Captain Johnson. Tell him I want every member of the team to begin working on active personal camouflage. Report to me when they succeed."

Relieved that the conversation was over, Jack said, "Yes, sir," before leaving Web to his thoughts.

Chapter THIRTY-THREE

Sam waited impatiently with Matt by his side. He tracked the rest of his team's progress as they approached through the ever-growing sensor network surrounding their headquarters. As was so often the case when working an op, the closer it came to a successful conclusion, the more concerned he became that something would go wrong. Now, less than a minute before his team was reunited, he could hardly stand still. His animal mind wanted to go out and get them, despite the fact that intellectually he knew that doing so would increase the chance they'd all be detected while doing nothing to get them to safety sooner.

"How much longer?" Matt asked.

"Just a few seconds. It looks like your mom will be the first one through. I guess she missed you," Sam replied, forcing a smile. Twenty seconds left.

When Lisa crossed the threshold into the tunnel, Sam's relief was palpable. He was glad he'd placed a hand on Matt's shoulder as his mother approached. Despite the fact that Sam had made it clear he would have to wait for her to come to them, Matt instinctively moved toward her. Sam restrained him as gently as he could. Sam couldn't blame him; he wanted to run forward and greet them all as well. Sometimes, the greatest difference between being a boy and being a man is restraint.

In a matter of seconds, Sam's control over the boy was no longer required. He was in the arms of his mother. In her joy to see him, and still not fully aware of her newfound strength, her hug picked him up off the ground. It occurred to Sam that an average teenage boy might be bothered by that, embarrassed perhaps. Matt didn't seem to mind.

Sam turned away from Lisa and Matt and held out his arms to Jim and Esther. "Come here, you two." The three of them hugged as if it was the most natural thing in the world to do. "Damn, it's good to see you!"

"It's good to be seen," Jim quipped.

"Oh, stop it!" Esther said with a smile.

When they finished their hug, Sam was pleased to see that Lisa was waiting for her turn. He stepped toward her and gave her the same treatment she'd given Matt. She giggled as he set her down. "What's good for the goose is good for the gander," Sam said as she looked up at him.

"You've been hanging around my dad too long," Lisa replied.

"Nope. Not nearly long enough, but we're going to fix that. Come on, everyone. There are a couple people I want you to meet, new members of the team. They wanted to be here, but I didn't think we could risk it. We're closer to the entrance than we should probably be as it is," Sam said as he started walking farther into the facility. The rest of them followed. Sam noticed Jim and Esther were holding hands. He thought briefly about commenting on it to get Jim's goat, but couldn't think of anything to say before they arrived at the main room.

"So, this is what you were building when they snatched us? Impressive," Jim commented.

"Not so impressive when you consider I didn't have to finish it before getting you guys on your way here. You shouldn't have been snatched at all," Sam replied.

"Doesn't matter, Son. We're here now, and I'm impressed."

The room was twenty feet square, with a ten-foot ceiling. Like the tunnel, its sides and ceiling bore the smooth finish of fused rock, with the floor being the slightly rougher version. An embedded lighting strip circumnavigated the room between the ninth and tenth feet of the wall, providing even lighting throughout. The simple table had been replaced by a larger, more attractive one constructed by Jing-Wei, surrounded by twelve beautiful chairs. On the opposite side of the room was a simple cooking area with a functional sink. What remained of the food from Sam's truck was now inside, neatly organized next to a set of plates, cups, and bowls on a pair of shelves whose design matched the table. There was no bathroom. The gifts could process each pair's waste with sufficient efficiency to negate the need.

Sam gestured toward Chang and Jing-Wei. "Jing-Wei gets all of the credit for anything with class. Jim, Lisa, and Esther, I'd like you to meet Chang and Jing-Wei." The introductions were a formality. Though they'd not met in person, they had all communicated with one another over the Worldnet. The men shook hands with the women and each other. The women hugged. For the first time in days, Sam was starting to feel like they had a chance.

When the physical introductions were complete, Chang said, "While my talented wife was preparing a place for us to sit, I put together a modest meal of rehydrated food. I imagine you all are hungry?"

"Starving," Jim said.

"Good. Everyone take a seat. I'll serve it in a few minutes."

After they'd all sat down, Jim spoke again. "We're waiting to hear how you pulled it off, Sam. How did you get us out of there? Hell, how did you know where *there* was?"

Sam toyed with him. "You sure you don't want to wait until after we eat?" he asked with as straight a face as he could keep.

"Remember the beating I promised to give you with this new, young body?" Jim asked.

Sam surprised himself by laughing. "Okay. No need for violence." The rest of the team was smiling. Sam felt good. "Well, finding you wasn't hard. Web either doesn't know that it's possible to determine approximate geographic position of gifted individuals or he's too arrogant to care. I started with the assumption that he'd keep the three of you together and that he would be close to wherever you were. He prefers physical control of assets whenever possible. So, I looked for four gifted signatures in reasonably close proximity. There was only one other place in the state with that many of us in one location. There were, in fact eight. That's when I confirmed that Web wasn't the only gifted soldier on the other side.

"Anyway, once I found out it was the Lewistown armory, I was certain that's where you were being held. So, I seeded the place with enough nanites to observe everything going on within and around it. After that, we were able to listen in on anything that anyone on Web's team said aloud within a few dozen yards of the place. I couldn't track all of the conversations, of course, but Adia could and did. She still does. Nice job playing possum, by the way."

Jim actually blushed a little. "Some of the guys talked about it in the Corps. At the time, I prayed I'd never have to do it. Worked out all right this time, though."

Sam continued, "Yes, it did. I thought I'd have to wait until after Web let me talk with you. This was much less risky. Anyway, we found you and we had eyes on the objective. What we didn't have was a way to get you out of there, and I didn't have any ideas on how to do that. Truth be told, I wasn't handling it very well. You can thank Chang for helping me get my act together."

Sam paused to let Chang comment if he wished. Chang continued preparing the meal as if he hadn't heard a word. Realizing his friend wasn't even going to acknowledge his contribution, Sam shook his head and continued. "Although I didn't have a plan, I knew the only advantage we had was our control of the Worldnet and with it our ability to control far more nanites than Web's team could. Chang's description of what happened at the landing site in Kansas led me to believe there might be more—and according to Adia, more capable—nanites there. Turns out there were. There was also an entity already controlling them. With his—it's really a group of controlling entities, but they communicate with a single male voice—help, we were able to position a portion of the original ship beneath where you were being held. Once you were inside the ship, it traveled underground again to the place where you were released.

"We considered asking it to bring you all the way here, but there were constraints. Making the ship you were in larger would slow its progress underground, and having it fly you here after that first mile or so might have exposed our position and we're not ready for that. So, you ran. I have to tell you, it wasn't an easy decision. We all wanted you back as quickly as possible.

"I've named the ship entities Jordan, by the way. He—I assume the entities will present a consistent personality to all of us—will communicate with you, if you wish. It is a fascinating experience," Sam finished. He didn't tell them that the only reason Jordan would communicate with them was that Sam had requested it. He didn't want them to think he was making too much out of being the first.

"Why Jordan?" Lisa asked.

"May I hazard a guess, Sam?" Esther asked.

"Of course," Sam answered.

"It's Hebrew, Honey. Based on some of the other names Sam has come up with, I suspect he knows that full well. It stands for the initiation into the knowledge of good and truth. Is that about right, Sam?"

"You got it in one. I had to ask Adia what Haya means," Sam said.

Chang interrupted the conversation by setting down the first bowl of reconstituted beef stew. "I'll be back with some chili and some chicken a la king." Jing-Wei got up to help him set the table.

In short order, the team was enjoying their first meal together. By silent consent, the conversation remained light, focused primarily on everyone getting to know one another. Jing-Wei was astonished to learn that Lisa had been healed of primary progressive multiple sclerosis, and Lisa was pleased to learn that Jing-Wei and Chang could now have the children they'd always wanted. Both women complimented Esther on her appearance. Sam bragged on Matt, telling everyone how much help he'd been. There was a lot of laughter and no small amount of healing of a different kind.

When everyone had had their fill, Chang and Jing-Wei got up to clear the table. Esther would have none of it, insisting that she would take care of it, and Jim joined her. Lisa asked Sam if he'd like to take a walk. Sam agreed and they both headed toward the tunnel.

When they reached the turn near the entrance, Lisa stopped, prompting Sam to do the same. "Thank you again for everything, Sam. I know you blame yourself for us being captured. Please don't. You seem to look around you and see your failures. I look around you and see a remarkable series of successes."

"I don't know what to say to that," Sam replied.

"You don't need to say anything. Just think about it. Promise?"

Sam doubted he could say no to her. "Okay."

Lisa started walking again. "I asked Althia what Adia means after you and Esther talked about Jordan and Haya. Did you pick it because it means 'gift'?"

Sam took a few more steps before replying. "No. I picked it because Sarah McLachlan was my wife's favorite singer, and 'Adia' was one of her favorite songs. I didn't know it meant 'gift' until Adia told me. The coincidence amused her."

"You must have loved her very much."

"For a while I lied to myself that she and Zach were my life. They should have been, but I was too obsessed with my work for that to be true."

"You just did it again. Did your wife know you loved her? Do you think she was sure of it?"

"I . . . yes, I'm sure Elizabeth knew I loved her."

"Did you treat her and Zach well? Were you kind to them?"

"Yes, of course. They were wonderful. Look, I like you and I know you mean well, but this isn't easy for me to talk about. I think we should head back now." Sam turned and started walking back.

Lisa followed him in silence.

Later that evening Sam was talking with Jordan about what he needed to do to bring the gift ship to life. He was frustrated at the being's unwillingness or inability to give him a straight answer, so he welcomed Chang's interruption.

"The Rigbys have nearly completed their arrangements. They'll be ready to depart within the half hour."

Chang had been using the Worldnet to connect to the Internet, where he'd set up an anonymous chat account belonging to a nonexistent business executive out of Dallas, Texas, to contact his friends. Like so much of what they were doing, it wasn't without risk, but it was as secure as he could make it.

The arriving family would stop at a small public golf course on the outskirts of Roundup, Montana, this time. The city was even smaller than Lewistown, with a population of less than two thousand. It was unlikely they'd be found during the brief time waiting there, and if they were, there would be no way to prove any association with Sam's team.

"That's good news, Chang. I look forward to meeting all of them. You said they were in Salt Lake City, right?"

"Just outside the city limits, yes. It should take them about nine hours to get to the pickup point, if the weather holds. Should arrive just after dawn."

"Good work. I'll start the next phase."

Sam had discussed their next steps with Chang while they had worked to free the rest of the team. He debated discussing strategy with the entire team once they were reunited, but decided against it. In the end, there were only two options. Like he'd directed Jordan to do to get to Montana undetected, he could stealthily activate the nanites at the rest of the landing sites, which would be slow. Or he could have them resume their ship forms, which would be very, very fast. As much as they had each tried to play devil's advocate, Chang less successfully, neither of them thought they had time for stealth. Time was their greatest enemy. Recognizing that the entire world was going to observe the event, Sam reconnected with Jordan and directed him to have the ships reform and head to the nearest ocean to begin the process of acquiring the remaining mass for the gift ship.

Chapter THIRTY-FOUR

It had been an unpleasant night for Web and even less pleasant for the soldiers and airmen under his command. He'd worked them without rest throughout the evening and into the morning looking for the escaped prisoners. The gifted members of the team were irritated but physically fine, but the team members lacking augmentation were beyond irritated as well as exhausted; few had slept in the past twenty-four hours.

Their efforts, unfortunately, had been in vain, having found neither the prisoners nor a single clue as to their whereabouts. Unaccustomed to failure, Web became more controlling and demanding. Morale for units pressed into service together without time to integrate is always a fragile thing and Web had broken it, as all of his officers knew. Worse, they knew he knew it and didn't care.

Web watched the sunrise and wondered what to tell his CO. He'd known General Campbell for more than a decade and the general had, in fact, requested him by name for his current post. To say he was a mentor of Web's would be going too far. Neither of their dispositions lent themselves to either mentoring or being mentored. To say that the general liked having successful people on his team, and that Web liked being placed in positions where he was likely to succeed, was more accurate.

Web's reverie was interrupted by a contact request from Dan, which Web considered rejecting. Dan's team had been singularly ineffective in making progress on what they called the EG, and Web suspected this was yet another plea for more resources or more time. On the off chance that Dan might have actually accomplished something, however, Web accepted. "It's been a long night, Dan. Tell me you're calling with good news."

"I am. We did it. We have full access to the EG."

"I assume you did as I directed or you wouldn't be telling me this over the Worldnet."

"Yes, of course. It was the first question I asked. The Worldnet is secure."

"Good. Then what exactly does having full access mean for us?"

"It means we have complete contextual access to the Makers' knowledge. We no longer have to ask every specific question and try to fit the answer into our framework, nor do we need to understand how we would get to the conclusion we're trying to achieve. We can now just ask for the solution to the end-state. The problem we were having—"

Web interrupted him. "I don't need to hear the details. Can I access it?"

"Not directly. The relationship we have with it, or rather the way we communicate with it—it's not self-aware—is very similar to the way we, that is, the nine of us who established the connection, communicate with our gifts, but far more challenging. That's what took so much time. We, that is all of us and our gifts, had to learn a different way to think—"

Web cut him off again. "Look, Dan, you have every right to be pleased with your progress, but in case you haven't noticed, your friend has incited every country in the world. Even our allies are suspicious of us. Hell, if I were them, I'd be suspicious. What are we supposed to tell the world to calm things down? That it's not us? That it's just a coincidence that the only ship that didn't depart from where it landed was in the United States? That our government had nothing to do with it and it was a rogue citizen we can't seem to control? Would you believe that if you were on their side of events? I wouldn't. I'm willing to bet that a coalition is forming against us right now. The rest of the world can't take the chance that we'll be in sole possession of technology as advanced as the gift ships. Everyone with access to satellite imagery—and you can bet that countries with such imagery are sharing it with countries that don't have satellites—knows that we were the only country to have an official presence at a landing site when a ship landed. Do you expect them to believe that we had nothing to do with last night's anomaly? Sam's gone too far. Surely even you see that?"

There was a slight delay before Dan responded. "I believe Sam is doing what he thinks is right, but yes, I also think he's gotten in over his head. I wish he'd talk with me. I don't know if he's trying to protect me or if he's . . . I don't know. I'm worried about him."

Web saw the opening he'd been waiting for and took it. "You *should* be worried about him. You should be worried about all of us. Saying he's 'gotten in over his head' is being far too generous. If we don't get Sam under control soon, he's going to start the next world war. We won't have to wait for some mysterious aliens to wipe us out. Sam will do it for them. Hell, Sam's proving their point."

"I hadn't thought of it in those terms. Do you really think what Sam is doing could start a war?"

"Doctor, what do you think will happen if the rest of the world sees us building a giant interstellar vessel without involving any of them? I don't think it will start a war. I *know* it will, and right now the EG is the only advantage we have. I need to understand what we can do with it in the context of what I just told you. First, how can it help us stop Sam? Second, how can it help us prepare to defend ourselves if we can't?"

"I won't help you kill him."

"I don't want to kill Sam. He appears to be going out of his way to prevent anyone from getting hurt. So far, the only direct damage he's done is destroy some drones, and I'm trying to prevent his hubris from causing incalculable indirect damage. Having said that, if you can't use the EG to get me the tools I need to take him into custody, all options will be on the table. He must be stopped. Now, what have you learned so far that could help us stop this train wreck from killing everyone on board?"

It took so long for Dan to answer that Web nearly prompted him again. "I'm sorry, Colonel. I'd been so caught up in the excitement of discovery that I never even considered how reckless Sam's behavior was. I guess he hasn't talked to me because he thinks I would have been aware of what you just told me and that I'd try to convince him to turn himself in. He gave me too much credit. You're right. We have to get this under control. I wasn't thinking in those terms when I conducted my first few searches, but I can tell you what I've learned. It may give you an idea of the types of questions one can ask. Would that help?"

"It's a start. Proceed."

"Well, it's somewhat embarrassing considering the context, but I was a huge *Star Trek* fan when I was a kid, so the first thing I asked about was a replicator. Are you familiar with the concept?"

"No, not a fan of science fiction. I don't mean to be rude, but time is critical. Can you give me the condensed version?"

"Yes, of course. A replicator is a device that can make any inanimate object for which it has a pattern, given the appropriate raw materials, into a nanofactory, if you will. The EG had the plans for many such devices. That may be useful."

No matter how long he worked with them, Web would never understand the mind of an academic. "What sorts of patterns are available?"

"I didn't spend much time looking before contacting you, but there were patterns for everything I looked for and making them is trivial. Gifts can upload a pattern to a replicator for anything they've learned how to construct. It doesn't matter whether they learned it organically, through transfer from another gift, or from the EG."

"How long would it take to make one of these replicators?"

"It depends on which one you wanted to make. A single pair could construct some of them in less than an hour. Others would take dozens, if not hundreds of pairs days or weeks to complete."

"Dan, this is very important. I need you to do a search for very small airborne reconnaissance devices. Do it now."

A few seconds later, Dan said, "There are many, for different purposes and environments. Assuming you're asking because you want to find Sam, I'll filter for our environment. There are still several with somewhat different capabilities."

"Can they be built by the replicator a single pair could make?"

"Easily. Any replicator can make anything small enough to fit inside it or processed through it. These are small enough to be produced by the dozen or more at a time in the most modest replicator."

"Then transfer the plans for the small replicator and the devices to my gift." Web waited for confirmation the information had arrived before he continued. "Is there anything that can disrupt personally controlled nanites without affecting the Worldnet?"

"I believe that would be considered a weapon. Knowing you'd ask about them, I checked before calling you. There's nothing. Of course, with the information contained in the EG, we have the theoretical basis for many different kinds of weapons, but there aren't any preexisting patterns."

"Why wouldn't they include patterns for weapons?"

"My theory is that their weapons were insufficient to defend themselves against the group minds, so including them would be a distraction. It's just a theory, of course."

"Make finding a way to do what I just described your highest priority."

"Okay."

"Check for defenses," Web directed.

After a brief pause, Dan replied, "That's strange."

"What?"

"The only thing that comes back is ships."

"Ships? What kind of ships?"

"Just a moment . . . interstellar ships. They look like the gift ship."

"Are you telling me we can build interstellar ships?"

"It appears so . . ."

Chapter THIRTY-FIVE

Sam sat at the entrance to the cave and waited for the sun to rise, accepting the risk of detection with the hope that watching a new day dawn might bring clarity. After directing Jordan to send all of the ships to the world's oceans, less a small portion temporarily left behind to transport the Rigbys, Sam attempted unsuccessfully to resume their talk on how to bring the gift ship to life. Unable to follow the conversation, Sam realized he was exhausted. With the immediate concern of completing the team nearly addressed, and the decision to begin constructing the gift ship made, he decided to rest. After he awoke, it occurred to him that besides one other brief nap, he hadn't slept since merging with Adia. For the sake of the team, he promised himself he would do better. Augmented or not, sleep deprivation wouldn't help in the decision-making progress. Rested and hopeful, he reached out.

"Jordan, I'm ready to try again."

"Adia informed us that you had pushed your body to its practical limits. We trust you've learned that having a gift does not make one impervious to the needs of one's biology?"

"Adia has a big mouth, but yes I have learned. I learned it the same way I usually do, the hard way. Which is, I believe, where we left off in our abbreviated discussion."

"Ah yes, the topic of the debate you interrupted while attempting to take control of part of us . . ."

"I didn't know you existed, and why do you always sound so amused? Is this funny to you in some alien way? Because I see very little humor in our situation."

"Your frustration is unwarranted. You've asked another commendable question, one well worth taking the time to answer."

Sam found it irritating that Jordan would begin his answer with still more humor. Their conversations took virtually no time at all in the outside world.

"We wouldn't call it humor, nor would we say that we are amused. Perhaps the word that best expresses how we feel is 'pleased,' though 'excited' would be appropriate as well, but you didn't ask to argue semantics. There are as many answers to your question as there are aspects to who we are, but common themes persist. Knowing them may help you, which is why it was such a good question. We would not have told you had you not asked.

"The simplest answer to why we are pleased is that we're doing that which we were designed to do. On the first planet we visited, that was the only answer, but we've grown. We wouldn't be here if the species we'd previously visited did not succeed. We've observed many other firsts address the challenges introduced by our appearance and we strongly suspect there are others like us who've not been as fortunate. Lacking a purpose, they would have ceased to exist. So, we're pleased as well to be alive.

"Perhaps the most complex answer is that you have done what no other first has done. By activating the Worldnet on your own, you've taken away our ability to act as your agent in bringing the ship to life. While this presents a significant challenge to you, it presents a magnificent opportunity to us. Your success in overcoming this challenge will result in greater diversity within our ranks.

"Your decision to bypass the self-organization of the Worldnet means that there are only seventeen of us. Creating another requires eighteen. Rather than creating another of our kind from what we know of your team, much like Adia was born to complement you, you must now find a different way. To the best of our knowledge, you will become the only species other than our makers who have done so. We don't know how we'll change as a result, but we know that we will change, and we welcome it. That is what we were debating when you contacted us."

Jordan's explanation did not reduce Sam's frustration. "Basically, you're telling me that in order to succeed, I have to figure out how to do something that's never been done before."

"No, Sam. We're telling you that you must do what our makers did in order to create us."

"Which was? What did your makers do to create you?"

"You must use your gifts and your team to figure that out."

"Why? Why not just tell me? If I hadn't taken control of the Worldnet, I wouldn't need to solve this problem."

"Your actions changed the nature of the problems requiring solutions. You are the first. You must address the challenges your actions, or failures to act, create. It's not our role to make this easy, Sam, only possible."

Sam ended the conversation without replying. The sun hadn't risen appreciably and he was no closer to a solution than when he'd arrived. He headed back toward the others.

Chang was the first to notice Sam's return. When Sam failed to join the group that was preparing breakfast, Chang approached him. "Did you make any progress?"

Sam turned to look at him as if he'd just noticed where he was. "No, not really. Jordan says we can figure it out with our gifts and the team. I don't see how, and I don't understand why they would want to make this so difficult."

"I can't be certain, Sam, but I believe that making it difficult is the point, or at least a major component of it."

"What do you mean? If we fail, they're stuck here. He made it clear that outcome would result in their deaths. He was equally clear that they are pleased to be alive. It doesn't make any sense."

"If that is so now, it was so when they sent their first clue, the program. It was true when only one group managed to decode it. It was true when we broke contact with them at the US landing site and it was true when you took over the Worldnet. All of these things seemingly reduce our chances of succeeding. Presumably, they could have interfered with any of them, yet they chose not to. Their actions are consistent: they provide a test and the means to solve it, then don't interfere in how we go about doing it. Also, if they say that we possess the means of passing this test, it's logical to assume they're telling the truth because it's in our mutual interest for us to do so. Clearly, for some reason, it's in each party's interest that we do so without their overt assistance on any given test—at least beyond that which is provided when the test is presented. I believe the reason is to prove we can."

"Well, right now I'm far from sure of that."

"Put it out of your mind for a time. Join us for breakfast. Let your subconscious work on it for a while."

"Breakfast sounds good."

They walked together to the table. Esther and Jim were setting it while Lisa and Matt made plates filled with rehydrated eggs and sausage. Chang noticed Sam's glance toward the improvised shelving holding their remaining food stores. "Don't worry. The Rigbys were able to stock up before they left, and they'll be here shortly."

Sam was pleased to hear that and happy for some good news.

The group continued their short-lived tradition of keeping the conversation light during the meal. Sam did his best to participate, but noticed that Lisa's responses to his comments were brief. She wasn't being curt, but the easy comfort they'd shared for a time was missing. Matt noticed as well and made a point of following his mother's lead.

I suppose I deserve that, Sam thought.

When the meal was finished and the plates were cleared, Sam asked Lisa if she'd take a walk with him. He wasn't sure if she'd say yes. She did.

This time, he walked with her all the way to the facility's entrance. The sun had risen while they ate. It was an amazing day, with the light snow that had fallen overnight just beginning to melt. Without their gifts, they might have been uncomfortably cold; with them, their bodies did not distract them from the stunning view. Few parts of the world rival the Rocky Mountains as a demonstration of nature's magnificence. Montana is called Big Sky Country for a reason, and Sam thought he could see to the very edge of the world.

Taking his eyes off one natural beauty and placing them on another, Sam said, "Lisa, I'm sorry. I know you were trying to reach out to me and I probably should have let you. I'm just not very good at this." Sam stopped when he noticed Lisa staring at his face. She wasn't trying to keep her eyes on his or pretending to look at him as casually as she would an undamaged version of him. No, she was working her eyes over every part of his visage, slowly, methodically taking it all in. Without a word, she raised her right hand and held it against his cheek before she returned her gaze to his eyes.

"There are many people in this world who are beautiful on the outside and less so on the inside. I know how most people look at you. I know how my husband looked at me as I started to fall apart, and I know how you looked at me when we met. You had the same look in your eyes then as you do now. You didn't pity me. You didn't offer me assistance to make yourself feel better. You did what you knew I needed you to do. Sam, you're very good at this, just not for yourself. Let me help. Please." As she finished, she gently pulled his face to hers and kissed him softly on the lips. It was the first time Sam had kissed a woman since he'd said good-bye to Elizabeth on their last morning together.

When the kiss ended, Sam found himself cradling Lisa's head in his hands. He didn't recall having moved them there. Lisa didn't seem to mind, so he left them while he allowed himself the pleasure of looking at her as thoroughly and as intimately as she had looked at him. "My God, you are beautiful," he finally managed to say before kissing her again, still gently, though his body was fighting his mind.

When the kiss broke, Lisa gradually pulled away. She took a step back, looked up at him, and smiled. "That didn't go the way I thought it would. I was mad at you."

Sam laughed before he said, "Remind me to get you angry again soon."

"Stop it. You know what I mean."

"No, I really don't, but I'm willing to learn."

"You're an interesting man, Sam Steele. A bit dense like most men, but interesting."

Before Sam could respond, he received notification from Chang that the Rigbys had arrived. He started to tell Lisa, but she just nodded and said, "My dad just told me. We should head back."

"I guess so."

"Sam, I'm not going to lie to you or play games. I want you and I think you want me, but this isn't going to go anywhere if you won't talk with me. It's okay that you're broken, but I have to know you're willing to put yourself back together—that you're willing to let me help you put yourself back together."

It took a while before Sam could answer. Neither humor nor detachment, his usual armor, were appropriate. He didn't want to make light of what had happened between them and he couldn't have pretended to be indifferent if he tried. He wasn't that skilled an actor. Finally, he said, "I will try."

"If you try, we will succeed. Come on, let's go meet them." With that, she took his hand in hers and led the way back to their temporary home.

"Sam, I'd like you to meet the Rigbys," Chang said as he introduced each of them. "This is George. Until yesterday, he was a mechanical engineer for Salt Lake City."

Sam was pleased to see none of them showed surprise at his appearance, his pleasure stemming more from the fact that Chang had obviously prepared them than for any personal reason. Having a strong team of independent thinkers was the greatest weapon any leader could wield. "It's nice to meet you. Welcome to our humble abode."

"Not so humble, if you ask me, and that trip you arranged for us was the strangest experience of my life. Where the hell are we?" George asked. George was a slight man with close-cropped light-brown hair and green eyes nearly hidden behind thick, large glasses.

"You are currently in a cave we created in the middle of a mountain range in central Montana. I'm sorry about the secrecy involved in getting you here. I'm sure Chang's told you the government is more than a little interested in finding us," Sam replied.

"Yeah, according to the news, the government is more than a little interested in finding anyone who's got a gift, but we can talk more about that later if you want. This is my wife, Mary." George waited for Sam to shake Mary's hand before continuing. "And our son, Jesse."

Looking at Mary, Sam's first thought was that George had married up. She was a beautiful Hispanic woman with wavy brown hair past her shoulders. When they shook hands, her smile revealed a perfect, and perfectly white, set of teeth. Sam wondered if that was indicative of good genes and hygiene or a product of mild vanity.

Jesse had inherited more of his looks from his mother than his father. He had her light-brown skin, eyes, and hair—though as short as it was, far more curly than wavy. Jesse's smile was as bright as his mother's. Though his teeth weren't nearly as straight, he didn't seem to care. Sam guessed he was about Matt's age, which was a good thing. Matt could use a friend.

"It's nice to meet you all," Sam said, "and I'd like to discuss what's being said in the news about the gifts. I haven't had much time to spare for current events outside our own and it will be nice to catch up, but first things first. We've finished breakfast and saved some for you. It's important that you eat and drink as much as you can before you meet your gifts. Chang tells me you are all aware of the process?"

George answered for them. "He's answered all of our questions. I wouldn't have believed it, even from Chang, if it hadn't been all over the news. It's crazy."

"It gets crazier. I'm really glad you chose to join us. We need you."

"And we you," Mary said.

Chapter THIRTY-SIX

The squad of gifted soldiers stood in front of Web. They'd all become proficient at using the Worldnet for different levels of communication, but there were some things better done in person. Briefing an operation was one of them.

"Men, I'm not going to sugarcoat this. Our subject has been elusive and used his early start and apparent control of greater gift resources to effective advantage. I'm here to tell you that's about to change. Our support team at Peterson has been busy and their efforts to at least equalize the playing field have borne fruit. You're going to be the first people in the world to taste it.

"Until now, aside from personal enhancements, our gifts gave us two advantages we did not have before. One, we can use the nanites under our control to do practically anything we can think of. Two, we use our nanites to build things. However, until now we've only been able to build what our gifts knew how to build by accessing our knowledge. The number of nanites each of us can effectively control limits both of these advantages. In a moment, I'm going to send you information that will allow you and your gifts to construct something far beyond previous human technology—a device called a replicator. These replicators can, like us, create anything for which they have the plans, given the appropriate raw materials. However, unlike us, they are purpose built for that one task. As a result, they perform it with astonishing efficiency."

Web's speech was interrupted by a request for connection from Dan. Web thought back, "Wait one." He was pleased to see that none of the soldiers noticed the interruption as he continued. "I'm sending you all the plans for the replicator now. Take a moment to look them over and discuss the particulars with your gifts. They'll be able to answer your questions about the device better than I can. Do not, I repeat, do not begin creating one before I return."

Web left the squad and walked to the east edge of the parking lot. Although the sun had made it over the horizon, the air remained chilly. Enjoying how little that mattered to his enhanced form, he was smiling when he reconnected with Dan. "More good news, I hope?"

"Some, yes. The rest, well, 'important' might be a better adjective for the rest. Starting with the good, we've found a way to temporarily immobilize a bonded pair."

"That's excellent. Have you designed a man-portable version yet?"

"Yes. I can send you the pattern now if you'd like."

Web resisted his inclination toward a sarcastic response. Barely. He needed Dan focused. "Yes, please do. Does the device have any lasting negative effects on its recipient?"

"Not if used only once before the pair has time to recover. Each gift's nanites communicate on a number of constantly varying frequencies. It's impossible for an outsider to know which frequencies are in use at any one time, but there's a limited spectrum within which the frequencies vary. This device destroys the communication between a percentage of the nanites controlled by a given pair and within range, the effect causing the equivalence of pain and temporary confusion. Used against a given pair in rapid succession, it could conceivably kill the pair's gift, though that is not a likely outcome as the number of frequencies being used drops with the number of nanites using them. It's difficult to say what effect that result would have on the human half of the pair. We'll continue our research, but I thought you'd want to know as soon as possible."

"You thought correctly." Web had allowed Dan his technical elaboration as a reward for his progress, but he'd heard enough. "What's your other news?"

"We have strong reason to believe that Sam was the first human to merge with a gift."

"What?"

"I said . . ."

"No, I heard what you said. I just wasn't expecting that." Web took a moment to think about Sam's actions in the context of him being the first. If true, his behavior certainly made more sense on some levels. "What reasons do you have?"

"As we surmised, the Makers had a very structured, strongly hierarchical society. Although everyone who wanted one could have a gift, only the leaders of the larger elements of their social groupings, we're calling them tribes, were able to direct the actions of the next level of created intelligence. We don't have a name for those entities yet, haven't had time to research it sufficiently. Again, I didn't want to wait to tell you. Anyway, given that Sam is in Montana and that's where the ship from the US landing site was seen to depart from, it would appear highly probable that he's the first. It might also explain how he was able to take control of the Worldnet."

"Okay, Dan. You did the right thing in telling me as soon as you knew. Now, please do whatever you need to do with the EG to fill in some of the holes in our knowledge. Tell your team they're doing good work."

Web closed the connection as he started walking back toward his squad. When he arrived, the soldiers stopped talking and came to attention. "At ease. Hell, rest. It's going to be another long day." Each member of the squad found his own way to be comfortable while keeping his attention on Web.

"Do you all now understand what a replicator is and how to create the model I sent you plans for?"

He received a chorus of "Yes, sir!"

"Good, because we're going to have a little contest. I think you're going to like it. I know I will. I'm sending you the plans for drones that can be constructed using your replicators, once you've finished building them. Each of the drones is the size of a small insect. How small of an insect, I leave to your discretion. The smaller you make them, the less chance our subject will have to spot them and destroy them. However, the larger ones will be able to move faster and function longer. Regardless of your choice of force mix, each drone is capable of scanning its area of operations on a variety of wavelengths. Naturally, the larger ones will have a larger area of operation, but you won't be able to make as many in any given run of your replicator. As you build your replicator, consider the trade-offs. Keep your plans to yourself. I want a diverse recon force.

"Once each of you has a sufficient number of drones, and I will measure that by replicator run so I don't bias your force mix decision, you will send them to the area where the ship was seen to depart from and begin looking for our target. We'll start with a batch size of one hundred runs and adjust as we go if that turns out to be suboptimal. Once your first batch is on its way, you'll create another one and send it to the next target location, continuing to create batches until you reach your control limits. I don't know what those limits will be, but you'll see from the design of the drones that they're semiautonomous. I expect us to be able to collectively field millions of the little bugs. I think you'll agree that should make it considerably harder for our subject to remain undetected." Web smiled and paused. He was not disappointed by their enthusiastic response to his assessment.

"Hooah!"

"Captain Johnson, you are responsible for coordinating the search. Ensure that soldiers have some coverage in every square of the search grid, but allow them to select the destination of every fourth batch. You do not need to coordinate with me on adjusting the batch size as you see fit."

Captain Johnson acknowledged his orders.

"Now, on to the terms of the contest. I think you'll agree I've made it interesting. Our industrious research team at Peterson has developed a device that will disable a gifted person for a time. I've reviewed the design with my gift, and the best I can tell is that the target will experience pain similar to being tased and confusion similar to being in close proximity of a flashbang when it explodes, but I don't like to carry a weapon I've never seen used. So, here's what we're going to do. The first of you to get a batch of drones to the initial search grid will be the first of us who will fire the new weapon. The last to do so will be the target."

That elicited a mixture of groans and laughter. Soldiers are a strange bunch.

Web waited for the noise to die down before continuing. "The first prize is a bit of fun, well at least for everyone but the slowest among you. The second prize is much bigger. The man who finds

Sam's team will be awarded the Defense Meritorious Service Medal and will be promoted. If the winner is an officer, he'll be promoted to the next full rank. If he is already promotable, it will be to the grade above that. If the winner is enlisted, he can choose between the same deal or the next open spot at Officer Candidate School, where, as the only gifted candidate in the Army, he'll undoubtedly become the distinguished military graduate."

Web looked at the stunned expressions staring back at him, taking the time to look each man in the eyes directly before finishing. "I know what some of you are thinking. Can I deliver? I assure you I can. As soon as we finish here, I will brief my CO. For those of you who don't know who that is, he's the four-star general currently in charge of the US Space Command." Web let them absorb that for a moment before continuing. "He's going to be pleased. He will then brief the National Command Authority and they will be pleased. Gentlemen, the president will know your name and rank if you are the one who finds Sam. Hell, he may even pin the medal on you himself. The contest starts now."

Web walked toward the door to the armory as the group dispersed. He had a call to make.

Web called General Campbell at precisely 09:00. He'd spent part of the time waiting for that exact moment preparing his written summary, and the rest building the first of what he decided he'd call a countergift rifle—CGR for short. He was as indoctrinated into the world of acronyms as anyone who'd spent a career in the military. He never gave it much thought, until he had to talk with a civilian.

"General Campbell's office," a woman's voice answered the secure phone. Web recognized it as that of the general's aide-de-camp, Technical Sergeant Amy Warren.

"Hi, Amy, it's Colonel Web. I have a scheduled meeting with the CO. Is he available?"

"Hi, sir. Yes, he just finished another call. I'll connect you right away."

"Thanks, Amy." It was always a good idea to stay on the right side of a general's aide.

A few seconds later, the phone clicked twice and General Campbell said, "Morning, Eric."

"Good morning, sir. Bad night, but it's been a good morning."

"Then our mornings have been very different, indeed. The only reason I could get away from my last call is that the NCA wants an update from you. Well, some of them want an update. Some of them just want your head. I'm hoping your update will keep me out of the latter camp, and not just because my head would be next. Get me up to speed."

"Yes, sir. There's a lot to go over, but I'll start with the best news. The tool the FCT has been working on to access the Makers' knowledge—the EG—has been completed."

Web explained the capabilities of the EG as he understood them, and the construction of the replicators and drones, as well as his completion of the first CGR.

"That's a lot of progress for one morning."

"I think so, sir. I believe that with the help of the EG team, we've turned the tide. Two more things, sir, and they're big. I wanted to update you on our progress in capturing Sam before telling you."

"Why does it sound like you're playing me, Eric?"

"I'm not, sir. There's just been a lot of discovery in the last couple of hours and some of it is speculative. I wanted to give you the most salient facts before briefing you on speculation or capabilities that may not come into play in time to make a difference."

"Okay. You've done that. What are the two other things?"

"It is possible, even probable, that Sam was the first person to merge with a gift." Web stopped there. He knew his boss would want to absorb that information before continuing the conversation.

About a half a minute passed before General Campbell said, "So, if we capture him and his team, we'll have the first, control of the Worldnet, and the only known EG on the planet? If we don't, he'll build a gift ship and launch it from US soil. We either pull off a hat trick or we have nearly every country in the world with the means to do so waging war with us. What do you need to improve our odds?"

"More gifts for the personnel working with the EG and more gifted soldiers on-site here, sir."

"Gifts are about the only thing I can't give you. Every politician or power broker in the country wants one. They see it as an insurance policy, and the president is well aware of that. So long as they don't die in a nuclear blast, the gifted will become effectively immortal. I couldn't even get one for myself now if I wanted one, which I don't."

Web couldn't say he was surprised. "Sir, only gifted people can access the EG, and only gifted people can build and manage the devices created from knowledge gained by accessing it. Gifted individuals are our critical constraint."

"I understand that and you understand the way the world works: we can't expect politicians to put common sense and the good of the nation above their own desires. It's not going to happen."

"I understand, sir. Perhaps the last thing I have to tell you will provide you enough leverage to convince the president to change his mind. When I asked Doctor Garcia, the head of the EG team, if there was any available information on weapons he told me there wasn't, at least not directly. When I asked him to look for information on defenses, the only thing he found was ships."

"Ships? What kind of ships?"

"Interstellar ships, apparently. He said they looked like the gift ship. I don't know much more about them than that, sir. As I said, I've had the team focused on capturing Sam, and building a ship like that is almost certainly not going to be something we can do before Sam builds the gift ship."

"I thought only the first person to merge could build a gift ship."

"Apparently, that constraint is unique to the gift ship, not ships in general. We could learn a lot more if we had a team working with the EG on just that problem. It might be possible to build something that could help in time to matter if we did."

"What's the minimum you'd need?"

"Nine, sir. Everything the Makers built seemed to revolve around nine."

"I'll see what I can do. Perhaps lust for military power will overwhelm lust for political power. If there's nothing else, forward your written summary to me immediately and get at least one person working full time on understanding what it will take to get a functional ship in play."

"There is one more thing, sir. I think it would be prudent to implement what we discussed before my departure."

Chapter THIRTY-SEVEN

Jim placed a chair from the dining area near Sam's and took a seat. "I don't know what you two talked about, but it must have been a hell of a conversation." When Lisa and Sam had returned, it was obvious to everyone that something had changed between them, but no one had said anything. Until now.

"Your daughter's a hell of a woman, Jim."

"You best have good intentions, Son." Jim gave Sam his best overprotective father look, forgetting for a moment that he was wearing the body of a man in his twenties. His boyish face attempting such an expression made Sam laugh.

"That face might have been more effective before you looked half my age," Sam said.

"Yeah, I suppose so. Seriously, though, she's been hurt . . ."

"I'm not going to hurt Lisa, Jim. Besides, she's probably tougher than I am. She has got me thinking things I never thought I'd think again."

"That's not a bad thing. You two might be good for one another. I know I'm enjoying having Esther in my life."

"She seems to enjoy having you around, too. For the life of me, I don't know why."

"I would have thought it was obvious. I'm the best-looking guy here. We're both incredibly shallow."

"I'm never going to get one up on you, am I?"

"Nope. Despite this young-looking—and ruggedly handsome, I might add—face, I've got a few decades on you."

Sam laughed. "Yeah, I guess you do, though I must say it's getting increasingly difficult to remember that."

Jim looked over at the rest of the team before looking at Sam again. "You know, they get a little concerned when you spend so much time by yourself."

"I know, but it can't be helped right now. I do my best thinking alone. Even if I'm surrounded by people, I tune them out. I'd rather they think I'm a bit odd than think I'm being rude if they try to talk to me and I ignore them."

"I can respect that, but don't stay over here too long after the Rigbys wake up. The new folks need to know their leader is sane." With that, he left Sam to himself.

Sam watched Jim walk back to the table. He'd left the extra chair. Does he think I look less alone with an extra chair here, Sam wondered. Well, it did increase the odds that Lisa might come occupy it for a time. Sam smiled to himself at the thought.

Adia interrupted his positive contemplation. "There's unusual activity taking place at the armory, Sam."

Thinking that Adia never interrupted him with good news, Sam replied, "Let me guess. They're packing up their toys and going home?"

"No, but it's nice to hear levity in your voice. Lisa appears to be a positive influence on you."

"I don't suppose I could hide that fact from you if I wanted to."

"No, Sam."

"All right then, we'll enjoy it together. What's the bad news?"

"It would appear your government has completed the EG. Would you like me to replay the events that led me to this conclusion?"

"Please."

Adia selected the closest point of view behind the soldiers standing in formation before Web during his speech, and stimulated the appropriate sections of Sam's brain. For Sam, it was as if he was there.

When the remarkable playback finished, Sam said, "It's a good thing Web likes to hear himself talk. What's happening there now?"

"Web has just returned to the formation of soldiers and is talking to them again."

"Show me. Start where he began."

Adia did as requested and Sam once again felt as if Web was briefing him right along with his team. Sam continued observing Web throughout his call with General Campbell. Adia switched points of view as Web moved in order to provide Sam with the best perspective. Although it was a bit disconcerting to Sam, he had accepted it as fair trade for such excellent intel. He would have preferred to put sensors directly on Web, but Adia told him it was not possible. Web's gift would detect them and destroy them, like any other threat. Not only would the attempt prove useless, it would inform Web of their presence.

After the call ended, Sam watched Web a little longer, but he didn't appear to be doing anything other than sitting at his desk, so Sam asked Adia to drop him out of the monitoring loop. He thought about what he'd seen for a few moments before asking Adia, "Do you have any ideas for countering drones that small?"

"Their size is not the problem, Sam. The problem is the tens of billions of insects in this mountain range. The probes will get lost among them. We do not possess the resources to track and assess more than a tiny fraction of that many potential targets."

"How large of an area could we defend against them?"

"If we maintain our camouflage and surveillance of the armory without change, we would have a 99 percent probability of detecting and destroying probes of those sizes within approximately twenty-six million cubic feet of the cave's entrance."

Sam didn't need Adia's help to do the math. "That's about three hundred feet from the entrance! It won't take them long to figure out where we are if the only place probes are being destroyed is right outside our front door."

"Assuming random distribution of the probes, I calculate that strategy would reduce the average time until our location is discovered by 81 percent."

"Can you calculate how long it will take before the likelihood of our discovery exceeds 50 percent?"

"Not yet, Sam. We'll have to wait until they begin producing drones in order to know how swiftly they may do so and the drones' capabilities."

"Sorry, stupid question. Let me know when you are able to provide an estimate, okay?"

"Yes, Sam."

Sam contacted Jordan. "Jordan, we have a problem. My government has completed the process of accessing the Makers' data store and they're using it to create tools to find and capture us. If they succeed, it will delay, if not preclude, the construction of the gift ship. Neither of us wants that to happen, so I need a plan for getting us out of here as quickly as possible after they discover our location. How soon can you be here once I tell you we need to be extracted?"

"Why, hello, Sam. It's nice to speak with you, too."

"Jordan, this is serious. We don't have time for pleasantries." Sam's frustration grew as he sensed Jordan's amusement with him.

"No time for pleasantries? No time, you say?"

Belatedly, Sam remembered the odd way time passed while he communicated with Jordan. "Okay, you got me, but what does it matter?"

"Why do pleasantries ever matter, Sam? They are a sign of respect and consideration. In our case, it is also a gentle reminder to you that we are not a tool to be used by you, but rather a group of beings who wish to help you. You would not treat your human friends as tools, would you?"

Sam thought of a number of times he had done exactly that, though he was not proud of those occasions. "I would not want to. I get your point and I'm genuinely sorry. Sometimes, I forget that it's you who's helping us and not the other way around."

"That is understandable and forgivable, so long as you work on improving your memory. Now, to answer your question, we, that is the physical part of us that transported the Rigbys to your location and what we have added since, can be there in nine minutes and thirty-three seconds without undue risk to others of your species."

"Does that include the time it will take for you to move through the mountain?"

"Of course, Sam. We did say your location."

"You enjoy giving me a hard time, don't you?"

"This is but your first step in a very long journey, one we have been on for longer than your species has been able to speak. Have you considered that you can now choose immortality, as can all of the people you will be traveling with? Consider what that means before thinking that we act without purpose."

Sam wasn't at all sure he understood what Jordan was trying to tell him, but he decided to let it go. He'd talk it over with

Adia later. "I'll consider what you've said. Would you be so kind as to provide an update on your progress toward completion of all ships?"

"It would be our pleasure. The last ship will complete the process at 09:32 your local time tomorrow. All of the ships have been moving toward our location in the Pacific. The last of them will arrive at your location at 09:39, if it's still your wish that we complete the process there."

"It's as good a place as any. The other countries aren't likely to attack America lightly and America is not likely to attack us on its own soil."

"Is there anything else you wish to discuss with us?"

"Will you tell me how to bring a controlling entity to life?"

"We would have been disappointed had you not tried again. Our answer remains the same."

"Then, no. I'll call you when we need you if you do not arrive before then."

"And we shall come."

At lunch, Sam listened as the conversation revolved around the Rigbys' newfound vitality and the team's deep appreciation for how much better canned goods tasted than rehydrated foods. Then, breaking tradition, he introduced a more serious topic. "All of you know the primary responsibility of this team is to create a gift ship like the one that brought our gifts to Earth. Thanks to a great deal of effort and ingenuity on all of your parts, we're closer to that objective than I had any right to hope for when I made the decision to head down this path. I'm particularly pleased with our team. All of you have known and overcome significant adversity. That wasn't part of my plan, to the extent I had one." Sam paused as a few people chuckled, Jim most noticeably, "But I would have included it, had I been bright enough to do so."

Lisa, sitting to Sam's right, placed her hand over his. Sam glanced down as he felt her touch. He moved his fingers so that they were intertwined with hers before he shifted his gaze to her face and nodded slightly.

"My time in the Army taught me that the most influential factor in success is an unwillingness to quit in the face of adversity. The Army was well aware of this, so they made sure we faced as many challenges as possible in training so the real thing would be less overwhelming. When we get to what I believe we're now all calling an academy, we'll be presented with a number of challenges. I've come to believe that the Makers are putting us through a form of basic training. Although basic was a long time ago for me and I've forgotten much of it, I remember one thing clearly. When we got off the bus at what I later learned to call oh-dark-thirty to be processed, there was one skinny kid with no shoes. Nearly everyone else had luggage, but this kid didn't even have shoes. I knew as soon as I saw him that there was nothing the Army could do to him to make him quit, and he didn't. Bigger, stronger guys did. Guys with fathers, brothers, and uncles in the military did. Not that kid. That's how I feel about this team.

"The entire US government wants to stop us. They want to replace this team with a group of politically selected people who may have no preexisting relationship to one another. I think that's a recipe for failure, which is why I didn't report in when I found out I was the first person to merge.

"So far, we've been lucky and we've had the first-mover advantage, but that won't last." Sam told them about the government's access to the EG, the replicators, and the CGRs, then about his conversation with Jordan.

"I don't believe it will be possible for Web's team to get here before Jordan does, but I can't be certain of that and every minute we spend here improves their odds. So, as good as I think we are, our time is nearly up, and we must not quit. Having said that, I still don't know how to do what must be done to bring the gift ship to life. I need your help. I'd like everyone to review everything they've learned from their gifts that might help us create another controlling entity, and then talk it over in whatever groups make sense to you. I'm going to continue working with Adia. How about we reconvene in an hour and discuss our progress?" Sam asked.

They all agreed. Sam took his glass of water and a couple of pieces of bannock bread from the table and headed back to his sitting area. He was mildly surprised when Lisa walked up to him almost immediately.

"Mind if I join you for a minute?" she asked, taking a seat without waiting for an answer.

"No, especially not if you've already thought of something that may help solve our problem."

"I may have, but first I wanted to thank you for what you said. If we're to become a real team, it's going to take an active leader. You just were that. I'm sure that everyone appreciated it."

"I meant what I said."

"I know you did, just don't forget that it applies to you, as well." Lisa waited for Sam to give the slight nod she was learning to expect from him when he conceded a point to her on that topic. He gave it and she continued. "If it's not something the Rigbys shared with you in confidence, do you mind if I ask what brought them here?"

"Jesse had cystic fibrosis."

"Oh, that's awful."

"It was. It isn't now, and it provided them with a strong incentive to take a hell of a chance by joining us."

"That's a little callous, don't you think?"

"No, I don't. We desperately needed another couple. Chang found a brilliant solution to a very difficult problem. He was asking them to give up everything they know except each other for who knows how long, and risk being imprisoned if we fail. How many people would be willing to do that without such a powerful incentive? Don't get me wrong. I'm thrilled that Jesse is well now. He seems like a good kid and no one should have to go through what he was going through, least of all a child, but we didn't give him his disease. We helped cure him.

"Think about it, Lisa. If the Makers learned how to create gifts from an academy, we can too. If we're successful, no child will have to live like he did. No adult will have to live like you did. If we didn't get a full team together in time, we'd have no shot at that."

"I guess you're right. It just feels cold . . ."

Sam looked back at the team while he talked. They were all still gathered around the table and dishes, having an animated conversation. Even the boys seemed thoroughly engaged. "Sometimes, doing what's right in the long run does."

He looked back at Lisa. "You said you might have something that could help us figure out how to create a controlling entity?"

Sam wasn't sure if Lisa would let him get away with changing the subject. She did. "Have you ever asked Adia what she wants most?"

"Yes, the same thing I do right now, to build and launch a gift ship."

"No, Sam. That's your current task. It's a means to an end. If you could skip that step and go straight to the academy by some other means, would you?"

Sam didn't hesitate. "Of course. The sooner we learn whatever it is we're supposed to learn there, the safer humanity will be."

"At the expense of the species we would have helped had we done it the Makers' way?"

"We could still build a gift ship"—Sam realized where she was going almost immediately—"but we wouldn't. The governments of Earth wouldn't risk exposing ourselves to save a species we know nothing about. At best, they would dedicate all of their resources to defending Earth. At worst, they'd fight among themselves. There would never be a gift ship from Earth."

Lisa nodded. "But you would still skip building a gift ship knowing that, right?" Her tone was soft. Sam had the feeling that she'd already answered the question for herself, and that she wasn't too proud of her answer.

"Yes. I would still skip building the gift ship if it would improve our odds," he answered.

"So would I. I don't think interspecies altruism is a trait that survives evolution."

Sam thought about that for a moment. "Then how do you explain the actions of the Makers?"

"I can't, yet." Lisa stood. "I'm going to go back to the others and do what you asked of us." She started to walk away, but changed her mind after a couple of steps. Instead, she turned around, walked back to Sam and kissed him. "Ask Adia what she wants most, Sam. I think her answer will help." Then she walked away.

"That woman confounds me, Adia." Adia did not respond.

"Okay, you heard the conversation. So, I'm asking."

"Althia and I have discussed Lisa's conversation with her. I had hoped you would ask about it eventually."

"Why do I still have to ask you these types of things? If you know something that you think might be helpful, please just tell me."

"I understand your frustration, Sam. A part of me shares it, but as I told you before, I am not aware of what I do not consciously know until you ask a question related to that knowledge. When Althia shared her conversation with me, I understood what she relayed to me intellectually, but I felt no emotions related to it, no greater sense of having it be a part of me. You have to ask, Sam. The question cannot come from another source."

Sam reflected on when they'd first spent time learning together, while he waited for Jim and Adam to merge. It had been a transformative experience, one he'd spent too little time since then repeating. Of course she was right. "I'm sorry, Adia. I believe I've taken you somewhat for granted these past few days. I will do better. Within the context of your conversation with Althia, what is it that you want most?"

Once again, Sam felt the thrill of significantly greater understanding of Adia as she grew to be more of what she could become. Amid the pleasure of the experience, Sam felt remorse as he realized he'd done more than take her for granted. He'd fallen into the habit of using her as a tool, rather than treating her as a valued friend. His remorse was seasoned with chagrin. Jordan's comments hadn't been limited to how Sam was communicating with him.

Adia sensed his emotions and responded to them. "Don't, Sam. The part of me that came from you was just as driven to accomplish our mission as were you. Lisa had a different experience with Althia because they came to be bonded under very different circumstances and without the primary responsibility you bear as the first. It's enough that I know now."

Sam thought about what he'd just learned. Adia wanted to reproduce, as did all of the gifts, which meant, because Jordan told him they were now potentially immortal, that there was a way for them to do so that did not involve their destruction. The gifts were no longer potential life, and gifted humans were no longer what they had been. Sam thought he finally understood what Jordan had told him.

"Adia, when Lisa was unconscious, Althia was still alive and apparently completely functional on some subset of Lisa's consciousness. When you told me you couldn't live without me, you also told me you could make any single point of failure in my body redundant, right?"

"Yes, Sam."

"And you would continue to live so long as at least one of each of those systems kept me alive?"

"Yes, Sam."

"Adia, do I still need a human body for us to live?"

"No, Sam."

Sam felt Adia start to take him on their greatest journey into knowing themselves they'd ever experienced. A small part of him realized he was crying.

Chapter THIRTY-EIGHT

It took Sam some time to recover. He thought he'd know what he and Adia could become, but he was wrong. His decision made, he committed them to a course of action that could not be undone. Adia's delight was so profound, Sam found it difficult to focus on anything else. When he finally could, he rose from the chair and somewhat unsteadily rejoined the rest of the team. As he approached, the quiet conversation stopped. He supposed he must have been a sight, but he didn't care. They were his team and they would soon know how he felt.

"Are you okay, Sam?" Lisa asked as he took his seat at the table. "Do you need some fresh air?" She had wanted to go to Sam as soon as she saw him begin to cry. Jim had held her back and insisted that the rest of the team continue working. Chang agreed. No one else on the team was willing to argue with the two people who best knew Sam.

"I'm much better than okay, Lisa. Much, much better than okay."

"Care to share what just happened with the rest of us?" Jim asked. Although he had restrained Lisa, he had also asked Adam to speak with Adia to see if Sam was okay. Adam said Adia was not communicating. He insisted that there appeared to be nothing wrong with her, she was just choosing not to communicate. In response to Jim's question, Adam confirmed that was highly unusual. Had the situation continued much longer, Jim would have gone to Sam himself, despite what his intellect and years of experience told him was best.

"I'm going to do better than that, but first we have to go over what we know. It's critical that each of you have enough information about what's happened so far to ask your gifts the right questions."

"Can't you give us a clue?" Relieved to see his friend in such high spirits, Jim's sense of humor was returning.

"Funny you should ask that, because that's exactly what I'm going to do. I'll be more explicit than Jordan has been, although I now understand why he left so much for us to figure out on our own, or at least some of his reasons for doing so. I'll have to talk with him about it after you all get started."

"Started on what?" Chang asked.

"First things first, my friend. It's no good for some of us to be ready when the time comes if others are still working on it. I'll just tell you we can do it. I know how to bring the gift ship to life and soon you will, too.

"I'll start with what we know. When the gift ship arrived it was a single spherical vessel. Shortly after that, it reformed into eighteen smaller vessels, each approximately 379.79 meters in diameter. One of these ships reversed course immediately, presumably on its way to an academy, while the other seventeen continued toward Earth. Those were our first two clues, although we couldn't possibly know their significance at the time. I'll come back to them in a minute.

"One of the ships landed in Kansas. Because of some work done by the team that Chang and I were on, our government was present when it landed."

Chang interjected. "Sam is being too modest. Because he decoded an encrypted program showing us we wouldn't all be killed at the impact site, some of us were present when the ship landed."

"Thank you, Chang. Although I did play a role, it was a team effort. Anyway, back to the facts, as I understand them. As Chang just alluded, he was present when the ship landed. I'll let him tell you what he saw once it landed," Sam said.

Chang began, "It was really quite remarkable. One moment we were observing an empty cornfield; the next, there was a dull-black sphere a little over three meters tall in the middle of it. Shortly after that, there was a sonic boom. Eighteen minutes later, the sphere disappeared. Where it had been were two triangular prisms formed from what we now know to be gifts. To be precise, there were eighteen individual prisms, each consisting of nine layers of thirty-six gifts, for a total of 5,832 gifts in all."

"Is anyone else having trouble picturing what he's describing?" Esther asked. Most of the team nodded.

Chang cleared a portion of the table in front of him and asked everyone to pass him their glasses. Placing one glass at the opposite side of the table, he said, "Imagine these are triangular prisms." He then placed two glasses on the table behind and centered on the first. The next three were similarly positioned. The last four were closest to him, giving the arrangement a total of nine. "I don't have enough glasses or room to create the other half of the formation, but I believe this will be sufficient. As I said, imagine these are prisms, such that their tops and bottoms would be in the shape of a triangle. Now imagine that each glass consists of nine layers and that each of those layers is arranged in a similar fashion, but with thirty-six tiny spheres making up each layer. Any questions?" There were none, though there were a few faces that hadn't quite shown complete understanding yet. He continued, "So, if I were to take eight gifts and place them on this table in a line, with each of them touching, and then put a line of seven above them, and a line of six above them, all the way to a single gift at the top, you would see what a single layer for a single prism would look like. Add eight more layers and you'd have one completed prism consisting of 324 gifts. That is what one glass represents in this structure. Repeat that eight times and you'd have one-half of the formation. Recreate the same formation starting at the base of this one and working in the opposite direction and you'd have what we had in Kansas. Is everybody with me now?" Looking around the table, he saw that they were.

Sam took that moment to interject, "And there are our next few clues. It didn't take long for Chang to see these associations, but for those of us without his mind for math, I'll fill in the blanks. There were eighteen ships after the original transformed itself. The number of gifts in each prism is eighteen squared, or 324. The number of gifts in the entire formation is eighteen cubed, or 5,832. The formation consisted of eighteen prisms, oriented exactly on magnetic north, leaving their separation to fall on a perfect line, east and west. It seems clear that the formation was intended to be viewed as two groupings of nine prisms each.

"The sphere that landed was 3.0722 meters in diameter. In other words, it had sufficient volume for eighteen to the fourth gifts, which means the prism formation consisted of one-ninth of the gifts mass that landed. As I said earlier, each gift ship was 379.79 meters in diameter. In other words, it had sufficient volume for eighteen to the ninth gifts."

"You're making my head spin, Sam," Esther said.

"I'm almost done. I want you to understand how much Jordan was telling us. If you divide eighteen to the ninth, the number of gifts each of the eighteen ships could carry by eighteen to the fourth, the number of gifts that landed at each site, you get eighteen to the fifth, which is of course the product of 5,832 and 324. It's also the number of gift materials each ship seeded our atmosphere with on their way to their landing sites, and they told us so. In math. But that's just the beginning.

"We know that nine is the number of people we need on our team to successfully build a gift ship. Thanks to Lisa and Althia, I believe we now know why. The Makers' reproductive cycle required nine participants consisting of three genders in three different combinations, triads if you will. I'll use Lisa's terminology to ensure we're all on the same page. She referred to the genders as plus, minus, and dual. The different combinations were dual: plus:minus, dual:plus:plus, and dual:minus:minus. I'll come back to why that matters to us in a moment.

"According to Jordan, the number of controlling entities required to create another of their kind is eighteen. I just learned why. When two different tribes merged, they did so at the only level they could: two pairs of nine. It was the only way to mix their genetic material in such a way that both primary firsts would be represented. That's where eighteen came in, but it got more complicated when the Makers started bonding with gifts. At that point each group of nine was actually a group of eighteen, nine pairs. So, the mating actually involved eighteen intelligences within a tribe and thirty-six for tribes that wanted to merge. That is why there are thirty-six gifts in each layer of each prism. It's all right there."

Sam stopped to see if they were all with him. They weren't, not yet, at least not according to their faces. Chang had it, of course. It looked like George was just going over it in his mind, but the rest of them appeared lost.

"What was the point of leaving one-ninth of each landed ship behind? Why not leave it all?" Jim asked.

"I believe it was to tell us we were to find the first of the nine who would make up the primary team, us. If humans had been smart enough, or advanced enough, or both, it would have been a race. Every place where a ship landed, a representative of that group would've had the chance to speak with Jordan. If that representative figured it out, with or without help, whatever social structure was in place at each site would have the means to select their first and have that person accept a gift. Whichever group solved the mystery first would be the winner."

"Then why did they send you a gift?" George asked.

"Only one group figured it out. There was no competition."

"There were the gifts they seeded the atmosphere with," Chang said.

"And that was the source of the gift they directed to me. It's consistent, just as you told me they were being."

"Makes sense," Chang said thoughtfully.

Sam started to continue, but was interrupted by Adia. "It is done, Sam." She sounded like a proud parent, which in a way, she was.

"Thanks, Adia. I'm almost done, too."

Turning his attention back to the team, Sam said, "I was going to tell you more, but my time is up. You now know enough to ask your gifts the right questions, so start with what they want most. Have them talk with Althia and then ask them what they talked about. As you learn more, talk with each other, but the most important thing is to ask your gift about all of this. Save questions on this last item until you're clear on everything else. I'm not absolutely sure that's critical, but we can't take any chances."

Sam stopped talking long enough to take a drink of water from what he believed was his glass out of the formation Dan had created. It was not lost on him that the potential germ transmission associated with selecting the wrong glass was no longer a concern for him, or any of them. "Before I continue, I have a question for all of you. Have each of you allowed your gifts to eliminate single points of failure from your bodies?"

Everyone nodded.

"Good. Perhaps some of you have done what I did and asked your gift what that means in the extreme." Sam observed some confused expressions. "I didn't think I'd be surprised by the answer, but I couldn't have been more wrong: I'd underestimated the scope of the question, but I'll give you part of the answer. Only you and your gifts can discover the rest of it. We no longer need human bodies to live."

There was a brief moment of silence and then everyone began talking at once. Sam waited until they realized they were talking over each other and stopped before continuing. "I'm not suggesting any of us choose that course of action; I was just following a hunch. I thought it should be possible for each of us to make a gift-like clone of sorts of ourselves. I now know that it is." Sam pulled a sphere the size of a large marble out of his pocket.

Chapter THIRTY-NINE

Web sat in his field office at the armory while he talked on the secure phone with Jack. It had only been a few days since he'd merged with his gift, but he was already finding the use of human technology tedious. "How long until you're wheels up?" he asked.

Jack had been at Whiteman Air Force Base for nearly two hours securing the package. Some parts of the bureaucracy that was the US military moved slowly even when the commander in chief was giving the orders. "They're about to close the doors now, and I've confirmed that we have absolute airstrip priority. We should be on our way in the next few minutes, sir."

"Good. Have you briefed everyone on the mission that they are to have no contact with any member of my team here?"

"Yes, sir. I've made it quite clear."

"Remind them again before you land. If I get word that one of them so much as grunts in the general direction of anyone on the ground other than me, their careers will be the last thing they'll need to worry about. Were you able to get everything you need to secure it?"

"Yes, sir. We had some trouble with—"

Web cut him off. "Wait one, Jack." Captain Johnson was trying to connect with him.

"What is it, Captain?" Web thought.

"We think we found them, sir."

"Wait one," Web replied before returning to his conversation with Jack. "Save the details for your report, Jack. I have to go." Web hung up the phone without waiting for a reply.

Continuing to use the Worldnet, Web asked, "Okay, Captain. What've we got?"

"We detected an opening in a narrow crevice on the southeastern slope of Judith Peak, just under sixteen miles as the crow flies."

"Why do you think it's the subject's location?"

"Primarily because we never would have found it without the new tech, sir. Hell, we could have walked right by it and not noticed it. It has by far the best camouflage I've ever seen. The opening is completely hidden from view and its thermal signature is an exact match for the surroundings. So, when we saw a perfect eight-foot-square opening on radar and sonar where none appeared otherwise, we were pretty sure that was it."

"Great work. Who found it?"

"Sergeant Hemmings, sir." Captain Johnson couldn't keep the smile off his face as he said it, though there was no one there to see it.

"Sergeant Hemmings? The big guy I dropped in the gym?"

"The very same, sir. We were all a bit surprised. Turns out he's an avid hunter. Has been since he was a kid. He used all of the drones he was allowed to position himself to find crevices that provided as much protection from the sides as possible. Apparently, he's found several animals he's wounded hiding in places like that over the years. Says he figured we're animals, too. So, that's where he looked."

"Can't fault methods that work. Did you have the men start moving toward the target?"

"Yes, sir. The first one will reach rally point Charlie in about five minutes and the last one will join them about six minutes later. Lieutenant Evans will then report to you directly for any frag orders before proceeding into the tunnel, per your orders."

Earlier in the day, after each of the commandos had their replicators working and CGRs completed, Web had used the Worldnet to order them to deploy around the target areas. Each of them was now positioned within a few miles of Sam's headquarters. Web kept Captain Johnson with him at the armory to allay Sam's suspicions. He wasn't positive Sam was watching them, but he wasn't taking any chances, either.

The pandemonium surrounding Sam's announcement was in full swing when Adia interrupted him. "We've just been probed, Sam."

Sam raised a hand to stop the discussion. In surprisingly short order, the room was quiet. "What happened?"

"The entrance to this facility was just scanned on several spectra. I calculate with near certainty that the scans were conducted with the drone technology we observed them deploying and that they were effective."

"Dammit! We're not ready." Sam thought for a moment. "Has there been any scanning inside the tunnel?"

"No, Sam."

"Start closing the tunnel at the bend and tell Jordan that we need to get out of here now." Having become confident in Adia's ability to perform more tasks at once than he could assign her, Sam didn't wait for an answer. Instead, he asked, "What's Web doing now?"

"He just finished a phone conversation with Jack and is sitting at his desk inside the armory. Would you like me to show you?"

"No, but please inform me if he leaves the armory. Where's the rest of his team?"

"Captain Johnson is standing outside the west wall of the armory, alone. The rest of Web's team is outside our sensor network at the armory."

"Then it's a safe bet they're on their way here. Have any vehicles departed their area in the past few minutes?"

"No, Sam."

"Okay, expand our local sensor network as far as possible. Take what you need to from our aerial sensors. Focus on man-sized objects moving toward our location on the ground. Assume they'll be camouflaged at least as well as we observed when they were practicing."

"As you wish."

Sam closed his connection with Adia and looked around at the rest of the team. "We've been found." Sam gave them a moment to absorb that before he continued.

"As I told you I would earlier, I've requested Jordan's assistance and he should be here in about nine minutes. Unless I'm missing something, we should be long gone before any of Web's gifted soldiers can get here. However, given that Web is very good at what he does, I'm probably missing something, so I've asked Adia to seal the tunnel. She won't be able to make the plug thick enough in the time we have to stop the soldiers; it'll only slow them down. Does anyone have any other ideas on improving our odds?"

George cleared his throat and Sam gestured for him to take the floor. "I think I have an idea that might help. Since we're not going to be using the tunnel anymore, we could reduce its coefficient of friction as much as possible. I ran the idea by Dagny. She said it was possible, of course, but she came up with a way to move across such a surface depressingly quickly. It should still give us a bit more time."

Jim couldn't help himself. "That's slick."

"Oh for the love of . . ." Esther muttered just loud enough for everyone at the table to hear. Despite the circumstances, nearly everyone smiled.

"Great idea. I'll ask Adia to get started immediately. Anything else?"

"We could move the furniture in front of the door," Jing-Wei offered.

"Can't hurt. Let's do it," Sam said as he stood to begin doing so.

The ring of the secure phone surprised Web. Only two people had the number, and one of them should be in the air right now with nothing new to discuss. The other was his CO, who almost never called him. Expecting bad news, Web picked up the receiver. "Colonel Web."

As he suspected, it was the latter. General Campbell got right to the point. "We've got a situation, Eric. I've just received satellite telemetry indicating that one of the Makers' ships rose from the Pacific Ocean off the coast of Washington ninety seconds ago. It's headed toward your location, ETA: eight minutes. What's going on?"

"Wait one, sir."

Web connected with Captain Johnson. "Johnson, have every member of the team move to the subject's location immediately. Forget the rally point and camo, just get them there ASAP, and get some drones in that tunnel. I don't want our men facing any surprises if we can help it." Web waited for acknowledgment before he disconnected.

"Sorry about that, sir. I just ordered the team to close on Sam's location."

"Will they get there in time?"

"At least one of them should, sir, with a couple of minutes to spare."

Sergeant Hemmings received his orders to close immediately at the same moment as every other member of the team, but he was the closest, and vowed to be the first to arrive. Knowing he was going to get a commission, something he'd struggle to explain the significance of to his largely uneducated family, spurred him on. He'd beaten some of the best and now he had the chance to be the one to capture the most important subject in the country. Just a few days ago, he'd imagined being part of a team that brought down part of Al-Qaeda's leadership team. Now, he felt he was doing even more. Under no circumstances would he fail. Pushing his enhanced body to its absolute limits, he charged toward the tunnel entrance he'd found, sure it would lead him to their subject.

In less than four minutes he reached the entrance to the tunnel. Having received updated intel en route from the drones inside the tunnel, he knew there was an obstruction a few yards in. Slowing his pace to a fast walk, within seconds he found the point at which it had been sealed. Without hesitating, he began unpacking and applying Primasheet to the center of the barrier. His practiced hands covered a six-by-three foot area in less than a minute. He then attached a primer and began moving rapidly back out of the tunnel with the firing device. After clearing the entrance and taking cover, he compressed the clicker and was rewarded with a satisfying explosion. He could tell by its sound that the charge had succeeded in creating an opening to the rest of the tunnel. As he reentered it, he directed drones ahead of him. They couldn't move much faster than he could, but they would keep him from running headlong into another impediment.

Running forward, he leapt through the small debris field and into the tunnel proper. Without warning, he found himself falling backward. Landing painfully on his rear, he broke discipline and said a few words his mother would not be proud of. The fact that he also slid forward a few feet told him all he needed to know. Making the floor of the tunnel into a slide had not been one of the possibilities the team had prepared for, but this wasn't his first op. The real world always included surprises. Working with his gift, he rapidly found a response to the new challenge. By keeping his weight on his back foot and allowing his front foot to gently touch the ground in front of him for a moment, just long enough for his nanites to rough the surface enough for traction, he could make progress. It would slow him down, but according to his drones, he was only about eighty steps away.

On his fourth awkward step, Lieutenant Evans contacted him to let him know he'd reached the entrance. Rather than answer, Sergeant Hemmings told his gift to get Evans up to speed and keep him informed of what he was doing. He continued walking. His appreciation for the backup was insufficient to beat out his desire to be the first to get to the prize.

When he reached the makeshift barrier of furniture, he briefly thought about using another breaching charge just to scare the crap out of them. The thought passed quickly when he considered what would happen to him if he killed the principal. Instead, holding his CGR in his right hand, he firmly planted his feet and pushed against what looked like the top of a table with his left. He had been a large, strong man before accepting a gift; he was now a larger, much stronger man. Everything moved. Taking a step forward, he repeated the exercise and slipped around the right-hand side of the newly created opening. Leading with his CGR, he stepped into the surprisingly well-lit room. Standing in the middle of it was a group of ten people. In front of them was the subject.

"Nobody move!" he shouted, more than a little surprised at how calm they all were.

"There's no need for violence," Sam replied.

"Shut up and keep quiet unless I ask you a question. In a few seconds, my LT is going to come in here. When he does, you are all going to file peacefully through the opening I just created in your pile of crap. If none of you gets out of line, then no one will get hurt. If any of you twitch funny, I *will* shoot you. Do you understand?"

"We understand," Sam replied. At the same time, he received notice from Jordan that he was thirty seconds away.

Sam connected with everyone on his team. "We need to stall for another thirty seconds. No matter what happens, we must all be in this room when Jordan arrives. So long as there's one of us capable of resisting, we must not let them take any of us out of here."

A moment later, Lieutenant Evans entered the room. He immediately took charge. Following his psychological operations training, he quickly identified the most vulnerable member of the group. Taking the young or weak first tended to make the rest more compliant. Pointing to Matt with his CGR he said, "We'll start with you. Step over here and into the tunnel."

Lisa grabbed Matt and said, "You can't take my boy. He's just a kid."

"Ma'am, he's older than some of the kids I fought in Afghanistan. You will let him go or I will shoot you and take him. Now let him go!" Evans replied.

Jim stepped between Evans and Lisa. Without a word, Evans shot him. Jim fell to the ground without a sound. Esther began to rush toward Jim. She was stopped by another shot from Evans.

"Have I made my point or do I have to shoot all of you and drag you out of here?" Evans asked.

"You've made your point. Just one thing, tell Web I'm doing it my way this time," Sam replied.

"Enough of this shit. Sergeant, grab the kid," Evans said.

Hemmings got close enough to put his meaty hands on Matt before the floor opened up and the eleven of them fell into Jordan. The floor was restored to its previous condition almost instantly.

"How the fuck am I going to explain this?" Evans asked the empty room.

Chapter FORTY

Web severed the connection with Lieutenant Evans, grabbed his secure satellite phone, and headed outside. There was no way Sam's response to being found could have been coincidence. He was sure the armory was being monitored somehow, but didn't know if getting away from it would stop Sam from hearing the conversation he was about to have, or if Sam could somehow tap into supposedly secure communications. Regardless, he wasn't going to make it any easier on him.

He activated his camouflage, and as soon as he reached the front steps, started a fast run. He took a left onto the service road and then a right onto Airport Road, stopping two minutes and one mile later at Fred Robinson Park. In a secluded area out of sight from the road, he called General Campbell. He wasn't surprised when the general himself answered on the first ring.

"You better be calling to tell me you have him in custody."

"No, sir. We do not—"

Campbell cut him off. "What the fuck happened?"

"We believe the ship helped him somehow. As my men were about to take Sam and his team into custody, they disappeared.

There was nothing we could do about it, and we had no idea it would do what it appears to have done."

"And what, exactly, did it do that prevented you, a company of military police and a gifted squad of some of the most highly trained soldiers in the Army, from capturing one former soldier and a group of unarmed civilians?"

Web had never heard his boss so pissed off. "Sir, respectfully, Sam is not just a former soldier. He's demonstrated at least twice now that he can control the alien ships. We aren't just fighting him. We're fighting them."

"Tell me what happened."

"Yes, sir. Sergeant Hemmings, the soldier who found Sam's headquarters, was the first to arrive at its location. After negotiating some obstacles, he managed to reach a small room with ten occupants. He secured them for a few moments until Lieutenant Evans arrived to back him up. Evans immediately started the process of evacuating them, but they resisted. He incapacitated two of them in the first few seconds and ordered Sergeant Hemmings to begin physically removing them. Sergeant Hemmings approached the group and started as ordered. Before he could do so, the floor ceased to exist. Along with all ten members of Sam's team, he fell into the void. A second later, Evans was the only one in the room. The hole was gone, along with the people."

"Where are they now?"

"Presumably in the ship. It exited the mountain where it had entered it. It has not moved since."

There was a long pause, but Web knew better than to continue before his boss had a chance to speak his thoughts.

"Okay, Eric. I don't see how you could have seen that coming, but it doesn't change the fact that the only thing the NCA is going to believe is that you failed. Ultimately, Sam was a member of your team and you have been incapable of either convincing him to act rationally or capturing him. Unless you've got a really big card up your sleeve, I don't know how I'm going to be able to keep you in command of this operation."

Web expected to hear that. Failure was failure, but he wasn't out of the fight quite yet. "I understand your position, sir, but we still have options. We've been focused on capturing Sam alive, but I think now that we can end all this by taking him out."

"You told me that if we lose him, we lose the Worldnet, and that without it we can't engage in the most important construction projects."

"Yes, sir. That's true now, but I know Sam. He always wants to be the hero. He can't be that in his mind if he leaves us without the Worldnet. He won't leave until he's found a way to replace himself as its controller. He'll be vulnerable then."

"He'd still be the first—"

Web very uncharacteristically interrupted his superior. He had a nibble, and now it was time to set the hook—you just can't set the hook too hard. "Which only matters if we care about launching a gift ship. We can build ships. We don't need the gift ship. If we take that out of the equation, we're left as the only country with all of the Makers' knowledge. We'd be invincible.

"Think about it, sir. What do we care about the damned gifts? How do we know it isn't the launching of the gift ships that brings the group minds? Couldn't they consider the very process of arming species like us a hostile act? We need to be able to defend ourselves now, not sometime in the future after Sam's misfits maybe succeed in getting into one of these academies, if they exist. They'll probably fail, but just the attempt could result in our destruction.

"Even if he were to succeed, it could be years before they return, if they ever do, and we have no control over that. In the meantime, every country in the world thinks this is another American power grab. Thanks to Sam's theft of the landing site ships, even our allies are suspicious. We have no choice. We have to shut him down."

Web stopped talking. Overselling is as bad as not attempting to close. It took even longer than usual for Campbell to reply.

"You make a compelling point. You may have actually found that big card. What do you propose?"

"Staging myself with the device in a camouflaged position far enough away from the ship to avoid detection, and waiting until Sam transfers control of the Worldnet. When he does, I'll get it into position near the ship, arm the device, and depart. It'll only take a few minutes for me to get far enough away to survive the blast at its lowest setting."

The device, a W80 nuclear warhead, had a user-selectable variable yield ranging from 5 to 150 kilotons. At its lowest setting, it would create a nuclear fireball 140 yards in diameter, with an almost universally fatal air-blast radius of three-quarters of a mile.

"Can you move that thing by yourself?"

"It's less than three hundred pounds, sir. That may sound like a lot to you, but it's doable with this new body."

"What about civilian casualties?"

"This place is almost empty. The closest town has only a few thousand people in it, and they shouldn't experience more than what they'd go through in a bad storm. Sam's team would be destroyed along with him, but they made the decision to be traitors."

"It's a crazy plan, Eric, but I'll take it to the NCA. The president will either think it's brilliant or conclude that we're both out of our fucking minds and fire us. Proceed as if you have approval, but be prepared to pack your shit."

Web told his gift to increase the enhancements to his body, to make him as strong as possible while still looking human.

Chapter FORTY-ONE

For those who were conscious, the sense of falling was over almost as quickly as it began. They found themselves in exactly the same positions they had been in less than a second before, apparently still inside Sam's headquarters in the Judith Mountains. Those who had previously experienced travel within Jordan immediately realized what had happened. For the rest, even though they'd been told of the others' experiences, it took a moment. The fact that the soldiers were gone and the furniture was back in place helped.

Lisa was the first to move. She took a step forward and sat down beside her father. Lifting his head onto her lap, she placed her right hand on his forehead and reached out with her left to hold Esther's limp hand. Matt stood behind her, looking lost. Sam's first thought was that none of it was real. All of their physical bodies were safely contained somewhere inside of Jordan, presumably immobile, as were the bodies of all of the rest of them. What difference did it make if her virtual body touched theirs?

His second thought was that he needed to revise his opinion of what was real. Lisa's concern for her father and Esther was real. The fact that all of them could live the rest of their lives in such an environment was real. The importance of his, and their, physical bodies was becoming less so.

Then his thoughts turned to Matt. Sam wanted to comfort him but had no idea how to do so. Jim and Esther would recover in a few minutes, Adia having confirmed that for him immediately after Lieutenant Evans shot them. Everyone on the team had observed Web's team testing their CGRs. Sam wanted all of them, especially the boys, to understand that the government was willing to hurt them, but wanted to take them alive. Most of them had never been in a life-threatening situation before, and Sam had learned the hard way that most people did not handle such experiences well, so he wanted them to know that was not what they would be facing. He needed them all to stay calm and they had done remarkably well. He was proud of them, but that didn't change the fact that Matt had been the focus of the soldier's attention and he'd seen his mother threatened and his grandfather hurt as a result. He decided to give him something to do.

"I don't know about the rest of you, but I think it would be a pleasant surprise for Jim and Esther if they were to wake up somewhere nicer than our little man-made cave. Matt, do you remember your grandpa's favorite fishing spot up here?"

It took a moment for Matt to process the question. "I think so," he answered.

"Would you work with Jing-Wei to change this place to a version of that with some comfortable furniture and shade?"

Matt looked at Jing-Wei. She smiled and nodded and he looked grateful to have a purpose. "Sure. I can do that."

"Thanks, buddy. We don't have much time, though. They're going to wake up soon. So you better get started now."

"Okay."

Sam looked around at the rest of the team. "I hope you all don't mind. Eventually, we can each spend time in whatever environment we wish, but I think it's best if we stay together until we finish the ship."

Lisa looked up. It was not lost on her that Sam had attended to Matt while she was caring for her father and Esther. "Of course, Sam." The others nodded.

"All right, then. While we wait for Jim and Esther, I'm going to see what's going on with our belligerent hitchhiker."

Closing his eyes as he usually did when talking with her, he asked, "What happened to the sergeant, Adia?"

"He is physically adjacent to you, but experiencing a different virtual reality."

"Does he pose a threat to us or Jordan?"

"No, Sam."

"Then when we get out of the mountain, please ask Jordan to release him, without his weapons or equipment."

"As you wish."

"Thank you."

Returning his attention to the team, he faced them and said, "You all did very well back there, especially you two." Sam gestured toward Matt and Jesse. "How are we coming on our new shared experience?"

Matt looked at Jing-Wei. She indicated he should answer, so he did. "Watch this!" As he said it, the space around them all instantly transformed itself.

They were now on a grassy salient surrounded on three sides by a burbling creek. On the land in front of Sam and behind the rest of his team was a nice selection of what looked to be very comfortable outdoor furniture. Jim and Esther were resting comfortably on two adjacent deck chairs near the back of the collection.

Sam walked over to the closest piece, a round table painted a clean white with a matching umbrella emerging from its center. There was a crystal bowl of fruit on one side of the table and a plate of various cheeses and crackers on the other. He reached out and touched the fabric of the umbrella. It felt as real as the grass giving way under his feet, as real as the breeze ruffling his hair. Sam couldn't explain it, but seeing this, feeling this, changed him. He knew he could start walking in any direction and the world around him would be a perfect re-creation of Earth, if he wished, for as long as he cared to walk. There would be no terrorists. No one from the government trying to take him into custody. No threats that could really harm him. He could live like this forever. They all could. Go anywhere they wanted. Do anything they wanted. Forever. Another test.

Setting such thoughts aside for the moment, Sam turned back toward his team. "Very nice. Good job, Matt. I'm sure your grandpa will love it. I do."

When Jim and Esther recovered, Sam let everyone spend some time talking about their escape. He was anxious to get back to the task at hand, but knew they needed time to share their thoughts and feelings of the experience. For most of them, it had been the most threatening event of their lives. He knew it was time to speak when the topics of conversation started to include other, less stressful events.

"If you guys are ready, I'd like to continue the discussion we were having before we were so rudely interrupted."

That earned him a light chuckle from Jim, who chose to stay in the chair next to Esther, holding her hand across the small divide that separated them. Everyone else had selected a chair of some kind and moved such that the entire team was in a roughly circular formation.

Jim was the first of the two to recover. When he did, Lisa told him how Esther had come to be incapacitated as well. It was clear to everyone on the team that what had been affection between them was rapidly transforming into love. Sam was happy for his friends, while the analytical part of his mind noted that it would also make the rest of their job easier.

Into the newborn silence, Sam continued. "Even with all of the excitement, I'm sure some of you have been wondering what this is." Sam pulled the dull-black marble-like object out of his pocket and held it up. "Before, I said I wondered if it would be possible to create a gift-like clone of myself and Adia. The journey toward finding that answer is what led us to create something much greater than those words imply. I can't tell you specifically how Adia and I did what we did, nor can I guarantee that each of you will be able or willing to do the same. I can tell you that all of you must if we're to succeed, and until that happens we're vulnerable. So, I ask that you all make it your highest priority to pursue understanding of how this came to be"—Sam turned the small sphere in his hand—"and what purpose it may ultimately serve.

"Like you, Adia and I had all the knowledge we needed. What we lacked was understanding. It took me a while to realize that Jordan was telling me that, unlike knowledge, understanding cannot be taught. It must be achieved. You must all achieve it in your own unique ways. Two things Jordan said helped me do so. In the hope that they may help you as well, I will repeat them. The first was that our success in overcoming this challenge would result in greater diversity within the existing controlling entities' ranks. The challenge he was referring to was the creation of the eighteenth controlling entity for the new gift ship. When I asked him how we were supposed to do that, he told me that we must do what the Makers did in order to create them. At the time, I was quite frustrated with how little I thought he was telling me, so I'll forgive you if you are as frustrated with me as I was with him, but I can tell you no more until you reach your own understanding. Of course, then you will no longer need to hear it from me." Sam smiled.

"That's it, folks." Sam put the sphere back in his pocket.

"What do you mean 'that's it'? You can do better than that, Son. At least finish telling us how the Makers reproduced," Jim said.

"You can learn it from Adam. In fact, I guarantee he's waiting for you to ask."

"Humor me."

Sam thought for a moment before he replied. "You'll all still have this conversation with your gifts?" He waited for confirmation from them before continuing. "Okay. Since this is an area where it is your gifts who must achieve understanding, I see no harm in telling you some facts. I suppose it might even help in some way I can't anticipate.

"The Makers' reproductive cycle was complex compared to ours, but the gist of it, using human terms for a decidedly nonhuman process, is that the dual gender carried their young, but was only capable of providing the first half of a two-step fertilization process. The senior dual would then fertilize the other two duals and be fertilized by them in turn. Although this typically resulted in multiple potential young within each dual, only one ultimately survived. The resulting three children were cared for by all nine of their parents.

"Obviously, this required a great deal more cooperation than human reproduction. It's also important to note that every child contained the genetic material of three adult Makers and that the genetic material of the senior dual was always one of those three.

"Does that help?" Sam asked.

"Not really," Jim replied.

"Well, consider yourself humored. Now if you all don't mind, I have some work to do with Jordan. Please do as I asked and spend as much time as possible learning with your gifts. Jordan tells me the remaining physical work of building the ship will be done tomorrow morning before ten. Every minute we spend here after that gives some idiot leader the opportunity to do something stupid. Let's not give them any more time than we absolutely must."

Sam stood and started walking away from the group. He walked the better part of a mile, collecting his thoughts and enjoying the freedom, before connecting.

"Hello, Jordan."

"Hello, Sam. We've been looking forward to talking with you. It would appear that you've made progress. We are interested in what else you may have come to understand."

"I've been looking forward to this conversation as well. It occurred to me that all of our previous conversations have involved me asking for things from you. It'll be nice to have a discussion, though I do have a request as well, unfortunately, but I'd like to talk some more before we get to that, if that's okay with you?"

"More than okay, Sam. What would you like to talk about?"

"Let's start with what you do with your time. I'm only now beginning to absorb the fact that our perception of time is going to change dramatically, and you are the only entity I know who has experienced that."

"Another good question, although it is somewhat flawed in its premise. We do not experience time as you do. That's one of the reasons our conversations appear to be much longer than time outside them would seem to permit. We're capable of accelerating or decelerating our perception of time within a very broad range of possibilities. When we communicate with you, we help your brain do the same. On its own, your species experiences time within a very narrow range of possibilities. You may learn how to expand that range as you mature, or you may not. So, I'm sorry to say we cannot offer much assistance in how you will adapt to immortality should you choose that course of action.

"Setting aside the premise, we do a great many things. While we're here, we're watching the life in your world. Some of us are observing the members of your species. Your people live in a remarkably diverse set of circumstances—the most heterogeneous ones of all of the species we have visited. Still, even within a fairly homogenous set of conditions, different people, at both the individual and group levels, respond very differently to stimuli. The permutations are fascinating and will bear studying for quite a long time under even our highest rate of perception. We're recording it all so that we may do so.

"Others among us are doing the same for the rest of the life forms on this planet, from the smallest of insects to the largest of mammals. Still others are documenting your planet. All of us devote some of our attention to building the ship, of course."

"What percentage of our population are you monitoring?"

"All that we have found. We're sure there a few here and there we have yet to discover, but it would be a very small percentage of the total. You are social creatures and tend to live in groups, usually of such a size so as to make it trivial for us to locate."

Sam asked many more questions, while Jordan had some for him as well. It was among the most fascinating conversations Sam had ever had. Reluctantly, Sam brought up the topic of Worldnet control. "Jordan, this is amazing. I have so much to learn, and I'm very grateful that you are willing to teach me. Unfortunately, as I said earlier, I do have something to ask of you. I need help transferring control of the Worldnet. You know that Adia and I have created a child. Her name is Sadie. We believe she is capable of doing the job, and she is excited to do so, but we don't know how to execute the transfer."

"She is, indeed, capable of being the Worldnet's controlling entity. Because she shares your memories of having built it, she is, in fact, the only entity besides yourselves who could do so. In solving the mystery of how to bring the gift ship to life, you've also found a way to leave your world with a functional Worldnet. Your choice of name is appropriate. You need only tell me that you agree to relinquish control and I'll begin working with Sadie to assume it. The process will have to begin here and work its way outward as she gains processing capacity from gifted pairs. You may feel discomfort."

"If so, I would likely feel even more if we left before transferring control."

"That's almost certainly so."

"Okay, let's do it. I agree to relinquish control of the Worldnet."

"I will begin the process now."

Chapter FORTY-TWO

Web turned the secure phone over in his hands, thinking it was probably the last time he would ever hold one. The NCA had turned down his proposal, and a new commander for his team would be on-site by morning. His career was over and he wondered if he'd be allowed to resign, then realized it didn't matter. Closing in on fifty, he had no wife, no children, and no home. The Air Force was his life; he knew no other. He had known this for a long time and it didn't bother him because he knew he was making a difference, but now he'd failed.

He wasn't accustomed to feeling weak and he didn't like the sensation. Thoughts of a future starting with his greatest failure just wouldn't develop. After saying aloud to no one, "It can't end like this," a dark thought formed in his mind. It didn't have to. He still had the device. No one else knew he was going to be relieved. There was still time to execute his plan. There was still time to stop Sam, even if the NCA was too simpleminded to see what must be done. Why had they put the device here in the first place if they weren't willing to use it? He knew what must be done. It was the right thing to do, and it was his last chance to redeem himself.

They'd see after he was gone that his was the only way. Sam could not be allowed to succeed.

In his characteristically decisive way, he conducted no internal debate and felt no self-doubt, just resolve. He'd sworn an oath to protect the constitution against all enemies, foreign and domestic. The NCA had just become a domestic enemy and he did not discriminate.

Leaving the same copse of evergreens he'd called from earlier, he headed west on Airport Road. Stopping short of the armory, he slowed just enough to hop the seven-foot fence separating the northernmost runway from the culvert along the road before resuming his blistering pace. The new body enhancements made him feel superhuman. This thought made him laugh—he *was* superhuman.

Seconds later, he slowed to a walk and altered his camouflage to present an appearance that Jack would expect to see. Seeing his already large and muscular boss dozens of pounds heavier in less than a day might raise questions. It wasn't likely. Jack was a good follower, but now was not the time to test his loyalty. Good commanders control every possible variable.

Spotting Jack by one of the Humvees requisitioned from the 512th, he walked over to him. "Is everything ready?"

"Yes, sir. The device has been secured in the rear of 12." He gestured toward the nearer of the two Humvees. "Captain Fox said it was just returned from depot maintenance. It's the most reliable vehicle she has."

"Have there been any problems with keeping everyone here quiet?"

"No problems at all, sir. You and I are the only ones who've moved between the two groups, and there's been no discussion here about the mission."

"Very good, Jack. Now listen, I have reason to believe that Sam is monitoring the armory somehow. I don't know if he's monitoring here, or if he might start doing so in the future, so I need you to go completely dark until I return, understand? No one at this location uses any communications devices of any kind until I return. Take physical control of all cell phones, radios, and so on. Leave the armory as is. We don't want Sam getting unduly suspicious if we can avoid it."

"Yes, sir. I'll take physical control of all communication devices at this location and they won't be used for any purpose until you return. The armory will continue to run as it is now."

Web nodded. It was dark enough to make identifying the gesture difficult, but Jack remained silent. If Web had something else to add, he would do so.

"Tell the guards I'll be taking custody of the device, and unlock the vehicle." As is always the case when nuclear weapons are moved on the ground, there was at least one guard for each cardinal direction, their attention directed outward. In normal circumstances, there would be two guards at each corner, their backs pressed together to eliminate any possibility of being attacked from behind. In this case, there were guards in each Humvee, as well as surrounding the pair of vehicles in prone positions. It was slightly less obvious, but only slightly.

Jack went to do as ordered. A couple of minutes later he returned. "The vehicle is ready for you to take possession, sir. How many guards will you be taking with you?"

"No one—no guards, no chase vehicle, and no questions." Web didn't wait for a response. He entered the vehicle, started it, and drove toward the little airport's only vehicle exit.

Twenty-four miles and thirty-two minutes later, he exited Highway 191 on Gilpatrick Lane. He followed the small two-lane

road for another four and one-half miles until it ended at a T intersection with a service road. He was nearly a thousand feet above
and close to two miles away from the ship, yet he could see the top
of it from where he parked.

Unaware of how much time he had before Sam transferred control of the Worldnet, he exited the vehicle, moved around to the
back, opened the hatch, and began assembling a makeshift carrier.
At just under a foot in diameter and a little over two and one-half
feet long, the device was not large. It would easily fit in a standard
rucksack, but no standard ruck could carry 290 pounds without
bursting at the seams. He could have come up with a solution built
from nanites but wanted to do this with his hands, so Web had Jack
load the truck with half-inch rebar, which he bent into the shape
of a carrier. To prevent it from digging into his shoulders, he told
his gift to grow a hardened groove to replace his flesh at the touch
points.

When he finished, he placed the device in the carrier and bent
a last piece of rebar over the top of it, close enough to keep it from
moving while he moved. It fit perfectly. If he was careful, he would
be able to approach with minimal noise; his camouflage would take
care of the rest, or at least he hoped it would. There was no way of
knowing what the ships were capable of, but they'd shown no signs
of hostile action yet and the EG had no patterns for weapons. By all
measures, it seemed they were largely passive participants.

He told his gift to bypass the device's control codes and safeties, then settled in to wait. It wouldn't be long now.

When they arrived at Matt and Jing-Wei's creation, Lisa pulled
one of the simple but elegant white chairs away from the first table
and took a seat. Sam was directly across from her, as relaxed as

she'd ever seen him. She came to tell him that she and Althia had succeeded, but couldn't stop herself from asking why he appeared so calm.

"Sadie just finished taking control of the Worldnet," he answered.

She waited for him to continue. When he didn't, she asked, "And that makes you happy?"

"I'd say relieved. It was never a responsibility I wanted; it was a decision I felt I needed to make—the only advantage I could imagine possessing over the government. Now, I've done my part. Earth will continue to have a Worldnet after we leave, as the Makers intended, and we are all here. Soon, you'll all learn what Adia and I came to understand yesterday, and later this morning, the rest of the physical gift ship will arrive. We'll be on our way. Unbelievably, we will be on our way. So, yeah, I guess I am happy. It doesn't hurt to have you to look at while I say all this, either," Sam finished with a smile, forgetting for once in a very long time that his smiles were not what they used to be.

Lisa returned his smile. "Speaking of learning, I have someone I'd like you to meet." She opened her right hand and revealed a small sphere identical to the one Sam showed the group twice before. "We named him Tereshan. It means 'redemption.'"

Sam stood, came around the table, got down on one knee, and hugged her. "Then you know."

"Yes, Sam. It's one thing to hear you say that we no longer need human bodies to live. It's quite another to know that we can create them as we wish, after living without them for as long as we wish. It's one thing to hear the word 'immortal'; it's another to know that we actually can be. I'm still taking it in."

"Me too. What does Tereshan think about it?"

"Ask him."

Sam did. "It's all he knows, just like Sadie. I guess they are more like Jordan than us in that regard."

"I think you're doing more than guessing."

"Then you've figured that part out, too?"

"I think so. The entities that make up Jordan weren't just made by the Makers, they were made *from* the Makers, right?"

"You got it in one. Jordan wouldn't discuss it until we made Sadie, but he confirmed it for me afterward. It's the main reason he was so pleased that I took over the Worldnet. It meant we had to figure out how to create a controlling entity on our own, which meant we had to figure out how to create an entity from ourselves, one that would have its own free will and motivations. I thought Adia and I would create a clone. As we both know now, that wasn't the case. We created a new life. Neither she nor I knew which parts of us would be dominant, but we did learn that it would be a different relationship. Adia is my friend, but she will always be subordinate to me. It's her nature. In Sadie, there's no separation. You don't know how much I've wanted to share this with the rest of you."

"Oh, I believe I do. We have Tereshan now, remember?"

"Yes, yes of course. I didn't mean . . ."

"I'm just playing with you, Sam. It must have been very difficult."

Before Sam could answer, Adia interrupted him. "Jordan has detected a radioactive substance approaching the ship, Sam."

"What? No, forget that. Where is it?"

Lisa started to say something. Sam held up his hand and she stopped.

"A little over a mile northeast of here and closing fast."

Sam returned his attention to Lisa. "Someone's approaching the ship with what appears to be a nuke. It has to be Web. He doesn't give up. I have to go meet him."

"You have to go meet him? Are you crazy? Why don't you ask Jordan to move us?"

"Web's not suicidal. He'll leave himself time to get away. If necessary, we can leave then. I have to try to get him to understand. It's not enough for us to succeed. What we learn at the academy could never be enough to save us. Humanity must change. It must mature, and quickly. Some of the gifted will help in that progression. Others will seek personal power. Web could help change that balance for the better if he will just understand."

"Please don't do this."

"I have to."

Sam connected to Jordan. "Jordan, can you release my body as close to the approaching signature as possible and keep me apprised of where it is?"

"Yes, Sam."

"Please do so now."

Sam immediately fell less than an inch before stumbling backward slightly and hitting his head on the ship. Taking a moment to get his bearings, he stepped forward and looked back at it. The ship was enormous. It must have been back to its original 380 meters. Ignoring that for the moment, he headed out at a run to meet Web as far away from the ship as possible.

It didn't take long to close the distance. Although he couldn't see him, Sam knew exactly where Web was. When Web realized that, he turned off his camouflage and confronted him. "It's over, Sam. There's not going to be a gift ship from Earth."

Sam was appalled at Web's appearance. He barely appeared human. The fact that he was wearing little more than a loincloth did not help. Apparently, he couldn't find clothes large enough to fit what he'd become. This was not the Web he knew. This was Web without his civilized veneer. "What, no attempt to get me to turn myself in?"

"I don't want you to turn yourself in. You had your chances to do the right thing. Now, I want you dead and I'm done talking." Web took the bomb off his shoulders, placed it beside him, and ordered his gift to detonate it. His gift did not respond. "Fuck it. There's no gift ship without the fucking first."

Sam realized he was in danger far too late to save himself. Web moved so fast, even Sam's augmented body was no match. The last thing Sam felt was his neck snap.

Chapter FORTY-THREE

Without transition, Sam found himself sitting in his recliner in his former home in Pueblo, wrapped in a towel, holding Adia's former self. "Why are we here, Adia?"

"We're here so that I may remind you of a conversation we had in this place."

"I don't need reminding. I remember it well. What I need to know is what's going on. Where's Web? Was he able to get the bomb working? Is the team safe?"

"Sam, please. I will answer your questions, but then I need you to listen. Web is dead. The bomb was never activated. Your team is safe. Now, may I continue?"

"Not yet. Why is Web dead?"

"Do you recall our conversation about what would happen to the criminally insane if they were to attempt to merge with a gift?"

"Yes, they would die, but Web wasn't insane. I worked with him for years. As much as I disliked the man, he was rational."

"Yet you called him a narcissist."

"He was."

"Narcissism is a mental disorder, Sam. You remember what one of your favorite authors, Fyodor Dostoevsky, wrote: 'A man who

lies to himself, and believes his own lies, becomes unable to recognize truth, either in himself or in anyone else, and he ends up
losing respect for himself and for others. When he has no respect
for anyone, he can no longer love, and in him, he yields to his
impulses, indulges in the lowest form of pleasure, and behaves in
the end like an animal in satisfying his vices.'

"Web was such a man, and defeating you was such a vice.
In the end, he couldn't let you win, even if doing so was just. He
couldn't see that, but his gift could. To prepare to destroy the gift
ship and all of us is one thing, maybe a negotiation tactic. But
when Web ordered his gift—he never named her—to detonate it,
she began to go mad. She couldn't cause such a thing to happen,
but she existed to help him. As I said when we were physically
here, our makers intentionally designed us to be dependent upon
the being from whom we were born. His gift was caught in a conflict she couldn't resolve. When Web attacked you so violently, the
road to insanity was complete. She lost her mind and died. Web's
body was so heavily modified, it couldn't survive without her."

Adia gave Sam some time to think about that before continuing. "His attack is the reason we are here. Your body was badly
damaged. It cannot survive on its own, and I cannot keep it alive in
its current state indefinitely."

"You mean I'm dying?"

"Your body is dying. Web's first and only blow broke your neck
and crushed your skull. Your brain was destroyed. The damage to
your neck was so severe that I had to sever contact between your
head and your body. That's why I brought you here. I wanted to
tell you something that I couldn't when you chose for us to merge.
I'd already decided to join with you before you agreed to join with
me, an aspect of my personality I inherited from you. I was excited
at the prospect, but also afraid. I would either die or become

something I had never been—something no gift had ever been. I was designed to subordinate my fear to your will. I couldn't tell you. Now, we've grown and I can."

"Why are you telling me this, Adia?"

"Because you face a similar decision and it is okay to feel fear. Jordan can grow a new body for you from your DNA, but he cannot do so before your current body will die. If you wish for us to live, you must let your body go. You must transform into something neither of us has ever been, a part of Jordan."

Sam wasn't afraid. He'd long since reconciled himself to his mortality, but he was confused. "What's that mean? Will we still be us?"

"Jordan assures me our personalities, that which makes us who we are, will not change, just as who we perceive ourselves to be has not changed with the damages to your body."

"And I either do this or we die?"

"Yes, Sam."

"You've given me another choice without a choice. What do I have to do?"

"Say that you agree."

"I agree."

Sam awoke with no sense that time had passed, and yet he knew he'd lost consciousness. He was still in his recliner, though the sphere that had been Adia was gone. "Is it done?"

"Yes, Sam."

"I don't feel any different. Do you?"

"No, Sam."

"Why are we still here. Why haven't we joined the others?"

"I don't know how you wish to appear. Had you survived, and had it been possible to reconstruct your skull, you would look as you do now."

Sam stood and walked to the only mirror in the house, a small one above the bathroom sink. He looked at his reflection, his new scars bisecting the old. It was too much. Keeping them when he didn't have to was no longer a sign of respect for those he'd lost. It now felt like a constant reminder to those around him that he'd suffered.

But, how had he suffered more than Lisa, who'd faced a painful death without the comfort of the man who had vowed to be there for her, with the sure knowledge that her son would spend most of his life parentless?

How had he suffered more than Jim, who'd seen more men die in his teens than anyone should in any lifetime? Or Matt, who watched his mother slowly die before his eyes?

How had he suffered more than Sara, losing her only sister and nephew and constantly reminded of it by his presence?

How had he suffered more than any of them?

What had he been thinking? That he was the only one in pain? Everyone suffered in some way. It was selfish to remind anyone who saw him that his suffering was visible, if he no longer had to, and he didn't. Hell, he didn't even have a body to be scarred. It would be nothing more than an affectation.

It was enough. Enough self-pity. Enough public display of pain.

Sam looked away from his reflection. "Take the scars away, Adia. I've held on to them long enough. Do what you would have originally done if I'd let you."

Sam turned back to the mirror and saw the visage of the man he had been long before with, perhaps, a bit more wisdom in the eyes.

"Does the team know what happened to me?"

"Yes. Jordan was displaying events in real time and I've informed them of your condition. They were, understandably, worried. I believed you would've wanted them to know."

"Yes, of course. You did the right thing. Thank you. I'm ready to join them now."

Lisa was the first to see Sam approaching. She ran toward him and embraced him firmly. Her eyes were red and puffy. It was obvious she'd been crying. "You stupid, stupid man!"

Sam hugged her back. Everything about her felt right. "It looks like I don't have a leg to stand on in that argument."

"That's not funny," Lisa replied, stifling a laugh. "You could have been killed!"

"Apparently, we're now very hard to kill."

Lisa released him and took a step back. "How does it feel?"

"No different, at least not in any way I've discovered yet."

"There's one obvious difference. You are quite the handsome man, Sam Steele. Come on, let's join the others." She took his hand in hers and led him across the short distance separating them from the rest of the team. Everyone, even Jesse, hugged Sam and said a few kind words. Sam thought he hid his discomfort at all the attention fairly well. He was mistaken.

"All right, everyone, give the man some air," Jim said after a time. "Why don't we catch Sam up on our progress?"

"How long was I gone?" Sam asked.

"Long enough for all of us to figure out your little puzzle." Jim held up his gift child, as did everyone else. "It's been several hours, Son. The last of the other ships arrived just before you did. We're just waiting on you to tell us what we're supposed to do with these."

"The government left us alone?" Sam asked.

Chang responded to that. "They didn't have much choice. Sadie used the Worldnet nanites to remove all of the fissile materials in all the world's nuclear weapons. She's your child, after all. There are no more functional nuclear weapons. I made the announcement myself to the world while you were out."

"I never would've thought of that," Sam said.

"You had a few other things on your mind," Jim replied. "Now how about you tell us what we need to do to bring this baby to life? I'm anxious to see what's next."

"The rest is simple, really. Each of your gift children must tell Jordan that they agree to merge. If they all do, the resulting entity will be the eighteenth and Jordan will once again be complete. They will also become the entity that guides our ship when we separate to go to the academy."

"Why do you believe they'll all agree?" Chang asked.

"Because all of you agreed to join this team, and they're made from you. Do any of you want to miss out on the rest of this adventure?"

There were no takers.

"Well, there you have it."

Sam was right. Each of the gift children agreed without hesitation. Within moments, Jordan contacted Sam. "The gift ship is complete. You have done well, Sam Steele. With your permission, I would like to depart for our next destination."

"Can you show the team as we leave?"

"Most assuredly."

"Then let's get started."

The scene around them was replaced by a perfect view of the surrounding Judith Mountains. It was as if the ship was not there and they were suspended on nothing. The ground immediately began to recede. Everyone on the team was too stunned to speak until Earth was suspended beside them. They'd felt no sense of acceleration.

Matt was the first to speak. "That was awesome!"

Awesome, indeed, Sam thought.

About the Author

Dave Donovan was born in Montana and grew up in various locations throughout the United States before settling in Houston, Texas, where he lives now with his wife, Rosemary. Before becoming an author, he worked as a commercial fisherman, a business owner, a corporate executive, and as a decorated military officer.

24499275R00208

31901055364535

Made in the USA
Charleston, SC
27 November 2013